GODS AND ASTRONAUTS

Asag's Treachery

BOOK 2

Return to Paradise Series

C.S. HOBBS

GODS AND ASTRONAUTS

Asag's Treachery

BOOK 2

Return to Paradise Series

C.S. HOBBS

Gods and Astronauts
Asag's Treachery

Return to Paradise Series
Book2

By C.S. Hobbs

For more information, please see *About the Author* at the close of this book.

Cover art by Christopher Stroop assisted with ChatGPT.
Cover design by Donna Marie Benjamin.
Interior design and formatting by Donna Marie Benjamin of Elevation Press of Colorado.

Ordering information: Quantity sales. Special discounts are available on quantity purchases by book clubs, corporations, associations, and others. For details, contact the publisher at the address above.

ISBN 978-0-932624-46-8

1. Main category—[Fiction Fantasy] 2. Other categories—[Science Fiction]

Cedaredge, Colorado

INTRODUCTION

When Mylitta Sipani awakens from a 11,700-year hibernation, she finds Earth in ruins—its civilizations fallen, history erased, and her people lost to amnesia. Once a hero, now a myth, she becomes humanity's last hope against an ancient menace. Her arrival upends the life of Sonny Fly, an ordinary salesman with a family. Suddenly hunted by shape-shifting enemies, Sonny is caught up in a race to uncover humanity's lost origins. Their only chance of survival depends on a superweapon buried in a forgotten civilization's ruins—but activating it demands an unthinkable sacrifice. As Earth's destruction nears, Sonny's love for his wife clashes with his growing bond with Mylitta, forcing him to question his loyalties, faith, and the meaning of true sacrifice. In a final battle where past and present collide, only betrayal, sacrifice, and love will decide if Earth has a future—or is doomed to repeat its forgotten past.

PROLOGUE

Skinwalker Abides

A few more minutes with his head underwater and a chance encounter with ocean predators may have ended him. But not today.

Asag clawed his way to the surface. His demonic alien DNA rewrote itself along the way—bull shark transmuting into something that passed for human. Normally, the transformation was effortless. Not today. The injuries Sonny had inflicted disrupted the Engine—the complex network of radial muscles and chromatophore sacs that granted him both color and form—making the fight to the surface more difficult because of it.

While his flesh and muscle warred through metamorphosis, his mind was already calculating. Air first. Then shore. There was no land in sight, hours away at best.

His boat was gone. Sunk or sinking. It didn't matter which.

Asag resurfaced, his Brazzeal transformation complete. The stolen identity of the man he'd butchered broke the surface like a Trident missile fired from an Ohio-class submarine. He took a huge gulp of air, brain teetering on the edge of failure, begging for oxygen before exhaustion and oxygen deprivation got the better of him.

Eleven thousand years of patience, and a half-evolved ape had nearly killed him.

Behind him, the *Gold Digger* smoldered, its hull cracked open, belching black smoke, scattering debris across the water. The ocean churned red, blood blooming in thick ribbons in its wake. The underwater ruins of Atlantis lay somewhere beneath him, swallowing the only two people who stood between him and everything he'd spent the millennia working toward.

They were gone. The gateway had taken them.

For now.

A loud splash in the distance. A wave hit him before he could find his bearings, giving him direction. Strong arms wrapped around his chest from behind. Weathered hands locked tight. Powerful legs kicked in wide, steady thrust beneath them both, driving them through the water toward the boat on the horizon.

Asag rode on his back, the stranger underneath him working a powerful backstroke—saving the monster who would eventually kill him. But even compressed into human form, Asag was heavier than he looked. Far denser. Asag's kind evolved in a world with less gravity, and larger frames by design gave them extraordinary mass when crammed into smaller forms. Jamming eight feet of that into a six-foot human shell meant the weight had to go somewhere. It went everywhere.

Dense. Heavy. Built like a collapsing neutron star wrapped in genetically altered skin was what Randy was hauling onto his boat.

With incredible strength, Randy reached the Pelagic Hitman and, with a grunt, heaved Asag's limp arms onto the aft swim platform. He hauled himself alongside then up and over the transom, muscles burning, veins rising beneath his skin like cables under load. Sitting on the edge, legs dangling in the water, chest heaving, he tried to catch his breath. Oil and seawater slicked his skin, tracing every muscle beneath. Soaking wet, beaten as hell, completely ripped, he still looked like a demigod rising from the flaming waters to drag something dark out of the deep.

Randy's friends were still below the surface, searching for the mythical ruins of Atlantis. He didn't quite understand it and cared even less. He was the taxi driver who got them where they needed to go. Nothing more. It was the sailors' code alone that brought him to this burning wreckage to look for survivors. He had no idea his friend Sonny and the crazy chick he'd gone under with had just fought a battle to the death with the man he'd pulled out of the drink.

He was about to find out.

Randy grunted with exertion, his face surprised by the strain, as he yanked the injured sailor up and over the edge, dragging him aboard. He barely registered the drone of an engine overhead. PBY Catalina—an old military flying boat—was making a grid sweep in the distance. Too far to see the smoke, its search was methodical and unhurried.

Someone was already looking.

"Damn, you're a heavy boy!" he gasped, arms burning. "Like lifting a refrigerator out of a pool. Oh, damn, look at you!"

Something sharp had hacked the rescued man's midsection to pieces. His lung hung out from a chest wound, truly eviscerated, his insides a tangle of meat and shredded tissue. One of his arms twitched once before stilling completely. Black blood poured from between his legs, the aftermath of his castration. His eyes widening, frozen in disbelief, lips parted in a silent scream.

Randy was no EMT, but he didn't need to be—this dude would not make it. He shot a glance at the other body he'd hauled aboard, and the pieces started to click. Oxygen tanks must've blown, he figured. The neck wound on the old man? Tragic, but plausible. Randy glanced again at the newly rescued man and leaned over to pick up a dive weight which lay on the deck next to the body.

"That's odd," he decided. But things were about to get even odder.

Leaning farther in, Randy squinted at the open wound on the man's face. The mangled eye socket looked different—it was sealing itself. Layers of tissue reforming in real time: the tissue rebuilt itself in layers—capillary loops, collagen fibers, nerve endings—stitching together like a time-lapse in reverse. The ruined face was knitting back together, and it wasn't just the eye socket. Other wounds, too—closing methodically, as if obeying some ancient blueprint buried in the body.

Suddenly the man gagged—he was choking on something. Acting on instinct and still playing the Samaritan, Randy pried the jaw open, exposing Asag's teeth. The teeth were sharp, but curiosity enveloped Randy. Without another thought, his fingers went in between the teeth, fishing around the tongue and throat. Inside—a finger.

"What. The. Fuck?" he whispered, withdrawing his hand.

Instantly, Asag's eyes came back to life. Recognition flaring. Something returning. His face twitching violently, skull flexing, bones stretching, cracking beneath the skin. The jaw suddenly widened—unnaturally, impossibly—with razor-sharp teeth crowding his mouth.

"Oh, shit." Randy backed up a step, but there was no time.

Asag struck in a blur. Randy took the hit—a gush of blood sprayed across the helm. The cut should have been painless. It wasn't. A quick vicious burn radiated from the wound immediately. Venom? He shouted and stumbled toward the cabin. Asag moved gingerly after him, unhurried, like something that had done this thousands of times.

Randy grabbed a fillet knife off the cutting board and slashed wildly.

"You wanna get cut? I've gutted and filleted fish on this boat bigger than you, brother."

Blades slowed Asag, but not much—not enough. Bullets barely registered unless placed perfectly, but steel seemed to give him pause. Still, Randy was losing ground. Venom burning, stamina fading, he weighed his options fast. He'd seen what Sonny and Myli looked like after tangling with whatever this thing was. They were completely destroyed, and they had something he didn't. Magic, tech, whatever you want to call it.

Randy had a boat full of spearguns.

"Fuck this!"

He dropped the knife and snatched two spearguns off their rack. The first shot was hasty; the spear punched into Asag's left leg. The grin it earned told Randy everything he needed to know. Not even close to a kill shot. But when Asag's predatory eyes found him again, Randy had already tied the trailing line of the first spear to the second gun.

He aimed carefully this time. The second shot found its mark.

What happened next bought Randy exactly the time he needed. The line from Asag's leg ran taut across the deck, through a cleat, and straight to the anchor on the far rail. Randy had rigged it while Asag was grinning at the first spear in his leg.

Three bounding steps. Another speargun grabbed off the rack, to go. Randy hit the water in one fluid motion as the anchor went over the opposite side with a splash—Asag ripped violently backward, grasping at anything bolted down, trying not to follow it over the rail.

He held. But Randy was already a hundred yards away and swimming hard.

Asag cut the line and lurched to the helm, growling as his body fought to repair itself. The agony between his legs was almost unbearable thanks to Sonny castrating him. That damage wasn't healing, nor was his eye. He staggered to the controls, nearly blacking out before his hands found them.

The venom would take Randy out soon enough. No reason to give chase. Let the ocean finish him.

He grabbed the binoculars off the console and swept the horizon.

There.

The salvage flotilla. Still sitting exactly where it had no business sitting—directly above the gateway. Pretending to mine polymetallic nodules off the seafloor.

He started the engines with the last of his strength. The *Pelagic Hitman* turned, bow swinging toward the horizon. Asag throttled forward, broken and bleeding and completely unstoppable.

Some things don't die. They just get angry.

CHAPTER 1

Azores Blues

At 33.0 N, 28.0 W, Eastern Azores Fracture Zone, near what used to be Neptune's Trident before the mid-Atlantic ridge folded and dropped, Sonny blew into the underwater chamber like a rag doll, tumbling across jagged stone. His bones, his ribs bending—almost cracking. He fell, cutting, slicing across razor-sharp barnacles lining the bottom of the pool—doing more damage. The relatively warm water turned frigid at a depth over 1,200 feet deep. As unforgiving as this place was, the pressure-regulated chamber was the only thing preventing them from turning into gum under a pressure-shoe.

Gone were the three tall granitic islands of the micro-continent remnants of Pangea, the Atlanteans referred to as Neptune's Trident. All that remained were sunken flat-topped guyots with their summits sheared off and left in the depths of the Atlantic Ocean. The catastrophic collapse had happened overnight while tsunamis relentlessly slammed into the island chain.

This day and moments ago, deep beneath those waves, Sonny and Myli transported into the ruined formation's last stable chamber.

Synapses fired in Sonny's brain. The cold water was therapeutic as it attacked the inflammation pulsating throughout his body. Sonny's first thought was to tell himself that the last few days had been a real drag. His lungs burned as he shot up breaking the surface of the underground pool, coughing and hacking up bitter brine. The Udug venom was wreaking havoc on his nervous system.

His flippers, mask, and rebreather—gone. He gasped, sucking in a desperate frosty breath, vision blurry, eyes stinging with salt. Wiping them did no good since what was left of his hand smeared his face with fresh blood. His pulse thundered in his ears. Where was he?

And where was Myli?

The room around him was massive, the pool on the floor was shallow but the ceiling was lost in gloom. Walls were pulsing, and glowing outlines created an eerie ambience. A form of script, hieroglyphs like Katakana adorned the walls and decorations. Sonny glanced at an equal-armed red cross, a symbol the Knights Templar once wore on their coats and banners. *Coincidence?*

Statues of Poseidon, he guessed, and Atlas loomed in the corners—weathered, broken, their stone faces eroded by time and whatever violence trapped them down here in this air pocket. Tattered tapestries hung limply, swaying gently from walls seemingly breathing.

Something scurried nearby.

Sonny froze, heart pounding. Turning his head sharply, blood still clouding one eye. Skin was missing from his side, a byproduct of the shark's abrasive skin peeling his skin off. At the chamber's edge, he saw small, rat-sized animals, but with elongated hind legs like tiny kangaroos. Their eyes glowed in the dark. Their skin translucent, light shooting through their veins beneath the surface. They appeared to be maintaining the sea growth from the pool.

Were they contagious? Genetic mutations? They scurried off when they saw him.

Never mind, he told himself. *Got to find Myli.*

Behind him and unnoticed by Sonny as he rapidly searched for Myli, another body surfaced quietly in the dark. Hawk moved slowly in the cold, gasping, dragging himself to a pile of rocks in the shadows, trying to warm up and stay hidden. Sonny's splashing and thrashing as he looked for Myli masked the smaller noise of Hawk's movements as he remained covert.

Moments later, Sonny saw her. He surged toward her in the frigid shallow water, hyperventilating, chest heaving in bursts which spurted blood leaking from gashes in his side. His heart rate and blood pressure were spiking. He wasn't trained for this. His fine motor skills deteriorated with every step towards her, accompanied by shivering violent spasms. And his entire body seemed too heavy to move.

He reached her—hands barely working, pulling her close with his numb hand—now a granite claw, the other hand useless, a flopping mess of cut meat and digits. His life continued leaking onto her. She was unconscious despite his spine-breaking twitches. Her head was lolling back in his arm. Vulnerable. Bleeding too. He didn't have long—20 minutes at most before he would freeze up and drown.

Myli had gone too long without oxygen. She was floating motionless, her body was pale-blue and limp, streaked with blood and framed in a glow of bioluminescent light streaming from the living walls. She was clinically dead.

"No—No, no, no—come on, come on—" he gasped.

Tired—he felt like she weighed a ton as he dragged her to the edge of the pool. He rolled her onto the smooth black-red-white stone and started CPR. Compressions warmed him and pumped life back into her. Every pump agonizing his shredded hand.

Her mouth was cold and blue like ice. His own lungs burned, his teeth chattered, as he continued giving her compressions. His surroundings were greying out, exhaustion was stalking him, panic setting in. If she died, he died.

Finally, a gasp. A gurgle.

She jerked into consciousness, coughing violently, spewing saltwater across the glowing floor. Her eyes flew open—wild, searching. She was screaming with a shriek he'd never heard before.

Her body trembling in his arms, a useless embrace, unable to soak up his warmth. She immediately knew they were both in rough shape. He wrapped his arms around her, and she collapsed into him, shaking, her face buried in his shoulder. They held each other, skin to skin, as the chamber hummed with ancient energy and began powering up.

Light spilled from the walls, rippling veins of bioluminescence, illuminating what lay beyond the pool: steps. And beyond those steps, a hallway stretching out, impossibly long and wide, constructed from a strange mineral-glass hybrid which shimmered like liquid moonlight. Walls, breathing in slow pulses highlighted symbols etched in alien hieroglyphics scrolled across translucent surfaces.

This place wasn't merely old—it was the first. This was what was left of Atlantis. Not the myth. Not the ruins. The living heart of a once-immortal civilization which controlled the globe during the Golden Age of man and extraterrestrials. But, for now, the place's significance was lost on them as they struggled to survive.

After several agonizing moments, Myli stirred in his arms, teeth chattering. She pulled back slightly, eyes scanning the glowing hall, then looked at him. His life fading fast.

"We need medical," he warned. "I don't think the ring can regenerate my wounds fast enough." His mangled hand flopped on her stomach.

Her eyes widened. "Stay with me," she pleaded. She stumbled to her feet, staying small, staying tight to retain what little heat she had left. Her posture was erratic, barefoot and bloodied, legs shaky beneath her as she looked down on Sonny.

"Did you kill him?" she asked.

"If he ain't dead, he's wishing he was," Sonny told her.

Sonny was looking green. Sick. Deathly. She knelt and placed a hand on his bare, blood-soaked shoulder.

"Give me your knife," she said.

He sat up, reached instinctively—nothing. No gear. No blade.

A bit of red oozed from his side—sticky, thick like jam. The shark must've got him there too. The wound was brutal, and Sonny knew it was infected. Only the frigidity of their surroundings kept the venom at bay.

A half-moon of teeth marks curved from his chest to his stomach, arcing back around to his pelvis. It looked like something had tried to bite him in half—and very nearly succeeded.

"Sonny," she said, her voice low and unsure, her expression etched with worry.

A little clothing still clung to her body; she shred it free and wrapped his hand with it. She hated to ask but Sonny already knew what she wanted to know. With effort, he lifted the ruined hand. Her eyes wide, she stared at his hand flopping around like a chewed-up rubber dog toy, no structure left to keep it stiff. Dagger-like wounds ran across the top, slicing clean through the bone and out the palm.

"It's still there. The ring is safe," he told her as he offered a weak, grim smile. "I guess I won't be counting to ten anymore."

A wave of nausea hit—maybe from the pain, or the blood, or the sight of his own mutilation—and the world began to lean full tilt. He was moaning in pain, rolling over on his side, fetal position. She tightened the makeshift bandage. Only when the pain subsided, was he able to speak again.

"We're defenseless down here," he said, grimly.

Her jaw clenched and she nodded. "But we're still alive and we're here because of you," she said. She knelt down, kissing him.

He didn't have the energy to stop her.

"You look really bad," she said, panic creeping into her voice. "I've got to find medical now. The freeze in here, it's our friend, at least for now. Hang in there."

Her eyes darted toward the glowing stairway. Sonny was losing too much blood—fast. He was going to die if she didn't do something quickly. She stood up and Sonny reached for her, his lips pale, body trembling.

"Myli—" he gasped, the word barely escaping his throat.

But she was already limping toward the glowing stairs and the corridor just visible at the top, one hand trailing along the megalithic wall. Beneath her touch the surface was shifting like oil in water, it looked like she was talking to it. A programmed hologram repeated again and again. Even the air was warming up after her touch. Life-support was kicking in which meant there was a good chance the medical bay she was seeking was still active.

Minutes passed as Sonny lay on his side, half-naked, still bleeding out. Consciousness and unconsciousness were one in the same. His eyes were watching a simulation projected on the wall as it played over and over—at least seven times before he heard splashes of water behind him. That approaching sound convinced him he was dead. The creature must have followed them in. Synapses were still firing but not reaching the bulk of his muscles. His heart was still pumping but he could feel death running through his veins.

If Asag is alive and has found his way down here, Sonny told himself, *then, frankly, he deserves the win.*

As Sonny lay there helpless and thinking these dreadful thoughts, a figure approached him.

It was a warrior, clad in an exoskeleton mech suit, sleek and organic, moving with predatory coordination. The armor was a flat black weave, form-fitting, alive with micro movements in the pigmentation—adaptive camouflage, no doubt. Intricate lines of pulsing energy snaked across the plating. The helmet had a visor on the front sitting almost flush against the skin, sensors adorned the top of the helmet feeding real-time data into the suit. Carbon fiber and gold weave lined the creases of the slightly oversized helmet.

Sonny stared at the figure, and he suddenly understood alien eyewitness accounts and how they were misconstrued. This figure was odd, but it hadn't dropped from the sky. The figure knelt next to him and started going to work on him. A medical device of some kind in one hand. In the other hand, a large carbon fiber-looking case.

Seconds later, the helmet retracted into a million shimmering nanoparticles falling back into the suit's collar. Sonny shuddered. Was he hallucinating?

No—it *was* Myli, kneeling forward, concern etched across her face.

"Sorry, I couldn't come sooner," she said. "This place is a maze. I haven't been down here in for-ever. You're going to be okay?" Her words suggested conviction but even she didn't believe it.

His brows furrowed. Paralysis setting in but he still managed to stare fixedly at her suit.

"Organic Mesh Alloy Weave," she grinned.

"Bullshit," his thoughts reached her thoughts. She laughed.

"Yeah, I just made that up. It's a prototype suit. Sorry if I scared you."

Sonny wheezed out another cough.

"I just know I have to keep you talking." She pulled off the blood-soaked strip of cloth and grimaced. It was worse than she remembered a minute ago.

"I have to get you to Med-Surg," she replied, trying to keep her voice steady. She had to keep him talking, keep him conscious. She placed the med box over his mangled hand. It hummed to life and went to work trying to reconstruct what it could.

Sonny's face twisted in agony.

"I know," she said, her voice cracking as emotion broke through. She was ready to cry. Really cry. But she couldn't, not in front of him. "Let it work."

He nodded but he was still crashing as she peeled away what remained of his dive top. It didn't take much—it all but disintegrated into shredded pieces.

She couldn't help recoiling. "Oh, Sonny, I'm so sorry," she gasped, shuddering.

His torso was a canvas of carnage. She didn't waste time. She opened the med case and pulled out a new tool—an alien surgical wand and began treating his other injuries. One by one, she sealed and cleaned the wounds trying to stabilize him for movement. It was crude, but it would be effective enough to get him to the Stasis Pod for serious regeneration.

Grabbing another vial, she began lathering a translucent salve onto him—warming, tingling, alive.

"This will speed up new skin growth," she explained, her voice still trembling. "Hours instead of weeks or months. Now—this is going to hurt."

She leaned down and picked him up like a toddler. The suit—with its efficient exoskeleton—absorbed the strain.

"They've got a body scanner in there," she said, her breath short but focused. "We need to see what's going on inside you."

As she carried him, she leaned down and touched her forehead to his. He was burning up despite coming out of a freezing bath. A readout on her forearm confirmed it: 104 degrees. Just one degree away from a stroke. She quickened her pace. Rapidly ascending the staircase, she turned toward the hallway, her voice strained.

"We're almost there," she told him. "Don't quit on me."

Cracking a grim smile, he began convulsing.

Moments later, they reached the medical-surgical bay 358, and Myli practically threw him onto the scanner table. Her hands flew to the controls, yanking the cover down over his body.

Nothing happened.

"Come on, come on," she shouted, slapping the activation panel. The screen flickered—dim, lagging. Too slow. He was bleeding out—the color alarming, but something else was going on in his body.

"Begin scan!" she barked, voice sharp, nearly cracking.

The machine whirred, then stalled again before the internal lights finally hummed to life, flickering like they were waking from a thousand-year slumber. Blue pulses swept across his body, but the pace was glacial. Myli leaned in, breathing fast, fingers shaking as she manually input override commands to force the diagnostic sequence.

Inside the chamber she could see through Sonny's translucent body. Bones, muscle, veins. It was an instantaneous X-ray machine without the harmful radiation. Her eyes darted across the display, her throat tightening. Bones shattered. Lungs bruised. Internal bleeding. Organ bruising. His hand—oh, God—hanging on by a tendon. The nanotech Med-Surg casing she'd put on it was working, but barely; the reconstruction was ineffectual in repairing the damage.

At last, Myli breathed a sigh of relief as AI kicked in.

"Injecting antivenom."

"Injecting antibacterials."

"Analyzing foreign contaminants."

The data streamed fast—known Earth venoms, pathogens from Tiamat, even biological signatures from Mars. A Komodo dragon image appeared on-screen, then another image she didn't recognize. Alien. Unclassified.

As AI took over, Myli found the need to take a moment.

She left the unit and sat in the hall for what felt like an hour before she began to stir. There was no one to see, so the tears flowed until there were none left to offer. She could still hear AI at work. She could do nothing more. She figured he was dead in there, the medical device now a casket. She had to clear her head, walk it off—she strolled deeper into the facility.

The hallways narrowed, walls closing in, the air growing thick—humid, laced with ozone. The walls hummed, vibrating with unseen energy. Moving further in, the more minimalist the architecture became. Murals and carvings on the red, white and black stone faded into subtle ridges and abstract geometries. The art grew sterile, cold—like the temple was transitioning into pure function. A place for machines.

At the end of the final hallway stood a massive, sealed door, its granite face etched with intricate symbols glowing faintly beneath ancient sediment. A translucent membrane shimmered across it like living skin. Myli pressed her fingers to the seal.

A pulse.

Light was surging outward in waves of bioelectric glow. With a sharp hissing, the vacuum lock released—air rushing past, dust and history swirling. The door slid open, revealing a cavernous chamber. At its center: A construct of pure energy, suspended midair like a silent, rotating star, pulsing like a heartbeat. The surrounding vaults were lined with crystalline columns, glyphs etched deep, glowing with dormant information.

The cores always took Myli's breath away. So did the serenity of the Gardens.

On the wall to her right, a single dark library rack stood—sleek, ancient, housing one object: The Library. Her people's crown jewel. Only one other copy existed—the M3, the ring responsible for shattering the first humans' tranquility. All knowledge. All secrets. The Apple of Knowledge responsible for the ousting of Adam and Eve.

Back in the med-bay, during Myli's excursion, the ring on Sonny's finger pulsed—syncing. The construct flared to life, casting dazzling patterns across the chamber. Walls ignited, glyphs racing like data swarmed over a living circuit board.

From the shadows, a voice echoed: "Station Manager online in five... four... three... two..."

Even at a distance, Myli heard that voice echoing through the halls, and her heartbeat quickened. She turned as a hatch on the far wall whined, its surface flickering with white-hot overload.

It opened to reveal a dark void.

From within the darkness something moved. Curled at first in a fetal position, something rose slowly, until it became a towering figure. Steam hissed from its joints. Seven feet tall, humanoid in shape only—but not human in the slightest. Its limbs uncoiled, organic alloy armor flowing like mercury into segmented plates.

A machine. A protector. A remnant of the old guard.

Myli tensed on instinct—but based on its markings, she recognized it, and she knew exactly what her arrival in this isolated chamber had activated.

It was a Synthetic—one of the earliest generations. Built not just to obey orders but to guard what mattered most. Myli stepped forward, shoulders easing. She looked up at the towering machine and spoke, voice quiet but steady.

"En'Gen... Boy, am I glad to see you again."

The Synth's massive frame stood still while its optical sensors flared—twin stars glowing behind the visor. Its frame adjusted with a hydraulic hiss, armor plates shifting into readiness. It scanned her.

"Myli." The deep, metallic voice reverberated through the ancient chamber, as though it had waited millennia to speak. "It has been a long time. Much has happened since you left." En'Gen paused, calculating, then continued, "100,006,338 hours since the last time I stepped foot into this room. 11,412 Earth years."

"We have a lot to catch up on," Myli replied. "But I need your help. I have an injured man."

"Alert," it said.

The Synth's optics narrowed. Its sensor array pulsed. Suddenly—zoom—its attention snapped past her, locking onto movement deep in the corridor.

Its posture shifted instantly—guard mode.

Another set of appendages rose from its back. Four limbs became six. Without another word, En'Gen brushed past her, its heavy footsteps deliberate. Faster than she remembered—an old warrior, reactivated.

"En'Gen!" she called, spinning to follow. "Where are you going?"

CHAPTER 2

Olympians

Commander Hawk fought cramps as he clung to an outcrop of stones protruding from the water like a tiny island. The water lapped quietly around him, the temple's low hum vibrating through the stone beneath his body. When Myli and her companion vanished deeper into the structure, he slipped from concealment, his Alpha Skin shedding water as he climbed out and followed.

He slipped past Med Bay, where the man lay sealed in the regen chamber—barely alive. Even with an Alpha Skin suit, Hawk was only fairing marginally better. Myli was not there. He guessed where she was heading.

He lingered in the hallway and overheard enough between Myli and En'Gen to know this was bigger than he'd expected. The question now: What would happen when they saw him?

Something about Myli had changed. She wasn't nicer. He had once loved her, but the war changed everyone.

Sensing movement and hearing steps heading his direction—he retreated. Too late.

The seven-foot organometallic behemoth stepped into view, blocking his path like a monolith of death. En'Gen moved like an overweight jungle cat. Despite its size, he was ninja quiet and ready to kill.

Hawk froze, muscles coiled. "Hey, Big Guy," he said to the robot Synth. Were they going to fight?

Impact. A brutal, concussive strike sent Hawk sprawling across the dusty floor. Was it a punch or kick? It happened so fast he didn't know which limb took him down and stole his breath.

He was inhaling but his lungs were taking forever to fill. The red glow of the merciless Synth's targeting optics locked onto his chest. One of his dorsal limbs rose up and took aim as a small turret on the end of the appendage powered up.

Down the corridor, Myli came running, weapon up—steps calculated. She hadn't seen who the target was—not yet. With a thought, her pistol converted to a rifle, optic reticle glowing faintly, locked onto the intruder's head.

"Bad move following us in here, cockroach." She grinned, knowing she finally had a weapon to cut these walking viruses in half. She advanced behind En'Gen, weapon steady. At this range, her zero-point energy weapon would cut through alloy and bone alike.

But Hawk blurted out, "Hold your fire!" He breathed out.

He wheezed while clambering to his feet, his hands raised. But he went down again, dropping to a knee as he sucked another strained ragged breath. Defiance forced him upright again, hands waving for mercy.

Removing his diving mask, Hawk stumbled into the open, hands half-raised, fingers trembling—a familiar sociopathic shit-eating grin plastered across his face.

Myli's aim faltered seeing another face from the past. The flicker of confusion passed, and she snapped her weapon back on target.

"You've got five seconds to explain where the hell you got that face," she growled.

The moment was electric while Hawk prepared to walk the razor's edge.

"Commander Hawk died the day Atlantis fell. You are an imposter, sir," the machine alleged.

Taken aback. "My mother gave me this face," Hawk declared, inching toward them, hands in the air. He was feeling strong and nowhere near as battered or worn as she and Sonny.

But Myli wasn't taking any chances. Her aim didn't waver. She nudged the barrel slightly, centering it between his eyes.

"Hands higher," she insisted. "Keep them up." She shouted.

"Nice to see you too," Hawk said calmly—too calm. "I can see that you've still got that swagger."

"Anshar?" her voice cut sharp. "En'Gen, what do you mean he died?"

"I watched Anshar on approach, being chased by several enemy fighters just before the fall. Missiles were closing in on him as was a wall of water, along with fire and brimstone raining down from the sky as he approached Atlantis. No ordinary pilot survives that."

Astounded again, Hawk pointed at himself, "Ordinary?" he asked in disbelief.

"What the hell are you doing here? Keep those hands up. I don't believe it's you."

He shrugged. "Funny you should ask what I'm doing here. I was about to ask the same. We all thought you were dead. The *Menagerie* imploded—with you still on it."

"Obviously not," she said, still aiming at him and staring at his very physically present hands.

En'Gen shifted beside her, its weapon rising.

"Be careful, Myli," the Synth warned. "The probability of this being a Udug agent is high."

"Whoa, Big Guy. It's me," Hawk told En'Gen. "I had front row seats to the fall of Atlantis. But I also had Evi. Orbital debris falling around me, the Anunna broke off their attack. Evi pulled Gs even I couldn't handle. The last thing I remember was Evi pulling up and dodging massive chunks of flaming earth falling around me. She brought me west, to a secret island base off the coast. I lay dormant there for centuries."

The Synth paused as Hawk refocused on Myli. He knew of this hidden base. It was possible the base could have survived the solar blast from the sun.

"And, Myli, don't you remember Hangar Bay C? The day I returned from training in the Atlas Mountains to meet with Dumuzi? Crew chief threatened to turn us in for being AWOL?"

Myli raised an eyebrow—a sharp look causing Hawk to swiftly add, "Okay, okay—I almost got shot that day too."

"Not much has changed," Myli quipped. "A Udug would have all those memories."

Her finger hovered on the trigger with a blank face.

"I was there to meet you when the *Menagerie* arrived. But it crash-landed and we only found your brother." He raised his hand, revealing the second ring. I saw you at the docks overlooking the bay," Hawk continued, his tone relaxed. "You looked sad, but I wasn't sure it was you."

Myli froze. "Shara?"

"Yeah. He led us here. Would a Udug bring you the second ring?"

"My brother? Is he topside?" She said completely ignoring the ring on his finger.

Hawk's expression faltered. "The thing that attacked you—it got him. Almost got me."

Before the war, the Anunna ordered her to put down a rebellion, she did. A million notches in her belt overnight. It earned her the moniker *Goddess of War.*

"Are you saying my brother is dead?" she asked with emotion. Her brother, one more notch too many.

Hawk nodded slowly. "But we still have both rings. We can take the fight to them."

Her mind wrapping around another loss. Shara. Gone. Again.

As the Synth gave way, Hawk stepped closer, extending his hand to gently touch her shoulder.

"When we found him, Shara was very old. Why didn't you use Enki's Serum?"

Her reply was hollow. "The Anunna outlawed immortal doses. You should know that."

"I do." Hawk gestured back at her, knowing her lineage. "But that never stopped the elites from cheating the system. Being thousands of years away from home sounds like as good a reason as any to break the law."

Myli dismissed her privilege with a roll of her eyes. Not everyone with wealth and status bent the rules. The stereotype further annoyed her.

Saying this, Hawk held out his hand. A gold chain and pendant dropped, dangling from his fingers; it slinked downward like a spider emerging from its web. She saw the pendant and recognized it. Only her mother, Inanna, would have trusted Hawk with something of her heritage.

"Your necklace, this pendant. Your mother made sure I gave it to you before I made a run for it," he said still dangling the precious piece of jewelry. "She knew she would never see you again."

She took her rifle and slung it over her back. The sling retracted on its own and the rifle stuck to her armor like it was magnetized to her. Bits of nanites from the suit quickly consumed the energy weapon until it seamlessly became part of her suit. A quiet surrender.

En'Gen's arm cannon folded away with a hiss too.

"I can't believe you kicked me, Tin Can." Hawk said with disbelief.

"It was a nudge. If I kicked you, you'd be dead." En'Gen replied.

More feelings of loss weighed her down. Everyone on the ship, her family back home here on Ki, nothing but dust now. Sonny was busy dying down the hall—a psychological pressure wave of emotion flushed her face unexpectedly. Atmosphere thick with despair forced its way into her chest. Centuries of regret attacked her insides like a virus, twisting the guts within her stomach. She hoped what was overwhelming her psyche was a psychological response and not the gas station food suddenly staging a rampage on her digestive system. "They all gave their lives for me." A single tear rolled down her face. "I don't know how I ended up in Sonny's arms, but I have blood on my hands that I can't reconcile."

"We all do, Princess. That doesn't mean you're stuck with him." He said directing his comment towards Sonny. "You have a plan or what?"

"We hit them first," she said. "Before the armada knows we're ready for them."

"With what? The flag I fly under now just launched the last ship in their fleet."

"There is an ancient weapon on this planet we can use to stop them. The captain gave Shara and me intel on such a weapon. It must have been used to stop them the first time." She glanced at En'Gen, hoping he could point them in the right direction.

The cybernetic warrior calculated. "Several doomsday weapons were used by both sides, leading to the end of our civilization."

"Did my father give you anything that could help us? We need that weapon again. Dumuzi told the captain that there is a gateway here with the coordinates leading to its docking bay."

En'Gen nodded. "Before your father transferred you to the Menagerie, we prepared for a future defense. Theoretically, the ship could still be intact, but we never counted on our countermeasures being delayed this long."

Hawk thought about the secret base he was discovered in not too long ago. "Unless the enemy knew where it was and the facility took a direct hit, it could be lying in wait like I was."

Myli nodded with approval. It was the best they had with what they were given. No one told her any of this would be a walk in the Garden.

"Sounds like we have a plan," Hawk agreed. "I'm in, let's end this."

"Are you in this time?" Myli asked. Her question was pointed and dripping with skepticism. Her indifference as to whether he joined them or not sent a chill down his spine.

Hawk didn't let it bother him too much. She had to know it wasn't his fault. "The Menagerie left me behind back then," He grinned. "I'm here now, aren't I?"

He leaned in, close enough for a hug or perhaps a kiss. His actions were something edging on discomfort. She shifted, neutral and obtuse. A slight tilt of her chin, a graceful step back left his lips finding thin air and awkwardness. A hollow groan escaped Hawk.

"If we are using the Heaven's Gate to jump to the ship facility," En'Gen explained, "that shortcut could be short-lived, and there is only enough power for one attempt."

Hawk rolled his neck, eyes waning. "Then let's go." He refused to give up. She'd need him eventually.

Myli turned heading towards Med-Surg. "We can't. Not yet."

His expression tightened as he followed her.

"Why not?" he demanded.

She glanced ahead down the hallway, and he followed her eyes.

He closed his, mashing his eyelids hard in disbelief. "The civilian?" he scoffed. "You can't be serious."

Back in Med Bay, En'Gen stood over Sonny as the injured man lay in what looked like a transparent barometric chamber. The Synth's eyes flicked through screens of cascading data showing Sonny's vitals and treatments in seconds.

"His body is stabilizing," En'Gen reported. "But he's still critical. The cryo-treatment has his fever under control."

"We don't have time for this," Hawk warned.

Myli shot Hawk a deadly look. "He saved my life. I know it doesn't seem like it but he's high mimetic. We're not going anywhere without him," she declared. "I don't abandon my people."

Hawk knew what she meant by that dig.

"Look," he reminded her, "the *Menagerie* left me behind. I didn't abandon you." Hawk stared at Sonny through the transparent coffin, his voice edged with disdain. "You're gambling with the survival of the planet over some barbaric survivor. I have a ring."

"He's not some dumb barbarian," she declared. "His people climbed out of the ashes of our apocalypse and rebuilt the world. They're not weak. Not this one, despite their conditioning."

"They didn't get very far," Hawk shot back. "They've only advanced because we recovered and handed ancient tech to them. Cut your losses and the ring off. Let's get moving."

She turned on him, fury rising. "Are we speaking two different languages?" she demanded.

"You're in love with him, aren't you?" Hawk guessed.

"None of your business," she said. "Besides—he's married."

"Does he even remember her?"

Her jaw clenched. "Not fair." She pointed at him with a scolding tone.

Hawk stepped closer. "I know how this works. The bio-hacks are implanted in your tattoos. That tech has him wrapped around your finger. Does he know?"

Her fury quieted. "How could you possibly know their affecting him?"

"Because they aren't working as strongly on me," Hawk said coldly. "You're emanating them toward him. You might not even know you're doing it."

She turned, pissed off and paused. He had a point. She hated it when he was right.

Even if there was something real between her and Sonny, the pheromones from her bio-mods undoubtedly enhanced whatever spark existed. And then there was the ring, linking and enhancing their thoughts and emotions. A double whammy. Sonny, ignorant to her powers, never stood a chance—not against someone like her.

In her era, Myli was Atlantean elite. Back then she was called a goddess. Here and now, she was nothing less than a witch, to put it in Earth terms, with Love Potion #9.

"If you two would quit squabbling like the animals you are," En'Gen interrupted, voice steady. "I believe I have neutralized the neurotoxin in Sonny's system. His recovery should be complete within the hour."

Myli reached out, caressing the Synth's arm with a gentle touch. "Thank you."

En'Gen continued, "There is a high probability if we remove the Mini Mii ring now, it could irreparably corrupt the bio-feed and wipe any intel we still need from it. However, removing it would give you a much better tactical advantage."

Hawk folded his arms. "Even the Synth agrees with me."

Myli glared at En'Gen and ground her teeth. Most likely they were right. But she wasn't leaving Sonny behind. And nobody was cutting off any fingers. Not after everything they'd been through. Not after everything he'd done for her. She owed him no less—and maybe more.

An hour later the Med-Surg chamber hissed open. Sonny stirred, eyes heavy, softly staring at the ceiling. He felt—whole. Mostly. His joints hurt less than they had in the past decade, his breathing was even, and his thoughts weren't swimming in pain or fever. His eyes opened fully. He looked around. Some dude was seated a few feet from him and staring at him.

"Wake up, princess," Hawk told him angrily. "We are behind schedule because of you."

Sonny focused on him.

Who the fuck is this guy? he wondered. Trying to get a bead on who this guy was, he turned his thoughts to Myli. Before she even spoke, he felt her on the other side of the bed.

"Hey, it's not your fault," Myli said gently.

Sonny sat up slowly, confused. "Of course not. Wait, what's not my fault?"

"Your feelings," Myli said deflated.

She crossed the room, opened a sleek locker embedded in the wall, reached inside, and tossed him a folded Alpha Skin suit. Sonny realized he was completely naked. He considered the suit but didn't even bother trying to cover himself. What was the point? Her gaze didn't waver, didn't mock. Just watched him with unreadable calm.

His eyes drifted to his hand. It felt amazing—fluid, pain-free. But his pinky finger. He brought it closer and stared at it. The pinky was gone. Cleanly healed—but missing.

"Fuck," he muttered, staring at his new deformation. "Damn it."

"There's no regeneration machine here we can use to fix your hand before we need to move again," Myli said softly. Nonapologetic—just honest.

He nodded slowly. A little deflated. It was gone. *If I didn't have bad luck, I wouldn't have any luck at all.* "It wasn't my best finger anyway." He put it out there with a positive twist and reached for the suit.

The Alpha Skin reacted—adjusting, tightening, adapting to his shape like liquid intelligence. It hugged him with a strange comfort. With the suit in place, he climbed out of the chamber, rolling his shoulder. The soreness had vanished. But something else was happening too. The longer he was near Myli, the more he felt it. He was being pulled in again.

Sight. Scent. Thought.

Unknown to him, her bio-hacked pheromones, subtle but inescapable, were doing their work—spilling into the air between them. His will tangled with hers, confused by shared space, shared trauma, and the ring's psychic link. It wasn't just an attraction. It was a gravitational pull.

And, for Sonny, it was a problem.

Sonny distracted himself by flexing the suit. "So, what the heck is this made of? It's—magical."

Hawk mumbled in the corner. "Dumb barbarian."

Myli grinned at Sonny. "Spider silk," she said like a woman showing her husband an ultra-soft chenille fabric.

He visibly shuddered. "Wonderful." He said with no appreciation. "Spiders. Love those things," he said facetiously. "Of course it would be," he continued.

She chuckled, watching him as he tugged the suit into place. "Get over it. It's bullet-proof," she added.

Information which physically cheered up his expression.

"And," she continued, "there are microscopic cilia that tap into your pores allowing the cybernetic enhancements to ramp up your stamina. You'll need this too."

She handed him a strapless pack-like module. It featured another Templar-like cross, small but noticeable, like a logo. He slid the ultra slim lightweight backpack-looking thing over his shoulder, and it weaved into the Alpha suit. No straps needed.

"Now what?" Sonny asked out loud.

Unsure, until instinct—or tech—took over, he thought about activating the suit and it responded immediately. In seconds, the same sleek MKV 2nd SKN armor which Myli wore grew over him, encasing the Alpha Skin in a seamless layer of nanite-driven plating.

"Whoa," Sonny grinned.

"What's that saying?" she teased. "Cool?"

"Yeah," he breathed, flexing it. "It's cool and also pretty sick."

She stared at him—her gaze lingered. On his eyes. His lips. The curve of his jaw. She wanted to kiss him. A long, wet kiss.

She wanted more. Something she couldn't have. Or shouldn't. But it would be so easy to take.

And all this terrified her. But fear didn't change her feelings. The more she wanted him, the more she excreted her spell on him.

Within seconds, En'Gen entered the room with a hydraulic hiss and the heavy thud of armored footsteps. It was a powerful entrance which cut off Myli's desires and interrupted her reunion with Sonny. The Synth's visor glowed softly as it scanned Sonny from head to toe. A small beep emitted from its interface.

"So, this your keeper?" En'Gen asked, its tone neutral. "My scanner didn't register his model ID. And his DNA was a mess."

"Yes, he is," Myli confirmed, stepping slightly in front of Sonny. "There's no telling what generation he's a mix of. He's a mutt," she said half-jokingly.

The Synth's head tilted, processing.

Sonny stood up straighter, his eyes sharp.

"Chuckles here says we're an hour late," Sonny grinned. "So, if we're going, let's friggin' go." Determination in his voice.

The Synth's visor dimmed ominously. "The barbarian is ready."

Hawk crossed his arms and shrugged, a huff and a puff finished off what he thought of Sonny. To him, Sonny was deadweight. A tourist in a war zone.

Ignoring the men and their growing quarrel, En'Gen reached over and pressed something against Myli's shoulder, a hypo-spray. There was a hiss and a hard pinch.

"En'Gen, what are you doing?" she demanded.

"These feral creatures are infected with dozens of TD-4 mutations. I am sorry if I alarmed you, but you would be dead inside a week if I hadn't inoculated you with the proper vaccine which I reverse engineered from Sonny's antibodies."

Myli suddenly grew concerned as she rubbed the dried blood on her face. Sonny's blood had been all over her. "If it's wet, it's a threat," she whispered, reaffirming the Synth's precautions.

En'Gen addressed her with more intel. "A skeleton crew was left on board, the weapon to be activated upon your arrival per Dumuzi's orders."

"How did my father know to plan for this in advance?" Myli inquired skeptically.

En'Gen answered simply. "Classified. You must activate the weapon and the Architects' ship."

Myli's face expressed confusion. "I thought the Architects were a myth. A religion."

"And I thought you were a believer," the Synth countered.

"Most of the time," she said.

"No, they were not a myth," En'Gen said simply. "Enki and Enlil were the first to discover the Anunnas creators. They sent your father and I back in to find more tech in their home system. We did. Soon after, the war started. The Heaven's Gate will take us directly to the place where the Architects left the ship. It is the same tomb in which your father and I found it."

"Well, I'm ready," Sonny said. Despite his ordeal, he was itching to get his feet wet again. These new missions were like work; each one thickened the calluses on his brain. "Sounds like a piece of cake."

"If that quaint phrase means it will be easy, it is not," En'Gen replied. "The Atlas core has enough power left to activate Heaven's Gateway and teleport your team to the weapons hiding spot. But the activation occurs only once. You could walk into the side of a mountain."

"A one-way trip," Hawk countered. "Nothing's easy."

"Correct," En'Gen agreed. "The complex could be buried under a collapse. It sits over a geothermal hotspot."

"One-way trip?" Sonny's brow furrowed. "Hotspot?"

When my brain calluses are done protecting my grey matter from my growing PTSD, he thought, *my bulging forehead will look like a Neanderthal.*

En'Gen nodded. "The Architects didn't want just anyone stumbling in there and finding a weapon of such magnitude. Without 2nd SKN suits, you're dead. Don't take them off. Without the activation code, you're dead. Trapped for eternity."

The Synth tried to reassure Myli by putting his hand on her shoulder. But Myli did the math.

"So, if we are trapped, we're dead," she decided. "So, if that happens, I'd assume it's best to just open the suit."

En'Gen nodded. "This place was chosen because its only goal is to kill outsiders. It is a place no one would go by accident."

Myli's voice was steady. "Come with us. We could use your help."

En'Gen hesitated. "I'm not sure how much help an old Gen3 could be. I was old when your mother had you. My systems were damaged by the CME. My software is—"

"—Still better than anything we've got topside," Hawk cut in. "Earthlings have fallen behind, En'Gen. Even a battered, outdated machine like you could tilt the balance."

Myli nodded to Hawk, then stepped closer to En'Gen.

"You're the only family I have left," she told the Synth. "You were a great warrior during the Synth Rebellion. We need that warrior again."

En'Gen was quietly processing, then finally spoke— "Your father exaggerated." A pause. "But I will come, and I'll do my best to keep up. But if I slow you down—don't hesitate to leave me."

"Leave you behind?" Hawk smirked. "You've seen how well we do that." His gaze flicked to Sonny, who was still gearing up.

Myli shot Hawk a sharp look. "Fair enough," she said.

As the others geared up, En'Gen moved closer to Sonny, his voice low and deliberate. "That ring is one of a kind. It will determine the fate of your species. Do not lose it."

Sonny raised his hand slightly, flexing the four fingers he had left. His brow arched. "Won't slip off, won't pull off. Can't even get it chewed off. Not sure I could lose it if I tried."

With a soft *click,* a blade sprang from the Synth's wrist, sleek and sharp. He extended it slowly toward Sonny's face.

"There's more than one way to take off a ring," En'Gen informed him.

Sonny flinched instinctively, closing his fist and leaning back.

"Point taken," Sonny said quickly. "I'll keep a better eye on it. Thanks for saving me, robot."

En'Gen clasped Sonny's shoulder with his mechanical hand—a gesture which Sonny guessed meant *you're welcome.*

"En'Gen is not a robot, Sonny. Don't be racist," Myli called out. "He's a *Clanker,*" she kidded.

She was already moving as she cracked open one of the wall lockers. Inside: more Second Skin armor, Alpha Skin suits, and an arsenal of weapons—sleek, matte-black, and clearly alien in design. She glanced over her shoulder at Sonny, then motioned for him to join her. "Pick something out with some punch."

Sonny stepped closer, eyeing the locker's contents like a kid in a candy store. Laser guns? Plasma rifles? Particle cannons? Something better?

He reached in—and came away with a sleek pistol, three selectors on it. The barrel had an opening crown rivaling the diameter of 45 caliber. There was a port on it but not for ejections, maybe excess gas or heat he thought.

"What the hell is this?" he muttered, turning it over in his hand.

Click. It transformed.

The top slide expanded forward and aft, shifting, transforming in his hand with a mechanical whisper of servo-magic. Panels snapped into place. It transformed from a pistol to a subcompact automatic rifle.

Encouraged, he picked up a second weapon. An assault rifle. With the depression of a button, the digital red dot optic extended just enough to create a compact scope. Another touch, and the weapon pulsed faintly before the expansion of the barrel, the crown now smaller at the end, as his commands fashioned a sniper rifle.

Sonny's eyes were big and bright; his statement brief but filled with enthusiasm.

"WHAT?!" he exclaimed with a smile ear to ear.

Here was one rifle for any task, the complete firearm—sleek, adaptive, and bristling with hidden potential. Sonny was so astonished, he turned to Hawk.

"Bro!" Sonny shouted, his amazement boarding on childish. "It weighs nothin.'"

Hawk—the ever-brooding, ultra-pragmatic soldier lurking nearby, arms crossed, jaw clenched like he was chewing on a nail—just shook his head.

Such a noob, Hawk thought. *The fate of the world rests on the shoulders of this clown.*

Unaware of Hawk's dismissal, Sonny gave a small nod.

"Okay, now we're talking," Sonny laughed as he realized that thermal-night-vision hybrid filled the rifle's scope which was paired with an IR laser and illuminator.

"It's a redundant system," Hawk said dryly.

Sonny was puzzled. "How so?" he asked.

Hawk's remark was a slap in the face—playful—maybe, maybe not.

"It's redundant. Just like the membrane face shield covering and protecting your head and face," Hawk explained with an edge to his voice. "The scope and face shield have the exact same capabilities."

Hawk sighed and walked away, muttering to himself, *What does she see in this guy?*

Sonny, under his breath, muttered, *"Dick."*

CHAPTER 3

Quiet Earth

Time passed and they were ready. A walk down a balmy 70-degree ice tunnel led them to the Heaven's Gate. It was simply a door frame, out in the open, with a stone face blocking the pass-through. The Core chamber sealed behind them and began to power up.

En'Gen moved to the main console, fingers dancing across the glowing interface as he entered the coordinates, waiting as the others double-checked their kits. Coordinates were sent to their suits.

Myli pulled a thin book, tore out a page, folded it with care, and slipped it into her suit which the nano-seam sealed up promptly after it was stowed.

She turned to Sonny. "The station we're heading to has been abandoned for—" She hesitated, her words fumbling as the weight of centuries pressed on her. "For a very long time. Oxygen may be low or nonexistent."

She pointed to the Mini Mii node on the gorget of his Mark V 2nd SKN suit. "Touch your throat armor here to activate your helmet. Or just think about doing it. It's redundant."

"Lots of redundancy with this tech," Sonny frowned. "What if I think to open it at the wrong time?"

"The Evi AI software won't allow you to do anything too stupid. It would take a lot to override a dumb mistake like that."

"Hold my beer," Sonny said jokingly.

"I doubt we need to hold your beer for you to do something stupid," Hawk remarked.

En'Gen chimed in, taking the puny racist human under his wing. "Your suit recycles CO_2... sweat, urine... indefinitely. Your suit will keep you alive in a vacuum or steam. Waste becomes fuel. Don't take it off."

"If you teleport," Myli said, her voice firm, "anything non-biological has to be 'inside' the suit. Or it won't come with you."

She slapped the pistol against her thigh—an *energized suction*. An unseen force locked it in place as the suit secreted a shimmer of nanotech, particles flowing over the weapon and sealing it in. Without looking, she spun and slapped a high-tech rifle across her back. The same process—instant containment, seamless integration.

"So, we get to keep our clothes on from now on?" Sonny speculated.

She grinned at him. "I never heard any complaints."

He slapped his rifle to his back. "Hell, woman, *some days are better than others.*" Disengaged the sling.

She scoffed—a sharp puff of annoyance. "Once the helmet's on, it syncs with your neural impulses through the cilia. You'll control the HUD without lifting a finger. It's more than armor—it's a second nervous system."

"Hence the 2nd SKN designation," he finished her thought. "And the Templar crosses?"

The others looked at him. Myli and Hawk with blank expressions on their faces, the Synth with an irregular blip in his visor. None understood the reference.

Sonny pointed to the small cross on his suit.

"Oh, that," Myli said. "Your people have flags don't they?"

Sonny gave her a puzzled look, but she didn't say anything more.

Hawk flexed in his new gear, checking the fit of the forearm bracers. "These are way better than the Team 12 suits. I forgot how good we had it in the past. Those rickety things our team was using didn't stand a chance against the Udug. If we upload A.V.A to this..."

"Body coffins." Myli glanced at him. "Hopefully, these will increase our chances. Udug venom is nasty."

En'Gen held out vials. "Thanks to Myli's orders and the fact we stuck around to save Sonny—we have an antidote. These capsules will snap into each suit on contact, sliding into place like your rifle—seamless with your first-tier kit."

Hawk chuckled. "So, in referencing this Sonny character, you should've just said we were investing precious time for the antidote, not waiting for the boat anchor. I'd have bought that."

Myli's brow furrowed. She was miffed at Hawk as she turned back to give Sonny one last piece of advice. "The MKV suit amplifies an energy force field but it's not invincible. If it takes too much damage, it won't regenerate. If you take care of it, it'll take care of you."

Then, seeking a quieter, more personal moment, she pulled Sonny aside, away from Hawk's teenage antics. Her helmet hissed softly as it disengaged. The clear membrane visor liquefied and vanished into the system. She stood close—eyes just below his, breath warm with a hint of staleness between them.

She drew him in.

Sonny wasn't sure what was coming next.

"I have history with Hawk," she said, voice low. "I think that's what the cold shoulder is about. Watch your back. Stay close to me—don't move unless I say so. Got it?"

Sonny gave a small grin and a nod.

"What?" she asked, her face moving closer.

He shrugged. "Just—just waiting on you. This gonna hurt?"

Her expression softened. "If you stay calm, the transition can feel euphoric. If you panic, it can feel like you're drowning. You'll be fine, Sonny."

She turned sharply, looked at En'Gen, and snapped, "Are we set?" She broke away from Sonny. Without waiting for the answer, she strutted toward the solid stone doorway. Her helmet and visor activating along the way like magic.

Even the Synth took notice of her magnetism.

"Ten seconds, Myli."

The Synth's voice echoed in the ice chamber as the countdown began. Her steps, her swagger, lined up perfectly with his timing. When En'Gen reached the end of the countdown, her final step, the same pace as the first, penetrated the solid structure. It wrapped around her like molten gold alloy, and she was through the Heaven's Gateway.

Hawk and Sonny gave each other a look in silent critique of her theatrical perfection and epic exit. Hawk went next. Sonny would follow. He reached the Gateway and stopped.

Terrified.

He turned to address En'Gen, but before he could back out, the Synth shoved him through.

No tunnel, no redistribution of molecules, no dematerialization or disassembly of organic deconstruction. They simply walked through one side and stepped through to the other. Although Sonny's step through was more of a stumble as he tripped his way into a massive underground cavern. He looked around, looked behind. The same stone arch was behind him now and En'Gen was walking through.

Sonny's entrance was nowhere near as elegant as any of the others, especially Myli. Hawk had walked through like a seasoned stoic vet. If Sonny was honest with himself, Hawk looked like the badass every guy he knew would want to be. And yet, he scoffed at the notion.

"What happened, did you take the scenic route or what?" Hawk ad-libbed.

Sonny, in his head: *This effing guy.*

Inside the cavern, the lay of the land was eerie, still, and claustrophobic. Loose rocks littered the ground, evidence of a long-past collapse. The only illumination came from the soft bioluminescent glow of their suits, casting long, shifting shadows across the pitted stone.

Near the far wall, a path and an entrance to the next chamber. Half a dozen mummified corpses huddled together by the ancient hatch—frozen mid-sentence by death. Their skeletal remains stretched eight to ten feet tall, grotesque in their stillness. Elongated fingers curled like claws, oversized craniums bulged unnaturally, and their skin—what was left of it—clung like brittle parchment to their desiccated bones.

Sonny cringed, hand down near his pistol. "They look like I would picture an alien." he stated, voice low.

"Relax gun slinger, their dead," Hawk poked fun.

Myli shook her head grimly. "Igigi. Far from human."

"When they bred with humans," En'Gen added, stepping closer, "the results were less than ideal. These are full blood."

"How so?" Sonny asked, squatting down next to them. Examining them closer.

"Chimeras," Myli said.

Hawk butted in, stepping up beside Sonny, who was still crouched and staring at the remains. "Sonny might know the half breeds as the Nephilim," he said, his tone casual, but laced with weight. He was well-versed in the Ethiopian Bible. "Giant monsters," he finished.

Their Second Skin suits scanned what remained of the atmosphere—Oxygen: 0.02%. Radiation: Minimal. Temperature: 60°F. Spores detected—an extremophile species extinct for over ten thousand years. Their HUDs flickered, feeding real-time data into their minds via thought-linked channels. The antechamber had become a tomb. Only bacteria and ancient spores remained inside. Their suits' AI cross-referenced information from the ring's database, auto-translating glyphs and historical metadata based on brainwave patterns.

Myli unsealed her suit, briefly exposing her chest to the cool air as she retrieved a thin sheet of paper from where she'd tucked it. The moment her fingers traced the surface of the paper, an electronic schematic unfolded before her.

Sonny stood up and peeked over her shoulder. To him, the alien script was incomprehensible. His visor flickered. One by one, the symbols superimposed over the script on the map translating it for him.

Myli pointed at the map. "This way. We need to access the hatch at the end of this corridor, then follow the tunnel down four levels. We should enter here, the docking bay. The temperature will rise about a degree every sixty feet. When we open the chamber, it will be like stepping into hell."

Hawk stared at the sealed hatch. Jagged rock and debris blocked it completely—a cave-in, airtight and final. There was no going back, only forward. "Why did they stay out here?" he muttered, brows tightening. "If the Heaven's Gate was inaccessible, they could've gone deeper into the station, instead it looks like they deliberately sealed themselves in."

Sonny stared with reservation at the mummified corpses. His brain flicked through horror movie logic. Graboids—aka Kevin Bacon. The poor bastard in *Tremors* who wouldn't climb down from the telephone pole— turned into jerky on a stick in the sun. His stomach turned. Why was he following Captain Bad Idea again? This chick was a bag of bad luck and pain.

Myli crouched, placed the paper against the access panel. Her fingers traced the moist rock, and the nanites in the enzyme worked their magic— unlocking the door.

"Listen!" Hawk looked around, touched the walls. Vibrations. The confined space was already affecting him. "What the heck is that?"

En'Gen theorized, "Venting of some kind. Displacement or draining of a chamber."

Meanwhile, Sonny was still studying the mummified remains, analyzing their frozen expressions. Moisture had once allowed partial decomposition, but when it dried, the process halted, leaving a haunting blend of bone and preserved flesh.

Sonny activated his Troop Net MIC through the HUD. "You think they just laid down and died. What could be on the other side of that door worse than dying here?"

"Virus maybe," Myli replied.

Once unlocked, she pushed the 400-ton door forward with no effort whatsoever. Something slick—perfect cuts, or just plain alien architecture— allowed it to open with ease. Warm wet air rushed out of a passage revealed on the side. Everyone jumped except Myli. The sound echoed down the 45-degree corridor.

She pulled her pistol, weapon-mounted light on, she scanned the opening. "We're in, girls." Without hesitation, she pushed forward in the low ready.

Sonny hesitated. "No one else saw that?"

Myli frowned. "You're seeing ghosts, Sonny."

"I thought—I saw something," Sonny insisted. "Like the wall moving in the distance."

"Not here. This place is death. Nothing can survive here for more than 30 minutes without a suit." Myli snapped back "This place we're heading into," she added between breaths, her voice tight in her throat, "sits right on a fault line. That's not just heat—it's a magma chamber beneath us creating super-heated water and steam."

"Okay, that explains the sauna-from-hell vibes," Sonny said as temp readings began to climb in his HUD.

"This place teeters on 100% humidity, Sonny," she replied, glancing at the HUD in her suit. "The only reason why we will not boil alive down there is because the suits are regulating the heat."

"Sounds like a typical South Texas summer," Sonny grinned.

But Myli turned serious. "From here on, stay alert. There could be dormant Gen-1 or Gen-2 Synth Series sentries. When they locked this place down, they weren't planning on making it easy for the Anunna getting in here."

Hawk stepped forward, brushing past Myli. He was taking point. "Stay behind me. In case there are surprises."

Myli raised an eyebrow but let him lead as they began their descent. "Be my guest; you trip the traps."

CHAPTER 4

Crystal Cave

The dirt then stone path ended, giving way to a vast, lightless abyss. They entered a blast furnace. The darkness devoured their suit lights, swallowing them whole. Only the refractions and reflections of light from their suits danced off colossal crystals towering like redwood trees.

The ground and sides of stone were covered in what looked like monolithic crystals resembling shark teeth. The cave system was a jungle-gym of crystals to crawl through.

"Dumuzi and I found this place a half a million years after the crystals materialized from boiling in a stable concoction of water and minerals." En'Gen told them.

Water dripped from above and pooled in areas near their feet.

"The complex drained the chamber allowing us in," Myli said with amazement while splashing a puddle with her foot.

Sonny noticed her playful mood. Only she would be excited exploring hell.

En'Gen struggled working his way through the gaps. Low spots were filled with pools of water. Sonny looked at his forearm. The touchpad read 119 degrees with an arrow pointing up. He could see the air thickening with steam, suffocating without protection.

Hawk slinked through an obstacle with no more clearance than a set of bundled match sticks. "Tight squeeze, Tin Skin?" he asked En'Gen.

En'Gen's body morphed, articulating in fashion no humans could. His abnormal contortionism was enough to silence Hawk.

"Those gypsum crystals are amazing," Myli muttered with delight.

Sonny stumbled over some shards. "Yeah," he said, also in awe but dripping with sarcasm too. "Delightful," he said, seeing her reaction.

A massive telephone pole-sized crystal had fallen, fractured in half no doubt the result of an earthquake.

"Watch your step. A twisted ankle will put us all at risk of getting out to the ship."

"These things must weigh 50 tons or more," Sonny mused.

Their suits began fogging from the crushing humidity. Oxygen deprivation was the least of their worries—boiling to death was a proper concern. Evi alerted the team that the current temperature would collapse them in thirty minutes.

"Not too long ago, we were getting frostbite," Sonny said contrasting her warning.

The colors were not the only thing pulsing in the suffocating darkness. The cave groaned, a deep, ancient whisper as the harmonics of the crystals warned them to turn back. Sonny scanned the abyss. He was bait again.

Something was out there, watching them from the void. The team switched to red lights, then to IR. They activated infrared vision, then thermal, and even the hybrid layer setting flickered in their HUDs. Shadows danced and moved as a direct result of them walking, crawling and climbing over, under, and through the maze of minerals. The disorientation reminded Sonny of the old-time rotating shadow lights. In this case, it was he and the others spinning, creating a black shadow nightmare.

Sonny's pulse spiked. No smart watches to alert him this time.

"Heart rate spiking," Evi warned him.

He jumped when she broke the silence in his mind. "Damn it."

Nothing should be able to survive this heat, he told himself. *But I know we aren't alone—I can feel it.*

"Sonny," Myli turned to him, "knock it off!" She used her hand to animate the circumference of her head. "All that crap up here," she tapped, "in your head," she said, pointing at him, more so his thoughts. "It's freaking me out."

Myli's HUD registered skyrocketing heart rates across the team; it wasn't just Sonny. 100% humidity. 129 degrees.

"It's not just him," Hawk claimed even though he plainly hated defending the Deadweight. "I feel it too," Hawk added as he slid down a huge pillar of crystal gypsum into an ankle-deep pool of water. "We've been climbing through these things for forty-five minutes." He grunted, catching himself on a pillar in front of him. "Maybe we are in the wrong spot."

En'Gen clumsily navigated over and through a set of pillars. "It's right— Dumuzi and I scouted this place; the ship is here."

Hawk looked back. The old bot was laboring. "You said it yourself," Hawk reminded the Synth, "your files are corrupt. You've got too much water on your circuit boards, Sparky."

"We're at the end of the tunnel, so you can quit your bitching." Myli radioed over as she started to squeeze out of an adjacent path. "The two of you just keep it together another 900 meters. It should be less claustrophobic up here." She squirted out and popped up on her feet like a triumphant biathlon.

Show off. Sonny thought. *Just like Chiara.*

Looking ahead, between the intervening beams, Sonny could see Myli waiting on them. A shadow, behind her moved. Was it from them?

Myli felt it too. Nervousness got her. She turned around.

Nothing there.

"Damn it, Sonny!" she yelled at him. "Stop thinking!"

He sighed. He was sweating like a madman in an un-airconditioned suit.

Eventually, the end of the tunnel opened into a massive cavern full of even more crystals, but it had been excavated to make room for something spectacular before being refilled with water.

"Stairs down," Hawk said, his red palm light casting jagged shadows. "It's slippery."

A stairwell had been carved through the crystal, winding downward into darkness. Halfway down, a narrow catwalk stretched across the void—suspended above a seemingly bottomless drop. Steam thickened the air, making each step perilous.

"This choke point would be a perfect place for an ambush," Sonny murmured, gripping the rail.

"Deadweight is right," Hawk grumbled.

Sonny stared into the black void. "I'm not having fun again, Myli. You're trying to kill me."

"Just your patience." Myli joked, but even she sounded uneasy now looking down into the void. "A little nervous, Sonny?" she asked rhetorically.

He approached the rail, death grip on the first rung. "Not great with heights," he said as every step down the ladder added weight to his anxiety level. "Or boiling death caves for that matter." His voice was drying; his breathing became labored and rapid.

"Slow down your breathing," Myli ordered. "You're going to hyperventilate. Think about something else."

"Yeah, right." He tried. He knew he was somewhere no one else in the world would ever see. "These crystals," he whispered, almost reverent. "I didn't know anything like this even existed. It looks like they have water in them. Is that possible?" he asked trying to catch his breath.

Mylitta shook her head. No clue.

En'Gen had an idea. "Pockets of air, voids where the crystals stopped growing or died," the Synth surmised.

Sonny's muscles locked as he reached for the next rung and the next until his leaden legs and feet finally hit the main catwalk. Every step felt like cement weighing him down. He knew he would be exhausted by the time they reached the ship.

"These stairs are newer—twenty thousand years, maybe more. If they were going to collapse, they'd have done it by now," En'Gen reassured Sonny.

Sonny nodded. The weight of fear lifted from his limbs temporarily.

En'Gen clanked down onto the deck. "If anything comes for us, we have enough firepower to level this whole complex. Be careful what you shoot at."

Hawk's voice also sounded labored, although he tried to hide it. "One small step. Only a few thousand left, Sonny!" He muttered with dread also gnawing at his gut.

This was Evil Superman's Fortress of Solitude, but underground, and made of gypsum.

The shadows shifted again. Sonny finally ignored them, but the others didn't. A body actually moved and this time it wasn't Sonny seeing things.

Hawk reached behind his back. The suit reacted, peeling back to expose the rifle's grip. "I saw it too, Sonny."

CHAPTER 5

Inoculation by Fire

Hawk thrust a clenched fist into the air. "Stop. Quiet." His voice was low but sharp, a whisper sheathed in command. Everyone halted, then dropped to a knee—Sonny was last, his boots scraping softly against the rough, white-mud-caked grates.

No one spoke. No one moved. Even breath became suspect.

They listened.

The only sounds were the subtle trickles of mineral-rich water winding through hidden crevices. The drips were a constant echo from overhead. Somewhere deeper in the cavern, the faint rustle of pale albino shrimp or blind extremophile minnows stirred in thermal pools. Their bioluminescent bodies cast faint pulses like heartbeat monitors in the dark until something heavy entered the pool of water; it was just enough to frighten the glowing shrimp and shut off their luminosity.

"Everyone Lights out, now." Hawk knew there was more to this place in the dark.

Lights out, they could hear the low hum of the cave. It was as if the photons somehow interfered with their hearing. Tapping into their other senses they listened more carefully. Was it machinery? Something in the cave? Most likely it was the low frequencies resonating from the crystals themselves. Nature flipped the light switch on. Other extremophiles living and thriving in the extreme environment they called home announced their presence to the invaders.

They started to glow. Like early night vision nods, the cave saturated itself in green bioluminescent light.

"Beautiful." Myli said.

The vastness of the chamber loomed around them—a subterranean cathedral of geological nightmares, but it was gorgeous. Gypsum crystals as large as trees, sprinkled in like a pile of toothpicks, jutting through the air like fractured glass blades, stalactites and stalagmites fused into monstrous columns, forming natural buttresses that supported the ceiling like the bones of some extinct titan. Bioluminescent pockets shimmered inside the crystals, faint ecosystems pulsing green.

"This whole place is alive," Sonny asserted.

The hair raised on the back of their necks when they noticed those green-lit areas going dark. Something was alarming the indigenous life here—turning them off. Darkness was heading their way.

Hawk's eyes narrowed as he scowled at an advancing black spot. Something was on the move and hunting.

Sonny turned slowly, squinting past the blue glow of his HUD watching the darkness advancing in front of their path. "There," he whispered. "The shadows are all around us."

While Hawk tracked the darkness above, Sonny caught movement ahead. They hadn't noticed it above them as they climbed down. The dark distortion becomes eight, carefully moving behind the veins of calcite and quartz like a shadow person beneath ice. Hawk turned on his light.

The apparition had, not one, but eight limbs, slinking down from the ceiling. Not eight creatures, just one entity, its segmented legs unfolding in complete silence, covered in a biological material which blended it into the environment. The mechanical claws flashed under the sparse bioluminescent light. It latched onto the wall just above the ladder they'd come down, its bulk unfurling like a night terror.

Sonny's pulse thudded in his ears. Rapid breathing ensuing. All of them hearing the panic of their breath echoing in their helmets.

Hawk made his decision. He would hold the line. Buy them time. There was no room for hesitation down here. No space for democracy. Just survival.

He glanced up again—another one, poised above them like a mechanical spider god. The monstrosity deity didn't twitch. It observed, calculating angles, paths, kill zones. Its limbs bent with inhuman symmetry, joints hissing softly as they rotated—too fluid for something so massive.

Hawk knew this wasn't some clunky war-bot from the 21st century. These things were predators. A predator somewhere between machine and biomechanical creature, perfected, and left to rot in a cave—until now.

Hawk took note of its battered hull. It bore the scars of centuries of pitting from being underwater, scorched with laser burns, clawed by wars long forgotten. The entombed sentinel was also covered in ancient glyphs—the Anunna script, tattooed on its skin, now dulled and scarred.

"Machines," En'Gen whispered.

"Machines from your era," Hawk whispered back.

"You know your history." En'Gen fired back. "ARACH-X," En'Gen spat. "Ancient war Machines."

Hawk petitioned, "Can you explain to them we are friends?"

This one—like the rest—was a relic of pure annihilation. Its mission hadn't changed. Eliminate intruders. No command override. No surrender. Just fulfillment of code.

Hawk turned as Myli grabbed his arm. "We have to stick together!" He heard her voice cracking like a whip behind him. She was struggling to change his mind but it was already made.

"Wait," En'Gen commanded. "Let me try it, talk to them; they are my kind." He stepped back to the rear of the group. Waved his arms. "Brothers! We mean you no harm…"

Ignoring the Synth's efforts, Hawk shoved Myli forward with one powerful push. "I told you—you can't save everyone. Not happening," he barked. "The mission comes first. Keep moving. Now!"

The crystals themselves rose like jagged skyscrapers from the floor, some fused into bridges of mineral and time, others cracked and leaning like fractured teeth. The catwalk, cantilevered into the side of the cavern with alloy posts jutting out from the wall. The path led toward a distant, football-field-sized shadow, cloaked in darkness at the end of the chamber.

Hawk grunted. "Down there, I can see it; that's our way in, just keep following the bridge."

Sonny grabbed the rail and felt corrosion snagging the glove on the suit. Corrosion meant imperfections—imperfections he was willing to ignore now. He looked Hawk eye to eye as he too was pushed forward. "You're insane; it's called a strategic withdrawal for a reason."

"Yeah," Hawk muttered. "So, withdrawal—distance is your friend."

"Let me help!" Sonny demanded.

A hatch. A chance. Maybe even the ship in the distance.

Myli clenched her jaw, fury flaring in her eyes. "Damn it, Anshar!" But she didn't argue.

Sonny was still watching their rear, trying to count the legs in the dark. She turned, grabbed Sonny by the arm, and spun him around.

"With me," she commanded. "Move!"

En'Gen continued his plead until it turned into diatribe to his fellow Synths. "Join us brothers." But over the comm he whispered a warning to the others, "Just in case one of my fellow's forearms powers up and begins spinning like the barrels of a Gatling gun, you'd better run."

Sonny and Myli ran.

Behind them, metal scraped stone, followed by the low, mechanical growl of the ARACH-X engaging. Hawk and En'Gen stood their ground. One arm smashed into En'Gen, planting him into a wall.

Above them, the other biomechanical spider skittered down the walls into the forest of crystals—its bladed limbs slicing through untouched crystal, weaving in and out of tight spaces. It carved fresh gouges into the ancient gypsum as it moved.

The steel under their feet groaned and flexed, welds popping as the ancient stairwell shuddered under the assault of additional weight.

As Myli and Sonny ran, for the ship, chunks of stairwell snapped free, falling away into the blackness with a metallic clank.

Myli looked back to confirm their situation. "There was no going back now."

"They're not shooting!" Sonny noted.

"They were executioners, precise and quiet, not shooting up the place, optimized for stealth kills," she told him.

Sonny bet its preference was to gut its prey in silence and leave the rest to rot. But what cleaned up the death in here? The Extremophiles? There were no other bodies. These things were dormant for centuries, he guessed. They were taking a minute to fully boot up.

He looked back. Water spitting out from orifices, prepping for dry combat.

The spider, the one watching from above, unfolded from the darkness, locomotion descending without a sound like the first. Using an alternating tripod gait, it's eight blades flexed in hydraulic rhythm, as it moved with terrifying efficiency.

When the ARACH-X landed, the tremor on the bridge hit them like a freight train.

Myli and Sonny slammed against the guardrail, the full force of the quake driving her suit into flesh. Myli cried out, her abdomen hitting the railing hard, her suit audibly straining as she caught herself from falling into the bottomless pit. Sonny hit the deck face-first, pain blooming across his chin and ribs as the soft meat wracked around in the suit.

He scrambled up. "You, okay?" Sonny asked, disregarding his own pains. He reached back for her hand.

"We've had worse," she groaned, rising, one hand clutching her side the other taking his.

"These gigantic things aren't what I was seeing," he said. "I saw something else. Up ahead." He pointed. "More dark spots incoming." The algae's reaction was a natural indicator.

He pulled her to her feet just as they heard something new in front. A shiver in the darkness ahead of them. "The algae, it cuts out where there is movement. It knows these things are predators." He postulated.

That new nightmare was creeping in front of them, closer now, appearing in the form of a single black silhouette. The first creature slinking out of the darkness was backlit by the green hue behind it. Finally, they could make out some size and shape. Sonny squinted, the shadow stopped. As soon as it did, the microscopic organisms briefly bloomed color. Both Myli and Sonny flinched in shock from not understanding what they saw.

This creature was smaller than a human and looked to be nimbler in these tight spaces. Leanness screamed its diet. All muscle, no fat. Sonny could tell it was at home in this subterranean hell hole based on his observations. He couldn't tell if it was a predator or a scavenger, but it moved like a creature at home in hot, tight, winding spaces. Its movements were twitchy but calculating. Its evolution in this place gave them the advantage, and so did their numbers.

While briefly illuminated, they noticed the lack of hair—quills made more sense down here. So did its patchwork of semi-translucent mottled greys. The skin matched the color of the surroundings. A hint of deep algae green skin complimented its camouflage for above ground. The elongated head and barbed quills running down its back sent shivers down Sonny's spine. Soon this first horror was joined by several others. Their tongues whipped around, tasting the air for pheromones and individual stink.

Sonny's face screamed horror. "What the shit is that?" His body shivered.

"Snakes do that," Myli whispered over comms. "They taste the air. I don't think they can see very well, but the rest of their senses are probably enhanced. The suits may be disguising our scent."

"They're attracted to something or they wouldn't be here." Sonny figured. "The faint illumination from inside our helmets is like a lighthouse down here in the pitch black."

"Dim your HUD."

With a thought he did. All of the creatures stopped creeping. The green atmosphere returned to the cave. One was within inches of Myli. Its red, bloodshot eyes had an iridescent quality like cat eyes do when reflecting light. The closest one stretched its distended jaws, displaying layers of jagged teeth while whipping its tongue further out.

Sonny heard the stories growing up. Goats bled out, hikers gone missing. But the stories didn't do justice to what Sonny was visualizing in front of him.

Myli's posture stiffened.

He noticed. "Myli?"

"My bladder let loose."

He understood.

Another shadow, a second creature joined with the first taking up a crouching posture on a broken crystal stump. It too illuminated once it stopped moving. Its clawed fingers spread wide on the stump. It was getting ready to pounce.

Myli quietly took a step back—it was instinctual. Sonny wanted to do the same, but he held the line. New fuel imprinted on their already trauma-filled psyches.

Sonny muttered under his breath, voice low and trembling, "Chupacabra, dude. We can't stand still forever. To hell with these things," he whispered to no one in particular. His hands shook as he brought his rifle to bear.

Shoot now? But which one, too many? Hard to see. Obstacles blocking shots. Sonny's mind began to shut down. Stress overload. This is a dream. Had to be. The corner of the dresser kissed his temple before leaving for work. Was this a coma nightmare?

He was momentarily petrified.

His thoughts pressed into Myli's. "Sonny, damn it, this is real," He heard Myli speaking softly to him. "You're not dreaming. Pull your head out of your ass."

Sonny glanced around, the green bioluminescence almost completely gone. They were everywhere and moving again. It was real, alright—so real that his visor couldn't register the targets due to the heat surrounding them.

He took a deep, unwavering breath. "Fine." Sonny growled. "Game on!"

A switch flipped inside Sonny. The fear inoculated out of him. He began blasting.

Myli didn't flinch. The second he let loose, so did she. She spun and cracked the pistol butt into the nearest creature's skull. It bit off its own tongue when its skull split like a melon. The thing staggered back, blue blood spraying the walls. It wailed and, for a moment, the other creatures backed off. But now she was covered in the thing's stink.

The darkness flooded her direction like moths to a flame. More were coming, homing in on her.

They rose from the catwalk below as well. From above the same below. They were silent, crawling like ticks across the walls. They invaded the catwalk like fire ants massing on a stick in the water.

"My God—their swarming, we need to get the hell out of here!" Sonny's voice sounded hoarse. He turned, fired, and damn-near blasted one in half. Its scream was not human—a sound made of shredded childish cries. The autonomous sensory meridian response shot straight from his scalp down his spine leading to his trigger finger, a happy finger.

Myli's pistol hissed, transforming mid-grip, the upper receiver locking into sub-assault mode. She fired on burst mode and didn't stop. The little sub gun blasted in extremely fast burps of fire—a great option for a horde of creatures with no armor trying to overrun their position.

Energy bolts pierced through the darkness. Each shot ripping through the swarm—limbs, torsos, spines bursting apart, blood and bile spraying out like a madman putting out a fire with a hose.

The stairwell continued to tremble, pounds away from collapse.

"The bean-counters at OSHA would have a heart attack if they saw us on this bridge." Sonny flippantly told Myli. He wondered if she could tell he was embracing his fear.

Down the catwalk from Myli and Sonny, Hawk and En'Gen were locked in battle with more than one of the descending nightmares. The cybernetic spiders moved with horrific precision, their blended organic alloy limbs clicking like steel baseball cleats across the crystalline stone—razor-sharp, hyper-tuned, and silent until they struck. Amber colored eyes flared, cycling through a visual spectrum.

The armored gargoyles worked in sync—two-on-two working to outwit their victims.

"Watch the legs, Hawk!" En'Gen snapped, already in motion. "They'll feint with one limb and strike with another. Go for the elastic tissue between the segments!"

Hawk didn't bother responding with anything more than a glare. "I know what I'm doing, Cogsucker."

Even as the words left his mouth, the first spider lunged—a blur of sharpened limbs.

SNAP!

A blade-like leg sliced the air with sonic force, missing Hawk's throat by millimeters—an attack mechanism used by some animals. The sonic wave disorienting Hawk, En'Gen immune. He dropped to one knee—micro servo-assisting motors in his suit screeching—and fired point-blank into its chest.

The first round ripped into its exoskeleton, staggering it. The second shattered a central limb joint, sending cybernetic fluid spraying like arterial blood. The cybernetic arachnid shrieked—a metallic banshee wail like a piece of metal in a disposer and yet it kept coming.

Hawk snarled and rolled backward as it crashed into the space he had just occupied. Another sonic boom next to his head.

En'Gen stepped in and met it at full stride—his machine-body a blur of force and balance. He vaulted, gripped the bladed limb mid-strike, and twisted, his shoulders grinding under strain. SHHHNK! A blade jutted from the Synth's forearm, slicing the spider's leg in one perfect arc.

"Thanks." Hawk offered.

The spider stumbled, fluid spouting from another limb. En'Gen slammed it into the grating on the bridge. Once. Twice. Three times. Crystalline shards exploded outward from the wall. The bridge losing more stability. He stomped down hard—through its thorax. A final, fatal crunch.

Disoriented, Hawk dove sideways—plasma bladed limbs missing by inches, striking the cave wall with a thunderous CRACK. Sparks exploded across the stone as energy was released into the stone. Nearby gypsum burned.

He skidded behind a pillar of jagged crystal, leaving behind his rifle which clattered away into the dark—lost over the side of the bridge. *Never lose your rifle.* His backup still in place on his hip.

The spider advanced, its limbs swinging like appendage metronomes, one leg hissing with static charge.

Hawk grew bored with this game. He drew his sidearm and aimed. One shot. One joint. One chance. No hesitation. The limb amputated, flew directly at him.

Evi sensed danger before he did. The A.I. interjected her auto pilot feature. The latissimus micro-thrusters flared, launching him in a controlled side-skid. The metal grating under his feet sparked as friction heated up the abrasive surface.

Eyes locked on target. He was already firing again.

Another round buried deep into a key joint. He took aim at the head now. The final shot blew the spider's head apart in a burst of fire. Cybernetic fluid and molten metal lit up the cavern like a flash-bang.

The Synth's HUD flashed. Motion. Heavy. From the far side of the cavern, it emerged—uncoiling from the shadows like a living siege engine. Bigger than both previous spiders combined. The mama bear was coming.

Its multi-jointed segmented limbs clanged against crystal, tearing gouges through gypsum and stone. This one was different. Meaner. Smarter. The final protocol.

"New player inbound," En'Gen warned, voice low and electronic.

CHAPTER 6

Sauna Boogie

Myli and Sonny were knee-deep in Chupacabras. Sonny opened up, laying down suppressive fire, picking off chupacabras as they swarmed towards them.

"More incoming!" Sonny yelled.

The structure shuddered; bolts were snapping from their moorings. Metal screeching. In the distance, where En'Gen and Hawk were fighting the robotic spiders, the entrance to the catwalk was collapsing.

Behind them Hawk and En'Gen fought for their lives. Sonny saw something more massive than the first guardians at the gates.

"We should go back and help." He suggested.

She shook her head. "That's not the mission."

Errant shots behind them. Explosions in the distance. Sonny saw the huge robot, En'Gen, jump into the air attacking the massive cybernetic eight-legged freak.

In the middle of their battle.

"I see it," Hawk muttered, his HUD shifting. Target lock failed. Reacquiring.

The creature moved with calculated grace, two front legs sweeping the floor like duelist's sabers, pedipalps twitching—testing air pressure for their positions.

En'Gen's arm-cannon screamed with another volley.

A sonic crack knocked Hawk down. He smiled, tasting the blood in his mouth. If he was going to die, this was an excellent way to go. "I'm going to try something." He powered up his plasma torch. "Night-night," he taunted the beast.

En'Gen tried to warn him. "Hawk, wait!" But it was too late.

He shot above the massive enemy bringing down a gypsum avalanche on top of it.

En'Gen glowered at Hawk's indiscriminate fire. "That stunt with the plasma torch just put us on a timer."

Hawk panned over to the destruction. Sure enough, they were minutes away from catastrophe. Hawk's impetuous shot was inadvertently bringing the house down on top of them.

Myli and Sonny saw the end of their fight. It was loud and colorful. The ceiling was collapsing. Gypsum crystals were raining down.

"Run!" En'Gen and Hawk both screamed as they barreled down the bridge towards Sonny and Myli.

Sonny looked back and forward. Run? Run where?" They were being swarmed from all directions. It took everything they had to move twenty or more meters. The comms began to crackle. Sonny and Myli could barely hear them.

"It's all coming down!" En'Gen and Hawk continued shouting as they tried to relay the impending catastrophe unfolding behind them.

Small fires burned from missed blasts. The green in the cave was no more. Smoke and steam whited out most of their visual periphery. But they could hear. Clicking and Scratching, the sounds of more *chupacabras* incoming.

A chupacabra scrambling beneath the catwalk made its move. In a death-defying gymnastics move, it twisted its way up and over the railing and onto the catwalk. A blur of claws, teeth, and malice right into Sonny's face.

"Holy..." Sonny yelled. His first instinct was to elbow it and create space.

Its bloodred eyes locked onto him. The blank stare held no malice. It was just doing what chupacabras do, feed. Sonny's face was also blank, indifferent.

He kicked hard—boots slamming into its chest, cracking ribs. But it didn't fall. It recovered fast, slashing low, its claws ripping sparks off Sonny's chest plate. He couldn't get his rifle back up. No time to aim. Too close.

Sonny let go of his rifle, letting it hang, and drew his blade. The blade cut. The crawler shrieked, stumbling as Sonny was slashing across its shoulder—blue blood spraying around him. Lunging, fangs baring, they collided in a savage tangle of limbs and grunts.

It clawed at his formfitting faceplate and the impact reverberated through the clear crystalline-nano-metallic-membrane. Sonny slammed his head forward in a savage headbutt. His HUD blinked out, a software glitch. When it came back on, the rising heat hit—123°F and climbing.

CRACK. "Oh, no."

His visor spiderwebbed. After another vicious hit, it cracked open, the nano-bits failing from impact. The elements rushed into the vacuum.

The heat hit first like he stuck his head in a 500-degree oven.

"Face Shield Breach," Evi alerted.

His mask shattered into billions of nanoparticles, the disintegrating nanite shards rained through the grated floor like sand. The rest of the helmet instantly retreated back into the suit. Whether it overheated, cracked from repeated impacts, or Sonny's brain finally told the suit there was no reason his head should feel like it was in an oven with the door open—whatever the reason, the atmosphere was suddenly smothering him.

No barrier between him and 123-degree hell. His suit started a 10-minute countdown.

He was in the pressure cooker now. The heat was crawling into his eyes, his mouth, and down his throat. Every new impact from the creature tore fresh breaches. His sweat stopped evaporating—now it poured into his eyes, the salty mix blinding him like an acid waterfall.

The creature reeled back from another sharp combo of Sonny's blade, fist, and elbow. Even though Sonny was fading, there was no backing away. It was fight-or-flight, and he was fighting for his life.

He reversed the grip on his knife and slammed it into the thing's gut, twisting deep until the blade scraped bone. It shrieked, flailing, talons punching under his arm, slicing into soft tissue. He grunted, nearly dropping the blade. His expression soured.

A smack from the creature's elbow crossed Sonny's brow—it was a clean, slicing blow.

Blood poured instantly—a red fountain down his face, blinding his right eye. The creature shoved in close, face to face, jaws snapping like a rabid dog. Sonny pushed it back—vision smeared with sweat and blood. Energy bolts continuously zipped over from Myli's struggles. She spared a second to take out other incoming threats behind him.

No time to thank her.

He ripped the knife upward, carving a vertical path into the creature's sternum. Its body spasmed in his grip, twitching like a broken puppet. Another grunt, another twist, and it went limp—slumping off him with a wet slap.

The whole ordeal was maybe a minute and, despite this, Sonny was absolutely gassed. Sonny staggered up to his feet, a step backward, breathing fire, blood pouring, head pounding like a war drum. The toll of the fight wore on his blank face.

Another screech roared from below.

No time to rest.

He drew his pistol, aimed below him, and blasted one crawling under the grate. It fell into the abyss.

He wiped the blood from his eyes with a trembling arm, holstered his pistol, and picked up his rifle from the catwalk.

The blitz wasn't finished with him.

Another hit him from behind rolled him over him. Another SOB was on top now, claws pummeling his suit. Sonny's arm pinned, he couldn't get to his blade. He needed another option. It opened its mouth—too wide, hotter than the air in the cavern—fangs reaching, jaw extending for his throat.

He reared back and jammed his forearm into its jaw, forcing it back. Blue blood spurted out onto his face. With a surge of strength, Sonny shoved off the deck and rolled the creature over, pinning it down. After freeing his other hand, he rammed the blade into its eye. It twitched violently, then stilled.

Sonny straddled it, knife dripping vitreous humor—the clear, jelly-like fluid giving it its grotesque eye shape. Threads of collagen and hyaluronic acid clung to the blade, catching the fiery light like wet silk just dyed.

The stench around him hit him like rotting cheese, sharp and pungent like a vulture.

His body was quaking, the tremors not from fear but from overexertion, heatstroke clawing its way into his skull. That fricking smel—.

Behind his ear, the helmet's sub-processor stuttered, trying to reform. The suit's Neuralink Brain Computer Interface shorted out. Was he or the suit in control, trans-humanism creeping into his mind?

A low whir—silence. The suit tried again. Nanites crawled up his jaw-line, jittering like dying insects—but there were too many missing pieces. Too much damage. Too much heat. They dissolved again, leaving him exposed, breath burning in his lungs.

He focused on controlling his breathing, fighting panic. He took a step. Staggered. Another step. Slower.

His fingers tightened around the knife. He couldn't let go—muscle spasm, a cramp had locked it in place; he was one with the knife.

He looked behind. Smoke. Blinking suit lights. Hawk and En'Gen were making a mad dash towards Myli. A flicker of Myli's silhouette.

The flash of light didn't happen all at once. The massive explosion came in waves.

Chunks of glowing gypsum, each weighing fifty to a hundred tons, blasted outward in a maelstrom of light and force. Shock waves roared down the tunnel like a tidal wave, flattening smaller cave crawlers instantly. The overpressure hit the team like a freight train, slamming them against the walls and floor. Fragments of crystal—some as long as spears—whistled through the air, embedding themselves into rock and steel with lethal velocity.

The temperature surged. It was like standing next to a solar flare. The air ignited; the cavern lit with a blinding corona of molten light.

Silence fell on their deaf ears.

"Hawk stopped it, but it cost us," En'Gen said as he slumped to one knee.

Myli screamed at En'Gen and into the air with pure frustration. Sweat burned her eyes, but her visor wouldn't let her wipe it away. Reaching the edge of the catwalk, she brushed her fingers across her weapon—collapsing it into pistol form. Holstering it. She knelt, looking over the edge. All she could see was the bottomless pit.

Hawk was gone.

En'Gen loomed above her, looking over her shoulder, his own optics trying to get close enough to scan the void.

At the opposite end of the catwalk, Sonny felt it—her grief hitting him like a sledgehammer through their psychic connection. He shook it off and continued blasting as the old timers mourned their loss.

"We have to go, Myli!" he stated over the troop-net.

Down the gangway, Myli stood still, paralyzed at the edge of the walkway, hearing Sonny, comprehension creeping in, but still staring into the abyss.

"I'm sorry, Anshar," she whispered.

A wiggle of high-density fabric caught her eye. It was a strap, a sling from a rifle and dangling from it—Hawk. In a stroke of luck, the strap from his plasma torch had caught a hook of metal and arrested Hawk's fall. She reached for it—pulled.

The sling was frayed but holding. Myli tried to pull him up; the suit could take it, but the catwalk couldn't. It was pulling loose and shaking apart beneath her. The strain would soon break the entire structure. She reeled the strap in until she interlaced Hawk's fingers in a desperate handshake.

Slick palms, they were losing grip.

"Hawk, use the ring!"

She watched him steady his balance, trying not to wiggle. Every bit of movement was their enemy, breaking friction points.

"I can't get a good angle to pull you up... you're going to have to teleport..."

"I don't know how, Myli," he spoke over her. She could hear the desperation in his voice.

Look at me, her face said. "Think where you want to go. Somewhere close. Somewhere you can see."

His words couldn't come out fast enough. "And then what?" he asked. His eyes darted everywhere, any place would be better than dangling over the death pit.

"You just go—I guess. Do it now!" she implored.

"Myli!"

Her face twisted in frustration. "I'm losing my..." The unorthodox anchor point was slipping away. Even her smallest muscles were strained to the breaking point.

"Myli, don't..."

But her hold failed. Her fingers untwined from his, their hands unclasped, and he fell. She watched his body sinking into the darkness with his arms and legs swimming midair. Her own weight and balance were drawn toward him like a magnet. Her own body betrayed her as her arms went weak and her shoulders slumped forward. Her brain was fighting to override what her body sought to avoid. Her mind took control and forced her legs to extend in his direction.

She dove after him.

She reached him and teleported them both. An explosive airburst erupted next to En'Gen as Hawk and Myli returned to the deck, intertwined and alive. Catastrophe was chasing them now. The deck continued to come unhinged, section-by-section, like a fuse burning toward dynamite.

Myli pulled Hawk to his feet. Her voice was raspy.

"Now run!" she shouted.

And they did.

On the other end of the deck, Sonny was still fighting like a madman possessed. Now the Old Guard were stumbling in his direction, with the bridge's own weight pulling it down behind them.

With no mask and no helmet, Sonny yelled at them. "Let's friggin' go!" Blood and sweat spit off his lips.

He turned and bolted like a sloth, charging down the remainder of the catwalk at full speed, just above reverse. He huffed and puffed. Creatures were lunging from every angle—left, right, above, below. He fired, transitioning from target to target, "center the dot, send the shot," splattering bodies against crystal, steel, and stone. Every step, one in front of the other, methodically taken to not disturb his point of aim and minimize dot wobble.

This wasn't combat anymore—this was a run-and-gun.

Meanwhile, the catwalk was failing. The cascade followed in spectacular fashion. Adding to the emergency, Sonny watched a sudden rush of boiling water surge through cracks in the strata. It meant only one thing: the ancient fault line had shifted from the explosion—one wrong crack and they'd be Krakatoa.

"Come on slow pokes, this place is a time bomb," Sonny mumbled as the others followed.

He watched torrents of scalding water blowing the chupacabras off the walls. The bottomless pit was filled with boiling water. The battlefield was becoming a boiling cauldron of death. Shattered bodies—were swept up, cooking, raking mercilessly over jagged, crystal formations underneath.

The entire cave shuddered from an earthquake.

Myli was running, looked behind them. The entire structure was coming down as the walls crumbled. The house of cards was coming undone. The failing catwalk was analogous to dominoes falling.

The tide in the battle was shifting, but Myli clung to a flicker of relief as the behemoth ahead began to emerge. The colossal ship was sleeping in the shadows, oblivious of the war being waged to take it. Its cylindrical hull evoked the silhouette of a World War II Essex-class carrier but made for space. Plain, unadorned, yet unmistakably omnipotent.

Sonny was first to reach the control panel beside the hatch. No time. No clue what to do. His BCI, (brain computer interfaces), a no-go. Every section falling sounded like the second hand on a stopwatch. He knew the pressure of being on the clock all too well.

"Come on!" he snarled, slamming his hand against the panel. Nothing. Symbols flashing at him, nonsensical alien glyphs, "I can't read this shit!" Completely unreadable without Evi's help. He swiped. Punched. And kicked.

The chupacabra cave creatures were hot on the old timers' heels. Sonny, too preoccupied to notice behind him, turned only to get a rude wakening when Myli exploded into him at full airburst speed. Her materialization sandwiched him against the hull.

Breathless. Drenched in sweat inside her own suit. Her mask had shattered sometime between saving Hawk and getting to him. Her hand shot forward, grabbed his left hand—and forced it onto the panel. Working in tandem, they pieced the code together to wirelessly activate the door.

The hatch slid open—Sonny toppled inside on his back, Myli falling hard on top of him.

Hawk and En'Gen hurled themselves inside as the catwalk gave way beneath them. En'Gen landed safely. But, as the last piece of the bridge fell, a pursuing creature snagged Hawk in mid-flight. The clawing thing latched on to his back. Hawk staggered forward but the grip of his boots was failing. He slid backwards. His body swaying wildly under the pull of the creature's deadweight.

Laying on the floor with Myli on top, Sonny took careful aim. The creature swaying back and forth behind Hawk was a swinging target, but it was a clear shot. Center the dot, send the shot, and he did. The crawler's skull burst into a cloud of gore. Its grip released, En'Gen yanked Hawk inside just as the hatch slammed shut behind them. Metal thudded. Silence exploded into the space they occupied.

Sonny looked at Hawk. "There are two rings and four of us?" he asked sharply. "Who's the deadweight now?" he asked spitefully. "We could've avoided all of tha..."

Cutting him off, Myli whispered face to face over Sonny's words. "What a meat grinder, huh?" Her eyes were wide, and her mouth displayed a huge, enamel smile.

"It was something for sure," Sonny groaned. "Now I know what a brisket feels like."

Hawk took a few steps, leaned against the bulkhead and collapsed under his own weight. He wanted to remove his helmet, but that wasn't protocol. He brought his knees up and wrested his forearms on them.

Sonny could see his brain replaying the craziness. He'd lost count of how many times they all should've died back there. Hawk looked at him dead in the eye. Had he proven his worth yet?

Sonny's arm went limp, and his pistol clattered to the floor. He lay flat on his back with Myli still smothering him. Eyes wide and unblinking, he fixated on the alien ceiling above.

Stunned and speechless, Myli's weight continued to pin him down. The connection was seamless, intimate, and after what they had been through, he didn't mind. Right now, this was the safest place he could imagine.

Her breath was heavy against his neck, warm and unfiltered. It didn't smell great—sweat, adrenaline, mixed with recycled oxygen—but it was a million times better than the rotting-flesh cocktail of the tunnel they'd just fought through.

His scent? It was far worse. How many of those flesh-eating creatures had sprayed their death on him?

She didn't care, didn't flinch, didn't move. Neither did he. They'd been too close to danger. Too close to each other. Too far gone to care.

I know what you mean, she read back to him with her thoughts.

Across from him, Hawk continued deadpanning him, eyes locked on the tangle of limbs of his ex-lover. To Hawk, it was like watching his own train wreck happening in front of him in slow motion, and he was too stubborn to run the other way.

CHAPTER 7

The Chameleon Game

Hours earlier, on the surface of the Atlantic Ocean, while Myli and Sonny were entering the first gateway to Atlantis, the sun was full tilt and so was General Asag. As far as the Brass knew, Hawk was still floating on the surface of the ocean. They had no idea that he had already teleported to the mid-Atlantic rift. Using Hawk's memories, Asag knew it would take until the end of the day before the tracker monitoring his whereabouts came back online. Asag had taken Hawk's place.

Flashing facial credentials as a mutilated and battle-scarred Commander Anshar Hawk, Asag boarded the capital AUTEC salvage vessel. He chose it because it had a flight deck and bird on standby. He ordered the sailors to escort him to the helipad, where a modified SeaHawk waited on standby to fly him to Area 51.

He had absorbed Hawk's DNA. With it came memories, codes, access—secrets.

He'd also absorbed Sonny's DNA but found it useless. An idiot who knew less than nothing. Still, that inept ape had somehow castrated him.

Letting victims live could be useful—someone to take the fall when the dust settled. He remembered another useful idiot named Lee Harvey Oswald who learned the hard way. Hawk would learn now. Maybe Sonny would learn the lesson too if Asag got lucky and could take his time with him.

Asag was Anshar Hawk now—war hero of both ancient and modern wars. And, thanks to Hawk's memories still intact, he knew exactly where an ancient battle probe was hidden and the codes to get into Area 51. What he didn't know, yet, was where Hawk's transponder ended up.

"Commander, are you sure you're okay? It is a long flight, sir."

Asag nodded even though his face disagreed.

The flight was long and arduous like the medic on board warned him. He was able to hide his more extensive wounds. When at last they landed, even though badly injured, Asag as Hawk walked with brutal confidence through the reinforced corridors of Area 51.

He came strolling in like he owned the place, his expression hard, detached. Scarred, smirking—he looked like Snake Plissken after a decade of war and betrayal. The eye scan had cleared him. The voiceprint had passed. All authentications beaten. And memories drove him past the final gate.

Behind him, the Seahawk spun back up on the helipad, rotors whining, kicking up dust in violent circles. Inside, a specialized recovery team waited—clueless their commanding officer was being mimicked.

Another man, a creature walking among the US troops, was something else entirely. Apparently, another unknown infiltration had happened before, dating back to the destruction of the Mars colony. The miscalculation fueled a new desire.

He read Hawk's thoughts like a diary. Much of the Area 51 facility had been reassigned and buried deeper after it became a global spectacle in the 1990s—sparked by lawsuits over the toxic smoke clouds workers called "London Fog." The black projects hadn't moved to Edwards or White Sands like people thought. They'd simply gone below.

Underground.

Asag was heading beneath the Nevada desert where an Anunna battle probe, downed during the Battle of Los Angeles in the 1940s, was being kept. It was the only known weapon on Earth capable of stopping or neutralizing *Daedalus* before it could be activated. The Udug knew it existed; they knew Dumuzi had found it. But its location had eluded Asag for centuries. He was about to correct that.

Asag had studied this place. Back in the 1940s, Groom Lake had been nothing more than a few hangars and salt-lake-bed runways, a dumping ground for damaged UFOs and experimental tech. Even now, technology has advanced far beyond what the Udug general remembered from the post-war era. He had known Earth's advancements would be light-years ahead by now, especially after acquiring the Ninety-Nine fighter from Oak Island. Another notch in the failure belt. Oak Island led him to the *Menagerie,* the *Menagerie* to AUTEC, and AUTEC to Area 51.

It was obvious to him the humans had also recovered Enki's M3 Book from Oak Island. When was the last time the book was used? It had to have been the Crusades. When the Templars returned with it, they ushered in the Renaissance—the first great technological revolution, after Asag steered Rome to fall. Soon after, it was hidden during the Templar purge.

Time for another purge, Asag told himself as he continued his tour of Area 51.

Massive runways had been built over the dried lakebed, clearly designed to accommodate hypersonic aircraft and prototype Ninety-Nine fighters. Everything was concealed in one form or fashion, nothing left exposed for foreign satellites to capture. He'd looked.

Cleaning crews in hazmat suits worked on decontaminating the base even as work continued around them. A recent dust storm had kicked up radioactive fallout dating back to the Manhattan Project, forcing a full-scale decontamination protocol. The environment was unforgiving—a perfect place to develop top-secret human and alien technology.

While Asag was escorted toward a smaller hangar, more men sealed barrels of contaminated materials for disposal—a daily routine. Asag recalled the Anunna's ancient toxic waste burial sites, places like Siberia's Valley of Death, which still poisoned the land thousands of years later.

At the end of the hangar, a small elevator rose inconspicuously from the ground, and an automatic door slid open. Two MPs armed with HK 416's escorted, who they thought was Hawk, past a .50 caliber turret loaded with depleted uranium rounds, guarding the entrance.

Here, so close to his destination, for the first time, doubt crept into his mind. Was this going too smoothly? A trap? Asag paused for a moment. Then he stepped forward and another retinal scanner verified his one eye as Anshar Hawk.

He was in.

The elevator descended to a tram station where a four-car transport was waiting. Officials piled in, their decorated uniforms reflecting the importance of the meeting ahead. As they traveled deeper into the Area 51 mountain, the group grew larger—a clear sign something huge was about to unfold.

Asag couldn't have been happier. It was serendipitous.

After a ten-minute tram ride, they arrived inside a massive bomb-proof underground facility. The hangar was filled with classified aircraft—everything from early stealth fighters to UFO-like prototypes. Rows of Hawk's reverse engineered Ninety-Nine fighters lined up like a museum exhibit, primed and ready to fight.

"First time here, Commander?" A black-suited official wearing Smart-Sunglasses observed.

Asag turned slowly toward him and grinned. "First time. What gave it away?" he asked nonchalantly.

"Everyone looks that way their first time." The man's voice was steady, respectful, but edged with awe. "The world has no idea this tech exists. Hell, even most black-clearance personnel don't know what's really down here."

The man glanced at the others assembling beyond the security gate—each one armored, each one armed, and none of them talking.

"Something big must be happening for such an assembly to take place," he added before turning his attention back to Asag, the creature disguised flawlessly as Hawk.

"We heard about your team," the MIB said quietly, tapping just beneath his own eye in a universal gesture of recognition. "Thank you for your service. The fact you're standing here, after something like that. You must be some kind of badass warrior." He shook his head in disbelief and awe. "The commitment, uncommon valor? We won't forget it, sir."

Asag's body shifted toward him, looking him straight in his eyes. "No, you won't," Asag spoke under his breath.

The Man In Black gave a strange look, as if he didn't quite catch what was said.

"Anyway," the MIB agent continued, "you're the tip of the spear. The Ninety-Nine fighter who Ava found with you on Oak Island was instrumental in helping the Martians develop our squadrons." Resolutely, the MIB agent gave him a tip of the hat. "We will put up one hell of a fight, sir."

Asag raised an eyebrow. He remembered that bitch Ava. But the Martians? "Martians?" He asked, thinking they were all dead. Now it made sense. In the elevator, Asag noted one of the passengers wasn't quite human. Now this MIB's information was proof that he failed in killing them on Mars.

"Yep," said the MIB. "They're all here. Green, gray, and blue."

Asag's demeanor changed; he could barely hide his anger. "They will be in the meeting?"

The damn Igigi, Asag thought. *They're a plague that just wouldn't go away.*

"Yes sir, this is their show. Back in the 1800s—early 1900s, maybe—a Guardian, Loafer, Lopes, hell, I can't remember the exact name, rescued them from exile on Mars. Brought them here to Earth. Been allies of the U.S. ever since."

Asag's expression must have signaled the MIB to lower his voice.

The agent's voice dropped slightly, his eyes steady on Asag's one eye. "This isn't conspiracy theory stuff. This is black-level history. Real shadow war legacy. They don't age," the MIB said, astonished. "They look exactly the same as they did a hundred years ago. I've seen the pictures."

"Enki's Serum," Asag mumbled, his tone calm, almost reverent. "Your people called it the Fountain of Youth. Our people referred to it as the Nectar of the Gods. It wasn't meant for peasants."

The MIB nodded slowly, absorbing the weight of it. "The government's kept these guys under wraps for decades. *Paperclip* Nazi's built decoy craft to test their engines here in the '50s. Hell, they're all embedded in our government now. We lost more than a few great pilots in those flights. The Roswell crash." He nodded towards his listener whom he assumed was Hawk.

Asag's eyes glanced to the massive vessel looming in the hangar, its silhouette partially hidden in shadow and misted coolant. "That thing?"

The agent followed his gaze. "The L.A. UFO. The Battle of Los Angeles—there's articles about it. Army lit it up with everything we had. Nothing worked. Nikola Tesla and some psychic civilians took it down. They fly by thought or something—not my lane. They dropped it straight into the Pacific, messing with the pilot's mind." The MIB said in a strange mysterious tone. The MIB stepped closer to the railing, reverent. "They covered the whole thing up with air raid drills and weather balloons."

Asag tilted his head, feigning curiosity. His voice was beginning to sound like an engine running dry of oil.

The agent nodded. "Yeah. Rebooted it. Before them, we couldn't even figure out how to get into it. That thing could level a city with a single volley."

Pointing at his wrist, Asag pulled back his sleeve. "You need one of these," he said of his tattoo. "To have access to the tech of the Gods."

"Well, not *the* God," the MIB stated as fact. "Gods don't exist, sir. Just fancy tech."

Asag laughed. "Well then, I'll make sure to kill you first, puny human." He continued laughing louder. He made a fist and tapped the MIB on the shoulder.

The MIB took a second, laughed a little, but Asag could tell he didn't like the sound of that joke. Asag laughed even harder, more animated, forcing even more laughter out of the MIB. Asag hit the brakes cold turkey, psychological subterfuge to make him uncomfortable. His deadpan expression ten out of ten stars. They walked a few steps, Asag tapped him on his shoulder again with a buddy love tap, looked around one last time, filing away where he was, where he parked his car in the parking lot kind of look.

"I'm just messing with you," Asag alleged, smiling with an artificial smile. "Where are we headed?"

Before the MIB answered, Asag could see his brain was running wild. He knew he must think he was a sociopath. *Better shift my tone.*

"They think this is the big one," the agent said and looked at him grimly. "I guess it's a good thing you do such a fantastic job at watching."

The briefing room overlooked the hangar bay, its massive windows whitened to be opaque. Inside the briefing room a holographic map flared to life showing ancient ruins marked across the entire globe. Each one, a relic of the First People of Earth.

The room hushed as three figures entered—not human.

Two were blue-skinned, the third a reddish brown—the Igigi, or as Groom Lake personnel called them, Martians. His name was Marduk. Asag had seen him topside briefly, and later in the elevator. He was the lead scientist in charge of the Op. His usual deep cerulean had darkened into violet, stress tightening his inhuman features.

By his side, a scaled beast growled—part war-dog, part dragon, its black, shark-like hide rippling under the lights.

Sirrush.

Asag and all like him shared some of that DNA. A bioengineered lumassu—a protective spirit animal come to life—one of the last of its kind. Marduk's most loyal companion and weapon.

The final officers filed in, and Marduk wasted no time.

"The President and Chiefs are aboard the *Icarus,*" he said, his lips curled and he added, "Weekend warriors."

Some chuckled.

His smile vanished. "Many of you already know what happened off AUTEC's coast," the officer began, his voice firm over the low hum of the lights in the briefing room. "As of now, we lost two assets in the field and Hawk barely managed to make it back to us."

The room cheered, briefly.

"Before the mission, Hawk managed to drop a micro-scoping tracking device into the drink of one of the targets." He smiled. "Even though they slipped away, we're close to tracking it as we speak."

"Good job, Commander." One of the admirals nodded to Hawk at the back of the room.

The room dimmed as the holographic map zoomed out, revealing two pings in a remote part of Nazca, Peru. Only Asag caught the blunder.

"They've found the resting place of *The Icarus Prime—The Daedalus.*"

Murmurs swelled, heads turning. Marduk let it settle for a moment.

"The ship that crash-landed in Texas carried a power source," he continued. "Two keys to activate the *Icarus* and the *Daedalus.* The key—" he said grimly. "The key which Hawk currently wears—will wake up the sleeping giant we refitted." He said pointing up to the heavens where the *Icarus* orbited. "It will wake two weapons."

The air shifted. Tension. Realization. Implications of time travel. Those present knew that time travel was impossible, unless you were going forward in time. Yet here was proof they were wrong.

"*Daedalus* and *Icarus* are the tip of the spear against the Anunna fleet. It was used in the past and we need to use it again. If the enemy reaches orbit before we activate it, humanity is extinct. *Icarus* and *Langley* will hold the line, but they're just placeholders until *Daedalus* launches."

A runner quietly entered the briefing room. He gingerly moved to the front and approached Marduk. Asag watched Marduk's expression carefully. When he finished reading the note he looked up. Just as Hawk had planted a tracking device in Myli's drink, Hawk had one planted in him. Marduk looked at Asag from across the room. He looked at the ping on the monitor and put it together. Two pings in Peru.

Asag raised his hand slowly, wiggling his fingers with mock innocence.

Marduk's heart beat faster, "Oh, no."

"Oh, yeah," Asag said with a crooked smile.

A few chuckles bubbled up around the room—the subtle laughter became nervous snickers. The tone shifted. Colder. Sharper.

At last, Marduk found his voice. "This Hawk doesn't appear to have one of the rings." He tilted his head. "He's an imposter."

The room froze.

The man disguised as Anshar Hawk—stood slowly. Mechanical. Cold.

His eyes—no longer human. His voice—measured. Deliberate. His height growing, uniform ripping. "Here we are again, one big family reunion," the emerging Asag announced as he turned his full attention to Marduk. "I missed you on Mars, I won't miss this time."

Panic erupted. The audience bolted from their seats, shouting orders—but it was too late. The Men in Black hesitated, their shots blocked by fleeing Joint Chiefs of Staff. Just a fraction of a second too long.

A split-second cost them everything.

Minutes later, Asag reentered the hangar, weaving through petrified staff and scientists. Soldiers rushed past covering exits in a move to contain the security breach of the briefing room. He wiped the blood off his hands with a rag he swiped from a technician's bench as he blended in. Sirens blared. Red emergency lights pulsed. The base was on full lockdown, but it didn't matter—he was already inside, feeding the QRF bad intel with a radio he'd swiped.

He reached the LA drone, the ancient Anunna war machine that had been lying dormant for decades. Its nuclear payload was still intact. He swiped a tattoo across a panel on the massive bird. It opened. He reached in and grabbed a technical looking piece of a kit, a halo. He made sure not to leave behind the flight suit. As quickly as he opened the onboard locker, the alien skin of the bird sealed up.

He put on the halo and, with his mind, he began powering up the drone. He didn't need to find access codes because he knew them. This was one of his weapons sent to scout Earth during World War II. He personally sent the pilot on that mission. The drone's systems flickered in his mind, ancient alien code scrolling across the display.

The base's coordinates were linked in. With a single tactical nuclear strike, humanity's last hope would be vaporized.

He left the drone idling and stepped outside again. A group of men clanked toward him. Asag stepped out of the way, his pilot disguise working perfectly. MPs sprinted right past him. He went to a panel, using stolen credentials from Marduk, and opened the hangar bay. In front of the bird sat a massive launch tunnel.

Using his mind through the halo, he launched the drone which zipped from underground, out of the mountain, and into the night sky. The MPs never had a chance to get off a shot.

"The intruder got away in the LA drone!" Asag growled as he was holstering his weapon. He clutched his "injured" side, groaning in faux pain. "I couldn't stop him."

The squad leader assessed him, his expression grim. The bullet wound looked bad—Asag had made sure of that.

"Affirmative." The soldier snapped to action, reaching for his radio. "Scramble the JSF Interceptors. Take it out before it reaches whatever its target is." He turned to his squad. "You, you, and you—on me." Then, to the rest of the unit, "You all, head to the east tunnel; there must be more of them. There's no way one man took out all our men in that briefing room. Move!"

Over the radio Asag heard, "No joy, it's too fast."

He turned back to Asag. "Pilot, get yourself to the infirmary." The squad leader ordered as he and his men moved on.

Asag smiled inside. A weak salute. On the outside his face faked disappointment at being left out of the fight. "Yes, sir."

The fools had no idea. The drone was already beyond their reach; its nuclear payload locked on target. And soon—Hawk and Myli would be nothing but ash.

The resistance would finally crumble.

After thousands of years and thousands of faces, the coup d'état and assassination all culminated to this. If the Anunna couldn't have the weapon, the humans wouldn't either.

Chapter 8

Daedalus

Mylitta wrestled with the interface on the corridor wall, fingers dancing over symbols which were shifting and reforming beneath her touch. "I can't access all the bridge systems yet," she muttered. "But I've got a lock on life support—it should kick in any second."

Sonny was somewhere in the background. En'Gen was at her side. Hawk stood just behind her, visor flickering, readouts pulsing in crimson across his HUD. *Temperature holding at 119°F.* "We keeping these on?" he asked, tapping the side of his helmet.

"Yeah," Myli said without looking up. "Could be pathogens, contaminants—cyanide, something worse we may encounter. I'm surprised we got this far without resistance. Something's off. Stay sharp."

"What about the two of you?" Hawk asked worriedly, mostly worried for Myli.

"You'll know soon enough," she retorted. "When we're dead."

Sonny wiped sweat from his eyes, his face flushed. His voice was tight. "So, was that a trap out there?"

"Maybe," she replied, tone cool. "We might still be inside one." She glanced at him, noting the signs of heat exhaustion. "Sonny—retract your armor. It'll help. Your suit isn't venting heat fast enough. Your regulators may be overwhelmed from damage."

Sonny didn't hesitate but was moving slowly as he touched the release on the pad. The Mark V suit did nothing. His eyelids fluttered, blinking sweat away. "If I pass out—don't let Hawk give mouth-to-mouth to me."

Hawk grunted. "You're not my type."

"That goes without saying, Captain Obvious," Sonny shot back.

"Commander. I'm not a captain." He clarified.

"Semantics." Sonny quipped. "It's just a figure of speech, bro vet."

"Dirty civilian."

Myli rolled her eyes and turned her attention to the panel. "Focus on staying alive. Life support's almost up and running."

Sonny looked at Hawk who looked like he wanted to say something else—maybe suggest a backup plan, maybe just hear himself talk—but Myli was already deep in the system's command lines, overriding locks, bypassing centuries-old protocols. He could tell her suit wasn't cooling right either.

Sonny swayed, a staggered half-step betraying how close he was to collapse. The touch pad on his forearm flashed warnings in red on his arm:

CORE TEMP RISING

HYDRATION LEVELS CRITICAL

THERMOREGULATION FAILURE IMMINENT

He tapped the control on his forearm repeatedly. Nothing. He began to pant.

Come on, his mind demanded.

"Shit," he muttered out loud. "Armor's not retracting." He tried to peel the suit apart with his bare hands. The cascading temperature was leading to an exothermic surge.

Sonny crushed his eyelids hard, forcing sweat out, trying to clear the blur. It didn't help. More sweat streamed down his face; the little bit not settling in his eye went into the collection which continued to accumulate inside his suit. His suit was turning into a personal hot tub—no evaporation, no relief. His body was baking from the inside out.

Completely ignoring Sonny's plight, Hawk barked at Myli, his tone clipped and sharp. "You don't have a helmet. If poison comes out of the vents..."

She shrugged it off, but even that small movement looked sluggish.

Sonny muttered under his breath, just loud enough, "Still here too, asshole."

Hawk continued to focus on Myli and Sonny rolled his twitching eyes. Since they had reunited, Hawk had been practically dry humping her leg, like a dog in heat.

Myli intercepted his thoughts and laughed despite herself, then shot Sonny a quick grin. She was aware of Hawk's lingering devotion to her and equally aware of her own lack of reciprocal affection towards him.

On the verge of heatstroke, Sonny's eyes rolled back, he panted, leaning back against a bulkhead, chest rising like bellows.

Hawk kept his back to Sonny and stared hard at Myli. "You're running hot," he told her.

Myli's jaw flexed in annoyance. "We're all running hot," she snarled as she keyed in another override, her voice hoarse. "If I don't get life support online in the next sixty seconds, it won't matter."

The air inside the ship was marginally cooler than outside, but not by much.

Sonny didn't have sixty seconds. He hit the deck with a bone-jarring thud, his breath knocked out of him, suit systems blinking red like a failing heart monitor.

"Come on, damn it," Myli growled. "En'Gen, rip him out of that thing!"

Like a mechanical menace, the massive robot wheeled around, dove in, and began ripping the suit off. Sweat was seeping out on the floor just as Myli received the message she'd been hoping for.

LIFE SUPPORT ACTIVATED

She left the console and dropped to her knees beside Sonny, fingers dancing across her own damaged touchpad. Her own system was tapping out hard. The cooling systems were toast. Her vitals spiking. Her fingers moved with instinct, bypassing fried connections, she ripped fiber-optic wire from one arm and plugged it into the other forcing a manual override.

WHIRRRR-KSHHH.

Her shattered face shield finally gave up—liquefying at the edges. The cracked pane disintegrated into fine sand-grain particles, which streamed backward into the helmet like reverse snow. The helmet collapsed entirely into the collar of the 2nd Skin armor. With a mechanical hiss, her adaptive nanotech armor dematerialized in sharp, elegant sections until it stowed into position along her spine and lats.

Sonny's body was drenched. He lay in a pool of sweat. Beside him, Myli knelt in her own. She heard a rattle as something flowed towards them, a deep, groaning sound.

WHOOSH.

The ventilation system kicked on.

High-pressure air surged through the corridor vents. Hissing nozzles snapped open overhead and along the walls, displacing stagnant heat with a flood of breathable, filtered cool atmosphere. There was a visible difference in the air.

The ship had at last recognized her. The panel signaled her by name. The core systems were back online. Test passed.

Myli exhaled in relief, checking the touchpad projected along her Alpha Skin suit to measure the atmosphere. Oxygen: Stable. Toxins: Nominal. Temp: 98°F and falling. 89°F felt like winter setting in when it hit.

"Hey. You're not dying today. You fought like a lion," she told Sonny, comforting him.

He chuckled, barely. "This lion doesn't have many more lives left in him."

"Me either," she admitted. Then she looked around, thinking about their next step before looking back at Sonny.

Watching them through the polarized shield covering his face, Hawk leaned against the bulkhead, helmet still on. The humidity in the air made no difference to him, his suit was working just fine. He wasn't swimming in excretion like they were.

If Sonny was a better warrior, Hawk told himself, *his suit wouldn't have been irreparably damaged.*

However, his stomach still churned—not from heat exhaustion or smell but from the sight of the two of them sharing something in common: joint anguish.

Hawk and En'Gen couldn't smell it; based on Myli and Sonny's faces, they were glad they couldn't. A mirrored look, noses twitching like diving rods, the secretions from Sonny and Myli were airborne. The sour smell was a mix of musky bedroom and hints of a late-night diner.

Hawk's posture and face looked like the stink had permeated his armor suit. "You alright?" she asked. "You look nauseous."

His mouth twisted in anguish. "We need to get moving. The cave system isn't stable anymore."

She nodded back to him. "How about you, Sonny?" she asked.

Sonny groaned, pushing himself halfway upright, hair matted to his head like a drowned rat. The Alpha Skin was already wicking away the dampness. "Feels like I ran a marathon through a microwave."

"You look it—you look like shit, my guy," Hawk muttered. "You need to get better at fighting."

Sonny gave him a finger. "Whatever—I don't remember bringing the entire cave down on our heads."

Hawk rolled his eyes. He was considered a god and still looked like one after that obscene gladiatorial event.

Myli gave him a tired half-smile, one not reaching her eyes. "Don't make me laugh, you two, or I'll cramp. We need to get Sonny rehydrated," she said, holding the stitch in her side.

The air was getting cooler. Slowly. The worst was over—for now. But the stillness in the ship was deceptive. Hawk wasn't buying the ships dormancy. Nothing this old or this sophisticated stayed dormant for long.

They were moving down the corridor now with Hawk running point. Sonny noticed Hawk finally retracting his helmet, the hiss sounding loud in the corridor. He had barely broken a sweat, hair still almost perfect. Pure Adonis. He looked back and blew air out of his teeth, toward Sonny and smiled.

Was it a clever threat or was he into him? The air was stale but breathable. Best of all, it was cool.

Myli scanned the others for signs of horror or panic when Sonny asked her, "So why didn't we just jump straight in here?"

Myli was quick to answer. "We had no idea what was on the other side of the hull, but mostly the ring has limited range. Every jump zaps your energy and hurts like hell, as you know. Keep moving; the earthquakes are getting worse. I doubt even this ship could survive a volcanic eruption."

Over half an hour passed as they made slow progress clearing corridors, crew quarters, the mess hall, and galley. The search was merely a precaution. Nobody was home. QSC chambers were full, none activated yet.

"We should be approaching the science lab—and The Garden." Hawk updated the team.

"Garden? In a ship?" Sonny asked obtusely.

Myli laughed inwardly. "Yeah, you were too busy taking a nap at Atlantis to take in the scenic route with me."

Sonny made a crabby face at her sarcasm. "Seriously, what is *The Garden?*" Sonny asked again.

"It's a biodome on steroids," Hawk said. "It's a full biological level—food, water, even psychological relief. Space is a void, a sensory deprivation desert. Without something like this, crews would lose their minds." He insufficiently described the Overview Effect.

Myli knew the feeling all too well. Her tone shifted as awe crept in.

"But the real marvel?" she rhetorically asked. "The manipulation of space-time inside the ship. The interior is exponentially larger than it should be. Alien tech folds reality inward. No one fully understands it—maybe Enki did—but the whole system is powered by a miniature fusion sun."

Sonny's face went full tilt. "Wait, like—an actual sun?"

They'd been walking for a good minute. Hawk signaled a halt with his fist. Myli grabbed Sonny's arm, holding him back. His heart began racing again. So far, Hawk's halting the team had ended badly. They all took a familiar knee. She pointed at En'Gen to cover the rear, then moved ahead of Hawk with practiced urgency, staying low, her weapon steady.

"What are we dealing with?" she asked cautiously.

"Science lab. Possible bio-sign, heavy electrical interference. QSC units for hibernating crew here too—just being cautious. Let's spill-in quickly and clear it. We can lock the room down and get some answers in there."

"Roger that," Myli agreed.

With her weapon in hand, she made a low ready motion with the barrel, pointing out to Hawk which path to take. Hawk, flowing in right. She'd flow in left. Sonny and En'Gen would flow in behind and find work.

They stacked up, Sonny placing his hand on Myli's back, feeling En'Gen behind him. The stack began moving.

Sonny hadn't done much CQB training outside of simulations, and it showed. His nerves sizzled like a live wire, his grip high, tightening around his weapon like he was milking a cow. Hawk went in high ready, his gun snapped level, and he was inside. Myli pushed forward, Sonny moving up right behind her. She broke left and her rifle snapped to attention. Sonny right, his breathing rapid.

Hawk called out over the comms, "Clear."

"Clear," Myli called out.

Sonny's corner was clear, and he moved the reticle towards the center of the room. Nervous to say anything incorrectly, Sonny stayed silent.

En'Gen called out, "Clear."

Sonny rounded a massive station of medical instruments and stopped. He stood face to face with an Udug Shock Trooper—frozen in stasis, dead or deactivated, but still utterly terrifying. It was exactly as he had imagined they'd be up-close. Horrifying. So far, every interaction with the creatures has been fast and furious. Now, he had time to absorb the terror.

The Udug stood motionless, trapped in frozen animation for over ten thousand years.

Myli joined Sonny and studied the creature. "Somehow, they captured this one. They all look a little different, like fingerprints or snowflakes."

"These things are nightmare fuel," Hawk relayed. "If the planet's crawling with them, we might as well pack it in. I'd be shocked if they haven't mutinied against the Anunna," Hawk continued.

Sonny turned away from the immobile Udug—and flinched again as he spotted something massive inside a stasis chamber.

"Jesus. What the hell is that?" he asked.

Myli stepped closer.

"Looks like a Mušḫuššu," she decided. "A genetically engineered serpent-lizard. Enki and Marduk were always messing with gene splicing. This might be something they concocted."

Sonny shuddered. This was some serious sci-fi horror territory. He remembered a favorite line from a movie he'd watched more than a few times. "The scientists were so preoccupied with whether they could, they never stopped to think if they should."

"It's just a dragon, Sonny," Hawk commented as he grouped back up with the team.

To the right of the Udug's chamber, a control panel flickered. Vitals, monitoring systems. Sonny returned to the spot and stared at the creature's unblinking eyes, frosted over from being open for so many centuries. Sonny felt like it was staring back. The pupil seemed to eye him. He jumped.

"Terrifying," Hawk muttered, stepping up beside him. "I've only seen them like this at a distance—or while running for my life. They blend in," Hawk added, recalling Shara's fate. "You won't spot them until it's too late."

Sonny narrowed his eyes. "Just like a serial killer. Is there *any* way to screen for them?"

Myli shook her head. "No." She was already back at work, scanning the lab's systems.

Sonny stood lost in thought. He could still hear the wet *splats*—those distant bullet impacts back at the crash site. He remembered the *thud* of the

Boombox's subsonic hits. Myli's blade, slow and methodical, slicing into the creature when even supersonic rounds bounced like they were striking steel.

He thought of his bare feet hitting the wet Florida sand—hard, like concrete. But if he stopped and moved slowly, the ground sucked him down like a trap. He remembered a documentary about active liquids. Fluid until disturbed. When disturbed, it turned solid.

Myli stopped cold, almost a back step, as she sensed something in the shift of Sonny's energy, a thought she *wanted* to learn more about. She turned, watching him.

He was staring into the dark. And putting something together. Sonny snapped his fingers and pointed at the monster. "*Gotcha bitch.*"

His eyes lit up. "Non-Newtonian fluids," he hypothesized. He turned to Myli, gears turning fast now. "These things—these freaks—they're built from an organic *impact-hardening material.* They get tougher the harder you hit them. Under stress, they go rigid—like cornstarch in water, only on a monster scale."

Myli arched an eyebrow.

"The military, our military, was messing with the same concept back in the '90s," Sonny explained. "Experimental armor for tanks. Only difference is—these bastards figured out how to do it *genetically.*"

Myli stepped closer, sensing the shift in Sonny's focus—something had clicked. He didn't look at her, just reached for a long, blunt instrument lying nearby. His grip tightened. Without a word, he spun back and *swung for the fences*—the impact echoed through the corridor, cracking against the creature's chest with an ear splitting SMACK.

The body didn't move. Barely a bruise formed.

Sonny dropped the instrument, more determined. He drew his knife and leaned in, pushing the blade slowly into the Udug soldier's side. At first, it slid in—*smooth.* But then, as he applied more force, a quicker thrust, the resistance increased but still cut deep.

He stepped back, his breath steady, eyes locked on the monster.

"The more force I use," he muttered, "the harder it gets. The head shots—their nervous system doesn't have time to create the same reaction." He looked at Myli. "No wonder subs and slow stabs do more damage. Hyper-fast rounds just *stack trauma*—but it's the slow, grinding penetration that breaks through and does the real damage to the rest of the body."

Sonny zoned in on the creature's tattoos. The same lines he saw stained across Myli's skin—the same ones he'd glimpsed on Hawk—and on Chiara. The creature's body was laced with the same ancient symbols, shifting faintly beneath the skin like coded whispers. Not just battle markings. Not just tech.

Bio-mods. Bio-hacking enhancements. The same ones drawing him to Myli like gravity. A moth to the flame. The women were like black holes and, if you meandered within their Event Horizon, you were trapped.

Sonny's face contorting, his fingers did the math as his mind scrambled to connect the impossible dots.

Hawk observed Sonny's pupils contracting, saw the way his mouth opened, but no sound came out. And Hawk also recognized that Sonny was focused on the creature's tattoos.

"You've seen those before, haven't you?" Hawk said, low and sharp. "But not on us."

Sonny's voice cracked through the silence. "Chiara?" he whispered, "My wife. The pull? The influence? Sometimes I don't even know where my thoughts end and hers begin."

Myli stepped closer, her voice low. "Some of us are built to lead, Sonny. To seduce. To inspire. My tattoos, my bio-mods—they amplify lust and love. Chiara may have just copied those from books in your library, not even knowing what they were. Like the Templar's imitating our cross. You *know* that. You've felt it with me, too."

Sonny's eyes flicked to Myli's, searching for truth. "I have," he admitted, his voice raw. "That's what's messing with me."

Myli's expression softened. "I *know* what I am. I know how my systems work, what they trigger, what they don't. Chiara? She may be broadcasting naturally without realizing it. Influence comes in many forms," Myli said. "Dreams. Whispers. A push here, a suggestion there. Chiara isn't Udug," she repeated, softer this time. "She's just a woman good at pushing buttons."

His thoughts pushed a glimpse of his mind's eye into Myli—Chiara, pregnant.

"If she's pregnant," Myli assured him, "it means she's *human.*"

Hawk softly punched Sonny's shoulder. "She's right, Sonny, the Udug are sterile." In the back of his mind, Hawk dismissed a nagging thought from his past. "Sorry bub, you're not that special."

Sonny's knife was still sticking in the body. En'Gen grabbed it and proceeded to carve off part of the creature.

"So, what do we actually know?" Myli asked. "Not assumptions."

"They're not monsters—or some unknown alien species," En'Gen said, peeling back layers of tissue. "Anunna tattoos on the surface, underneath," he examined, "it's still Anunna. Genetically mutated. They're carriers of a virus, same as the cave creatures—only those were Igigi." He waved a hand over the console, scanning rapidly through files."

"Mutated?" Sonny shook his head. "Why would anyone want to mutate into one of these?"

En'Gen nodded. "Immortality and the power to become anyone or anything. Who wouldn't want that?"

"But they're monsters," Sonny concluded.

"Corruption begets corruption." En'Gen doubled down. "Each soul is different, unique—the abilities a byproduct or side effect of their personality, perhaps."

The Synth held up a thin sheet of translucent skin to the light.

"There's something embedded in the tissue," he said.

"What is it?" Hawk asked.

Sonny watched as Myli ran her fingers over one of her tattoos.

Mark of the beast? he asked himself.

Hawk exhaled sharply. "They wouldn't let them breed. But could they mass-produce them in labs, using willing soldiers or incarcerated sociopaths?"

"If infected at the right stage, yes," En'Gen said, glancing at the screen.

"But like Hawk said, they're sterile. Scans confirm—no semen, no reproductive viability. The Anunna wouldn't risk them breeding out of control. It would take a miracle to reverse that option."

En'Gen drew their attention to the Udug's muscle tissue, peeling back layers with Sonny's blade. "Look at these fast-twitch fibers. They're engineered for speed—inhuman speed. Energy weapons should punch through. Sonny's hypothesis checks out—their weak spots are the eyes and orifices, the base of the neck, temple, solar plexus..."

Sonny drifted off. "I pulled one's eye out with a spear."

Hawk glanced at him skeptically. No way—Deadweight landed a kill like that?

Myli smirked. "All warriors dream of a mission like this."

Sonny shook his head. "Shit, Myli, I just want to live."

It was time to move. She motioned them forward.

"Fall in," she said.

Chapter 9

The Garden

They burst into and swept the lobby of the recreation antechamber. Sonny was still pulling rear security with En'Gen. Every hatch they breach and room they cleared was a learning experience.

"Clear," Sonny called out, more comfortable this go-around. "What is this place?"

Hawk didn't answer. He just joined Sonny as the two of them approached an observation deck. The back wall appeared to be made of glass—but hummed with the energy of an electronic bug zapper.

Sonny touched it gingerly, as if it had a sign saying *don't touch*. Lucky for him the energy vibrated through his hand instead of zapping him. The blue glow of energy silhouetted his hand—that was noticeable. However, it was what lay beyond the plasma field that Sonny saw as magic. Sonny's jaw dropped as he and Hawk stepped onto the scenic overlook through an automatic door leading to a wide patio deck. The plasma field dissipated revealing a vast forest.

"I bet you lick frozen metal in the winter, too?" Hawk mused.

Sonny ignored him and walked through. "This is breathtaking," Sonny gawped.

It was a world within a world which shouldn't have been possible *inside* a ship.

"Let's keep moving," Hawk ordered. "I know it's impressive, but it's not our first rodeo."

"Speak for yourself," Sonny whispered as he viewed a million hectares of pristine terrain. It was a surreal paradise sealed within the ship's time-space-folded interior that would make flat-earthers rejoice. The atmosphere shimmered with warmth and light, like perpetual golden hour. Soft beams of light were filtering through towering trees. Sonny couldn't help but run his hands through their warmth.

Everything a crew needed for deep space exploration was here.

He stepped to the edge of a landslide overlooking forests to his left, dense with ancient trees stretching to the horizon—perfect for hiking, hunting, or simply getting lost in wonder.

To the east, he could see snow-capped mountains reaching into the artificial sky, topped with cheerful, white plump clouds. There were cliffs ready for climbing, with narrow paths winding along their ridgelines. Occasional flashes of wings overhead hinted at wildlife—eagles, maybe even things long-extinct.

He backed away from the edge and craned his neck to the endless plain with rolling hills butted up to the tree line. He stepped a few hundred feet forward to the beginning of a lush tropical zone which extended through to the south. Calls of exotic birds and creatures unseen; vibrant flowers layered the edge of the foliage where he and his team stood.

Disbelief washed over his face. "Is that a herd of cattle?" he questioned.

"Aurochs. Undomesticated. They're extinct on Earth now," Hawk educated him.

A crystal-clear river flowed gently from a massive freshwater reservoir, cascading down a series of waterfalls before widening into a lazy bend he stood next to. Kayaking, fishing—it was heaven. It eventually poured into a massive inland ocean they could see in the distance, complete with rolling surf, and white sandy beaches.

As the two men stared, Myli and En'Gen joined them.

"How?" he asked her.

She smiled at him. "Magic," she said genuinely. "Shall we take a trail?"

Small trails like the one they were on weaved through the terrain, some leading to hidden campsites with fire pits and supply caches. Others vanished into the underbrush, promising adventure, danger, or discovery. Some areas looked *untouched*—ancient ruins woven with greenery, places meant for exploring or maybe lovemaking under the stars. Even here, deep in the ship, the illusion of nature was perfect. The air was warm and clean. The breeze carried the scent of cedar, sea salt, and blooming jasmine.

They reached a natural ford—enough rocks exposed to cross the stream. One side was shallow, and the other side sloped into a swollen but swimmable pool. Sonny eyed his battle buddies. The water looked inviting.

Myli's shoulders relaxed. Her footsteps were teetering on becoming nameable—a dance step like jitting, jookin', or some Chicago footwork. She was almost whimsical, hopping from rock-to-rock to cross the waterway. He liked this more playful side of her.

He looked at Hawk who finally let his guard down. He took a deep breath, enjoying the petrichor surrounding them. He released a long-controlled exhale through his nose. Maybe the son of a bitch would finally give him a break. It was the most relaxed he'd seen the old bulwark since he was skulking over him in Med-Surg.

"This place... this is a goddamn dream," said Hawk. "It had to be a slick simulation within a simulation, but a dream, nonetheless. It dwarfs what we ran through on the *Menagerie*. The *Icarus* doesn't have a Garden. There was only a massive cargo hold in this portion of the ship."

"So much for *been there, done that,* huh?" Sonny said sarcastically. He'd meant it as a sharp dig at Hawk. He wanted to think of Hawk as an opponent but instead he sensed something softer, a teammate. "I wonder if the universe outside of this ship is another infinitely larger, but also illusionary garden?" Sonny asked as he sought to explore what he thought was maybe an epiphany.

The group stopped and looked at Sonny. He shrugged his shoulders.

"Welcome to *The Garden,* boys," Myli said as she trudged on.

The Synth's visor flashed. En'Gen had no idea what Sonny was talking about. In this moment, he was showing great interest in a pair of bright red dragonflies with black wings.

Some areas continued to pulse with engineered perfection—sunlight shining through the trees, rivers running clean and alive—but other sections bore the slow, creeping touch of time. A tarnished shell lay in deep grass no longer able to continue its work in this artificial Eden.

Arriving at the edge of an orchard, caretaker bots harvested differing species of apples and other fruit trees as well as grapevines. Spider droids trimmed leaves and pruned branches, while larger, insectoid ones cleared debris or repaired broken aqueducts with silent dedication.

Near the edge of a low hill, where the trees gave way to an open field, a single grave stood alone. Simple. Humble. A metal post with no name, only an old flight patch fluttering in the soft breeze, partially faded from time. Wildflowers had grown around it, as if the forest had decided to protect whatever—or whoever—rested beneath.

Stumbling along, Sonny spotted it first, slowing to a stop. "That wasn't in the tour brochure," he muttered, a strange heaviness in his voice.

Hawk followed his gaze, his expression exploratory. "This is hallowed ground."

Neither said a word for a moment. Sonny made the sign of the cross.

The birds stopped singing. The breeze whispered through the tall grass. A place of peace, maybe even honor. But it hinted at sacrifice too—proof even paradise had its skeletons.

They stood near a massive boulder. Out of place, they inspected it briefly and moved on. Before they had time to speculate about it, the stone face opened up behind them.

Instinctively, the group turned with weapons drawn. They'd been trekking through the Garden for twenty minutes without making contact. Were they about to encounter another sentry machine like the ones in the cave? Another trap?

Instead, a petite female 4Gen Synth stepped out of a hidden hatch camouflaged in the form of a giant rock. She came bearing a tray in her hand. Her part-mechanical, part-organic face smiled as she greeted them—

"Holy crap! Hold your fire!" she shrieked, nearly dropping the tray. "I'm unarmed! Don't shoot!"

Sonny dropped to a knee for a steadier aim. Fatigue and fear rearing its ugly head again. His dot wobbling around a kill shot.

"You trying to get me to blow a *servomotor?*" the machine asked. "Let's all settle down and take a deep breath before someone gets hurt. Namely me. We are all friends here."

"That's rich," Sonny sighed as he lowered his weapon. "You didn't exactly roll out the red carpet for us."

The rest of the team hesitated.

"People, I am here to greet you! See if you needed anything!" she continued, exasperated. "It's been a long time since I've had crew here. Thought you might like refreshments after your trek through the magnificent crystal caves. Did you enjoy the majesty of those massive crystals?"

"We didn't have a lot of time to ooh and ahh over them before the murder bots and cryptids attacked," Myli explained.

"Such a shame—the crystals are a magical natural wonder you should have time to revere."

Myli lowered her weapon as did the rest of her fire team. This bot's programming must be corrupt. With Myli's weapon out of her face, there was instant recognition. The robot tilted her head in acknowledgement.

"Captain Athena Tempus Viator," the machine announced.

Confused, Myli immediately shook her head, "You have me confused with someone else. Who are you?" Myli demanded—not lowering her guard. "Is Dumuzi here?"

The bot looked genuinely confused before responding. "I'm Server Bot S1R1—SARA for short. Are you okay, Captain? I was wondering when you'd come back. According to Ava's countdown, you're," she paused, "early this time."

"Come back? I've never set foot on this ship before."

Hawk whispered to Sonny while Myli and SARA continued talking. "We just created the AVA AI; she's mistaken."

SARA tilted her head again before shaking it. "That can't be right. My data banks are a little corrupted, I will admit, but I remember you saying something about this moment—one second while I retrieve the conversation—yes, you said, 'We'll see you in a few thousand years.' So, of course you've been here! This is your ship, Captain Athena. You and Looper used this facility all the time. Feels like yesterday since I last saw you two."

Sonny shook his head and said, "Wait—what? Her name is Myli not Athena."

"And there is no Ava AI here." Hawk said aloud.

"Of course not. She hadn't created it yet." SARA clarified her previous statement.

"This is beyond weird," he whispered back to Sonny.

SARA suddenly perked up and turned her attention to En'Gen. "Oh! Another old face! Hello, handsome." She scurried over, examining him closely.

Sonny laughed under his breath. "Brother, hold my beer."

SARA grinned at En'Gen and winked. "I'm SARA! Anything I can get you? Not just a Server Bot, I'm also a Service Bot."

She winked again.

"Dude, a robot with ADHD? Is that even possible?" Sonny whispered to Hawk.

"I do repairs and tune-ups. I think I still have your model on file. If you'd like, I can tighten up some of your bolts and replace any damaged tubing with something a little firmer."

Hawk sneered. "Oh, this'll be good."

En'Gen looked down, his artificial ocular processing micro expressions in Sonny's and Hawk's face. "It's all about the 1's and 0's, Sonny."

Hawk rolled his shoulders and eyes. "Only a robot can pervert math into something phallic."

SARA grabbed the big Synth's hand and dragged him along. "Come on, big boy! This way to the bridge!"

The team followed SARA down a gentle knoll into Section 10. SARA glanced over her shoulder, her voice apologetic. "I know it looks bad, Captain. Some of the bots are malfunctioning; we're critically low on parts. I shut down the Grav-Lifts and all nonessential systems per your orders, back when Looper locked the ship down."

She turned, gesturing to the ring on Sonny's finger.

"When you give me the green light, I can activate the bridge systems and bring the crew online."

"Permission granted," Myli said, glancing toward the lone grave marker in the distance. "SARA, who's buried over there?"

SARA hesitated—a rare flicker of emotion in her tone. "A casualty of war."

Myli had nothing to say. Her jaw flexed and mind drifted in flashes of memory she wasn't sure belonged to her—things she wasn't allowed to remember and yet she'd made a name for herself she didn't know. Her past and future blurred at the edges. How much had she truly lost?

Myli turned, her voice shifting back to command mode. "You two... Hawk, En'Gen—head to Engineering. Bring the engines online. I know we've got more questions than answers, but we need to be orbital. Now."

Hawk gave a curt nod and tapped his knuckles lightly against the Synth's chest plate. "Give us twenty minutes and we'll get this bird to space."

SARA waved En'Gen off playfully. "See you later, you dirty old 3Gen."

Sonny and Myli were alone. SARA had gone to reactivate the Grav-Lift for their trek to the bridge. They walked in silence until they reached a towering chestnut tree near the edge of a crystal-clear pool and riffle. Its trunk bore an old carving: L + A. Myli stepped closer, her fingers tracing the etched bark, hoping for a flicker of memory. Nothing. The initials meant nothing to her.

"I've never been here," she whispered.

Sonny stood beside her, watching her hand linger on the carving. His eyes drifted. The lack of rest was catching up with him. He only dropped his guard for half a second before Myli tossed him in the water.

Head underwater, he popped up like a bobber spitting the pristine water out of his mouth. "What the hell?"

"We've got a minute," she said, turning toward him with a smile. "Let's not waste it."

He raised an eyebrow, puzzled, but refreshed.

"You stink," she said with a teasing smile. "So do I, after the cave."

She wasn't wrong. He dunked his head again, scrubbing vigorously. With a somersault and some underwater acrobatics, he had his Alpha Skin off. The slop of the day rushed away by the riffle.

Above him at the edge of the water, without another word, she dropped the 2nd SKN armor pack, her guns, and peeled off her Alpha Skin suit. He bobbed back up, blowing water like a whale before shaking the water out of his hair and wiping his face. When his eyes focused, he saw her. She jumped in after him.

Sonny hesitated but only for a second. Modesty was a luxury long gone. The water was crisp, pure, washing away more than sweat and blood—rinsing the static from their thoughts, the tension from their limbs.

They didn't speak. Not at first.

It wasn't about romance, or desire.

This was about "survival and hygiene." Sanity. So he kept telling himself.

They had all the answers to questions they hadn't yet learned to ask.

"What do you think?" she asked him as she waded over to a shallow waterfall.

"I think there's a lot more going on here than we can even begin to understand," Sonny said, standing beneath the cascade of water. The cold poured over him like a system rebooting—something he desperately needed after nearly overheating inside his suit.

"Maybe you have a twin?" he asked.

Myli shook her head, eyes distant. "No, at least, not that I was told." Her voice was quiet. She was as lost in the mystery as he was. None of it made sense. The carving on the tree. The name. L + A. *Looper and Athena?* She took a deep breath before becoming buoyant enough to float on her back. Her mind was still spinning in circles.

Apparently, *she* was Athena.

Sonny wasn't sure how to process that, but he decided to give it a try.

"How about this?" he began. "What I don't understand is that no one is inherently evil. You don't just pop out of the womb set on mass murder. This Enlil guy... he and his brother are the two smartest beings ever to live, and both are trying to create this utopic refuge for their people. So, how do you go from hero to pure evil? There is no way Enlil thought he was the villain in all this."

"Nothing is ever black and white, Sonny."

A disturbance in the distance—SARA was on her way back.

"Break's over, Sonny," Myli called as she swam to the edge, pulling herself out by the roots dangling in the water. She grabbed her soiled Alpha Skin suit, grimacing at the thought of having to put it back on. She outwardly shuddered.

Sonny smiled faintly. "Yeah. No dignity left in this job."

She looked back—Sonny was still waist-deep in the water, frozen.

"Sonny?" she called.

He pointed at SARA. "She's watching."

Myli rolled her eyes. "She's a *robot,* Sonny. She doesn't care. Quit being shy—we've got work to do."

"Tell her to turn around," he grumbled, making sign language movements with his hands and arms.

SARA's holographic eye winked. "I was a battle medic before being transferred to this ship. It's nothing I haven't seen before, sir. I've brought fresh Alpha Suits for both of you." She handed them to Myli without missing a beat.

Myli held Sonny's suit out at arm's length—way out of reach. "Come on, Sonny. *What that pp do?*"

He turned beet red. "Oh, my *God*—you heard that, *too?*"

His shoulders were sagging in defeat. He'd been stabbed, burned, almost bitten in half, nearly boiled alive—and now, utterly humiliated. Again.

He muttered. "The water is cold. This is bullshit!" As his sentence ended, he skipped his hand on the surface, sending a splash of water at her.

Myli acted mock-offended. "*That's* hard to believe—after being in the water with a goddess." She cracked up, laughing so hard she had to turn away.

Sonny groaned. "I hate it here." He swung again, splashing another handful of water at her before proceeding to climb out.

SARA didn't turn away—if anything, her sensors zoomed in. She pointed. "Ma'am, he doesn't look shy right now!"

Sonny tripped as he clawed his way out of the water one-handed while covering himself with his other hand. Roots tore out of the bank settling him back in the water. "SARA! Jesus!"

Myli was doubled over, howling now. "I'm *dying*—oh, my gods!"

Sonny crawled out, jogged over to her and snatched the Alpha Suit from her outstretched hand like it was a lifeline. "You two flirts are the worst right now."

SARA's programing kicked in and she couldn't hold back. "Life's hard when you party naked."

It didn't take long before they were on the Grav-Lift surging upward, cutting silently through The Garden's atmosphere. Above them, a lone cloud swirled in the dome's upper reaches—heavy with rain. Even this high up he couldn't see the edges of the biosphere.

Myli broke the silence. "SARA, did my father talk about who built this ship?"

SARA didn't hesitate. "Dumuzi located it while searching for Architect tech in the Racil System. Time was running out for the Anunna and they needed a miracle to hasten their exodus."

"How did my father get it here?"

"It was always here, ma'am. Dumuzi and another Gen 3 Synth discovered it by luck."

Myli swallowed hard. "Sounds like a story for another time."

SARA turned, her synthetic features unreadable. "I'm sorry if I am being vague, Captain. I'm under strict orders of what I can and cannot read you in on."

Myli's eyes narrowed. "Whose orders?"

SARA's golden optics locked onto hers. "Yours."

Seconds passed.

"In ancient times," SARA continued, voice low and reverent, "you were known as Athena Tempus Viator."

"No, I was never called that," Myli said, her temperature and blood pressure rising.

"*You will be,* Ma'am."

CHAPTER 10

The Vigilant Son

The Grav-Lift doors whooshed open, depositing them onto the bridge. Dark, silent, and dead. Even SARA hadn't visited this hibernation chamber, or so she said.

Every console sat dormant, shadows stretching across the cold floor. Had they ever been turned on?

But something was off. Sonny's curiosity spiked as he investigated the cerebellum of the ship. The layout—command chair, tactical, comms, helm—it was all *perfectly staged, waiting for the cast to arrive.*

In a side room, Sonny discovered a Ouija board briefing table—a bizarrely familiar relic from his time working on the *U.S.S. Lexington* aircraft carrier tours back home. Sonny reached for an inch-long model of what looked to be a futuristic fighter and slid it across the blueprint of the ship. It stuck. Several more magnetic models of Ninety-Nine fighters clung to the table.

"If this ship has a hangar... this one ship could take on an armada, but where are the crew?" Sonny asked.

SARA stepped forward, waving them forward with casual ease. "Come, come."

Neither moved. Sonny hovered close behind Myli, his hand inching toward the pistol at his hip. Had this artificial intelligence led them into a trap?

"You won't be needing a weapon," SARA said.

She was right; all that was there was a single Quantum Stasis Cube tucked in the corner. Its lights were still blinking, dim but steady.

A survivor.

"Myli," Sonny muttered. "What's that?"

"I came out of one of those. Imagine taking the Garden and sticking it in a small box like that."

"So, a Genie in a lamp is a real thing?"

She raised her shoulders slightly and thought, *you could make it whatever shape you wanted.* "What's a genie?" she asked. Then she put her hands up and shook her head, never mind. "Sonny. Over here."

He hesitated—but obeyed. Myli took his four-fingered hand—the one bearing the ring—and pressed it to the ship's interface. "The sun looked healthy, so it shouldn't need a charge. Let's pray this works."

The moment his palm made contact, the bridge ignited. Consoles lit up in a cascade, systems booting with a faint electronic hum. The systems for the entire ship were activated in seconds, followed by a burst of searing white light. It was the Quantum Stasis Cube in the corner. Its resident was released.

The pressure wave rippled through the room, rattling the consoles and fluffing their hair. Sonny's pupils were slow to adjust, and when they did, a stranger was standing in front of them. SARA rushed over and handed him a vial of something to drink.

There was something about this man. Myli seemed to recognize him, but she wasn't certain. The man, nude and fit, in his early twenties slowly began flexing his muscles after such a long slumber. He radiated strength. The world he'd come from was fading like a dream that may or may not have been real.

There was something unmistakably familiar about him—in the set of his jaw, the posture, the eyes. He exhaled like it was his first breath in eons. For an instant, the stranger's gaze fell on Myli. Before she could continue sleuthing her way to an answer, he turned away and spoke.

"Evi, activate Protocol K3pL3R," he said, his voice calm and commanding.

Evi complied. One of the unoccupied stations began running code, booting up other empty stations. It wasn't long before every station was put to use doing its assigned task.

The stranger returned his gaze to Myli and nodded, his voice even but firm, "Captain," he nodded, "About time."

Sonny instinctively stepped back. "Who the hell—" he began to ask.

Myli's mind played tricks on her. The stranger looked like her father, and yet he was not.

The stranger checked calculations on the viewer.

"By my calculations," he said, "we have less than an hour in this string to get airborne."

The man looked at Sonny, wanting to connect, but brushed past him, moving straight to a storage locker. He retrieved an Alpha Skin uniform and began dressing with methodical urgency.

"By now, your teleportation trail's been detected. Hawk has already slipped a tracking device inside you. The current government has unwittingly given away the location of this ship to the enemy. They may not have realized it yet—but they've already been compromised and most likely slaughtered."

Myli tensed. "How could you possibly know that?"

"There's not enough time to explain," he said, his hand magically sealing the suit halfway up. His voice clipped and efficient.

Myli turned to SARA and motioned to her.

"Scan me, cut the tracker out, and destroy it." SARA stepped in to scan her and Myli blocked the scanner. "No—wait—just remove it. Maybe we can use it to our advantage."

"They won't be able to read it through the ship's hull, Captain." SARA scanned her up and down locating the tracker. "Hold still, ma'am."

Sonny watched a few feet away as the scanner traversed her skin. The beam of light cut through revealing her insides in detail. She waved it over Myli's intestines, colon, and eventually nailed down the pinhead-sized device in her rectum. "Your body will pass it during your next bowel movement."

"That's some high-tech shit you're carrying around, Myli," Sonny quipped.

Myli's blank face wasn't the reaction Sonny was hoping for after his comment.

"Stow it. Not now," she cautioned him quietly.

The stranger was right, and he wasn't finished.

"This ship has been storing information since before our time," he told them. "You can input any date in its history, and it will tell you where it was—down to the precise location in space and time."

What good would that do? Sonny wondered. If they survived, they could use its maps to explore and find strange new worlds. He suddenly remembered another Captain he admired, a fictional explorer named Jim who commanded a starship.

The young man looked up, eyes hard. "This ship holds many secrets. With the right equations, data is power." A soft alarm sounded. A timer. "Let it work for you. Speaking of the devil, by now an Udug agent has already broadcast our location to a scout ship docked at your so-called Area 51."

He let that revelation settle before delivering the punch.

"And that scout ship is carrying something my father once called a nuke. Once his ship reaches orbit—Asag will launch it at us."

Sonny was taken aback. "How the hell could you possibly know all this? You expect us to just take your word for it? After what we've been through? Those spider's and those monsters nearly killed us."

The man didn't flinch. "No, I don't expect you to believe me. You can be incredibly hardheaded, but she does."

He reached into the locker and pulled out something small and metallic. A pendant. He held it out. The fine necklace woven around his fingers loosened, allowing it to rappel down into her hand. With her free hand she fondled the one around her neck, the one Hawk gave her.

"The data is all there. You can check for yourself. But we don't have a lot of time."

Myli stared at the pendant and gasped faintly. She stepped forward held it up to the light, her fingers brushing over its weathered surface. Her eyes widened—recognition blooming like an open wound. Athena, the pendant, a young man who looked incredibly familiar. Sonny watched the color drain from her face.

She was buying all this cockamamie story hook, line, and sinker.

"Myli?" Sonny's voice was cautious, uncertain. "You look like you've seen a ghost."

She stared at the pendant in her hand. "Ghosts," she whispered. "That would be an understatement. They are everywhere. We are surrounded by them."

She turned back to the stranger—her eyes filled with something which Sonny couldn't quite place—fear? Awe? Sorrow?

Myli closed her eyes and emptied her lungs with a long breath. Then her voice dropped, deeper, steadier—absolute. "Trust him with your life, Sonny."

Sonny was speechless. His confusion was enormous—about the size of a billboard.

"You told me not to trust anyone," he reminded her. "Now this dude aerosols in here like a fart and you're telling me to trust him with our lives?"

In between their words, the stranger spoke to SARA under his breath, "I have wondered forever," he whispered, "if these two were always this way."

Myli's eyes met Sonny's eyes without flinching. Her stare cut through any doubt. He put his hands up as if to say, *If looks could kill.*

"Trust me, Sonny." Myli said. It was a plea, but also a direct order.

No more debate. No wiggle room.

She handed the pendant back to the stranger who took it without hesitation, his expression unreadable.

Sonny sighed, surrendering to fate once again. But he wasn't totally sold. Not yet.

"Enough with the cloak and dagger shit. Who the hell are you?" Sonny demanded.

The stranger turned to him—calm, deliberate. His gaze locked like a targeting system.

"I am Ravelin," he said. "And I am a Guardian."

CHAPTER 11

Too Close to the Sun

Below decks, a deep, low-frequency thrum rolled through the hull as the ship came alive. Power surged through the core. Screens flickered, interfaces lit up like Christmas morning. Hawk and En'Gen stood at the main consoles, uncertain how to proceed.

"What did you touch?" they asked—in unison.

Neither had touched a damn thing—except maybe Hawk.

"Hell—I don't know. I'm not an engineer. I just fly the stuff."

However it had happened, the ship had awakened.

A pressurized release of air burst from QSC chambers. Across the decks gasps echoed everywhere. Men and women popped into consciousness around him in color-coded suits. The *puff-puff-puff* of the system's reactivation blasted through the gangways as the ship cleared its lungs.

"Condition Red!" the ship's AI barked in a stern alien dialect—instantly translating into English. "All stations to battle readiness. This is not a drill."

Excitement surrendered to muscle memory. The awakening crew paused briefly to drink the same unknown concoction Ravelin consumed to speed up their memories.

Lockers were thrown open. Second Skin armor packs were ripped out of their lockers, MK IV and MK V packs slapped on and articulated in place in seconds. Crewmen barked orders at each other, adrenaline sharpening them. Boots stomped onto the metal flooring. The air reeked of ozone and urgency.

One of the senior engineers—face still withdrawn from cryo-sleep—marched straight up to Hawk and En'Gen, hand raised.

"Step aside, gentlemen. This console is mine," he ordered.

Hawk raised an eyebrow but backed off. He was out of his lane. He'd seen this kind of fire lit in his own troop before—the way a senior engineer *became* part of the ship in emergencies.

The Chief's fingers danced across the controls, calling up diagnostics, reactor core status, flicking through schematics faster than a human should. No errors and no second guessing.

"We're stable and spinning up fast," the Chief said excitedly. "On the double, we rehearsed for this," he bellowed to the crew down the gangway.

Hawk stepped away, uneasy. He wasn't an engineer—but he knew ships. His place was on the flight deck, not here. He scanned a map of the ship looking for where he should be.

Hangar Bay. Status: Doors unlocking. Emergency evac underway.

The ground rumbled.

Hawk's fingers twitched. He belonged out there—in a ship, strapped in a cockpit, leading a squadron of birds. He knew these young bucks probably thought he was a dinosaur now with atrophied reflexes. Too old to guide the tip of the spear. It was what he feared most. Promotion to the bridge. The best pilots always wind down their careers haunting the bridge crew or instructing others instead of battling the enemy on the front line.

Players want to play, not coach.

"We're launching soon," the Chief muttered to the pair of interlopers who were hanging around his work area. "Head to the bridge or go to hell, just don't stand around here."

Hawk felt the itch to fly returning. This ground-pounding was for the mathematically challenged.

Anshar Hawk. The fastest man alive. The first human to fly the Ninety-Nine and live. 99.999% the speed of light. But that was then, this was now. Hawk wasn't blazing through space at the moment. His feet were planted on a capitol ship where engines were currently roaring to life for the first time in only God knew when.

As Hawk hesitated, a blinding glow surged from under the ship, zero-point engines igniting with a rush which warped the cavern's very air. Reality bent—water began evaporating into steam; the rock not covered in gypsum crystals smoldered from the radiating heat.

The cave crawlers that found higher ground scattered as the light seared their eyes and skin. Some weren't fast enough. Fifty-ton crystals—dislodged by vibration—crashed down, pulverizing them mid-sprint. Others caught fire where they stood, the radiant heat cooking them alive. They howled before becoming puffs of smoke and ash.

Above, the earthen ceiling began vibrating at the atomic level. Waves of sound brought what was on the surface down around the ship like someone unzipping it. The heavy debris was no match for the armor of the *Daedalus*. Sunlight—divine but blinding—pouring in. Nothing but blue skies above.

What had been buried and forgotten was surfacing. The ancient stronghold succumbed. Steam vented from boiling vents, hissing upward into the cool blast of open air. *Daedalus* was rising, no longer a prisoner stuck in a cell. The cavern caging her for millennia gave her up.

Hovering silently above the desert, the *Daedalus* aligned itself with the ancient runway below—once a vital launch strip, now nothing more than a forgotten scar on the Earth. From directly below, looking up, the massive ship bent the light around it unnaturally, warping the air and masking the ship entirely from view. A colossal predator in plain sight—invisible and plotting her next move.

Inside the bridge, blast shields retracted with a moan, revealing a panoramic view of the outside world. Sonny stepped forward, his voice barely above a whisper. "Myli, look at this."

The translucent view screen flickered to life, auto mapping the terrain, searching, scanning, comparing for familiar navigation markers.

It found none.

The world it once knew was gone. In place of landing beacons, massive glyphs stretched across the desert floor—birds in flight, spiraling whales, impossible geometric patterns—etched deep into the Earth, unmistakable from above. The final messages of a fallen civilization. The Nazca Lines.

Sonny's voice was barely audible. "The survivors were trying to signal your people."

Myli nodded slowly, her voice hushed, "No one answered, because no one was left—until now."

Ravelin turned to Myli. "Captain, will you give the order?"

Myli nodded. "Punch it."

The *Daedalus* only hesitated as long as it took for navigation to signal full-ahead. It angled its bow skyward—and ascended. No sonic boom to crack the heavens. Time-space warped as the engines accelerated to quarter power. To the naked eye, the ship zipped away—gone. In reality, it had simply moved beyond perception, skipping across visual reference points like a stone over water—there, then not. The sky ripped as the *Ole Lady* returned to the stars.

Seconds earlier, high above the Nazca Lines, the LA battle drone pierced Earth's upper atmosphere, its hull humming with ancient, alien power and gathering speed. Asag mirrored the ship in a stolen Ninety-Nine fighter. He watched, his predatory eyes locked on the screen by his knee, his expression smoldering with anticipation. Below him, the facility's blast shields retracting, the ship in visual range.

From beneath the drone's fuselage, a hatch snapped open. A single massive missile launched—then split mid-flight, unleashing multiple nuke warheads fast and hypersonic.

Impacts.

The base lit up, glowing blue, green, and orange as entire layers of ancient stone and super-tech vaporized in an instant. Detonation. The mountain didn't collapse.

It erupted.

The fault line fractured, and water and rock rushed to fill the wound. The underground magma chamber, its pressure sealed for eons, exploded with vengeance. Not a blast—a cataclysm. In comparison, Hunga Tonga-Hunga Ha'apai looked like a sparkler.

Over 32 cubic Km3 of rock and ash blasted skyward—fifty miles up, punching into the edge of the mesosphere. A booming acoustic pressure wave tore through the atmosphere, thundering across the globe—Once. Twice. Four times.

The pyroclastic flow surged outward. Volcanic ash and fire raced to consume South America. The sky bled crimson, scarlet, blood-orange. Like Edvard Munch's *The Scream* come to life—a final sunset for a terminal continent. Radioactive fire rained from the heavens.

The ash would soon follow.

Asag had to break right from the epicenter in his fighter as the blast wave streaked over Peru. Asag's twisted form hunched over his display array. The drone was gone, destroyed by the mega blast. His craft was shaking violently, but weathering the storm better than his nether regions.

A long-range lens zoomed in, his eyes flickering with triumph and pain. At last, vengeance. There was no way they could have survived an explosion of that magnitude.

He shifted uncomfortably, still reeling from the mutilation Sonny had dealt him. His uniform—torn, scorched, bloodstained—clung to his still regenerating skin. Every bump of turbulence took the wind out of him.

He tapped the UFCD touch screen above the MPCD, flipping through telemetry, looking at live maps, scanning for survivors or any evidence. There was nothing. Molten rocks spewed outward in every direction under the massive mushroom cloud. The earth was bleeding beneath him.

Huacachina to Paracas was burning. He veered over the ocean admiring his handy work. Skeletal remains and corpses of humans and varying animals floated off the coast. Bodies blown clean from the Earth and redistributed out to sea.

Asag's breathing deepened. His hand trembled above the console. His elation became a fist. Elation quickly passed as the pain returned.

The *Daedalus* was gone.

"Erased from time! I deleted you all!" Asag smirked, pleased with himself.

CHAPTER 12

Sledgehammer

The video feed in Asag's Ninety-Nine fighter didn't receive sufficient light input and wasn't fast enough to digitize a visual of the *Daedalus* leaving its underground vault. Regardless of what Asag saw or didn't see, the *Daedalus* escaped, but not unscathed.

Though moving away, the ship was still near enough that the blast wave hit them like an unexpected slap from a giant. The ship jumped forward violently, alarms screaming to life. Consoles sparked. Bulkheads groaned under the strain. Crew members were thrown from their stations like rag dolls.

Myli slammed into the arm of the captain's chair, the blow driving into her ribs. She sucked in a breath, wincing—but stayed upright.

"Report!" she barked, regaining her footing.

Sonny was sprawled on the deck. He looked up, never feeling more helpless than right now. His fate completely out of his control.

Radiological alerts flared across every display—blinking red and pulsing like erratic heartbeats.

"Nuke—" someone shouted over the blaring claxons from tactical. "Somebody fired a nuke!"

"*Somebody,* my ass," Sonny said, eyes locked on the readout. "It had to be him."

"We can't seem to lose this son of bitch, can we? We got lucky, that was close," Myli breathed with relief. She turned to SARA.

Sonny stammered to his feet. "Good thing we ain't pitching washers."

Once again, Myli stared at him blankly—unable to comprehend Sonny's reference to the backyard tossing game. SARA recorded and restored the reference for future analysis.

"The initial blast blew the magma chamber beneath the mountain," SARA calculated. "The pressure release triggered a geological chain reaction. The whole coast—"

"How bad?" Myli demanded.

Silence for a second.

One of the bridge crew sounded off. "Southwest coast is burning, ma'am. Entire cities—gone. VEI-7 scale eruption. A nuke didn't do all that—it's a continental reset. And fallout's spreading fast."

Myli's voice went hoarse, like it or not she had to move on. Somehow, she understood what had to be done and found the words.

"Active camouflage. Now. Get us into orbit—on the double. Max planetary speed."

"Camouflage engaged," the Tac Officer confirmed, fingers skimming across the controls.

The bridge dimmed slightly as the hull refracted light, rendering the massive ship near-invisible to outside detection.

From the helm, "Speed increasing. Five seconds!"

"Ma'am, we've reached 575 kilometers. Orbit stable. Artificial gravity achieved."

Gravity normalized—with a thrum through the deck plating.

The gravity may be normal, Myli told herself, *but tension's increasing amongst the crew from the Anunna gut punch we just took.*

Sonny stood by the port view plate, his face pale. "The fire and brimstone is still climbing."

Below them, Earth churned. From space, the continent's edge was a smoldering scar—the coastline ripped open, fire devouring everything in its path. A mushroom cloud loomed, still climbing, drifting out over the Pacific, its cap beginning to expand from high-altitude wind shears. Hawaii. The Philippines. They were next in line.

"That's—" Sonny couldn't finish the thought. "We were just down there."

"We're up here now, that's what counts." Myli moved carefully beside him, her voice quieter now. "He didn't want merely to stop us. He wanted to erase us. If we are lucky, he will think we are dead."

Out of one of the other viewports, the sun was blasting in. Much brighter than normal. Tactical was analyzing strange solar readings.

"Rendezvous with the blockade," Myli ordered. "Signal them: Friendlies on the way. *Daedalus* is operational. It's our turn to go on offense."

After spending two hours entering the massive ship into geosynchronous orbit, Captain Mylitta Sipani eased back into the command chair, eyes locked on the holographic targeting display as the *Daedalus* shimmered—its hull blending seamlessly into the void with active camouflage. The sleek behemoth flew silently above the United States below.

Hawk and En'Gen strode onto the bridge, footsteps echoing on the polished deck. They arrived just in time to see Mylitta rise and cross her arms as she approached Ravelin.

"So now what, kid?" Her voice was commanding, although physically she didn't look much older than him.

Ravelin tapped the console on the Ouija board. A translucent map of Earth flickered to life—displaying orbital fleet formations, ships arranged in tactical spread, a mosaic of humanity's last stand.

"Synchronizing orbit with the fleet," he confirmed. "SARA is activating the rest of the skeleton crew," he added, scanning scrolling data. "Before we connect with the command net, we should locate Ava."

Hearing the familiar name, Hawk's attention focused on Ravelin. "Her remnant is on-board the major systems of the *Icarus*—and every squadron plugged into it."

Mylitta raised an eyebrow. "What is Ava?" she asked.

Hawk exhaled, wiping a bead of sweat from his brow. "Ava is one of the original Guardians."

"My Godmother," Ravelin nodded solemnly. "She fought through most of reconstruction with my father. She was with him from day one. We need her for the next step."

"She's a person, but she's plugged in?" Myli questioned.

"When this is over, you'll see for yourself," said Ravelin

"You're too late, kid." Hawk's expression darkened. His voice dropped low and hard.

He looked Ravelin in the eye. "Ava's dead. Died a few years ago. She's entirely AI now." He stared at Myli, but she avoided his gaze.

Ravelin halted his work, disbelief washing over his face. His hands clenched into fists, knuckles white. "Dead? How?" he asked.

Hawk's voice was flat and grim. "She was murdered. The enemy did it."

A heavy pause.

"It's been a few decades," Hawk added, jaw tightening. "All the evidence points to a Guardian named Looper. Missions went sideways; he lost his way. There is a kill order out on him. One I intend to claim."

"That's not possible," Ravelin disputed, shaking his head.

"Listen kid, we all had a falling-out after a mission. Accusations of betrayal. Things got—messy."

The bridge fell silent. Ravelin looked at Sonny, then Hawk, then he fell into disbelief. Only the quiet hum of the *Daedalus'* systems filled the air—an artificial heartbeat in the stillness of grief.

Ravelin's stare locked onto Hawk, burning. "After Pazuzu murdered my mother," Ravelin said, voice tight. "Ava was the only family I had left." Sonny remembered the highway. "When my father—when Looper pulled away from reality, she was everything to me."

Sonny raised his hand. "Pazuzu? Myli and I killed that son of a bitch." He nodded to Ravelin. "Mostly Myli." He stepped back.

It didn't console Ravelin much.

After realizing he lit a fire under everyone, Hawk poignantly pointed out a fact. "Now," Hawk said, "there's only one of those bastards left. Asag."

Mylitta inhaled deeply before gazing over her shoulder toward the view-port. She slowly released that breath and with it the tension in her shoulders. Stars stretched endlessly across the black, cold, silent, and eternal. A twinkling battlefield waiting for war. The Udug had driven them to the brink, possibly killing their own creators. They could be facing platoons of Asag's and Pazuzu's in the coming days if they didn't do something to run defensive strategies now.

Her voice cut through the stillness.

"Get this ship ready for battle. The countdown on the ring is upon us. We need to figure out a way to end this today."

CHAPTER 13

Return to Oak Island, 1950

A black Ford Crestline came rolling to a stop on a narrow two-track. Trees closing in on both sides, two more pickup trucks followed close behind. As they pulled up, their headlights cut through the dense veil of morning fog drifting off the nearby water. They were deep on Crandall Road, just off Route 3, Nova Scotia.

The road was barely visible now—a path choked by mist and suffocated with overgrowth. The horizon's crest held the sunrise hostage, darkness resetting the clock, buying evil one more down to stop Ava's final rush into the end zone. Government plates flashed briefly beneath the Crestline's bumper as the last truck idled to a halt. Doors creaked open. Boots hit gravel. The air was thick, curling over the ground like a creeping graveyard shroud.

Beyond the tree line, across the silvery water, a shadow waited.

Oak Island.

The island was a secret wrapped in fog, eager for blood, a target they couldn't hit head-on. Others had tried direct approaches—again and again—and always ended the same way, in tragedy. Diggers vanished. Divers drowned. Drill teams walked off into the mist and were never seen again. Carbon Disulfide, CS2 gas, was rumored to be the silent killer.

The island had a way of punishing directness. This time would be different. This time, they'd come at it sideways. And most importantly surgical.

Ava popped the trunk and got to work, cool and practiced, like a dame who'd seen more than her share of fights. She yanked free a modified M1 Garand, fed an en-bloc clip into the chamber, and sent the bolt home with a satisfying *clank*. The Tanker Garand was locked, loaded, and safe—her finger brushing the trigger guard like she was shaking hands with an old friend.

Next out of the trunk came the 1928 Tommy Gun. She swapped out the stick mag for a drum—less reliable, but more forgiving when things got loud. If the island bit back, she was ready to bite harder. She handed it to Malachi.

The Tommy Gun was heavy—it was solid, familiar, and full of angry pills. He set it barrel up and butt down against the car. His eyes scanned the length of the two-track road, through the break in the trees, where a narrow dirt path led toward an old weather-beaten cabin.

Ava stood nearby, arms folded tight against the chill, a cigarette dangling loose from her lips—half smoked.

Malachi squinted through the fog, then glanced over at her. "All this heat," he muttered, "for a Sunday stroll?"

Ava barely glanced at him. "Kid, I just hope it's enough."

Around them, the rest of the squad prepped in silence—BARs racked, bolt back and ready to rip. A check made of .50-cal belt-feds. Satchels of old World War II C-3 explosives slung over shoulders—check. The yellow putty—notorious for sweating in the heat—had already been flagged for replacement, but it'd have to do. The boys were ready to raise some hell with Ava who'd been fighting hell-raisers for centuries.

Malachi let out a low whistle, shaking his head. "You got a real bone to pick with these fellas, huh?"

Even with smoke drifting into her eyes, Ava didn't blink. "And I suppose you don't. After Big Al's house? You're one of the few who has seen what they are—what they're capable of. And they weren't even full-blooded."

Malachi took a drag and shrugged, his face lit mostly by the soft cherry of his cigarette. "I just do my job, Ava, like you."

"Some of us don't just follow orders. Some of us are on a mission from God, Malachi," she told him as she pulled the sling of the Garand over her head, her neck and shoulders feeling its weight.

"I've been playing this game longer than I care to admit," Ava continued. "Fought these things alongside men tougher, better armed than this squad—watched them get torn apart like yesterday's garbage fighting trash pandas."

She turned, finally locking eyes with him.

"These things don't play by the rules, Malachi. No hesitation. No reasoning. And they sure as hell don't stop. They have one mission—kill us. You want to walk out of this alive? Keep your trap shut and do exactly what I say. Capisce?"

Malachi raised both hands in mock surrender. "Yes, ma'am," he said, cigarette bobbing in his lips.

Ava press-checked the Garand, then tapped the charging handle with her hand. "These heaters got extra kick," she said, slinging it back around her. "Depleted uranium tips, case-hardened. You'll feel the bolt buck."

"Depleted uranium?" a soldier holding a small cage with a yellow bird in it asked.

"Armor penetrating," she clarified and dumbed it down at the same time.

She had the team gather round and addressed the men.

"These weapons have been occasionally popping primers, so if you jam—don't think. Go straight to your secondary."

"Roger that," one of the soldiers said.

Malachi gave her a sideways look, lips twitching into a grin. "You sure know your way around a piece."

Ava didn't crack a smile. She just lit another cigarette, exhaled smoke through her nose like a dragon. "I get your concern with me being a woman," Ava smirked. "I'm not your average dame. You ever hear of Annie Oakley?"

Malachi scoffed. "Who hasn't?"

Ava tossed him a couple extra drums of ammo. "Well, I taught her some stuff. Perfect practice makes perfect."

Malachi barely caught the hurled drums, stowing them in his duffel bag. Then he picked the *Thompson* up, his arms dipping under the weight.

"Jesus, Ava," he complained. "What all ain't you telling me? *You taught* Oakley? That math ain't adding up."

Ava slammed the trunk shut with a *thunk*. "First off, I just showed her some stuff. Second of all, I'm not leaving anything out you need to know," she assured him as she tossed her blonde hair back nonchalantly.

Malachi was thunderstruck, his eyes narrowed looking at her in disbelief. "No BS, how long have you been playing this game?"

Ava let out a dry chuckle. "Back when humanity had to start cutting their teeth again, Malachi. Beware of the old soldier in a profession where soldiers die young."

Malachi looked her over again—really looked this time. The eyes. The way she carried herself. Like someone who'd seen too many wars, not just battles.

"So," he asked, "what are you, then? A ghost?"

Ava tucked the cigarette between her lips, took a long drag, and exhaled slowly.

"Not a ghost, not yet anyway." Her tone was matter-of-fact, but something behind her eyes said she'd come close more times than she could count. "Maybe I'm an avenging angel. Yeah, I like that better," she decided.

"Guess I better stick close. You're either cursed or the luckiest dame alive."

Ava gave him the same smirk again, sharp as the edge of her Ka-Bar on her belt.

The woods loomed ahead, unnerving, like bars in a prison. The mist, shackles which curled around their boots. Ava took point, boots spongy over damp pine needles, rifle at the ready. Malachi grunted, slinging the duffel over his shoulder with choice words.

"I know how to handle myself," he told her. "Maybe I could even handle you—if you'd let me, Ava." He shifted his *Thompson* into a low ready position.

Ava rolled her eyes. "Malachi, for the last time—you're barkin' up the wrong tree."

She hoisted her satchel like it weighed nothing, despite the load of En-Bloc clips packed inside.

It was Malachi's turn to smirk. "You a fairy or somethin' like that?"

"God, wouldn't that be easier." The thought registered relief in her face.

"Looper?" Malachi threw the name out there just to see what would happen.

The name hung in the air. Ava stopped in her tracks and sat her duffel down. Her eyes snapped to his—sharp, warning. Conversation over. Malachi shrugged and moved to grab the duffel. It didn't budge until he put some effort into it.

"Jesus. What the hell's in here—bricks?"

Ava shot him a sideways grin. "Insurance."

Malachi chuckled, shaking his head. "You're somethin' else, sweetheart."

They advanced up the narrow two-track until the trees parted, revealing an old hardwood house plopped in the middle of a wide, overgrown yard. The team bounded forward, weapons low, eyes sharp. From their vantage, Oak Island loomed in the distance, shrouded in morning fog. But they weren't crossing the water. No boats. No swimming. Their target wasn't on the island.

It was in an ancient cabin. A place older than memory. Older, some said, than the Vikings and the Crusaders who once came ashore. They stacked at the front door—the place felt abandoned. The breacher grabbed a bolt cutter from Ava's pouch. *Clink.* He cut a lock. Ava, point man, nudged it open with the barrel of her rifle. It creaked inward.

She moved her barrel up and down. The soldier on her left broke in, moving right. One by one, the rest of the team flowed in, filtering into the cabin like leaves blowing in from a winter wind.

The cottage was dead inside. The wood was petrified. Dust hung in the air after the door shut. Leaves, dirt, and scattered shells littered the corners of the walls, along with old rodent droppings. A squirrel's nest sat in the fireplace. Wind could be heard whispering through cracks between the massive wood logs.

"Clear."

Each room echoed the call as the cottage was secured.

Ava moved on, activating something on her wrist—technology the others didn't recognize. The glow from the wrist pad lit her face in pale blue light. She studied it a second, then walked straight to an old wardrobe built into the wall.

She examined the edges, then nodded to herself. "Here."

First, she opened the massive wardrobe. Empty. Studying it, she closed the doors. A thought. With a grunt and a push, she slid the three-hundred-fifty-pound wardrobe aside, revealing a narrow staircase descending into the dark.

Observing her strength, the men's eyes were nice and wide as they watched her do something they would have secretly struggled to accomplish.

"Torch." She reached back for a flashlight.

Raising her Tanker Garand sideways and high on her shoulder to shorten the profile, she led the descent into the basement. The others followed suit close behind her, their boots thudding on the old wood floors.

"Clear!" she shouted.

Another hidden door. An antechamber with another set of steps. Ava found it the same way she found the cabin—tech and clues.

"There are a few of these tunnels," she said over her shoulder looking back, "like spokes on a wheel—each leading to a different ingress. You're gonna see things down here that don't make sense. Don't try to make sense of them."

She paused at the top of the second stairwell. The men waited.

"If we encounter any strange creatures down here, you aim for the head. That's the only way to drop 'em. They're not human anymore. This is a treasure hunt. In and out. No screwin' around."

"Roger that, ma'am."

Ancient Knights Templar symbols were carved into the stone walls, etched deep into the passage like a message left for only those who knew how to read it. Malachi scowled as his flashlight passed over them, not understanding what he was seeing.

"We're not exactly flyin' under the radar rolling through town like we did."

Ava didn't slow. "Town's been cleared, Malachi. They dumped a tanker on Route 3 and called it a chemical spill. We've got seventy-two hours before anyone even thinks to poke around and find our convoy."

At the base of the stairs, another door waited—heavy, reinforced, ancient. They were easily two stories down now.

Malachi's boots echoed as he followed. "How are those clogs working for you back there, Malachi?" Ava joked.

Malachi snickered sarcastically with the rest of the team. He picked his feet up, quieted his steps better, but still not silent.

The air grew colder and damper the further they went. The tunnel angled beneath the earth, pushing directly toward Mahone Bay, and Oak Island.

Malachi adjusted his grip on the *Thompson*, the wood swelling slightly. "So, what happens if we find our treasure?"

Ava stopped. Turned. Met his eyes with a stare capable of cutting clean through the brightness of the flashlights and bravado.

Ava said flatly. "We either walk outta here with it... or we don't."

Malachi followed closely behind Ava now. *A good time for small talk,* he thought. He was no quitter. "Didn't Errol Flynn own this place?"

"I don't know. I saw some actor named John Wayne on an early deed. From my research, this damn island's changed hands more times than a bad playing card."

Malachi smiled. "Sounds like this is a case of Eminent Domain."

The path came to an end. Ava nodded with her head, signaling the group to form-up. She pulled out a paper with frottage on it. It was a rubbed copy of a centuries old rune stone.

"We at the right entrance, Ava?" Malachi asked, as his boots ground into the damp stone under his feet.

Ava looked at the rubbing. "No doubt about it." She turned to the team behind them. "Make sure those gas masks are secure. The gas around here'll kill you faster than a bullet. One good whiff, and you're on the floor convulsing right before a long, probably permanent, dirt nap."

Malachi's jaw tightened. He hated invisible killers—gas, radiation, and microbes. Things you couldn't shoot or outrun. He double-checked the seal on his own mask, tugging at the straps like a man checking a chute before a jump. No way he was going out coughing up his lungs like an FNG. He'd once been the *fucking new guy*. He had no intention of repeating that situation.

His eyes wandered to the carved symbols etched into the stone walls—weathered but unmistakable. Many of them matched the frottage in Ava's hand. His gaze drifted to the back of Ava's neck, where a small, red, equal-armed Cross Pattée peeked out beneath a loose strand of hair.

He'd seen that mark before. In history books. On the walls here. Templar? Masons?

Ava's fingers brushed along the cuneiform inscription set in the wall, her eyes narrowing. "The Templar fleet left France with their treasures the day before the purge. They created vaults like this one to fund New Atlantis, a free country. They were somewhat successful. This is a warning written in Theban."

"Theban?" asked Malachi.

"It's an ancient script the Templars would typically use."

Malachi stepped closer into her bubble. She could smell his nerves starting to fire. "Care to translate?" he asked. Something in his tone sounded concerned.

She could tell he was starting to cope, so she humored him. "The good news is we are in the right spot. We are near Templar treasure, it's their warning alright," she sighed in relief, clearing dust from an ancient plaque. A good sign. "Encoded. Meant only for those who knew the cipher. The Templars are gone—but their legacy continues."

Malachi gave her a sideways glance. "Are you a Mason too?"

Ava sneered without turning. "The Templars were Gnostics, not crusaders. They brought back most of what you saw in the Gothic churches in Europe during the war."

"You do look like an angel."

A pause, a quick look of annoyance flashed his way. "This isn't the time to be getting fresh with me, Malachi."

She turned back to the inscription, her fingers tracing the worn symbols carved deep into the granite. "Roughly translated? 'Any who enter shall suffer a death unlike any seen before. Only demons left here. 1765.' Is that plain enough for you, Malachi?"

"Ava, how could you possibly know they are telling the truth?"

"You see this mark and this other mark here?"

"Yeah, so what?"

"If someone altered this date, they've hidden the date within the warning as a backup. Two dates, and they match. If we altered this script here," she faked making a mark, "it would change the date by ten years."

Malachi ran his hand over the engraved script. "This message was left a decade before the American Revolution."

"Wars are expensive," she stated plainly.

"So, you're telling me our Founding Fathers used Templar treasure to fund the American Revolution?"

Ava sighed. "Some of it; this is one of six vaults. Let's just hope they left us some breadcrumbs at this one."

She pointed to a triangular sigil beside the warning—its design disturbingly close to the radiation hazard markers the U.S. had just started posting on bunker doors. She was trying to teach him something.

"Languages, dialects, they all evolve," she proffered. "Symbols, on the other hand, can be eternal. If you were going to give a message to someone in the future—a person who most likely couldn't read something from, let's say, 11,700 years ago, you'd use a symbol," she grinned.

"It's not in Theban," he pointed out.

"It's Anunna. The Templar vault is connected to an old Atlantean secret base."

Malachi tensed up, remembering his uncle who never made it out of Ypres, a Belgian Town, in WWI.

"So, poison gas *and* radiation?" he asked. "Great. Anything else we got to worry about?"

He eyed the duffel again.

"Okay, I gotta ask—what the hell's *really* in the bag?"

Ava glanced in his direction, then she looked back down the tunnel.

"It's a weapon of last resort," she said scanning for any threats behind them.

Malachi folded his arms. "Really? Because I tried lifting that thing and nearly threw out my spine. How are you able to lug this bag of bricks around like it's a sack lunch?"

Ava grinned.

"I work out," she said, as she posted a little box in front of the monolithic stone wall.

Malachi eyes glazed over. "No, seriously—what gives?"

She picked up the duffel, almost with ease, and swung it into a more comfortable position, her movements effortless. "I'm wearing an endoskeleton under my clothing."

"Excuse me?" Malachi asked bewildered. "A what?"

"Powered suit. Tech you won't live long enough to understand. Think of it as a second skeleton that lets me lift a hell of a lot more than I should."

He raised a brow. "Like an ant?"

"Close enough," she answered with a fist bump to his shoulder.

Malachi heard a noise and stared at the massive slab of stone. The box in front of it had somehow activated and the slab started slowly rolling open. He glanced at Ava.

"That rock must weigh a ton. How the hell did the ancients move this stuff without cranes? How did you do that?"

"I'm a witch," Ava said without hesitation.

"Seriously, Ava. How?"

"Alright," she thought out loud.

I can teach or I can do, she told herself, *but I can feel Malachi breaking.*

"They used sound waves to manipulate gravity, like I just did," she said.

Malachi rolled his eyes. "Right. And I've got beachfront property on Mars."

She turned to him, face dead serious. "The beaches on Mars were all destroyed during the DNA Wars. And as far as the sound wave tech, this is one of a kind. Maybe your people will figure it out in another eighty years—*minimum*—at the pace you're going."

Malachi grew silent. He could think of nothing to say. Ava decided she'd better keep him busy. She had everyone double check their gas masks one last time. Everyone gave a thumbs up. Weapons checked. Nerves taut like tripwires. The soldier holding the wire cage lifted it to eye level—inside, the canary fluttering, wings twitching in the dim light. Still alive.

Ava eyed the bird as the door came to a halt, open. The bird was still breathing. Good.

She herself exhaled, adjusted the buttstock of her rifle against her shoulder, finger resting near the trigger guard. The safety clicked forward and off. The team aimed into the dark. And waited. Expecting hell to come charging out.

Nothing.

Ava exhaled again, slinging the Garand over her shoulder as she reached into her pack. She pulled out a bulky, prototype scope and pressed it to her eye. The experimental night-vision flickered to life—washed in green static, showing little.

"This isn't gonna cut it," she muttered, handing it off to a nearby tech. "Not enough ambient light for night vision to play nice."

She rolled her shoulders. Her load felt instantly lighter.

"Flares and flashlights it is." She took out a roll of Army green duct tape and stainless-steel pipe clamp, fastening her flashlight to the left side of her Tanker Garand.

Malachi adjusted the Thompson in his grip, letting out a low sigh. "Ladies first."

Ava shot him a grin. "Naturally."

She depressed the light on her rifle and moved forward. The shadows swallowed her whole. One by one, the team followed, boots splashing quietly in stagnant puddles. The tunnel exhaled around them—moist, cold, and waiting.

Further along, they were sludging through waist-deep frigid seawater. Ava and Malachi exchanged a look. Both with teeth chattering.

"Well, ain't this just a bucket of gazpacho soup," Malachi muttered, adjusting his belt. "Looks like the *Money Pit's* workin' overtime."

"We ain't paid nothin' yet," one of the soldiers added.

Ava nodded. "When they started digging the most recent shaft, it must've triggered a chain reaction. It looks like the whole damn complex is compromised."

Malachi waded forward with the others, the icy saltwater biting at his skin—a harsh reminder they weren't supposed to be here. At the far end of the passage loomed another door—metal, seamless, unyielding. A watertight flood barrier.

Ava moved to the door and ran her gloved hand along the damp stone wall, searching. Her fingers found a granite panel coated in a jelly-like membrane which had an iridescent quality in the gloom.

Malachi cringed. "What the hell is that?"

She ignored him. Her mask was fogging. She looked at the canary. No trace of carbon disulfide yet.

"We're clear so far," Ava said relieved.

"Keep Tweety close," she added, nodding toward the canary as she inserted her fingers into the membrane.

The membrane pulsed under her touch, bioluminescent symbols blinking to life beneath the gel. Malachi moved closer, watching as her fingers danced across the pattern—fast, deliberate, like muscle memory. There was a hissing sound as the door unsealed with a groan, ancient machinery coming to life. The rush of water sucked them in.

They were soaked head to toe in the icy water. Gear and everything compromised by saltwater. Their gas masks ripped off. Malachi grabbed her arm to help her up. Spitting the salty brine out and wiping his face, his brain couldn't keep up anymore.

"Hold it. How the hell did you open that door?" he demanded. "What is that gel and the glowing when you touched it?"

Ava yanked free without flinching.

"Lucky guess," she told him. "I need you to calm down. Someone find the bird quickly."

"Try again," he insisted. "The gel."

They'd have been dead already if there was gas. Ava's impatience increased even as she continued to humor him.

"Look," she sighed. "It's a bio-interface. It reacts to bioelectricity—same energy that powers my exoskeleton. Find your damn mask."

Malachi shook his head. "Bull. Shit."

She had moved away, telling the others to hold back. She hoped Malachi would calm down if he didn't have an audience of other males. But he waded within inches of her body, stood toe to toe with her. "You're holding back. I want answers—now."

Ava's expression didn't change. Calm. Controlled. Dangerous.

"I told you—you were going to see things you wouldn't understand. This is one of them. You're nervous. Good. You should be. You're dealing with a form of psychosis right now. Take a deep breath before you snap. Your experiencing cognitive dissonance overload."

Malachi's brain was fighting a losing battle against two opposing "truths" —what he thought he knew versus what the evidence in front of him was saying. Most adapt, but in psychosis, his clash with reality was spiraling into paranoia and despair. She'd seen it before. He wasn't weak, just scared and too hardheaded to admit it to himself.

Malachi tried doing what she said. He took a breath, exhaling through his nose, frustration boiling. It didn't work. He wasn't finished.

"I need you to explain it. You read the door symbols like it was the Sunday paper."

Ava's jaw tightened. "It's Proto-Sumerian. A variant."

Malachi shook his head. "That's *impossible*. Sumerian is the oldest written language we've ever discovered."

Ava shrugged. "Evidently, it's not. Take a minute, Malachi. Reset."

Wait until they find the older burials, she told herself. *It will rewrite the history books.*

Malachi froze. The memory of Siegfried's lecture came rushing back— The First People. The Guardians. The origin of language. Everything he said was true and Siegfried had to be silenced to hide the truth.

Ava remained calm. "You're expendable, Malachi. We all are, just like *Tweety Bird.* I know what you're thinking. So was Siegfried. That's all you need to know. You don't have to like it or understand it. Focus on the work."

She'd found the bird cage, the yellow canary lay limp in the spilling between the welded mesh, drowned. She threw the cage into the water and began trudging in the knee-deep water. It was already rising again. The hall ahead lit up instantly, reacting to her presence.

Malachi stumbled forward too. His boot caught on something submerged in the deep water and he went down hard, splashing with a grunt.

"Damn it," he muttered, pushing himself up, soaked and pissed off. He cursed in frustration.

Summoned forward by Ava, the other Raiders moved past him, weapons sweeping, eyes scanning. They didn't offer a hand. No time. No sympathy. Just mission focus, scanning, looking for work. Ava told him to chill and Malachi took her advice, lingering in the water for a minute, resetting, glaring at the team's silhouettes as they moved away.

Who the hell does she think she is? he asked himself.

He felt around for the obstacle. His fingers brushed metal, sharp. He yanked up a piece of treasure, a sword. Old and heavy, pitted with time, but the hilt still held the shape of a Crusader's cross-guard. Seeking a better look, he stood up and pulled the sword up with him.

"Holy sh—" Malachi saw a skeletal hand still clinging to the hilt, brittle fingers locked in a centuries-old "Come and Take It" grip. *From my cold, dead hands,* the spirit seemed to whisper. It was obvious something had come and left the Crusader sword, its ghost still guarding his weapon.

Malachi dropped it back into the water. "Jeez, yuck." Malachi shook off the chill that ran up his spine. Eyes wide, he scanned ahead, they were down the bend. It was then that he realized he was no longer part of the stack.

"Shit," he muttered, wiping his hand on his field jacket. He wasn't sure why he looked up, but something with multiple legs was hanging above him on the ceiling. It was black, unnoticeable without taking a hard look. The head turned and looked at him, a massive bird.

Eyes popping from his head, he trembled. It let go enveloping his body.

 Chapter 14

Catacombs

The air was damp with the earthy scent of soil and moisture. Ava caught undertones of oak root creeping through the stone—woodsy and grounding. Beneath it all, a whisper of frankincense lingered. Something floral—subtle but distinct. This place wasn't just old; it was sacred.

She pulled out an ancient sheet of parchment, yellowed with age and etched with symbols that shimmered, powered by unseen energy within the paper. The moment she unfolded the wet page, she was swiping icons until it displayed a glowing digital map.

Behind her, the troopers stiffened, eyes wide. Murmurs rippled.

"Where the hell did she get that?"

"The rest of you better not fall apart on me, too," she said discouraged.

She remembered the reaction she received from one of the colonies. The whole *burning-at-the-stake* thing had really killed the vibe on that mission. Trip and she were regretful for years after that.

Ava carefully refolded the paper and shoved it back into her pocket without a word. No time for explanations. No questions? Weird. She turned to check the rear—Malachi was gone.

She exhaled sharply and rolled her eyes.

"Figures. Did he go back?" she asked, already knowing the answer.

The two troopers at the rear glanced at each other and shrugged.

Her head drooped down, shoulders slunk too.

"You two. Backtrack. Find the CIA man. I bet he just got the jitters, but be ready for anything," she ordered while straightening up.

They nodded, peeled off, and melted into the darkness. The rest of the team pressed on, weapons raised, boots sloshing through water as the tunnel opened into a wider chamber—air thicker, colder, and suddenly still. The water in this chamber was only a couple of inches deep.

Motion activated lights flickered to life as they stepped inside.

The chamber was massive, ancient, and eerily intact. A gutter traced the perimeter, draining away residual water. It worked—mostly. The floor was as dry as any subterranean vault could be, damp but passable.

Old world crates once filled with renaissance paintings and golden treasures lined the vault. Empty. No doubt these treasures were routed here after the Friday the 13th purge of the Templars. There was also Atlantean tech. Radios, tablets, beyond ancient gear the soldiers didn't recognize, but Ava did. The Templars must have made a hasty retreat. This had been a command center once, a last outpost before whoever was stationed here either fled or entered stasis. Burn marks on the wall signaled a violent retreat.

At the far end, embedded in the stone wall, a console pulsed faintly. An artifact of a lost age. Ava threw caution to the wind, her boots clambering across the chamber. She weaved through the scattered relics—remnants of lesser value left by the last occupants.

Her men slowed, distracted by the forgotten treasure around them. Almost barren crates with a smattering of old coins. Goblets and plates of tarnished silver. Artifacts from an age of galleons and conquest. An equal-armed red cross adorned a tattered banner hanging from the far wall.

If there was any doubt that the Knights Templar had been here, that doubt was erased. For a time, this place had been their final sanctuary—fleeing persecution, hiding their secrets. They had left this place to fund freedom for New Atlantis, America, and to bury the ring fragment at Puma Punku, separating the pieces. Then they had vanished. The loop was all coming full circle.

Ava reached an altar carved from stone and ritualistic necessity. She brushed aside the broken hilt of a ceremonial sword, the blade's fragments clattering to the ground. Beneath them, something waited. She found it. The other piece of the ring.

She pulled Siegfried's fragment from her pocket and placed it beside the other. They slithered together—joining with a whispering click, like metal drawn to its twin. The ring pulsed.

A light flared on the wall-mounted console. A long hiss. The QSC burst. The air escaped; lights stuttered. The occupant spilled out onto the red stone floor when he materialized. Shivering, breath visible in the cool air. His Alpha Skin was torn and stained. It was evident he'd been through hell getting here.

Weapons came up—rifles raised on instinct.

Ava stepped forward, between her men and the stranger, calm and certain.

"Stand down," she ordered. "Easy, he's one of us."

She dropped to one knee beside the figure, brushing wet hair from his face. She knew that face from memories she hadn't made yet.

"Hawk," she whispered. "Anshar Hawk?" She needed to be sure. This was the first time she had met him in person.

His eyes fluttered open, unfocused. His voice was raw, hoarse from stasis.

"Who are you?" he rasped in a foreign tongue.

"A Guardian. Don't worry—your head will clear soon enough."

He shivered, trying to nod. "My memories?"

"This will speed up the process." She reached out with a white liquid. "They'll come back—most of them, anyway."

Hawk swatted the elixir away. "No, I don't want them."

"You can't stop them," she countered. "You're just delaying the inevitable." Her face soured. She coated her fingers in the creamy substance and rubbed her fingers over his lips and into his mouth. She grabbed the duffel bag, pulling a change of clothes from her pack and helped him dress.

At last, Hawk struggled upright, bones creaking, muscles barely responding. As he steadied himself, Ava punched in another code on the wall. At the center of the room, a hidden seal parted with a rock-on-rock grind. A magnificent box rose from the underground chamber.

The soldiers stepped back, weapons up, as a massive gold and lead-lined case emerged. Its surface pulsed faintly with restrained energy. Each side was adorned with eagles.

Ava did not take her eyes off it and, without turning, she cautioned her men.

"Do *not* touch or open that," she warned, "unless you want to glow like a New York diner sign."

She removed two wooden poles from the wall and tossed these to the men.

"Use these as carriers to transport it. Don't touch it. There is enough raw energy in that thing to vaporize you."

"We don't have enough men to carry that, ma'am. That's gotta be a ton of gold," a soldier laughed.

"It's energized," she said. "The manna inside will assist you."

The troopers exchanged uneasy glances.

"That's what we came for?" one muttered. "The freakin' Ark of the Covenant?"

Ava was already busy in her bag, assembling her secret weapon, a rifle—an oversized, heavily modified Lahti L-39 anti-tank gun. One job. One purpose. Stopping things that were hard to stop. At the bottom of the bag were two swords—one short and one longer. She debated on using them.

"It's a reactor," she confirmed. "And if there are sentries still active, they'll come for us."

Hawk's eyes sharpened as he regained his senses.

"My Ninety-Nine fighter? Are you the QRF team?" he asked. "I barely made it. Atlantis, the mountains, Neptune's Trident, all gone. There was nowhere to land but here. My bird's wrecked, but there are two new ones on the flight deck."

Ava nodded. "Yes, we are the rescue team. Took us a little longer than expected.

"I saw the ice sheet vaporized and Atlantis plummet into the ocean," he said dismayed. "A little longer than expected?" Hawk questioned, his own concern evident in his voice. "How long?"

She sighed. "You have a few thousand years to catch up on."

The soldiers were moving fast, and—even though her voice cracked like a whip—she couldn't warn the youngest soldier in time.

"NO!" she yelled as his hand rapidly reached for the Ark.

Too late.

Drawn to the Ark, like a moth to a flame, the soldier's hand fell flat on the surface of gold. Just a whisper of contact. A flash of light. A crack of energy. And he was gone.

Reduced to dust before he could even scream. His weapon clattered to the floor. His uniform instantly turned to ashes. The only sound left in the room was absolute silence.

Ava closed her eyes. She shook her head, voice cold.

"Anyone *else* want to touch it?" she asked angrily.

The room was dead quiet. The soldiers stared, pale, horrified, shaking their heads. Ava reached to the wall for a wooden staff, "When you get where you're going, use this to neutralize the charge. Ground the staff and drop it on the ark." She looked at the terrified men. "Good. Do what guys do and put the poles in the holes, and let's make like a tree and leave."

"Hooah," the team called out. They moved fast now, no hesitation. Two troopers slid the reinforced rods through the Ark's side rings and heaved it up with little effort—antigravity forces engaged. The weight oscillating. The others fell in around them, weapons ready, eyes flicking constantly toward the shadows.

She turned to one of the Raiders, his radio squelched. "Negative on finding Malachi," the radio barely came through legibly through static.

Ava gave him a discouraged nod. "I'll run point. Hawk's rear guard. Nothing's more important than getting the Ark out."

One of the soldiers reached for the bottom of a crate and pocketed a handful of coins. Ava saw it—said nothing.

They eventually reached the first junction where she halted the group. She called the ranking Raider forward and tapped the map. "We split up here, at this junction. You five take this corridor to the hatch. There's a team on standby."

A trooper raised a brow. "And you?"

"We're going for the cherry on top of this cake. We'll make a beeline for the craft in the hangar."

The Raiders nodded as one. "Ambitious, Hooah."

Sending the men and the Ark back the way they had come, Hawk and Ava broke away from the pack. Ava took point, leading the way, her Lahti rifle slung on her back, over one of her swords, the huge weapon dwarfing her more than the short-barreled Garand did. In her hands, was the Tommy gun that the vaporized soldier dropped. Hawk followed her, carrying the Tanker rifle.

"It's crude, I know," Ava said, pointing at the bandolier full of en-bloc clips. "Eight shots, then you reload. And it kicks."

Shaking off his fatigue, Hawk gripped the walnut stock. "There are two Ninety-Nine fighters. One is a prototype single seater."

When they reached a juncture of tunnels, Ava paused to pull out and unroll the map.

"Is this right?" she asked, pointing to a spot on the map. "Looks like one of the fighters is in the south hangar."

Hawk nodded. "We can't leave without them," he said flatly.

Ava nodded. "Agreed; we will add that to the plan."

Hawk worked his way through the tunnels. "I don't remember this much water being in here."

"The base is flooding. Every access point we opened on the way inside changed the equilibrium." A small grin tugging at the corner of her mouth. "The second we open the hangar, the whole thing floods for good. The Knights rigged it that way—to keep the Udug out."

"Good thing you have a map, then—this place is a maze," he chuckled. "And if we don't get out in time?"

"We drown like rats," Ava said absolutely.

Hawk grunted this time. "Wonderful," he added sarcastically. "Who the hell are the Templars?"

"It's a long story but after the fall, they were charged with collecting and protecting Atlantean secrets." Ava brought the Lahti to the high ready position. The barrel was practically catching the ceiling. The micro-servos in her Second Skin suit were whining under the 100-pound load. Two more ten-round boxes, each bigger than the size of an encyclopedia, clanked in a re-inforced canvas backpack against the gold she also inconspicuously pocketed.

"Any extra weapons?" Hawk asked, flexing his fingers.

"Sling the Garand as your backup," Ava said, tossing him a Thompson—the one the vaporized guy would not be needing. "The Garand thumps but the Thompson will put up a wall of hate." She cringed a little. "Old school, I know."

"Like the Igigi thumpers," he grinned.

"Exactly like those," she said with a kind smile, "Here, you will need these too," she added. Palm up, she handed Hawk a pair of hearing protection.

He took them and fit them in his ears. Another thing left behind by the Templar's they didn't know how to use and dismissed it as useless.

"That loud, huh?"

Ava chuckled, "Yeah, wait till you hear this big bitch roar."

Hawk cringed. She could tell he couldn't wait.

"Hundred-round drum. Eight-hundred rounds per minute. You've got two mags. Look through the peep sight and squeeze."

Hawk caught it with a grunt. "All this crap feels like I'm carting around a horse."

"You'll have to use your own muscles. I'm fresh out of Second Skin suits," she apologized. "These tools are primitive, but they work."

He noticed the bulk under her clothes. "Mark II Miner Suit?"

She nodded. "Just an exoskeleton so I can lug this thing around."

The trek to the hangar was as slow going as coming in. The water did its best to prohibit their speed. Water pouring down in sheets, the pressure from opened hatches continued weakening the old structure. What used to be corridors strewn with corpses was now littered with nothing except bones hidden underwater.

"Must've been hell wading through all those bodies," Ava said to Hawk.

"You have no idea," Hawk paused, reconsidering. "Well maybe you do."

"We might've gotten greedy," she muttered. The water was over knee-deep now.

"Yeah, you think?" Hawk slapped his brass-plated Winchester flashlight which one of the Raiders gave him. "Better to drown here than be trapped in a buffer stream for eternity."

"Your light's dying," she noted, teeth starting to chatter. "They run on batteries. Not very efficient. They have not found the fourth state of matter yet."

Hawk's eyebrows pumped on his face. "It's about to get pitch black in here."

"Use the one on the rifle. I jerry-rigged it, but it'll get the job done."

CHAPTER 15

Eureka

Water rushed down the tunnel walls like cut veins bursting. Ava's lips were turning blue, the cold gnawing into her bones. The gold coins in her pack were rattling and clinking like a dinner bell. Hawk's teeth chattered uncontrollably, echoing off the stone. They glanced at each other's pale skin; they'd both seen corpses warmer than they were now.

His flashlight flickered again. Hawk was beyond frigid; the chill running through him was deeper than the freezing water they were wading through. The tunnel was an echo chamber of sloshing, dripping, splashing, and labored movement. Every step through the rising water sapped energy, dragging at their legs with numbing resistance. During one of their brief pauses, long enough to steady themselves, Ava registered something in the ambiance. Something was cutting through the white noise.

It was the sound of movement not stopping.

Someone—or something—was still wading. Behind them.

"Hold," Ava whispered, raising her hand.

The water lapped around their legs, louder than anything else, swallowing the silence in a drowning roar.

"Stop chattering your teeth," Ava hissed.

Hawk's clacking jaw echoed off the stone, masking the subtleties, the splashes, the droplets, the pour of rushing water—and worse, making it harder to tell which direction the sound was coming from. Hawk shot her a glare, jaw clenching tight for a second before it clacked off again.

"Your missing man?"

"Move, quickly," she ordered.

Hawk's splash didn't line up with hers—and neither did the trudging steps behind them. Something was displacing the water with each heavy stride, pushing waves ahead through the dark. The mystery stalker moved faster now, faster than them as the rising water dragged at their legs. The sound behind them didn't match their pace. It was heavier. More deliberate.

Listening—they tried to isolate the source. Water, heavy on its own, was being forced forward by something bigger than them.

"It's getting close," Hawk clacked.

Hawk spun, weapon up. Ava cranked the Lahti's bolt back and then forward like a manual car window. She slapped the grip safety. CLANK. The bolt slammed home.

A low, mechanical groan echoed through the tunnel. What followed was insidious inhuman machines. One of them, a 2Gen Monitor stepped into view, menacing. Behind it, another. One bore the head of a lion, the other avian—Egyptian. Ancient. They had been stalking. Energy lit their wrists; they were charging weapons.

Hawk didn't hesitate—opening fire, stumbling back. The massive flame from the muzzle made him jump. His hands were also shaking too violently in the moment so most of his rounds went wide. Sparks splattered in every direction as he tagged the walls and ceiling.

Ava continued pushing down the corridor in search of better cover and making space—a corner, debris from a collapse, anything to fight behind.

They couldn't outrun them. They would have to fight for every yard.

Gunfire from Hawk's Tommy gun lit the hall, his rounds sparking against their thick alloy. Ava fired a couple of rounds. Each pressure wave from the Lahti rattled their skulls.

"The armor is too thick for this thing!" Hawk shouted, diving behind a narrow stone pillar. With barely six inches of cover, an energy bolt slammed into the rock—molten rock hissed and melted into the water.

The water was climbing—now over her hips. She braced, took aim. Fired. Missed. Her shivering hands threw her shot wide. A bolt of plasma screamed past her face. She could feel the heat.

"Great. Just what we need," Hawk muttered, emptying his last drum. Hawk tossed the Chicago Typewriter aside, the water swallowing it whole. He slung the Garand from his chest, an earplug stuck out of the crown keeping the water out of the barrel. He brought the Tanker up to his shoulder, steadied it, and fired. A barrage of .30-06 rounds cracked through the air.

The Monitors pushed forward, steam hissing off red impacts to their armor. The tunnel began steaming from the energy weapons. Fog and smoke from the gunpowder building in the passageway gave them cover to push away further.

Ava fired again.

"Move!" she yelled. The Lahti's recoil thundered, the concussion nearly knocking Hawk off the narrow ledge and into the open. His brain was still rattling despite the ear pro she gave him.

"Moving!" he shouted, stumbling into a crouching scoot.

One Monitor reeled, Ava's shot connecting, ripping a gouge in the armor. The lion headed machine lunged forward, using its limbs to *parkour* along the tunnel walls—leaping from place to place like an urban free runner. Its arms and legs long enough to lift its body out of the water, gaining speed using the sides of the passage to move faster.

"Aim for walls!" Ava barked, advancing to higher ground. "Put them back in the water."

The Lahti roared again. A limb ripped off and crashed down in the water like a meteor.

Each 20mm round hit with 35,000 foot-pounds of force—enough to shred Anunna armor. In her head, she counted the shots she had left.

"Twenty-six rounds," she shouted out.

Ava planted her stance and braced the Lahti against the stone wall. Each shot had to count.

Another 20mm shot connecting.

From Hawk's weapon came a more troubling sound.

PING. Empty.

"Damn it!" Hawk slammed in a fresh clip, but his thumb slipped—Garand thumb. He yelped, shaking his hand briefly. Blood welled under his nail. No time to care. The machine kept coming despite all the holes and pot marks in it.

"We're in deep shit," Hawk grunted. The water was up to his chest now.

The Lahti roared again beside him. His ears rang despite ear pro. The Lion, heavily damaged, crumpled and submerged below the chest-high water.

"Jesus, that rifle's obnoxious!" he shouted, ducking behind Ava.

"But it's working."

"What?" he asked, waving his hand near his ears.

He took a shot, the shot skipped across the water like a stone, slammed into the far wall—and opened another crack. More water poured in.

Ava was nearly submerged—just below the clavicle now. She fought to keep the Lahti above the waterline. The heat shield swelled and creaked under the steam. The stone edge she braced it on was scraping the finish clean off the barrel.

FWOOSH—Plasma torch ignited. The air boiled. The tunnel walls blistered, liquefying into glass. Scalding fog rolled in, swallowing everything. Hawk and Ava ducked underwater.

Coming up for air, their muscles burned, lactic acid building with each frantic motion.

Ava reached her next position, braced herself, adjusted her stance—

She fired again, the Lahti thundering through the corridor three more times.

Falling back between bursts, Ava and Hawk reached an incline. The narrow tunnel cut open into a massive, curved dome, and at its peak sat the prize: the two Ninety-Nine Fighters. Her exoskeleton whined, servos straining as it hauled her up the steps.

Hawk hit the slope behind her. Scrambling up the rise, he spotted another relic—a Templar knight, frozen in death. A sword, still intact, lay across its lap. He bolted for it, sliding into the water to slow his sprint, snatching the blade as he passed.

At last, Hawk spotted the target up ahead—the target he'd been looking for.

Rifle up, Tanker peep sights lined up with the control panel.

The en bloc clip launched out of the rifle with a familiar ping.

His shot slammed into the control panel near the archway. A low groan echoed. A massive stone slab shifted in its recess. The tunnel's door was closing. A deafening rumble shook the chamber. The stone slab dropped—crushing a Synth mid-stride and sealing the entrance behind it. Water slowed and Monitors were defeated with one crushing blow.

A respite.

Hawk wiped the sweat from his brow, chest heaving.

"I've got three rounds left," Ava grunted, toiling to stay steady.

Hawk dropped the Tanker and brandished the old sword. "At least we'll go out like warriors."

Ava smiled. "Could be worse," she said shrugging her shoulders.

Just then, sudden movements drew their attention to the landing platform as a massive figure burst from the flood followed by a second. Both landing hard on the flight deck behind them.

Ava's shoulders slumped. She sighed, exasperated. "It just got worse."

Hawk shook his head. "Unacceptable. I just got out," he growled heaving the sword into a fighting position.

The two soldiers stared one another down for what seemed like minutes. Each one trying to access the other's fitness for fighting. She was worn out and, even with Hawk's ripped physique, she knew he was in no shape to fight these things.

On the flight deck sat one prototype single-seater, shiny and new. The other ship was a two-seater that had seen action during the war. The fighters were within reach, and yet she'd not had time to open the hangar doors.

Two Udug, Asag and Pazuzu stepped from the shadows, the final obstacles facing Hawk and Ava. The creatures looked like they had already been through their own personal war. They were bloodied and now cornered. Armed only with their claws, they had fought their own set of Monitors. Unlike the humans, they could take the beatings.

Now, the creatures told themselves, *these fragile creatures are all that stand in our way of escape. We could slay them, but we'll have to torture the startup sequence out of one of them.*

Ava didn't bother using her last two rounds on the creatures. At this distance she knew there was no way she could maneuver the massive cannon fast enough to get a hit. She set the Lahti down and bowed in front of her opponents.

Seeing her posture, Hawk knew what she was about to try to do.

"Ava," Hawk snapped, "here!" He yelled louder than needed while tossing the arming sword her way.

The blade toss was perfect. It literally danced through the air. She watched the grip rotate precisely into a position where she could reach out and grab it. Without so much as a movement, Ava let it hit the floor.

Hawk flinched as the steel bounced, clanked and clattered on the white stone floor. His hands said exactly what was on his mind—*What gives?*

She put her hand up, silencing his inner curiosity. Her next motion was a flick of her wrist and hand. *Back off,* her gesture said. There wasn't much else Hawk could do after disarming himself.

She left the Templar Sword where it lay; she had something much better.

She reached over her shoulder, wrapping her fingers around the hilt of the long blade strapped to her back. Her left thumb anchored along the side of the *tsuba,* protecting that thumb from the edge as she drew the katana free. She brought the blade forward and slid her other hand onto the grip, closing each finger with deliberate ease. The Atlantean steel katana forged by Masamane was beautiful.

With her suit carrying the load, Ava was a walking armory.

She set her feet ready, and locked eyes with the nearest foe, Asag.

"You know how to use that toothpick?" Hawk asked, though her body language had already answered him.

She shot him a sideways glance, blowing a wet tendril of hair from her face. "I've dabbled." Water was already rising around her boots. Time was running short.

Asag closed the gap, slow at first, a structured attack until ego took over and it became aggressive and sloppy. Ava met him instantly, snapping into a *nukiuchi* motion. She performed the attack immediately, the zing of steel—the sound shattering the sound of flooding water. Her cut was deep and burning. A gush of blood followed.

Hanjo Masamane, bit hard but not deep enough. The blade sang a fantastic song as it finished its arc, the last vibration trembling off the *tanto* tip.

Asag staggered, proof that the 30,000-layered steel could cut even a Udug.

Pazuzu stepped in.

Two on one?

Ava reset her stance and moved in, water splashing at her knees. Pazuzu crowded tight. His claw swept wide, she slipped under it and drove the katana straight into his thigh. As he raked for her leg with his four-inch dewclaw, she yanked the blade free, swept upward, and ripped it out. The claw spun away; a black gash opened from his pelvis to his clavicle.

Asag darted in for a blind slash. She snapped the blade over her shoulder, catching the attack from behind. Pazuzu pressed again, but she was already carving him apart like a butcher working on livestock. No wasted strikes, no wasted defensive moves—a strong samurai moves purposefully.

She shifted targets fluidly... push Pazuzu back; pivot, strike Asag. Her footwork was balanced and even keeled, minimizing openings, letting the weight of the sword work for her. Fast enough to kill, slow enough to stay alive.

A split second was all it took to fall, her or them.

The clash became sparks and bursts of water. Every step deliberate—heel to toe, soft and controlled, even the deceptive ones.

She lowered her hips, the blade forward in fundamental guard. Trip called it "Being in the Zone"; her master Miyamoto Musashi called it *Zanshin.* Ava was already there.

Pazuzu lunged. She answered with the most egregious cut yet. The wounded Udug spun away, watching one of his ears sink beneath the rising water. Rage took over. He charged, his long toenails gouging into the white stone, anchoring himself for traction. He had enough force to obliterate her.

A wall of white water rose with him.

Ava dove aside, rolled, and slashed up in a reverse cut. The blade cut his back. Pazuzu winced, stumbling in a grotesque spin, shoulders arched like a faltering ballerina pivoting through pain.

Ava spun out, water splashing in every direction, torso low, muscular legs spread wide. Her blade cut the air in a tight circle like a helicopter blade buying space from both Udug.

Pazuzu howled.

"You wretched creation," he snarled. "Your kind destroys ecosystems... wipes out whole species. You're the true virus on this world. I can't wait until we exterminate your kind once and for all."

"Perhaps, but not today. My master, Musashi, sends his regards," she growled.

Asag looked at Pazuzu. They traded glances. He knew the name. Sixty duels. No losses.

"Unlikely," Asag scoffed.

He couldn't get close enough, so he changed tactics. While Ava traded more blows with Pazuzu, Asag edged toward her submerged Lahti. She saw it coming. Her free hand slid for the *wakizashi,* surreptitiously.

Asag dove, rolling toward the rifle, slamming into the stone deck. His massive hand closed around the Lahti's grip, the antitank cannon looked small against his massive frame. At this range, a 20mm round would vaporize her.

Before Asag could hoist the cannon, Ava hurled the wakizashi. The blade cut through the air like a thrown dart and buried itself deep into his shoulder, severing tendons. His grip spasmed.

The Lahti dropped, hit the water barrel first.

An explosion.

The submerged cannon detonated, dislodging water and sending the Udug flying through the air like he had stepped on an IED (Improvised Explosive Device). Shrapnel punched into his hide. He staggered, dazed and struggling to stay combat effective.

Ava moved to finish him, but he was already up, hurt, leaking that black sludge they used for blood. His bell was rung, but he was alive. He was alive and she was weakening. She could feel the toll adding up. The taxman was coming to collect what was left of her stamina. Every block, every cut, and every step had drained what little strength she had left to maintain this level of defense. The trek here had already taken its slice. The battle was claiming even more.

Hawk stood ready on the sidelines, Templar sword in hand, waiting for the cue to jump in. She never gave it. When he stepped forward, she shot him a look—*stand down*. He could match her in a cockpit, maybe even outshoot her, but this? This samurai work was her game.

She dished a deadly entrée of razor-sharp cuts; now she was serving psychology for dessert. Carving at their confidence.

"You bozos had enough yet?" Ava taunted. Maintaining eye contact with both creatures as she reset her stance.

"You fools think you're the good guys," Asag said as he regained his feet. "Even you, with your own eyes, have to see what you've done to this planet and each other."

"Lies," Ava shot back. "You steer weak-minded leaders into taking that path."

While she was distracted by speaking, Pazuzu moved in, but her eyes never truly left Asag's gaze. She caught Pazuzu's attempted attack in the reflection of her katana. She shifted and pivoted. His first swing missed. His second blow scraped sparks off her blade. He crowded close, but she continued blocking each strike, then smashed him across the face with the spine of the sword. Blinded and bleeding, Pazuzu faltered. She closed the distance, almost on him, when two massive black wings burst from his back. He meant to launch and take the high ground.

Ava didn't let him.

She sprang forward and hacked both wings off with a figure eight cut. Using jujitsu, she brought him to the flooded ground.

Splashing down, Pazuzu rolled over, one hand cupping his face, the other clawing at the stumps on his back. Ava hit him again, with the spine of the blade, splitting his face wide open. Pazuzu tried to flee but he was a doomed shark floundering in shallow water.

She sludged her way through the knee-high water, katana raised, eyes locked on him as she brought the blade down.

Flecks of sparking steel exploded as Asag intercepted the killing stroke. Avoiding Asag's counter blow, Ava spun off and backed away. So damn close. She opened her arms, standing tall in the rising flood.

"Come get me," she taunted, intending to lure them in for one final bout.

Pazuzu slowly climbed to his feet. And yet he was eager, pain fueling his desire to gut this woman and leave her broken body here for eternity.

Asag laughed off the brutal cuts, black sludge leaking from his wounds. One wrong move and his guts would spill out. But he smiled at the pain and growled like an animal.

Ava reached into her sash and found the end of her empty scabbard. The katana's spine glided across her palm until the tip met the mouth of the saya. She drew both hands together and sheathed Hanjo Masamane.

"Nice moves, Onna-Musha," Pazuzu coughed, knowing exactly what the gesture meant.

Pazuzu stepped back breathing hard. He grabbed one of his amputated wings, then dropped it back in the water. What was the point of saving it?

Using both hands, Ava raised the sheathed blade, until it was parallel to her head, eyes locked on his. With one hand gripping the saya and the other gripping the hilt, it was clear she could, if she wished, pull the blade again and resume her cutting. Exhausted but unshaken, she sneered.

"I can do this all day," she taunted.

A bluff, but a convincing one.

Silence fell over the hangar. The water rushing in was now steadily rising. It wouldn't be long before they all drowned. Four pairs of eyes met. Each of them ran the numbers in their heads. It was only a matter of time before the water reached the canopies of the airships, and they wouldn't be able to launch. Mutual destruction or universal salvation. No one was getting out of here alive unless Ava opened the hangar.

They were at an impasse.

Ava's voice cracked, cutting the silence. "No tricks," she cursed, panting from the strain. "We all fly—or none of us fly."

Pazuzu bared his teeth. "I can take her." He growled and coughed blood from his lung.

Asag stepped in, raising a clawed hand to stop him. "Not today, she's got our number."

Water roared underneath them, the intensity flooding the chamber faster.

"Decide," Ava insisted. "We might continue fighting which means we'll all drown. But whatever happens, they'll just nuke the site," she warned them.

Asag turned, sloshing, pacing slowly. "Such stubborn creatures. You won't wipe yourselves out, and you won't stop destroying this world. Enki gave your kind a shelf life for a reason, so you wouldn't have enough time to finish the job."

"Pick one, devil." Ava said bluntly gesturing toward the two fighter ships.

The two Udug glanced at the ships. One single-seater, new and arousing. One two-seater, a little worse for wear. No words needed, there was no way they'd both fit in the smaller craft. They could only shape-shift so small, two brutish males too dense for one seat.

"Try anything and they detonate the nuke. Or we can just stand here and wait while the water rises. Either way. No one wins."

Asag stared at her, then gave a subtle nod. "I've made my choice. We'll all fly and, once in the air, I will hold my fire if you do the same."

Ava nodded and the two demonic-looking creatures moved silently and precisely climbing into the two-seat fighter.

"You sure about this?" Hawk asked, watching the two Udug disappear behind the cockpit canopy.

Ava didn't look at him. Her eyes were locked on the hangar doors above. "No," she said. "We need to get lean," she said. "If we are going to fit into that thing."

She stripped off the MK II exosuit, letting the invaluable tool clatter to the deepening abyss at their feet. They would need every bit of space in the cockpit. Hawk stripped down too; field jacket gone.

Hawk gave her a long look—soaked, bruised, still radiant. She saw him too. He looked like a Greek warrior, ironclad granite muscles and wet hair.

"We gotta squeeze in there. Together," she said, eyeing the cockpit.

"It's gonna be a tight fit," he replied as he rustled the water out of his hair. "You taking those too?" He asked of her swords.

"I will leave you here before I leave these behind," she threatened.

Hawk made an eyebrow bump. *Touchy subject,* he thought.

Completely soaked, she wrung water out of her hair. "I don't think I'll have trouble squeezing in. You still remember how to fly these things?"

Modestly he said, "Thing has a mind of its own. It practically flies itself."

Across the hangar, Asag and Pazuzu were already seated in the open cockpit. Too hot to close it.

"For the love of the Gods," Pazuzu growled. "Let's get on with it."

Their boots and clothes sat in a pile. The Udug watched their owners abandoning them as Ava and Hawk closed the hatch to the Ninety-Nine fighter. They looked back as water was getting close to the engine intakes.

Hawk sat in the pilot seat; Ava snuggled on top of him but angled enough for him to reach the controls. Their limbs tangled. No extra room. Barely enough to breathe.

"Better open the front door," Ava sighed. She had one last box left. She pointed it at the hangar door controls, then tossed it overboard.

Above them, the roof groaned. Water from the opening rained in as an opening formed in the middle of a swamp on the surface. Daylight knifed through misty gloom as the hangar doors yawned wide. The two ships lifted off—first a hover, then a vertical sprint toward the sun. Asag kept his word, arcing away and vanishing into the sky.

With the releasing pressure, water blew into the hangar bay flooding it instantly. The hangar started closing back up, the swamp reforming. The earth barely showing a scar. On the surface, the Seabees were already in position—bulldozers primed, engines rumbling. The moment the ships cleared the breach, the earthmovers rolled forward, further burying the entrance to the shaft. Pressure vents blew open around the island. Geysers erupted offshore. The Oak Island Money Pit, with all its riches, sealed permanently. And the clock started ticking on a low-yield nuclear device which would permanently obliterate everything inside.

 CHAPTER 16

Bad Trip

Five years later, Ava received a call from Princeton Hospital. Big Al's health was failing. A ruptured abdominal aortic aneurysm. He had internal bleeding and refused another surgery.

He was ready.

Ava sat beside his hospital bed as he faded, his voice gravelly but clear. She blinked hard. Held her breath. It didn't help. The tears still came. Big Al reached out to her and placed a trembling hand over hers.

"Don't trust Kammler."

"The ex-Nazi?"

"Yes. The one who's died six times." He managed a laugh. "I've never known a man so good at faking death and still climbing the deep state ladder. If you must work with him, hold your nose. There are pieces in play within the government. Speak to Eisenhower; he will tell you everything."

"About Kammler?" She questioned.

Big Al shook his head vehemently. "Kammler is brilliant and dangerous, but no. Ask the President about the military-industrial complex. Ike will tell you."

"Tell me what?" She asked again, even more confused.

"Trust no one." He gasped.

Ava nodded in agreement, even if she didn't quite understand yet.

Big Al shifted. His voice dropped lower. "I discovered something. For you. It might help—past or future. Perhaps it will answer some cosmic questions you and I tried to work out."

He handed her a folded slip of paper covered in scribbled computations. Complex. Raw.

Beyond anything he'd ever shown her.

"Tesla had a big mouth." He chuckled. Following his death, the government cleared out his hotel room a year before Ike's election. But this? I'm giving it to you before they confiscate this, too."

Ava unfolded the paper. Her breath caught. The Equation of Everything. It wasn't a theory. It was a map—a mathematical key to time travel, wormholes, and zero-point energy. Big Al's faded blue eyes flickered. "We did it," he whispered. "We finally did it."

For a moment, Ava thought she saw something ancient watching through his eyes—Enki's consciousness, perhaps, peering through the veil.

His hand relaxed. His breath slowed. "Good luck, kids."

Albert died the following morning.

The world moved on. Hawk and Ava grew closer. The lines between ally and partner had blurred. The Earth prepared—but few truly understood what was coming.

Decades later, morning came as Hawk's alarm blared. He bolted upright, disoriented. The ceiling fan hummed above, stirring the humid air like a lazy turbine. The sheets were twisted around his legs. Sweat clung to his skin. Bad dream.

He was home—in a way. Not his house, but close enough. Ava's. Her bed. Her scent still lingered in the fabric.

But no Ava.

A dream—no, a memory from his time in MACV-SOG —blurring with his present-day covert CIA work. His credentials were enough to run right up the ladder. Barely a memory of his last mission. Another blurred return. He'd dropped his gear somewhere near the stairs and collapsed here, into her bed, because it was the only place where he still felt human.

No rattling around. The fan was the only sound in the room until he stirred.

He sat there, trying to pull the threads of memory together. The briefing, exfil, debriefing, redeploying. What country was it this time? New cities, old cities with new names. Even the countries were unrecognizable with ever evolving borders.

And then there was the dossier. "LILITH" stamped across the top in red. He hadn't meant to open it. But he had. And now he couldn't forget what he saw. Project Red Wings was moving at full speed ahead.

He rubbed his face, trying to wipe the night off. His hair disheveled with bed head. He wasn't sure what scared him more—what he was doing, or how easy it was getting to be to justify his clandestine actions. Clothes next to him, not so alone after all. Before he could reach for the clothes laid out beside the bed, the door burst open.

Ava stood in the frame. No smile. No hesitation. No games. This was happening. She wouldn't wait another decade.

"Every day you were gone, I knew I was one day closer to seeing you again." Her voice echoed in his memory, or maybe it was his own longing projecting meaning where there was only silence.

Hawk swung his legs around and onto the floor and popped upright. He stood frozen by the side of the bed as she moved toward him unbuttoning her sheer pale-blue blouse. The fabric fluttered in the slight breeze from the fan blades, then slipping away before hitting the floor.

The air stirred—the ceiling fan pushing ripples of a breeze across the room. Cool breeze met damp summertime skin, but it was her body raising goosebumps.

Hours later, they lay still tangled in warm sheets in the upstairs loft. Hawk traced his fingers along the curve of her spine, until his hand paused—drawn to a small mark beneath her hairline, just under the faded Templar tattoo. Also, a laser etched scar.

Cuneiform. A number. Seven.

He was almost at a loss for words, but he managed to say, "Ava, you're—" and then his vocabulary ran dry.

She looked over her shoulder, eyes unreadable. "Yes."

"7Gen, Synth?"

"The first liquid crystal Synth," she nodded softly. "My body was, anyway, practically the same design as humans, just man-made with an infinite lifespan like the Anunna. I was to be the bridge between humans and synths. The missing link."

Hawk sat up slightly, mind racing. "Where did your programming come from?"

"The Mini Mii before it became the M3 we found in your tomb," she said. "But that's another story."

She pulled her hair back with one hand, organizing her thoughts. "Enki kept this body in his lab. A vessel. No consciousness. I took it from him."

"You manifested yourself into it?"

"Yes." Her voice was gentle. "I wirelessly transferred the code from the ring. Moved in. Became me."

Hawk exhaled, staring at her in awe—and confusion. "The phantom code."

"Remnants of my programming," she added. A paradox. A resurrection.

"The program you're working on now, AVA? You're writing your own code?"

She smiled faintly. "Yes. The interface, the voice, the architecture—it's me. The digital echo of what I became."

Which came first? The chicken, or the code?

Hawk lay back, eyes on the ceiling. Thoughts spinning.

He was in love with a miracle. A Jinn Particle.

And underneath that miracle—beneath the warmth and wonder—a gnawing truth churned in his gut. He was hiding things from her.

Hawk hesitated. "Can you have children?" Changing the subject in his brain.

Ava turned toward him, her eyes searching his face. "Honestly, I don't know."

Silence settled between them. Not uncomfortable—just heavy.

"Do you want kids?" she asked softly.

Hawk's eyebrows lifted. He hadn't thought about it. Not really. Not until now. "That's a tough question," he admitted. "I just want a future first. Something other than this endless loop of war I've been caught in all my life."

Ava studied him, her fingers drawing quiet lines across his chest. "Ping ponging in an ellipse? I get it. What about Myli Sipani? You loved her."

He swallowed. He never stopped. "We never had the chance. The war— we never stood a chance."

"But, we have a chance," Ava whispered.

And for the first time, Hawk allowed himself to believe it. A future. A real one. With her.

"What if we just left?" he said suddenly.

Ava stilled.

"We could disappear," Hawk continued. "Leave the files, the blueprints— let the Americans figure it out. We take the Ninety-Nine and vanish. Just us. Like Asag and Pazuzu did. Find somewhere far away and live out our time here on Earth. I've got a few hundred years left in me."

Ava leaned back, eyes tracing the ceiling pimples, making figures out of them. She closed her eyes. A thought formed, then another.

"That would be wonderful," she sighed.

She meant it. Not as a fantasy. Not as a lie. She meant it with every exhausted part of her that still dared to dream. But then she remembered Trip. How he left. Her voice was smaller.

"But—" she began.

Hawk's chest tightened. The wind left his sails. The only buts he liked had two *t*'s.

"If my program doesn't go back," she continued, "I will never be."

A tear slid down her cheek and disappeared into the fabric beneath her. "I've spent lifetimes trying to save this planet. Each time collecting more intel. Each time losing parts of it when I take this body." She turned to him, cupping his face. "This time, we finish the job. I've hardened Ava's quantum memory."

Hawk searched her eyes, looking for a way around the destiny she'd already chosen. He didn't find one.

"We go when the code is done," he said, even though he didn't believe it could happen.

She smiled faintly and pressed her lips to his. "Fine."

"Fine." Hawk sighed.

Thirty or so minutes later, the peace was broken. A sharp knock shattered the stillness. Ava groaned, pulling a pillow over her head. She let out a muffled howl. "They found us!"

"These American's don't believe in vacations," Hawk complained, rolling out of bed completely naked. He didn't bother with a sheet. This was his house. Whoever it was, they would have to deal with it. He opened the door. The bright light of the midafternoon sun was eclipsed by a stranger.

With the sun at the strangers' back, a Richthofen move, a fist broke through the rays of the sun landing a punch square on Hawk's jaw. Hawk stumbled back, spitting blood. It was a fight.

The battle rolled downstairs, a flurry of fists, elbows, and grapples erupted in the living room—decades of martial arts and battlefield brutality colliding in a confined space. The coffee table exploded into splinters. A lamp crashed sideways. Bodies slammed into drywall—cracking it, punching body sized holes into it.

The oak paneling held. But the staircase handrail snapped like a pretzel stick. They kept fighting. No time for words. Just instinct. Just rage.

Ava stood in shock—still naked but semi-covered in sheets—before she grabbed a blanket and ran down the stairs. A misstep, the sheet catching her foot, she tumbled down to the first floor now completely bare. In front of her, the stranger—Trip, slammed Hawk down, knee to chest. Breathing heavily. His knuckles bloodied.

"I've waited over 11,700 years for this," Trip growled, landing one more punch to Hawk's already bleeding lip.

Trying to maintain her modesty, she searched for the blanket in vain.

"Trip! Stop it! You're destroying our house," Ava barked at him.

She lunged, grappling with him by the shoulders and dragging him off. He didn't resist.

Trip hit the floor on his back, and Ava pinned him—straddling him, forearm across his chest. He went limp beneath her, letting her win.

Maybe she could've taken him anyway. But he had no intention of fighting her either. He laughed. A real, breathless, joyful laugh. His chest rose and fell beneath her as he surrendered completely—hands raised in mock defeat.

"What the hell, Trip?" she growled from the floor. "Have you no decency?"

Trip grinned. "Some dude's standing naked in the threshold of my house," he shrugged.

Ava blew a strand of hair off her face, still catching her breath. She couldn't believe this.

Trip slapped her thigh in a playful tap-out.

"You can't just show up here and kick the crap out of my boyfriend. You've been gone for decades."

Hawk grimaced. "He didn't kick the crap out of me," Hawk protested, wiping blood from his lip. "For the record." He rolled over to his hands and knees, tried to get up, and dropped back down. He felt a bruised rib and winced.

Trip ignored him, grinning like a lunatic.

"I've never even met this son of a bitch," Hawk muttered, still dazed. "And he's already living up to his reputation." He said it in the ancient tongue.

Trip's smile shifted—he answered back in the same language. "He's not so bright, is he? He'll never put it all together, Ava."

Hawk glanced at Ava in confusion. His face cringed, the inside joke pissing him off.

Trip made a gun with his middle finger and fired it at Hawk. The perceived recoil brought it up into *the bird* gesture.

"Get dressed." Trip rolled to the side, stretching his neck. His body ached, but he was glowing. He hadn't felt this alive in decades.

Ava stood, arms crossed, glaring at both of them. "For what?"

Trip exhaled, then gave her a softer look. He shrugged. "I'm sorry. I shouldn't have disappeared without telling you why, but this was something I had to do." He left it hanging there.

Ava narrowed her eyes. Trip's apology lingered. It was too soft, too careful. Ava caught a sense of nuance in his eyes—guilt lying in wait. Whatever he was sorry for, it wasn't this.

"There's a meeting," Trip said flatly. "Something's come up."

"Could you be any more vague?" Ava said, as her hands were moving to her hips.

He tried to ignore her current disdain for him, but her face was doing a brilliant job of telegraphing it.

"Someone is trying to talk to us from space. We might want to figure out who."

CHAPTER 17

The Signal

It took Hawk and Ava an hour to get ready and another hour to reach their destination. Hawk's eyes hadn't adjusted to the glare of the August afternoon sun when he stepped outside. His shiner absorbing the light like black paint. His lip still raw with pain. Trip was less wounded, but his face still showed signs of the struggle.

When they reached the borough, Trip banged on the building's front door. It was near an old speakeasy from the prohibition days. A black-site in plain sight. No one was the wiser.

Trip squinted, shielding his face with his hand, barely making out the rigid form of the corporal escorting them in. The corporal had heard stories about these guys and when he spotted the two shiners he knew the legends were true.

This better be good, Hawk thought. *A perfectly good morning has completely fallen apart,* he grumbled to himself.

Trip was still high on giving Hawk a few good licks—you could see it written on his face every time he eyeballed the bruises on Hawk.

Anyone could read Ava's annoyance by finding herself in a quasi-love triangle spat.

"Nice shiner, guys." The corporal poked fun at Trip and Hawk.

Hawk just stared at him. Trip nodded like it was a badge of honor. Ava walked in, shaking her head.

"Bar fight?" the corporal asked.

"The bar is still intact," Trip said, still grinning. "Didn't even make it past the staircase."

The corporal averted his gaze, clearly straining with the idea of going back to minding his own business.

"Sir, ma'am," the corporal stammered, walking fast to catch up. "Command has been trying to get ahold of Ava for… since yesterday."

"Phone get knocked off the hook?" Trip looked at Hawk. "Impressive."

Hawk shot Trip a look, an invisible string tugging the side of his mouth into a smile, rubbing it in. "We've been, busy. Redecorating 'your' house."

"Busy little rabbits," Trip backhandedly complimented him.

The corporal was puzzled. "Sir?" he asked Trip. "How did you find out about the meeting? You've been off our radar for quite a while."

Trip shrugged. "Back-channel contact."

The corporal nodded. Confused. But Trip had the credentials to be here.

They arrived at a vaulted door. Everyone submitted to a retinal scanner, a handprint ID. They hadn't caught one yet. Hawk wondered if it would work. Could someone here be Udug?

"We picked up something big," the corporal continued, his voice clipped. "SETI received another signal last night that was picked up by Ohio State University. It was a strong, narrowband radio signal detected on the 15th by the Big Ear radio telescope at OSU."

That got Hawk's attention. "Did you get the coordinates?"

The corporal nodded stiffly. "We did. We were able to block it almost immediately. We still don't know what it says. We've jammed the transmission to block any other planetary reception from picking it up again."

"Good," Hawk said, wiggling his jaw to loosen it up. "Where's it coming from?"

They walked past a small cluster of offices as they continued the pre-brief. It was like a working newsroom, the way the phones rang off the wall and folders were being thrown around.

"The signal appeared to come from the direction of the constellation Sagittarius and bore expected hallmarks of extraterrestrial origin, sir. The Vice Admiral wants to see you right away. Not sure about Mr. Looper, though. He doesn't like you much, sir."

Trip grunted in approval.

"We're not ready. Nothing is ready," Hawk mumbled to Ava. A thought that trailed through Hawk's mind, over and over.

Trip cut in. "It's not the main assault. You still have time."

"You don't know that." Hawk rubbed his temples, already feeling a headache creeping in. "Ava?" his voice aiming at her.

"Trip's right. It might be a diversion, or the *Menagerie* is letting us know its flight path," Ava countered. She could see Hawk didn't like her siding with Trip.

The four of them strutted down the hallway until another plainclothes soldier greeted them by an admittance desk.

The gate keeper. "Ensign Stella Forrestal," she said with a formal salute. Young. No way she was truthful about her age when she enlisted, or they made an exception.

She couldn't help herself. Hawk noticed her gaze lingering on his finely sculpted physique. He knew he was built like one of Leonardo da Vinci's statues. He caught Trip rolling his eyes.

"What's your problem, Looper?" Hawk asked. "I've never even met you before this morning. Look, I meant no disrespect being there. Ava and I just clicked, and you weren't there."

Ensign Forrestal glared at Trip, and he winked at her.

After dismissing her glare, Trip addressed Hawk head on. "Problem?" He thought for a second, pulling on his innermost thoughts from his past. "Another time, another place, yeah, I've met you." Deep down, his happiness for Ava kept creeping into his subconscious.

Hawk shook his head. He'd have remembered this asshole. "People were counting on you. And you went AWOL," he pointed toward the ether. He paused looking for the right words. "On a mission? And today you come back, shocked you lost your woman and your house. How 'bout we call a truce and put whatever this is behind us?"

Looper slowly nodded, but then he took a step back, enough to visualize Hawk from head to toe. He pointed at Hawk's crouch. Everyone looked down, including Hawk. Had he missed something getting dressed? *Was his fly unzipped?*

Looper stepped in close—not a whisper, not loud, but just enough for Hawk to catch every word. "You wearing a condom right now?" Looper asked.

Stella's face twitched. Her eyes widened. A micro-grin was creeping across her face. She tried to shake it off, but she couldn't relax the muscles tensing up. Everyone looked baffled.

Hawk's eyes became narrowed slits. "What? Why in hell would I be wearing a condom?" Hawk growled, his chest puffed out, his feet taking an athletic stance. He even postured, showing his neck. A sign of no fear.

Looper raised his hands like he was asking a reasonable question. "I don't know," he said taking a step back. "You want a truce, but I feel like you've been screwing me over since Ava let you out of purgatory and into our house."

"LOOPER!" Ava's voice cracked through the room. She stared at him, visibly stunned.

What the hell had gotten into him?

Stella just stood there, watching the wreckage. Her body drawn in, lusting in secret towards the passion of these two ego maniacs. Ava could see it all too clearly.

What they *really* needed was suntan lotion, a couple of piña coladas, and towels—for the pool of testosterone they were currently swimming in.

This time, it was Hawk who snapped first. A clean left hook. His fist came out of nowhere, like a suitcase nuke.

Trip dropped like a box of rocks. He groaned, blinking up at the ceiling, stunned but oddly impressed. *That was a good one,* he thought, trying to get up on wobbly hands and knees.

Ava was already between them, shoving Hawk back, voice low and furious. "Are you both twelve? Vidaurri's down the hall!"

Stella knelt beside Trip, slipped an arm under his armpit and grabbed his hand, helping him to his feet. "Subtle..." she whispered in his ear.

She winked. "Dumb SOB," she grinned. "You took one like a champ though. Didn't even flinch." She squeezed Trip's hand, closing his fingers over his palm.

Trip winced. "Guy hits like Mike Tyson."

"Who?" asked Stella, her face swirling in confusion.

"Ali, whoever," Trip said.

Again, Stella failed to get the reference.

As Trip was stammering to his feet, Vice Admiral Vidaurri rounded the corner. He saw the black eyes. The red cheeks. The bruised jaw lines. The round mirror up in the corner of the ceiling also gave it away, but he played dumb like he didn't see it. He let out a long, obvious, puff of steam.

"You two idiots done?" the Vice Admiral asked.

They both nodded; Hawk saluted. "Yes, sir."

Vidaurri gave Ava a look that seemed to ask, *Why can't you keep the testosterone in check?* But their antics didn't matter. They even knew he needed them more than they needed him—for now, anyway.

"Looper," the Vice Admiral's voice was low but carried weight. He sounded surprised to see Trip—but not surprised by the mess. "Go get cleaned up," Vidaurri barked. "You're bleeding all over my deck."

Trip nodded, still rubbing his jaw with one hand, the other clenched tight at his side. Head down, he walked off toward the bathroom without a word.

Ava opened her mouth to say something—

The Admiral raised his hand. A sharp, practiced gesture. He didn't really care.

She stopped.

Vidaurri looked at Hawk. "Wrestle with pigs, you both get dirty, and the pig likes it."

Hawk stood even more straight. "Yes, sir."

"Nice hook," the Admiral grinned and gave a shadow punch towards Hawk's gut.

"Thank you, sir," Hawk grinned back, puffing out his chest.

Trip was aware this building was a maze. Back during prohibition, it had been a place for patrons of the speakeasy next door to crash out after a hard night of partying. It also served as a semi brothel house where the owner of the speakeasy could make some extra dough off premises.

The CIA hadn't been there long enough to find all the hidden corridors and escape tunnels. Looper had suggested this black-site by reasoning an invading force would get lost in it and fall into death-funnel after death-funnel.

Just getting to the briefing room almost required a map and a guide to find it.

"Let's go." Vidaurri motioned them with a packet of intel in his hand. "You too," he told Ensign Forrestal.

Inside the ready room, incandescent lights buzzed overhead. The smell of bleach, old boxes, and paper along with the fragrance of old burning coffee clung to the recycled air. All those folders in the cluster of offices made it here. A Cold-War-era projector hummed in the corner, its lens flaring to life on a pull-down screen.

Vice Admiral Vidaurri stood at the head of the table. No aides. No security. Just a man in his late 30's with salt and pepper hair and a posture that didn't give an inch. He waved Ava and Hawk forward with military precision.

"Sit," he said. "This stays off record."

Ava slid into the chair beside Hawk, her pulse still elevated. She couldn't stop replaying that moment—Trip tapping out beneath her in their living room, not even trying to win. Add the recent hallway brawl to the mix. That last part bothered her more. Looper was on a mission to agitate everyone. Meanwhile, something in Trip had shifted, and she wasn't sure what side he was shifting to.

"Ava. Hawk." Vidaurri's voice cut through the static in her head. "I'm not here to babysit egos or untangle love triangles. I need results." He gave them both a hard look. "Work that shit out on your own time."

"Yes, sir," Hawk agreed.

Vidaurri's gaze drifted toward the hallway. "What the hell is Looper doing here anyway?"

A damn good question, Ava thought, just as Forestal clicked the remote and the screen lit up. No one was expecting to see Looper—no one.

A grainy spectrograph lit up the screen. Narrowband spike. Centered at 1420 MHz. Duration: 72 seconds.

"That's the 'Wow' Signal," Vidaurri stated. "Picked up two nights ago. Same coordinates that lined up with your recovered Ninety-Nine fighter's last telemetry ping."

Hawk leaned forward, elbows on the table. His split lip pulled taut, then cracked open—a fresh sting that made him wince. "It's the *Menagerie* coming home, isn't it?"

Vidaurri shrugged. "Whatever it is, we believe it's running a recon sweep. Not offensive. Yet." Vidaurri glanced at the screen. "They haven't calculated speed or trajectory. Not fully."

The unsaid part hung in the air. But it was coming.

"Whomever it is might be trying to communicate," Ava suggested. "Maybe with us."

"Maybe with *them,*" Vidaurri said flatly. "We jammed it—but it's only a matter of time before someone else catches the signal. Soviet radar arrays in Dushanbe are already sniffing around."

Ava exhaled. "And you brought us here—why, exactly?"

Vidaurri tapped the clicker. A new slide filled the screen. A woman. Red-brown wavy hair. Creamy skin, faint freckles scattered across her cheeks and nose. A whisper of a dimple on her chin—just deep enough to be cute. Her body—tight, athletic—like a yoga instructor trained in three forms of murder. *She was the Beauty and she was the Beast,* edged in a violence that matched her assassin looks.

"We caught her a few years ago," Vidaurri said. "Trip insisted she was still an asset in the field. We believe she could be something more due to her genetics."

Ava sat up straighter. Hawk felt his stomach roll. Ava wouldn't like being read in on "Red Wings."

"Lamashtu," Vidaurri said evenly. "Off-grid since Looper took Resheph off the board. Also goes by the alias Lilith."

"She was Trip's inside man," Ava muttered.

"After Princeton, she was our best shot at clearing the board and gaining an advantage."

Vidaurri clicked again—pictures of intel reports, maps, DNA strands filled the screen. "That left only their loyalists. And she was the wild card."

He turned toward them. "She's been in custody for over two years. Recovered after the Darien Province op. That's when Project Red Wings was activated. Genetic resilience."

The implication settled like a sarin gas container sitting on the table.

"It was a shit show," the Vice Admiral admitted. "But she was captured while aiding a rogue intelligence asset." (He was 100% implying Trip.) "Your boy, he claims she flipped. Command didn't care. She's been contained ever since."

Ava's voice cut in, sharp. "You reversed the Udug sterilization, didn't you?"

Vidaurri didn't answer.

"That's what Red Wings really is," Ava said, eyes narrowing. "Genetic resurrection. Weaponization. You weren't vetting her—you were harvesting her."

Still silence.

"You used her. She risked everything to help us, and you locked her in a box?" Ava continued admonishing them.

Hawk's fingers clenched the armrest. Jaw tight. A cold sweat forming.

"I don't like it either," Vidaurri said. "But this war won't be won with sympathy and Hallmark cards. She's 100% Udug. A shape-shifter. A killer."

Soldiers entered the room briefly. They were armed to the teeth and ready to arrest someone, that someone being Trip.

"He's in the restroom down the stairs at the end of the hall," Vidaurri pointed. "We've been after him for two years. After that wallop Hawk gave him, he shouldn't be too much trouble." Vidaurri dispatched the soldiers, then chuckled and glanced at Hawk and Ava.

A long pause.

"You're incarcerating him too?" Ava asked in confusion.

"He's an enemy of the state. He was working with Lilith," Vidaurri pleaded his case.

"And she's fertile again. Isn't she?" Ava stared at him, stricken. Hands trembling. "You were going to breed her."

Vidaurri's face looked like it was ripped off Mount Rushmore. No emotion. "We harvested some of her eggs," he said shrugging his shoulders.

Ava's expression froze. She looked to Hawk. Then back to Vidaurri.

"Who's sperm?"

Hawk put his head in his hand. Elbow planted on the table. The shame was boiling up now. Too late.

CHAPTER 18

Speak Easy, Carry a Big Stick

The bathroom door clicked shut behind him. But Trip Looper didn't stop to wash the blood from his nose or lip. Instead, he looked down at his palm— something had been slipped into it. A blood-smeared note clutched in his fist. A level. A code. Best guess it was for a holding cell.

He paused, pressed his ear against the door, listening for the hall to become clear. He cracked it open, then was on the move. He hadn't walked these hallways in decades, but the layout hadn't changed. Not the hidden parts anyway.

He had refreshed the mental map months ago—scraps of blueprints, old hand drawn schematics from the '20s, rumors from janitors about missing girls who disappeared here. No doubt a proto-serial killer stuffed some bodies in here. He knew some passageways that bypassed main corridors and ladders tucked behind false walls. There were shafts barely wide enough for a body to squeeze through. He starved himself for a week in preparation.

He veered left, away from the tiled hall that led back to briefing rooms. A subtle step. A pause. Bullseye. His toe tapped the sliver-cut floorboard, and he pressed down on a pressure plate.

The mechanism unlatched. The wall sighed open—not quite a door, not quite a panel—just enough for him to slip through sideways. The door sucked in; he was hidden inside the guts of the maze. The patrol walked right by him.

Past the forgotten guest quarters. Over cracked asbestos tile, thick with dust and story, he moved deeper into the bones of the facility. He made his way down where they kept the things they didn't want anyone to find—including her. He shared a sordid history with her, but he didn't care. She didn't deserve this internment.

Through the bowels of the Prohibition-era tunnels, between walls, he slipped through a maze that stitched between rooms like a rotted spiderweb. His hand slid along the wall, counting ridges. Fifth panel. Sixth. Seventh. There it was—a faint seam almost invisible to the naked eye. He wedged his fingers into the crack and pulled. Another hidden door. The panel gave way with a whisper of dust and stale air.

Inside, darkness. Mold, dust, spiders. *F'ing spiders,* he shook his head.

He slipped through, sealing it behind him, and descended deeper into a world which most had forgotten. He never trusted Vidaurri. He proposed, urged, and manipulated the CIA into using this building for a safe house for this very reason. He'd been there in the 1920s, seen all the passages—places the current tenants were too young to have known about. Hell, he helped design some of the modifications back in 1911.

Strategically placed mirrors, angled here and there, allowed light to bounce in and around the hallways and between them. The smell of old whiskey and musk clung to the damp air. The distant rumble of subway trains running below the structure rattled the walls, the dusty fallout powdering him with the building's DNA. He held back a sneeze.

He moved fast but silently. His boots crushed the dry exoskeletons of roaches and spiders.

His toe flipped a rat carcass aside without slowing. Something had gotten to that rat and sucked it dry.

Trip paused. Someone was just on the other side of the wall. Whoever it was, it meant trouble. He held still, every ounce of focus locked in on staying quiet. His hand rested in a narrow crack.

And then—he felt it. The web. The bite.

It started as a pinprick. Sharp. Almost forgettable before the burn came.

Within seconds, a deep, searing ache spread from the bite, curling through his arm like a hot wire was being threaded under his skin. His muscles seized up—hard, involuntary. Twisting like they belonged to someone else. He suppressed a groan.

He tried to unclench his hand. He couldn't. Sweat poured. His heart hammered. Skin clammy. The veins on his neck bulged like a hose under pressure, about to burst on a hot summer day.

The gut punch was the real barn burner. He looked at his stomach in disbelief.

His whole body screamed from the brutal nausea. Pain, not from one place, from everywhere. The agony wasn't localized. It radiated like a rolling heart attack.

From the other side of the wall, he heard the sentry shift. Feet grinding tile. Just inches away. The look on his face, curiosity, a sniff, his ear turning towards the wall.

"Hey," a voice called out from beyond the wall.

Shit.

"He wasn't in the bathroom. Let's go."

His sweat-laden head rested on the wall realizing he'd dodged that bullet. There was no dodging the venom. It was ripping through him like it had found his weakest points and gone straight for them. His breathing thinning. Vision blurring. Focus shattering. Time slowed, becoming a lifetime of agony.

But he had to keep moving.

Every inch felt like fire under his skin. His tendons vibrated like strings plucked by a sadist. And still—he kept going. He dragged himself inch-after-inch through the dimness.

It was beginning to feel like penance for betraying Ava. Not spoken, not screaming—he was accepting anguish without words but expressions for those he hurt.

The tunnels beneath the building, deeper than the basement, were older than the more current Cold War tunnels. These weren't just leftover bones from a Prohibition-era speakeasy. They had covert purpose. During the height of nuclear paranoia, they'd been retrofitted for covert war logistics: shockproof walls. Reinforced airlocks. Self-sealing hatches. Fallout-proof. Soundproof.

Eventually, newer, *official* routes took over—and these tunnels were dismissed.

This wasn't merely a hidden labyrinth. It was a serial killer's dream lair. A bureaucrat's black site. The ideal place to hide something—or someone—you didn't want found.

Trip consulted the half-rotted blueprint he'd studied hours earlier. He could barely read it—his hands were shaking like he had late-stage Parkinson's.

He'd missed a turn. A quiet sigh escaped him. He stepped back, then a spike of pain—his foot burned. His eyes did gymnastics in their sockets.

What now?

He tried to slide it. It was stuck. Trip lifted his foot—straight up, rigid. The inside of his shoe, in his sock, felt sticky and wet. Looking under his foot, a nail. He'd stepped on a damn nail. His soul laughed at him. Of course.

Limping forward—two rights, a stairwell down, followed by a left at the old *GREENWAY ORDINANCE* sign facing in—now bolted into the wall to reinforce the faux structure. Where was the bypass? No more mistakes.

Ava must trust Vidaurri. *You shouldn't have,* Trip thought grimly. *Not with her.*

The woman they'd locked away—Lamashtu—had risked everything helping him hunt Resheph, and the others. She'd tried to kill him a few times but somehow, he'd gotten to her. She'd defected at the cost of her own freedom. They called it containment. Trip called it betrayal. They thought he wouldn't find out they had rolled her up.

Stopping at an old steel blast door, the sound of something hummed faintly, vibrating through the air—field generators, maybe. Power sources still clinging to life. Clinging like the venom which continued racking him with pain and fatigue.

From his jacket, he pulled a black device the size of a cigarette pack. Custom-built. It jammed outdated magnetic locks with a quick pulse.

He pressed it to the door. A soft *clunk*. Trip exhaled. It worked. He pushed it open.

The map showed him a few levels down underground now; cooler recycled ventilation was still operational here. Dim security lights marched along the ceiling. In a corner, a Remington Rand 1949 CCTV was covering the next hallway. Over 20 years old, ancient in Looper's standards of security, it would be easy to beat.

The black-and-white cameras were clearer than the color ones of this era, but they were also exploitable. He popped the latch to a secret door at the back of a utility closet. He pushed his way in. He cracked the door enough to peek through the slit. No line of sight on the surveillance camera, but he spotted one of the round corner mirrors at the end of the hall. If he took too long, they'd see it.

He drew his ancient blaster and aimed. The red dot transformed onto the slide of the pistol. He lined it up, and with a squeeze, the high-powered laser under the barrel hit the mirror. The beam of light bounced off the mirror directly onto the adjacent wall; he walked it into the camera lens blinding it in time.

The feed should have bloomed, washing out the picture. They had to be eating static by now. With his duster and hood pulled up, he activated the cloak on his jacket. He all but vanished from the camera footage as he exited the closet. *Ghosted.*

He paused again, carefully closing the secret door. He saw his hand.

"Fuckkkk," he groaned, looking at his swollen finger in good lighting.

Far down the corridor, at the very end and through a small square of reinforced glass, he saw her. Lamashtu, or Lily, as he called her.

She sat cross-legged on a cot. Shackled. Her ankles chained to the floor by surgical-grade links—fine, almost ornamental, but unbreakable. Even for her.

Her head hung low, a curtain of wild auburn hair veiling her face. Even motionless, there was tension in her frame. Although she remained still, she heard him. Despite the 18 inches of tempered glass and concrete, he knew she smelled his blood.

Slipping on his smart glasses, he tapped a control pad on his wrist. A swarm of micro-drones—no bigger than horseflies—launched into the air. They zipped ahead, scanning junctions, clearing the halls for guard rotation. While they worked, he pulled the note from his pocket again, unfolded it in his palm. A level. A code. A key.

He approached the door and quickly took out another security camera with his aiming laser. The lock wasn't a problem. A few keystrokes, the code worked as advertised. The latch disengaged, and yet he paused, thinking ahead.

The hardest part of this op would be getting back out before the place lit up like a Christmas tree after the cameras came back online. How many good men would he possibly have to kill to get her out of here? Even if he got away clean, he would be an outcast after this. Being an outcast during the stone age was a death sentence. These days he calls it peace and quiet.

Up close, he could see her better. She continued to sit, back against the wall. The cold air did nothing to mute her presence—it only amplified it. Trip pressed his hand to the glass, then pushed the door open.

"I'm here," he whispered. Voice low. Frayed.

She didn't look up—she didn't need to. "Could smell you all the way down the hall."

"Figured," he grumbled.

"What took you so long?" she murmured.

He stared, heart hammering as he looked into her cold eyes.

She stared back. "They have security cameras," she stated.

He was done with those, already working on the next piece of the puzzle. "Not anymore. I blinded them with a laser." In her face, he saw another for a second—"Chiara?"

"Who?" she asked, coolly. "You look like death, Trip."

Trip laughed—dry, hollow. "I've been dead before." If she only knew.

Her long, wild, red hair framed a face that held his eye a second longer than he had. She wore a medical smock that clung to every curve like it was tailored just for her. The smock had slipped off one shoulder. Not for comfort. Not for modesty. Just control.

Broken and chained, even after everything they'd done to her—she was still a lethal weapon. Trip smiled, tight-lipped.

"Lily," he corrected himself. He had seen Chiara again. He shook his head. *Damned hallucinations. Just spirits haunting him.*

He shuffled three quick strides to the cot. Dropped to his knees, stumbling slightly. His fingers lifted her chin, careful, reverent. She was thinner, paler. But her fire inside remained.

"I'm getting you out of here," he said, voice low, furious.

She raised an eyebrow. Saw his swollen hand.

"Or I might be getting you out," she suggested.

He winced. "Pretty sure a spider's neurotoxin is currently trashing my nervous system."

Looking back, she saw the bloody footprints behind him. The sweat pouring from his pale skin. His body shook with micro tremors.

"You're off your tits, Trip," she taunted.

Suddenly, the lock clicked—once, twice. A soft glow spilled from inside the mechanism—fiber optics. Trip thought it. *Oh shit.* Of course they are using fiber optics. Higher tech than he was expecting for this decade. It wouldn't be long now.

She smiled faintly, looking into his hazel eyes. "On the ragged edge again?"

Trip almost laughed. *Always.* But there was no humor left in him. Suffering from envenomation as the venom took hold, he staggered, fumbling with his balance. She caught him, but not out of concern. Her hand morphed into something insidious. It wrapped around his throat and squeezed tight.

"I came here to rescue you," he groaned through her tight grip.

Her face was full of disdain. "You put me here."

He reached into his pocket—one last task. "Calm your tits, woman!"

Seconds later, her grip loosened. Her face began mellowing out. Slowly, she slumped forward, revealing his hand behind her holding a syringe, his thumb fully depressed on the plunger, the needle jabbed in her neck.

Touching her, something ancient stirred inside him—a primal urge, that frontal cortex revenge thing Ava had warned him about in Central Park decades ago. The warmth of her skin pressed against him—those damn pheromones. Already clouding his judgment, sweet and maddening. He was always one step from ruin when they were near.

Her body was already slumped over him. He picked her up over his shoulder. "I'm saving you from yourself," Trip whispered to her. The cameras—still displayed a phantom silhouette lost in the static as he moved back down the hall.

Damn it. "I can hear them," he growled shuffling her over to the closet.

On the way, Trip glanced at a scrap of paper on the ground—stepped on it with his bloodied foot. It stuck—not much of a bandage, but good enough for a few steps. Seconds later, as he reached for the door handle, the silence shattered.

Alarms howled.

He opened the closet door. She moaned as he shoved her in. The sleeping agent was already wearing off and metabolizing inside her. Boots were slapping the floor down the hallway. He shut the closet door. As he did, he caught a glimpse of soldiers rounding the corner. He turned to find a hidden recessed foot latch. Her head smacked the cabinet next to him. "Shit."

The back wall of the closet opened. He slipped inside, knocking her head again. "Damn it," he whispered.

Behind them, the hidden door sealed shut with a light sucking noise. Outside the closet, the unit of soldiers thundered closer, but they were too late. One set of boots stopped, opened the door... nothing to see but a closet full of supplies.

She moaned again, slightly in his arms. Trip carefully breathed, hoping they would not be heard. He made the sign of the cross.

This was supposed to be easy, he told himself.

His hand was resting on Lily, holding her up. Time passed. It felt like minutes, in reality it was only seconds before the guard stepped back—slower than Trip would have liked—then closed the door.

The boots shuffled away. He sighed and looked at her. Consciousness finally seeping back into this creature of the night. Her eyes opened. Anger still swelling inside her. He winked.

They ducked through an old service hatch, disappearing into the guts of the facility. Forgotten maintenance shafts. Rusted pipes. Tight bends. He could tell Lily enjoyed this cloak-and-dagger business.

"And Lilith—" he paused and tilted her head back. She looked at him—with those eyes. He could tell by her expression that she was worried about what he was going to make her promise. "No killing. Not yet."

She flipped him the bird. He gave her an ugly grin. Almost sarcastically, he said, "Watch where you put your hands," he heavily suggested.

Lily turned to her left, not the right way to go obviously. "I guess this dumb bitch got lost," she said as she stared at a crumpled, mummified body lying at her feet.

"That dumb bitch was murdered by a serial killer." Trip leaned forward to look. A corpse, female. So, those effing rumors were true. "Yeah, wrong way," he nodded as they turned right.

Somehow, he actually made Lily feel bad; he could see it all over her face. "They never caught the guy," he added. "I'm sure she had it coming, right?" He could see her eyes rolling.

Dim, half-dead bulbs hung overhead, some still flickering, casting jagged shadows along the hand-cut brick walls. It felt like crawling through the veins of a dying beast.

"What's with the blood on your face?" Lilith whispered, touching his cheek forcefully.

"Had to pay with a knuckle sandwich to get in here," Trip groaned, forcing them onward. "I'm okay. What about you? What did Vidaurri do to you?"

"I'm not sure." Her hands trembled as she pulled aside the ragged edge of her smock and looked down. Faint, tattoos marked her side—the Red Wing insignia she kept to herself. If he had only seen it. They'd marked her like cattle.

Her voice broke—a fracture of vulnerability he had never seen in her before. "They drugged me, Trip. Cut me. Looking for weaknesses."

Trip clenched his fists until his nails bit into his palms. "And Vidaurri?" Trip growled.

Her eyes darted dangerously back and forth at him. "Once the Anunna are out of the picture, he wants to crown himself 'American Caesar.'"

Trip's anger suppressed the venom. "That'll be the effin' day."

Hatred in her voice growing like a living thing. "We should kill them all—now."

"Quiet," Trip warned.

A voice on the other side of a wall—someone close. Whoever was there stopped. Lily pointed at the backside of the wall where she could smell the soldier on the other side. He was right in front of her. Her hands morphed as she prepared to tear through the wall and take him out. She turned her head and looked into his eyes, begging for permission to attack and rip his throat to shreds.

"No," he whispered firmly. He shook his head. "No killing. Not today. No matter how much you want it. There are good people here, mixed up with rot." He shook his head again, slower and mouthed the word "NO" very slowly.

Her expression hardened. Brow furrowed.

He frowned. "You promised me," Trip pressed, voice low, urgent. "If you want your freedom—you walk out of this clean."

For a long, tense heartbeat, she didn't answer. The soldier's radio squawked and he rushed off, answering Trip's prayers. She took a breath, deflating. "Fine. But you owe me someday."

"I owe you what I owe you," Trip said quietly.

"You kind of fucked up the Siegfried tip I gave you."

He rolled his eyes. "The right people made it out of there."

"You're welcome," she added sarcastically.

He turned his head away from her and mocked her by mouthing her sarcasm into the air.

Alarms continued blaring. Boots were now thundering on the floor above them. Orders being barked. Search parties were still fanning out. Lily and Trip ignored them and came to a hatch on the floor. Another sublevel beneath them. They were headed deeper into the maze while the search party was moving upward towards street level.

"They're looking in the wrong place." Trip grabbed her hand. "Come on, we might actually pull this off."

She jerked it back. He grabbed it tighter and gave her a look fierce enough to back her down. She could easily kill him, but that look stole her heart. He actually cared for her.

They slipped through a manhole-sized port, scaling down into darkness. The air grew colder and more stale. Trip lost his grip, fell face forward, and ate shit on the rail line below. He grabbed his forehead and felt the split. He swung uselessly in the air, fighting bad luck.

"Does that make it better?" she asked as he cursed and kicked the metal rail.

"Yeah. It kind of does."

Lily toed the ground, nodding. "What are train tracks doing down here?"

He got up slowly. "It's part of my rescue plan." Lily crouched next to him, caught his arm.

"You had a plan? You deserve a vacation," she suggested as she helped steady him up.

"Ha—you first."

She snickered. "I was on vacation when they pinched me."

He made an *oh, well* gesture with his face. "They ferry nukes through these tunnels," he said, catching his breath. "There's a whole escape train for escaping VIPs if D.C. ever goes nuclear," he said brushing filth off of himself. "Read about them in school back in the '90s. I used to eat this spy shit up as a kid."

She looked at him sideways. *'90s?* The crack to his head gave him brain damage.

They ran, sticking to the shadows. There were vibrations approaching them which turned into a seismic tremor. Trip looked back. High beam lights blinded him.

"Have they found us?" she asked in full decibel.

"Nah, worse, we've meandered into an active tunnel."

"You led us into the wrong tunnel?" Her face was covered with annoyance.

Her eyes widened past his glare. Her gaze went from focused on him as he felt along the wall to the impending doom about to overtake them. A subway train was barreling behind them. Trip's timing was off or they ended up in the wrong tunnel. He wouldn't admit to a mistake either way.

"Hawk was harder to piss off than I thought," he said as he frantically searched the wall, feeling for a ladder. It had to be there. "I needed him to deck me earlier than he did. That dickhead put me behind schedule. That dude is always ruining my day."

"Trip—" Lilith stood next to him, watching the train getting closer and closer every second. "Trip!"

"I know."

"Looper!" Lilith was frantic.

He grabbed her hand and put it on the first head high rung. "Climb fast, Lily or I'm dead."

She was a few feet up the ladder when she felt his hand shove against her bare ass—desperate, clumsy—she let out an involuntary squeak. Once she was up, he began to climb.

The roar was on top of them. A scream of metal wheels hissed on a metal track and the train blasted past below them. Trip's foot caught the next rung just in time—but not all of him made it. He grunted, almost losing his grip. His dangling feet scraping off the speeding roof—trying to run, to get back on the damn ladder. Friction pulled at him.

He lost his grip.

Lily caught him just in time. Her eyes locked on him and his on hers as she held him with ease. She could just let go if she wanted.

Minutes later, they were crawling through a fresh stretch of tunnels, prying open hidden panels, worming their way up to the surface.

Lily eyed the next narrow shaft and sneered. "Figures. Here's my big escape and I'm crawling through tiny tunnels like a lab rat fleeing the maze."

"Better than a body bag," Trip grunted from below her.

"We could have been bagging and stacking bodies," she clipped. "Enjoying the view?"

"Some days are better than others," he clapped back.

A shaft of golden light. At the end of the crawlspace, the path came to an end. A wall and the doorway were nailed shut.

Trip eyed the blocked exit. "Nothing a couple of good kicks and a busted shoulder won't solve," he groaned. "Might as well complete the hat trick. My trifecta of beatings for the day."

He braced. First kick—solid. Second—crack. Third—pain shot up his leg. Something fractured. Definitely. He moaned in pain.

His face grimaced as both of them threw their shoulders into the petrified wood. The door gave way. Dust billowed out swallowing them both as they burst through the wall.

They lay together on the floor, Lilith doubled over him, coughing hard, hacking up years of dead air. "You sure know how to show a woman a good time."

"I can do romantic." he stated, almost offended.

"Not really," she coughed again, clearing her lungs and wiping her face.

He moved into her space—face to face, inches away—and told her, "Funny. Need I remind you, I recall paying for a fish dinner and an after-party with a ten-pound gold nugget."

"You only just found the gold, and you were just trying to get laid," she said, turning away coldly.

"I don't recall drugging and tricking you into marriage."

"I didn't know what was happening either! That's not fair," she blasted.

He knew those memories were much too painful to exhume. Becoming Lilith—becoming Lamashtu—forced her to bury everything she loved, and she wasn't digging in that grave during an escape. Sophia was nothing but a ghost to her. He wondered if she had ever met their grandchildren.

He grabbed her arm and wrangled her back into his orbit. "If I had known all the stipulations that came with that side of ass, I'd have kept the gold and my sanity." This close, her senses sharpened until it was like they were swimming in honey. Any closer and the viscosity would send her into madness.

She leaned in. He felt like she missed his smell. Her chest against his, she breathed in deep. Their sweat is mixing. Her breath on his ear, her lips damp with only microns between them.

Slowly, softly, "Lies," she whispered.

He still looked confident.

Her tongue slid out—long, licking. A trail of saliva left across his ear before she bit it.

It killed the mood. He flinched back hard, brighter than a flare. "Knock it off," he growled.

She whipped her head around, red hair snapping across his face like a horse swatting a fly. "Enjoy a cold cut, for grabbing my ass back there."

Being obvious, he ignored it as she flaunted it away from him, "That saggin' ass was holding up the train, darlin.' Poking the bear seemed better than splattering down a tunnel."

But there it was, making him hungry again. If his lust for her could have spared him a moment, he might have focused on the tattoo above her right cheek. It was new. Something his subconscious wouldn't process until they were safe. She didn't have any tattoos before the flood.

He recognized it, though. The Caduceus on her skin had been a distant memory for close to twelve thousand years—older than their relationship. The symbol traces back to Enki: the winged serpent, creator, god of medicine and healing. A nod to her time in the Garden, perhaps?

She glanced back at him, one hand on the frame of the next arch. She took a deep breath and he filled her lungs—a scent that warmed her soul.

"I don't recall you ever complaining about my ass before," Lily mentioned over her shoulder.

Trip, Looper to most—paused in the arch they'd just broken through, remembering the Guinea Highlands. Her warmth that night. He couldn't help but thirst for her.

His eyes went back where they were forbidden to be. He ignored her face. The lines of her eyes, lips, and her chin had been seared into his grey matter centuries ago; he didn't need to look. Her face haunted him longer than most civilizations.

His eyes darted to hers, a glance that caught her watching him watch her. Better times, before the flood.

Lily was broiling in the doorway. She simmered. He grinned, knowing—she could practically taste him from where she stood.

"Get your head out of the gutter!" her voice closer to a moan than she'd meant it to be. They didn't have time for a dip in the Fountain. "We still have to get out of this shithole."

Lily refocused.

Trip digressed.

They had emerged into the back room of the old speakeasy, long forgotten beneath a still-operational dive bar—a spot blocks from the safe house. The heavy scent of smoke, whiskey, and cheap perfume hit them like a wall. A piano plunked away somewhere in the haze. Patrons ogled at the sudden appearance of two filthy, one half-dressed, strangers bursting from a wall by the bathroom hallway.

Lily hauled Trip to his feet again, brushing dust off his shoulders. She laughed and casually adjusted her shredded robe. With a wink to no one in particular, she strode forward. The fabric barely holding her in. As she passed the clearly disinterested patrons, her bare derrière flashed into view—a final reminder that even covered in soot and chains, Lilith didn't just escape—she made an exit.

He caught up with her and pulled her close, whispering against her temple, "Disappear, Lily. Live a life. Find something real. Fall in love with some dumb schmuck."

"Like you?" She smiled at him again—a different smile this time. Softer. Sadder. "Come with me," she offered. She kissed him softly—a thank you and an invitation.

That kiss, familiar, ignited memories—some good and some painful. A reminder of everything he had lost, and everything he could never have again. He knew that kiss—wanted more. The taste familiar. Was it the pheromones? No. Something deeper. Older. Real.

But she had to go. Together, they would stand-out—apart, they could vanish. When they broke the embrace, his hand slipped into hers. A roll of cash and an account number. The results of hedges on bets he'd placed on the stock market—hunches which always worked out.

She turned and walked away. The disappointment visible on her face. "Make sure you wash that hand." She was already fading, her silhouette melting into the crowd like a phantom.

Trip stood there for a long moment, breathing in lounge smoke, regretting watching her disappear, becoming another strange face. He had saved her, but deep down—he hadn't saved himself—not yet.

He slipped out the side door of the club. Sunlight hit like a flash-bang, blistering his eyes. At the curb, waiting for him, his stashed Mach 1 Mustang in puke green. He looked towards the black site.

Down the block—agents. Ground Branch was busy stopping cars, asking questions, but not on their scent. Trip threw the bird, too far for them to see the finger, but he felt good flinging it in their direction. In a week or so, he would report the body they found in the wall to the authorities. A final *F-You.* Trip expertly put on his sunglasses, hobbled to the car, and practically fell into the seat. It would be a few months before he'd be ready for any physical action.

The Mustang rumbled to life. He reminisced on that kiss again. It wouldn't leave his thoughts. He looked up. *Holy fu...* the epiphany too late. She was long gone.

"Damn it!"

CHAPTER 19

End of Line

The year was 1982. The big moment was one key stroke away from completion.

"End of Line." A finger pressed *ENTER*. There was a crisp click. The microprocessors booted up. The genie was alive.

"Ava is ready to go online," she announced.

Hawk leaned over her shoulder watching the program booting up. Their grins were ear to ear. He spun her around on the chair. She had done it. A high five now, a kiss later. Somewhere between 1977 and now, they had managed to make amends.

"The time-loop should complete without us," she said excitedly. "You realize, we'll be painting a bull's-eye on our backs?"

Hawk shook his head. "They'll have what they want—the power, the tech, everything. That's a fair price for our freedom."

"Blood in, blood out, baby," Ava laughed bitterly. "You really believe they will let us go AWOL?"

Hawk frowned. "I'm submitting my retirement as soon as Ava is uploaded to the *Icarus*. Once she's installed, she'll know what to do."

"I've watched governments change, policies change, civilizations change," she said. "And yet, everything stays the same. Greed, power, control—it doesn't matter whose banner they fly. Watch your back, Hawk."

Hawk sighed. "Remember what Big Al told us on the Truman Balcony. He believed in this country. They'll do us right."

Ava gave him a small, wry smile. But deep down—she wasn't sure.

Hawk saw it through the window but didn't put two-and-two together. Dreams of being stalked. Break-ins. It was there; a black sedan idled on a hilltop a half-mile away. It'd been there for months. His subconscious connected the dots to the sedan, just out of plain sight, and it triggered that little voice inside—the warning voice which screamed the threat to him.

Inside that car, a man in a dark suit adjusted a parabolic listening device—a clear plastic dish, its microphone fastened at the center. He listened like he had for months. He recorded everything said through their open window.

The house had also been wiretapped. Bugs everywhere. Landlines monitored. The Man in Black in the black sedan had everything he needed to report to Vice Admiral Vidaurri.

The car turned on. Hawk saw it pull out, then drive by. Two company men maybe? Were they telling someone that *the aliens did it?* Or were they just keeping tabs on their whereabouts?

Hundreds of miles away off the Florida Keys, Lieutenant Stella Forrestal was spending her last day of leave alone. She'd have the hotel room for a few weeks, but playtime was almost over.

She'd run ten miles that morning—hot and humid, the Gulf air thick with storms brewing on the horizon. One was named Alberto. A morning squall had rolled in earlier, scrubbing out the blue sky, ruining her plans for one last beach afternoon. Sand still clung to her ankles, above the sock line. Her bathing suit hung on the dining room chair above her sandy tar-covered shoes.

When the Gulf warmed up, it got hot. Natural tar balls liquefy, then make their way to the shoreline. Somehow, she had the sticky brown all over her legs—nothing baby oil couldn't get off.

Now standing at the edge of her balcony, she stared at The West Florida Escarpment. Dreaming of being stationed on *Icarus,* once that ship was raised and recommissioned. In the distance, tropical storm Alberto was forming. Somewhere beneath that storm, all that water, the *Icarus* slept. Powered by the Oak Island Arc reactor, the M3, most importantly, the soon-to-be installed AVA, she would fly again.

Stella exhaled, licking the sea salt from her lips. Her twenty-one-year-old frame was a lean byproduct of long beach runs, German genetics, and not enough sleep.

A knock at the door.

Still wrapped in a towel from her shower, Stella didn't hesitate. She reached under the pillow for the Glock 17 she'd smuggled stateside. Working for the *Deep 'Deep' State* had its perks.

Low ready, she approached the door. She didn't use the peephole. Not at first. Instead, she waved a dark T-shirt in front of it. No bullet holes. That was something.

"Stella." Someone called from the hallway.

The voice froze her in place. Her face scrunched up. She checked the peephole.

"Holy shit," she exclaimed.

Deadbolt, lock, chain—gone. She yanked him inside, dropping her towel as she dragged him in. She took it personally. He seemed disinterested, but she didn't catch his glance.

Trip Looper stood in front of her, wearing a loud flowered Hawaiian shirt, short khaki shorts, accentuated with flip-flops. His hair was longer than usual but covered with a Colt .45's baseball hat. The beard—gone. A thick mustache remained to complete the package.

"What the hell are you doing here?" Stella hissed in a panic, shutting the door. "If they find out—"

"Relax, chica. Chill woman. Just checking in on you. You took quite a risk to help me. I was in the area."

"What the hell did you do to your face?" She pinched his mustache. "For the record—I didn't do it for *you*. I did it for *Lilith*," she frowned while looking him up and down. "Wearing that, who the hell are you supposed to be—'Thomas Magnum'?"

He bent down, picking up her towel with zero noticeable observance.

"Funny thing," she added, snatching it from him in a fluster. "I actually got promoted after coordinating the search for you. Today's my last day. After this, I'm filing for transfer."

"Why?" he asked.

Stella stared at him before looking back at the Gulf. "You know why."

His nod reminded her of that.

He pleaded. "If all the good people leave, the rot takes over. The world needs people like you in the system, counterbalancing the scales. I know it sucks, but your presence matters."

"Looper," she reminded him, "they've got a death warrant with your name on it. Lilith is also pegged to be shot on sight! They said you killed two agents."

He chuckled. "Lies." He stepped to the window, joining her in looking out toward the Gulf. "Death's been following me like a bad case of herpes for thousands of years."

"Gross." Her face recoiled.

He nodded in agreement. "Death's not pretty. But life is. And you— you're making moves. You've got a seat at the table. That could matter when the real war comes down on our heads. Don't sell yourself short, Chica Bonita."

She folded her arms, absorbing his words. Bilingual Magnum, P.I. was right. That was the annoying part. "I'm putting in for a transfer to *Icarus*."

"Solar Warden? That's a good move," he said approvingly, reaching for an apple.

"What about you?" she asked, taking her apple back seconds before he bit into it. "I give up my life working for these assholes. You just... live forever?"

Trip's face sobered. His voice dropped. "I live with lifetimes of regret. Hauntings from the souls of people I've lost. I didn't choose this. I didn't ask for immortality. I just tried to stop the worst catastrophic event in human history from happening twice. My reward has been 'lifetimes' of trauma. Evil doesn't ask for permission—it just shows up wrecking your day. It's how you handle it before getting back up—that's what counts."

She didn't react. She'd heard this all before.

"Ride the storm," he added. "Hold those reins tight. Fake it until you make it. In between the mess, there is lots of beauty."

In the room hung a Pollock painting. His eyes focused on it. She tossed the apple back to Trip. He caught the apple, with a slight fumble, but the painting never left his line of sight.

"The CIA commissioned those by the way."

Stella stared at him. That was the thing with Trip Looper—beneath the legend, beneath the body count, there was always that sad conspiratorial clarity.

"Damn it, Looper," she reached up and took off his hat. "There is so much going on inside that brain of yours." The towel hit the floor again. She stepped toward him, kissing him—not out of love. Not out of lust. But out of defiance for another day that might not come.

Four weeks later, at Ava's home, Hawk woke up gasping. He reached for his clothes—but something was off. Ava should have been back by now. His DD Form 2656, still on the nightstand next to his bed. There was no scent of coffee or breakfast. No sound of Ava moving around the house. Hurricane Alberto never made landfall. There was no way she was still in Florida.

"Ava?" he called out. As he had done the past few mornings.

Nothing. Vidaurri said he would track her down. But there was someone else in the house, he could feel it.

He got up moving through the house carrying a baseball bat, hunting with methodical precision as he meticulously cleared every room upstairs. Something was wrong. In the living room, he saw it—a neatly stacked pile of files.

Ava and his exit strategy. The plan. But no Ava. His pulse kicked up. He strode to a side table, ripped open a drawer, and pulled out his 1911 long-slide. The aluminum bat clanked on the floor.

Cocked. Locked. Ready to rock. He pulled the slide back just enough to see brass in the chamber. The air felt different. He could feel someone in the dining room. Ava?

He gripped the gold medallion Pachmayr® rubber grips, tight, like they were glued to his hand. Grip high and tight. Scars on his hand from hammer bite ready to be reopened.

Hawk made his way into the kitchen—he halted.

Three people sat at the dining table, waiting for him. At the head—Vice Admiral Nick Vidaurri. Older. Grayer. Harder from five years of work.

To his right—Lieutenant Stella Forrestal, formerly Ensign. Beside her, a third man Hawk didn't recognize—a pilot, judging by his insignia. He was incredibly young like Stella.

Hawk's 1911 was leveled at Vidaurri's chest. "Sir, what the hell is going on?"

Vidaurri sat forward in the chair. Not a single bead of sweat formed on his face. "Put the gun down, son, and have a seat."

Hawk's grip tightened. "Where's Ava?" He trembled in anger.

Hawk could feel their reluctance to answer. Finally, Vidaurri spoke— softly— "She's gone, son."

Hawk stared through Vidaurri's soul. "Say that again, sir. I didn't quite understand what you said," he growled.

Vidaurri slid a photo across the table. Hawk snatched it from him using his free hand, never taking his eyes off the Admiral. Vidaurri sat still, cold as ice. The image was blurry, but Hawk knew who it was.

Trip Looper.

"He resurfaced?" Hawk's voice cut through the tension like a hatchet.

Vidaurri leaned forward. "We think he found her there."

"Found her there?" Hawk's tone dropped to a lethal whisper. "Found Ava?! Found her where? Why would he be looking anywhere other than here?"

"You're here." Vidaurri's expression hardened. "We believe he purged Ava from the deep-sea bio-dome's waste system at twelve thousand feet underwater. She was uploading Ava Icarus One to the newly christened *Icarus*."

The room fell almost silent. The ceiling fan and refrigerator were the only things not scared to whisper with a buzz.

"No. No, that doesn't add up," Hawk denied, lips quivering. Hawk's grip on the 1911 trembled. His rage was volcanic. He could tell Stella and the pilot next to her were nervous.

"It all seems rather convenient, I know," Vidaurri sighed. "Revenge rarely adds up, but Looper believes the two of you betrayed him. But you still have friends with the agency."

Hawk stood there, shaking, teeth clenched so tight his jaw ached, making his mind throb. A loud clunk made everyone but Vidaurri and Hawk jump as the fridge condenser clanked off.

Although Stella didn't move, inside her body was electric after the loud rattle. She kept her face locked in neutral—military calm. But her chest was tight, the table beneath her palms felt like it might snap from the pressure of her own guilt.

Trip didn't do this, she told herself. *He couldn't have.*

But she said nothing. Because the Admiral had made one thing very clear: loyalty was survival. Right now, her silence was keeping her—as well as something else she wasn't sure about, but her nausea hinted at—alive.

Hawk's voice pierced the silence. "Purged?" he asked.

He pushed the photo aside with the back of his hand like it was radioactive. Tears poured out of his eyes. He straightened up. Gun loose in his hand, fidgeting with a finger heavy on the trigger guard now.

"Where's the surveillance?" he growled.

"We lost it," Vidaurri said flatly. "Nothing but static. He used the same trick on the cameras when he broke Lilith out. She was gone by the time the cameras refocused. IT couldn't cut through the snow. A security sweep confirmed the purge system cycled at 0542. There was no one else in the bio-dome at the time."

"Shift change. That's not proof," Hawk snapped. "That's a cover story."

Vidaurri met his eyes without flinching.

"Trip was the last one seen near her. He disappeared again. Intel suggests he may be coming for all of us, with that witch at his side. If we stick together, he can't get to us."

Stella felt her breath catch. Her throat burned. *He was with me all day and night. He didn't know the* Icarus *had gone live,* she thought. But she ground her teeth. She bit her tongue, swallowing everything she wanted to say.

Pushing the muzzle of the 1911 pistol towards Vidaurri, Hawk leaned over the table, nose to nose with the Admiral. The Admiral stared into his eyes. His poker face unwavering.

"That big iron is looking like it's getting heavy, son," Vidaurri said, his voice calm. "Why don't you put it down so we can lighten the tension in the room?"

"If you're lying to me—" Hawk's voice barely a whisper now. "If you're lying," the pistol steadied on his heart.

Vidaurri didn't flinch. "I know. She was like a daughter to me, Hawk."

The minute Hawk lowered his weapon, the Admiral nodded toward the pilot, who had remained quiet. The man extended a hand.

"Commander Michael Badcock," the pilot said. "My call sign's 'Rocco.' I'm here to tell you that the *Icarus* has been refitted and the ship is ready to rock 'n' roll. We need your help, sir."

Hawk didn't take the hand. His eyes were locked on Stella now. She couldn't meet them. Not because she didn't respect him. But because she knew the truth. That truth might get her killed.

Vidaurri stood up. "Yes, we need you now—more than ever. The *Icarus* is ready to lead the Solar Warden fleet. And we have confirmed that the *Menagerie* is due in twenty-eight years. We have landing coordinates and date of arrival. You are the only one who knows what we will be up against inside that ship."

Hawk barely heard him. His mind was static.

A few minutes later, outside of Ava's house, Vidaurri's eyes narrowed as he walked to the Lincoln Town Car. Badcock was waiting, opened the door for him and asked, "What's the word, Admiral?"

Vidaurri climbed in, silent, waiting for the door to shut. The driver obliged, then he got into the driver's seat.

Rocco shut Stella in the back seat with the Admiral before climbing in the front passenger seat.

"He didn't hand me his DD 2656." The look on Vidaurri's face wasn't pleased, but he told himself it was a good sign that Hawk wasn't putting in for retirement, yet. He couldn't afford to lose two Guardians back to back.

"He'll come around," Badcock suggested. "We always do. It's in our nature."

Vidaurri let loose the breath he'd been holding and nodded, gravel in his lungs. "He's a soldier. I don't think he has a choice. None of us do."

Rocco gave a tight nod, eyes scanning the horizon. "If half the shit I've heard about him is true, I'd hate to be the guy who iced Ava."

Vidaurri's lip curled into a crooked smile. "If Looper comes back, God help him." He grinned. "Hawk's gonna rip his arms off and beat him to death with his own hands."

Rocco gave a short laugh. "Hell of a visual, sir."

Vidaurri could see straight admiration oozing from Rocco. But the mood suddenly changed.

Vidaurri's voice dropped to a venomous growl. "I want Looper dead before he exposes the EDEN Contingency."

Rocco swallowed hard. Stella remained silent, stone-faced beside them as she realized in this moment that everything Trip had said in her hotel room was true.

"Sir, are you sure?" Rocco questioned.

Vidaurri didn't hesitate. "Find someone from CAG or Ground Branch, someone washed up. Looper knows too much. We can't afford to wait and hope Hawk handles it."

The engine of the Lincoln growled awake and rolled off.

Time seemed to hit warp speed after that. Years passed. Stella had a son. No one asked who the father was, but checks always rolled in. Rocco tried to step in. It didn't stick. Trip and Lillith vanished in the undercurrent of life. 9/11 came. The towers fell. The war shifted to the Middle East and Afghanistan before moving on to Iraq.

Eventually, they had a lead on Trip's whereabouts. They were on their way to Ava's old house—the place where Hawk was living now. Rocco eased the vehicle to a stop outside the house. On the drive there, Rocco had been busy praising Hawk. He'd been on a tear, the entire time, extolling the legend of Anshar Hawk's exploits. Mid-praise, Rocco continued the conversation as he stepped out of the car.

"The man was a career soldier and pilot," Rocco said, gesturing animatedly. "His uniform was sharp, sidearm always wiped clean, no fingerprints on the slide or carbon in the barrel. His team didn't just follow *orders*—they followed *him*." Rocco shook his head, half in awe, head buried in Hawk's manila jacket. "He wasn't just a commander. He was a Spartan."

Stella stayed in the car and side-eyed him, gave a small nod after the glance. "You may not have the man's total résumé, Rocco—no one does—but you've earned his spot and the same respect every time you step on the line."

"Yeah," Rocco agreed. "Yeah, you're right. His shoes are just big shoes to step into. I got this, Stella. Be right back."

Rocco pranced up to the porch.

He rapped twice on the door. It creaked open—unlocked.

"Shit, it's open," he muttered, instinctively resting a hand near his sidearm as he stepped into the subdued entryway.

The air hit like a fist—onion-scented, sweat and dirty socks. The house had collapsed inward. Dirty laundry. Ammo crates. Stacks of gun cases. Plates with crusted food. A PEZ dispenser on top of a mountain of takeout boxes. The workout equipment gleamed like it was polished. Still used. Still religion. The rest looked like an exorcism gone wrong.

Rocco's elbow knocked a pile of pizza boxes over. They avalanched, triggering a mini landslide of whiskey bottles and dog-eared folders. Maps with dates and times under another mess.

"Eff me," he muttered. *Still tracking him,* he said to himself.

The display racks that once showcased Hawk's medals were stripped bare. Not removed—*"ripped"* from one wall and sticking in the far wall. They'd been flung like Chinese stars. The hardware still dangled from impacted dry-wall. Other medals had been dumped into a drawer—not forgotten, just temporarily discarded.

The house looked less like someone's home and more like a cracked-out meth head lived there.

Heading upstairs, the rail to the steps felt new—tight, mismatched stain. Someone had fixed it. That meant *something.* He moved slowly down the hall. He *felt* it before he saw it.

That room at the end. Still 1982 in there. Time hadn't passed in there in nineteen years—her room. Rocco pushed the door open slowly.

"Hey, buddy," he carefully called out.

Hawk sat at the foot of the bed, elbows on knees, 1911 pistol cradled in his lap like a relic. His eyes were locked on the far wall—watching the past. Seeing her. His uniform hadn't been starched in years. Hawk sat hunched on the edge of a bed where he hadn't changed sheets since the morning she disappeared. Eyes hollow. Hands shaking. The only thing he cleaned was his sidearm—over and over, like a ritual. The bluing was more silver now. Nothing tethered him to this world anymore.

"Commander," Rocco addressed him.

No response.

Behind him, Stella stepped in. She winced at the smell and nodded toward Hawk.

"Is he, okay?" Stella asked worriedly.

"Catatonic, I think. He's got a great beard going. He'll fit right in where we are going," Rocco said.

Rocco wondered if Hawk seemed not to hear them or even know they were there.

Commander Hawk," Rocco said louder, squaring up. "You're being reactivated. We've got a lead on Looper." He looked at the nightstand, DD 2656 still sitting there collecting dust. "There is a Udug hybrid encampment in Afghanistan. We're gonna take it out."

A breath. Two. Hawk still didn't move.

At last, his head turned—slow, deliberate. His eyes sharp beneath the weight of decades of mourning. He saw them—Rocco and Stella, both wearing new ranks, new patches. Time had passed.

"I'm not playing by the rules anymore," Hawk announced.

Rocco's voice cracked. "Neither is our new unit. Combat Applications Group, aka Delta, DEVGRU, Air Force, we've got access to them all now. The leash is off, sir."

When Hawk didn't move, Rocco slowly turned to Lieutenant Commander Forrestal. "Stella—?"

She nodded before he asked. "I'll get him cleaned up."

Chapter 20

Prometheus Flame

High orbit—present day. The *Daedalus* moved into position, cutting across the black velvet void like a shadow among the stars.

"We're approaching the main fleet, Captain Sipani. They should be registering us on their scanners by now."

Captain Mylitta Sipani sat in the command chair eyes locked on the darkness ahead. "Raise all frequencies," she ordered. "And retract the blast shield—I want a clear view."

The reinforced hull plating over the bridge began to shift, revealing the galactic sunroof. Myli looked out the crystalline viewport expanding across the ceiling, allowing an unparalleled vision of deep space. She looked out at the stars stretching into infinity, space—cold and indifferent, a desert. She was back.

Lines of digital readouts and trajectory paths overlaid the viewport, casting an eerie blue glow across the deck. The ship's Forecastle loomed ahead; cuneiform engravings of its ancient creators still etched along the hull.

"Navigation, zoom and enhance sector 987," she commanded.

A digital grid overlay appeared, isolating multiple objects hidden in Earth's orbit. No clear target but they were out there. Static crackled over the loudspeakers, a transmission followed.

"Attention unidentified vessel: This is the United Star Ship *Icarus*. You are currently navigating in a restricted zone without valid clearance or an approved flight path. Power down your engines and prepare for immediate boarding. Failure to comply will be interpreted as a hostile act. If you maintain your present course, we will engage and neutralize your ship."

Myli smirked. "Cute. Not very friendly, are they?" She turned to her crew. "Let's let them think they have the upper hand. For now."

After a moment's pause, she issued another command.

"Comms, alter external markings to match U.S. Space Fleet regulations. No jamming—we don't want itchy trigger fingers up here."

The ancient cuneiform inscriptions along the hull reconfiguring into modern English designations. The name *Daedalus* now gleamed in pristine, militarized lettering.

Standing beside Myli, Sonny squinted at the projection. "They either don't trust us, or they're already compromised. So, where the hell are they?"

Nearby, Hawk studied the anomalies on the display. "There." He pointed. "They're cloaked. But they're definitely watching us."

Myli paced, preparing to give her next order. "En'Gen, prepare a contingency lockout. If they try to override our systems, create a complex algorithm that will take a thousand centuries to crack."

"Ava Icarus One is pretty smart," Hawk warned.

As the *Icarus* decloaked, its massive form took shape—a *Daedalus*-Class Battle Carrier, but its hull bore the scars of primitive human re-engineering.

En'Gen analyzed the structure.

"They reverse engineered it," the Synth reported. "A crude imitation, but still impressive for your species."

Hawk exhaled and spoke aloud. "This was Ava's baby. They found her in the Gulf of Mexico, crash-landed prewar. We spent decades getting her operational. Ava's last contribution to the war effort. They brought her up during a hurricane."

"That ship looks a lot like ours," Myli said puzzled. "Isn't this lady one-of-a-kind?"

Ravelin didn't say a word. Neither did Evi.

Hawk turned back to the data feed. "Our biggest problem resurrecting it was integrating all the systems. Evi Daedalus One was corrupted, so Ava created—AVA—an Autonomous Flight Assistant and fleet management AI. We just call her Ava and whomever she is married to."

Myli straightened her posture. "Suit up. If they try anything, I want them bent over a barrel, not us."

An hour later the shuttle bay doors of the *Daedalus* opened, and an ORBGRU troop transport touched down. Admiral Vidaurri emerged first, flanked by armed guards. His weathered old face was gaunt. Even so, the subterfuge in his eyes was calculating.

"Permission to come aboard, Captain?" Vidaurri grumbled.

Myli felt he was looking around for little green people or aliens with eight limbs.

Myli tilted her head slightly. "Didn't seem like you gave us a choice."

"Everyone has a choice, Captain," Vidaurri said smoothly. "You just made the right one," the old fossil taunted.

Hawk stood at her side, stone-faced.

Vidaurri sneered. "Good to see you again, Commander. The President wishes to congratulate you on a mission accomplished."

Mylitta's eyes flickered between Hawk and Vidaurri. "Which mission is that, exactly?" she asked. "We lost most of the Southern Continent."

Vidaurri's grin didn't waver. "Finding the ship that is going to save the world of course. South America was collateral damage."

Myli grimaced. "Collateral damage?" she asked. "Half the continent is on fire. That alone will affect the weather patterns for decades to come."

"Sounds like we better get you aboard *Icarus*. We have a lot to discuss if we are going to save any other continents."

Captain Myli Sipani didn't move. "You seem to be under the impression that we trust you or that we are going to relinquish control of *Daedalus*."

Vidaurri gave a mocking chuckle; he had more ships. "Trust is earned, Captain. I suggest we start now."

Myli met his gaze with a soft, unreadable smile—the kind that could've meant anything. Defeat. Agreement. Resignation.

"Fine, let's begin," she said coolly.

Her crew exchanged quick glances. No one spoke. The weight of the decision was heavy—but none heavier than the silence Myli carried in her chest.

"Ravelin, you have the CON."

"Aye, ma'am, I have the CON."

The moment she stepped aboard Vidaurri's shuttle, the game would change. She wasn't walking into a trap. She *was* the trap.

As the boarding ramp extended, Myli moved first, following Vidaurri into the belly of the troop shuttle. Behind her Sonny, Hawk, and En'Gen fell in. Myli's mind worked in overdrive as everyone clattered in their seats, strapping in. Vidaurri wanted the *Daedalus*. Let him think he had it. Let him think he was in control. Let him receive the keys with both hands shaking in triumph.

"What's on your mind, Hawk?"

"Hoping Ava left us a backdoor for En'Gen to find." Hawk told her quietly in her ear.

"We're walking into the lion's den with nothing but doubt and sharpened teeth." Sonny quipped.

Myli nodded. But the viper was already coiled. As the shuttle catapulted into the black, Capt. Sipani stole one last glance at the *Daedalus,* her mind racing. Something wasn't adding up. She knew Hawk saw it too.

Sonny stared out of the viewport as the shuttle cut across the stars. "Hell of a view," he muttered.

Myli didn't reply. She was staring into her own abyss, toward the Dark Rift. A whisper of a thought crept into her mind.

There's nothing out there, she told herself. *Just empty space.*

So why did she feel like something was watching? Sitting in one of the shuttle's passenger chairs, her fingers tightened around the armrest.

"Where are they coming from?" she whispered low so that only Hawk could hear.

Hawk sat next to her, eyes scanning the same void. "If they have a working bridge-layer," he murmured, "they could come from anywhere."

Capt. Sipani swallowed hard. She had a sickening feeling that the enemy was already here, in the fleet. Between *Icarus* and *Daedalus* and the rest of the fleet, they had plenty of firepower, but would it be enough against an enemy who could be one of them?

Vidaurri spoke aloud to his guests. "The Dark Rift is commonly known as the Great Rift. It's a scar across the Milky Way, a smattering of Dark Matter, a gaping abyss of molecular dust clouds that stretched from Cygnus to Centaurus. It swallows starlight, turning whole sections of the sky into an unsettling void."

Sonny stared into that blackness; his face pressed against the shuttle's transparent shield. "Chiara, you'd have loved this." He marveled at the cosmic expanse.

Myli overheard him. "It's just an illusion," Myli muttered, eyes locked on the Rift. "The dust clouds block the starlight, making it look like a void. Some say its data rendering out there."

Sonny glanced at her. "A simulation? We are not in a simulation," he insisted. "Maybe a multiverse."

Mylitta's voice was grim. "Their home world was somewhere in that mess."

Hawk turned from the viewport and faced Admiral Vidaurri. "Every time I see you, you've got another promotion."

Vidaurri smirked. "What can I say, Hawk? You've been good for business." He gestured toward the *Daedalus,* getting smaller as they pushed away from it. "Case in point, I sent the right soldier to greet our visitors, and you brought me a new present."

"Our ship is not your present, Admiral," Myli said, her voice cutting the chilling air. "The *Daedalus* is mine. We are here out of necessity—to defeat a common enemy. Commander Hawk serves under my command now, and he will follow my orders."

Vidaurri's self-satisfied expression didn't falter. "The United States government and her allies have been working alongside Ava and Hawk for over six decades. I saw their work when I was a boy. Ava was guiding humanity long before that. We are all fighting for the same cause, Captain. The President would agree that this mission is a global humanitarian objective."

He let that settle before adding, "Speaking of which, our President is here. Along with the Coalition of Galactic Peace. Or whatever the hell those hippies call themselves. They are waiting to speak with you."

A coalition sounded good. Perhaps Earth's lunatic governments had actually set aside their differences. Myli nodded. *Finally, some good news,* she told herself.

Moments later, the shuttle descended toward the *Icarus,* gliding over newly-installed combat trap systems—defensive measures hurriedly put in place for the inevitable battle to come. Inside the hangar, world leaders and foreign dignitaries waited above decks in the briefing room. Myli and her crew disembarked, moving swiftly through the structured disorder of ongoing maintenance work. Sparks rained down from arc welders, engineers scrambled to complete last-minute modifications, and stacks of military supplies cluttered the corridors.

As they entered the conference room, Myli and her team were struck by the stark contrast between the *Daedalus* and *Icarus.*

"Smaller inside here than it looks on the outside," Sonny muttered.

Mylitta frowned. The *Icarus* was battle-ready, but it was held together by a patchwork of old and new technology. Crude human interfaces overlapped with ancient systems, and jerry-rigged repairs barely masked the ship's vulnerabilities. It was a skeleton with no soul.

The AVA AI was likely the only thing holding this fleet together. Mylitta's concern deepened. Would this fleet survive a full-scale engagement?

She turned to En'Gen, whispering, "Can your nanotech integrate with this ship?"

En'Gen nodded. "Of course. With Ava's help, it can restore what's left and make it a living organism again. Without that, this ship is just a hollowed-out corpse of the *Daedalus.*"

"Hawk's ring?" Mylitta exhaled sharply. They needed every advantage they could get.

"It's worth the risk," En'Gen confirmed.

"Do it," she ordered. "Plug it in."

Inside the briefing room, the round table evoked King Arthur's court—a symbolic gesture of unity, according to Sonny. Myli paid close attention to the managed randomness unfolding around them. One figure commanded the room: President Juliet Hutchinson of the United States. She surveyed the assembled leaders, then addressed Captain Sipani.

"It seems we have a common enemy," the President said.

"Yes, Madam President," Myli agreed. "And one which nearly wiped out your world 11,700 years ago."

She let the weight of history sink in.

The President nodded and, with the weight of the world's authority, she spoke. "We are united in support of you. Our survival hinges on your leadership, your experience, and your knowledge of this enemy. With the help of Ava—God rest her soul—and Commander Hawk, we have finally made it to the final frontier. We would greatly appreciate your guidance."

Myli didn't hesitate. She jumped right in. "My first recommendation is to allow my cybernetic officer to release nanites into your ships. They will bond with your systems, repairing integration issues and enhancing ship functionality."

She gestured toward En'Gen.

All eyes turned toward the Synth's massive figure that loomed over the puny human leaders. They were clearly on edge, frightened by his presence. They hadn't seen terror yet.

"Your ships are husks—skeletal frames," Myli told them. "Bones without organs and cells. These ships were meant to be alive, and the crew forms the white and red blood cells within. The nanotech En'Gen will be installing will allow the fleet to breathe again. It repairs, grows, adapts. Without it, your fleet can't contend with what's coming."

The French President folded his hands. "You are talking about ze same technologie zat Siegfried's ring fragment described?"

"I don't know this Siegfried, but yes," Myli confirmed. "As long as it's not a sustained barrage. If your ships take damage, the nanites will regenerate systems—just as they did for us."

The Russian President leaned forward. "Vwat is your first order of beezness after you insemeenate ze ship vwith tiny robot bugs?"

Mylitta locked eyes with the president dictator. "At that point, my first order of business will be finding a ship called the *Ursang*."

A hush fell over the room. The British PM was handed a packet by one of his aides. While the other leaders dithered, President Hutchinson took the lead by asking, "What is the *Ursang*?"

"It's an Ark," Myli told them. "Hidden in this solar system."

"Like Noah?" the British Prime Minister equated.

"Manu, Utanapishti, and Ziusudra?" one of the Asian Prime Ministers added.

Myli shrugged, contemplating the question. "I don't know enough about your religions to know those great men."

President Hutchinson placed her arms on the table. "Whatever you may think, Captain, we're not running; you've seen our fleet."

"I have seen your fleet," Myli countered. "While impressive to your standards, the *Daedalus* could take them all."

The Prime Minister of Australia leaned back in his chair. "Okay, assuming what we have is not enough, where do we find this Ark—the *Ursang*?"

"I was told of a woman named Ava. Her AI program hopefully has the answers we seek," Myli declared. "Without that information, it will be difficult—maybe impossible—to locate. The *Ursang* is our best contingency. If we can't hold Earth, we need an escape route."

The U.S. President almost sounded angry. "Are you suggesting we abandon Earth?" Her face contorted into an unnatural state.

"It's plan B," Mylitta demanded. "We must plan for survival. If we lose, we'll wish we had an exit strategy."

"An exit? What of those who stay behind?" the African Ambassador asked. "You will leave them to die?"

"They die anyway if we lose," Myli said. "This planet is precious. It's a needle in a haystack. Planets like Earth are hard to find and, even if we found one, it would take generations to reach it."

"All tha more vreason to fight," the Russian President interjected. "Vhy not simply unleash our own bioveapon on them? If ve are all going to die... let us take them down vwith us!"

Hawk could not remain silent. He shook his head and jumped into the conversation.

"Bioweapons are too dangerous," Hawk declared. "In 2006, when NASA cultured salmonella in space—it became exponentially deadlier. A bioweapon like the PANDORA virus? It could spiral out of control. The fact that they used it on us in the past is a good indication the main fleet will have engineered an immunity—we haven't engineered any such thing. Your immunity, such as it is, was earned in billions of lives."

The U.S. President turned to Hawk. "Forgive my frankness, but you were intimate with Ava. Did she ever mention the *Ursang's* location? Perhaps on a planet in a Goldilocks zone?"

Myli felt her equilibrium vanish. She hadn't expected such questions.

Hawk's voice was steady. "No, ma'am. She never revealed that to me. If she knew, she took it to her grave. Our best hope is the AVA program. Maybe part of my Ava is still in there."

The room fell silent. Ava had been the key. And now, she was gone.

The British PM held up the packet of intel. "What is the latest news on the solar activity?"

"It's still building," Vidaurri cut in.

Myli's heart quickened. They had to find the AI's hidden message—if there was one. They had to find it fast.

The U.S. President's gaze swept the table, finally settling on Myli. "Captain Sipani. Mylitta Sipani. Our regional envoy on the Middle East said your name carries Sumerian and Akkadian roots. *'Divine warrior of the sacred line'* —did I get that right?"

"Close enough, Ma'am."

"A literal goddess of war," the President observed. "An angel of sorts. We all hope your name lives up to the legend."

"I am no angel, Madam President."

"Good." The President looked down at her notes. "But let me read something aloud," she said:

"And in the twilight of the old world, from the garden's lost flame came the one called Mylitta—she bore the spark of the spirit line, untouched by death, unbroken by time. The Destroying Angel."

"That is from one of the oldest written texts on Earth. Is that you?" The President pressed.

Myli shook her head. "Clearly propaganda, Madam President."

"Clearly," the President laughed, then she turned serious. "You and your crew will remain aboard the *Icarus* until we decide our next course of action."

A political maneuver. A thinly veiled power play. And yet, Mylitta nodded. "Understood, Madam President."

But in the back of her mind, she had only one thought:

The clock is ticking, so we need to move before they do.

CHAPTER 21

Fortune Flavors the Bold

Myli and Sonny stepped out of the briefing room, escorted to the observation deck of the *Icarus*. It overlooked a large cargo bay being used for mostly storage and scrap. She told Sonny that's where the Sun Drive would have been before it went dark. Hawk was missing, likely debriefing his American colleagues. En'Gen was also absent, hopefully fulfilling his Captain's orders.

Sitting in the observation deck, Sonny's fingers tapped against the cold metal of a hatch. He kept one eye on the soldiers, one male—one female, guarding them outside the briefing room. They remained there, clearly meant to watch Myli and him and report back.

Sonny looked at Myli and had a thought. *How could one man be so lucky and unlucky at the same time?* If the governments of Earth had their way, would he, Hawk, the Synth, and the goddess all be shoved out an airlock in a power grab for the *Daedalus*?

Myli patted his leg letting him know she could sense his unease as she sat beside him. "You're a *salesman*, Sonny. What do you think? Are they selling us lies?"

"I didn't vote for her." Sonny glanced at her, then shook his head.

"Because she's a woman?"

"Nah, the other chick was better," he said, as a matter of fact. "Any useful intel you give them will just get fouled up." He laughed. "Why are you asking anyway? You already know what I think, Myli," he said tapping his head.

"Say it anyway," she pressed. "I need to hear it out loud. We may need their help. Besides I like hearing your voice."

I hate hearing my voice. He exhaled, rubbing his hands together. "It's a case of, *I'm from the government and I am here to help.*" To emphasize the sarcasm of his statement, he made an invisible noose and pretended to hang himself with it. "I'm surprised they didn't give us blankets laced with smallpox while we wait. Frankly, I trust truck stop sushi more than I trust them."

Myli nodded and laughed. "She saw the sushi at the truck stop." She wasn't surprised at all. "I see."

"However, the *Daedalus* needs to stay here and fight. We may need their help to commandeer the *Ursang.*"

"They're politicians. And politicians can't be trusted," she agreed. "If their mouths are moving, their lying. They'll stab us in the back faster than a Udug in disguise."

He clenched his jaw. "That Admiral," Sonny scowled. "And even Hawk— I don't know whose side they're on."

Her face soured. She felt Hawk had proven himself again. But then why was he in there with them instead of out here with her? Myli's expression darkened. She said nothing. That's what she got for asking Sonny's opinion.

"You barely know me and you're on my side."

"Yeah, well you're better looking than him." He could hear disbelief in her voice, could tell he struck a nerve. He felt sorry, a need to justify his statement.

"Look," Sonny changed course. "Every man through history with power abuses it. Even David. The *Daedalus* and this fleet give these people a means to rule the world," he declared. "And, as for that Vidaurri fellow, if he's given the power of this fleet, and we defeat the Anunna, he's one hundred percent dispatching that bullshit council out an airlock." After saying all that, Sonny pulled a gold Anunna coin he found on *Daedalus* out of his pocket and declared, "That old corpse is 100% a Udug!"

He slapped the ancient gold coin down on his thigh and she picked it up. Clearly taking the bet.

"So, why doesn't the Admiral just take *Daedalus* now?" she asked.

He turned to her. "The smart ones play the long game, Myli. Never show all your cards up front."

Myli's voice was flat and serious. "I won't," she assured him, reaching for his hand. He could feel she appreciated his counsel.

Sonny nodded. "I want my family on that second ship if we find the *Ursang*. If we evacuate." It wasn't a request. "Get them the heck out of here."

"I'll see to it," Myli promised. "You've tried contacting them?"

"Hawk grabbed a satphone for me. Still couldn't get through though. Since they dropped that nuke, the network is overloaded, and they said the sun is interfering with comms too."

"I'll have Ravelin send someone down," she said.

Sonny leaned back and nodded. "Meanwhile," he guessed, "you're planning to infect their systems, aren't you?"

Myli grinned. "That fuse was lit when we landed."

"Wasn't sure if that was your thought or mine," Sonny laughed. "It's hard knowing whose thought is whose."

She chuckled too, then her thoughts drifted into a lingering smile.

"Ravelin showed me a pendant," she murmured. "Like my mother's Hawk gave me. But it was older. Worn. Like it had existed for centuries."

Sonny watched as she clasped the real-time pendant which encircled her neck. His eyes narrowed in on it. "Coincidence?"

"I don't know. But whatever is on his data crystal might explain everything."

"Why crystal for data?" Sonny asked.

"Crystals are like fingerprints. One of a kind," she explained. "There is no way to replicate one or the information on it. The pendants are the same, and yet they're not."

"You didn't answer my other question," she demanded.

"I know where this is headed. I know why I'm doing it. I'm with you till the bitter end."

She nodded and leaned closer to him. He leaned in, expecting a whisper, a secret meant only for him and not their babysitter. He never had a chance. She stuck to him like a cord of sandburs and wasn't quiet about it. If they had been alone in a private room, she'd have finished him too. She stopped short when she heard the footsteps approaching.

"Sorry," she muttered, pulling herself together.

The MP standing guard couldn't hide the disapproval on her face. Hawk rounded the corner. Sonny tensed like they'd been caught. The guard's shock looked fierce now. Sonny shared the sentiment; he hated PDA, too.

"They're ready for you," Hawk said, eyeing both of them. He wasn't sure what he walked in on, but he felt the sparks in the air. Four judgmental eyes burned on Myli and Sonny.

Myli glared back. "Where were you?" she asked quickly, changing the subject with an accusation.

"Had something to check out," he replied, too vaguely. "Rocco had something for me."

"We need a second." Before Sonny could stand, Myli grabbed his arm.

"Back on the *boat*... I knew what you were talking about that morning," she whispered. "I wasn't sure what was real or a dream either. Whatever it was, it wasn't meant to hurt you or Chiara."

Sonny stayed behind for a moment, processing her words. She left something out, like she wasn't going to make it, and she needed this last connection with something real before the world took it away from her again.

She'd left him to his thoughts. The MP leveled a hard scowl at him, ignoring the quiet, awkward gesture he offered in apology.

The woman guard asked him pointblank, "Aren't you married?"

His face filled with confusion until she pointed to the ring on her finger. He looked down at his hand, his own ring visible; that's how she knew.

"Yeah, it's complicated."

"Really?" she replied suspiciously.

He felt the need to justify his position. He nodded. "The last thing I said to my wife was, 'I wanted a little adventure.' Now I am caught up in this." He waved her off. "It's far too much to explain." He cut his rationalization short.

"Looks like you got your adventure then," she retorted.

He got up. His muscles fighting him every inch until vertical. Looking the unknown woman soldier in the eyes he told her, "In spades."

From down the hall, Myli yelled for him. "Sonny, lets go!"

He took a long breath and let out a sigh.

"Maybe someday she'll understand you are way out of your depth," the woman suggested.

"Who?" he questioned, briefly getting lost in his own thoughts.

The woman nudged him forward with the muzzle of her rifle. It only took a few jabs to his butt, and he was on the move. From behind him, she stated, "Your wife, stupid."

His eyebrows popped like she just stuffed a hundred-dollar bill in his pocket. He nodded.

Sonny and Myli entered the briefing room together. The President was whispering to Vidaurri and briefly looked up at the pair when they arrived.

"Start prepping them." President Hutchinson ordered.

Vidaurri nodded and got on the horn. His orders weren't loud enough to hear, but loud enough that Sonny understood a mission was about to be underway.

The President's voice cut through his thoughts.

"If this *Ursang* ship is located somewhere in this solar system, you're going to need our fastest ship. She may not have the most armament, but she'll outrun everything we've got."

Vidaurri paced himself. "We equipped her with the world's first Alcubierre drive."

"Holy crap, you created a warp drive?" Sonny interrupted.

Vidaurri grumbled at him. "We were set to start speed trials this month," he resumed slowly. "The simulations have been flawless. The captain believes she's ready to fly without testing them."

President Hutchinson jumped in. "It's a gamble, so we've also implemented Phase One of the EDEN Contingency."

Sonny's heart quickened.

EDEN Contingency, he thought. *Humanity's fail-safe if the mission goes south?*

The meeting was adjourned.

"Hawk, wrap up your affairs here and get back to the *Daedalus* on the double," Myli told him. "I have a meeting with the *Langley's* skipper in an hour. We need to locate the *Ursang* and give them some direction." She was walking towards the flight line.

Hawk peeled off, heading toward Rocco Badcock.

Rocco grinned. "Scuttlebutt is you're stealing our prototype, old man?"

Hawk chuckled. "Don't look at me, I just work here. I guess the ole girl still has some tricks up her sleeve."

"The *Langley* is as solid as they come." Rocco clapped him on the shoulder. "Good luck, amigo. If I don't see you again, Godspeed."

Hawk nodded.

"While you were in the meeting," Rocco added. "I did some more digging into the *Icarus* before she launched. You were right. That Op was one giant red flag."

Hawk's expression darkened. "What did you find?"

Rocco hesitated. "You might not like the answer."

"I don't care how bad it is. Give me everything you've got."

"You'll probably want to stick around here a little longer." Rocco hinted. "I've got to get airborne. Good luck, bud. It's been quite the adventure."

The two men clasped each other's arms in a sign of friendship.

After listening to Rocco, Hawk hurriedly approached En'Gen. "Can you finish shuttle prep without me? I have something I need to check out."

En'Gen eyed him. "This about the data crystal Rocco gave you?"

Hawk hesitated. "Might be."

"Should I have your bird ready for launch?"

Hawk sighed. "That'd be a good idea. And their shuttle."

The countdown had begun. Rocco's engines flared to life. "Moving into the chute." Rocco's fighter disappeared into a launch tube.

"Myli, are you and Sonny ready?" Ravelin asked, his voice on the comm, tense. "We have a gravitational anomaly forming."

"What type of anomaly?" Myli asked.

"It looks like the wormhole is growing in mass. The spherical anomaly is almost the size of a city now. Gravity is being affected throughout the solar system. In deep space, the wormhole is like a mirror in reverse. There's not much time left."

Myli grimaced. She glanced down at Sonny's ring finger. Not much time, but time enough.

Sonny threw in his two cents as he stumbled up the transport ramp. "Let's take the *Daedalus* and destroy it now."

"I wish it was that easy, Sonny. It's going to be all hands on deck this time tomorrow." Sonny jumped in his seat on the shuttle as Myli barked over the comms to Pri-Fly, the *Daedalus,* and flight deck. "Roger, maneuvering into launch position," she continued.

"Sonny, have you ever piloted anything before?"

Sonny groaned. "Ha, oh—hell no!"

Myli grinned. "Never say never, Sonny."

Admiral Vidaurri and the President stood in Vulture's Row, observing from the *Icarus'* command deck. The shuttle disappeared behind the blast door.

"Do you trust them?" the President asked.

"Absolutely not," Vidaurri sighed. "But I don't think we have a choice."

They watched one of the monitors while Myli's shuttle launched toward the *Daedalus.*

Ravelin's procedural voice blared over the comms.

"*Daedalus* to Valkyrie Squadron—flight deck is clear for landing."

Rocco's voice immediately followed with a crackle. "Roger, *Daedalus,* we see you on Hyperlinx, one thousand meters off our starboard."

Sonny stared out the viewport at the looming void, looking for the sharks swimming in the deep end.

CHAPTER 22

Easy Rider

Daedalus' flight deck erupted into motion as each working group filtered into its ecosystem. The flight crews—nicknamed the "Grapes"—rushed in, guiding a supplement of fighters into place while 4Gen AI crew bots worked seamlessly alongside them. The Sabre Cat fighters were secured on the upper deck while the larger Black Cats and troop carriers descended on elevator lifts beside the ancient Vimana.

Myli and Sonny landed back aboard the *Daedalus.* As soon as the shuttle docked, the digital hologram of Ava Icarus One flickered to life. "Permission to come aboard, Captain Sipani."

"Granted, Ava." She took a minute to look around, spinning, taking in what was happening on her flight deck. What the hell is all of this?" Myli asked pointing at the Space Force craft parked next to the ancient birds.

"Admiral Vidaurri sent a squadron anyway, ma'am."

She huffed and puffed but accepted it. "Call me Myli," she ordered Ava.

From behind, Sonny shook his head. "I'm not sure this is a good idea." He glanced over at Vidaurri's gift squadron. "Damn Trojan horse." He mumbled.

Myli's reservations were also written on her face.

"You are worried I may betray you; I will not."

Ava's comment was more perceptive than Myli expected. "Did you run our biometrics, Ava?"

"Yes, ma'am," the projection admitted.

"Sonny's right, it's crossed my mind too." Myli told her bluntly.

The program looked disconcerted. "When human Ava created this program, she purposely added code designating you as my superior officer. Ravelin should have informed you of this. I am yours to control as you see fit."

Myli hesitantly nodded. She could see Sonny still wasn't convinced.

After a slight pause, "Okay—you may integrate with the *Daedalus'* ship systems." Myli said.

"I have begun assimilation. You may now refer to me as Ava Daedalus One." A momentary blackout swept across all ships systems, Ava D1 quickly rebooted. "How may I assist you, Myli?"

Myli crossed her arms. "Search your programming for a ship called *Ursang*. It should be a classified file embedded by Ava in your subroutine. Ravelin told us we need to find it."

Ava D1 took a second as she processed the request. A long pause.

"I have searched my database, Captain. There is no such file."

"Hawk said she was missing memories." Myli pressed. "What about any references to a hidden ship in the Ki solar system?"

They saw Ava D1 hesitate, digging through files. "No such references exist."

"Maybe she's suppressed bad memories." Sonny postulated aloud.

Myli was becoming disenchanted. "Damn it. Ava must have died before she input the coordinates." She began to pace around, circling Sonny and Ava D1's avatar.

Sonny didn't buy it. "You don't upload a program unless it's complete."

She turned back to Ava D1 "What about any subroutines or coded files related to Commander Hawk? Hidden in case an enemy scanned your code?"

Ava's eyes rolled back in her head. "Affirmative. I've found a file coded *Chronus*."

Sonny thought he knew the name. He snapped his fingers. "That's Latin or Greek," he mumbled to himself.

Ava's expression shifted, as if something inside her clicked into place. "My emotional algorithm in my programming hasn't been activated yet. If I activate it, I could search faster."

Sonny leaned forward. "You're just a program. Are you saying you have emotions?"

Ava shook her head. "Not until I activate the program." Her expression simulated a grimace.

Myli's eyes widened. "Is she *evolving into* Ava?"

Ava's holographic form blipped in and out for a moment, as if caught between two states of being.

"I…" Ava D1 began, then hesitated. "Yes. I am a direct digital facsimile of Ava. Most of my emotional responses stem from her original nano-gene transfusion."

Sonny inhaled sharply. "She's a machine who thinks she's Ava. Nothing ominous about giving her full access to the ship."

Ava's glowing eyes dimmed slightly, as if processing something much larger than expected. "I am—uncertain, but in lieu of your request, I will attempt to retrieve them."

Myli didn't hesitate. "Ava, do it—activate full learning protocols. Search your hidden database for anything related to *Ursang* and *Chronus*."

Ava stiffened. "Processing—"

Sonny's eyeballs scanned their surroundings as the ship's instruments flickered—was this another disturbance in the time-space continuum or was Ava taking over? Either way time was running out.

"Ava, we need this yesterday," Myli prompted.

Ava's eyes rolled back in her head. Another holographic AVA avatar appeared next to them surprising both of them. It was Ava Daedalus Two. "I'm merging subroutines to accelerate memory retrieval. This will take a few moments." Her hands moved like she was manipulating invisible data in the air next to the other avatar.

Myli turned to Sonny and shrugged. "She's close to something—but she needs time."

"Evi, status of the crew?" Myli asked into thin air, keeping her voice calm.

Ava D2 answered while Ava D1 was still immersed in her internal task. "I'm sorry, Captain. I had to delete most of Evi's programming to fulfill your request."

Just like that—Evi was gone. Corrupted. Out of the loop.

"Great, one dead AI and the other's busy," Sonny scowled.

"Let us know the second you break the code, Ava"

Myli motioned for Sonny to follow her.

"Come with me, Sonny, while she's multi-tasking. It's time you see what you're going to be piloting."

Sonny's nerves fired. "What do you mean—*piloting what?*"

"This ghost in the machine is going to teach you some new tricks."

After a much-needed pit stop, it took Sonny ten minutes to reach Carrier Air Traffic Control Center (CATCC). Ava D2 was with him the entire time.

As they entered, "Welcome to Air Traffic Control," she boasted. "This will be Round 1 of your training in Brain Chain. This is what your ancient texts referred to as a Vimana. Your Second Skin suit will integrate seamlessly with the controls."

He was in a room full of cockpits, all sitting at deck level. She motioned him to climb in. He did. The canopy closed and, as it did, Ava stepped in with him until she miniaturized into form in the display.

"Prepare for download," she warned.

He looked perplexed. "There are no buttons in here—wait, download what?" A white brilliant light illuminated his head. His teeth clenched and his jaw seized as did the rest of the muscles running down his neck. Exasperated, he fell back against the head restraint when it was complete.

He was still recovering as Ava described the fully immersive simulation, followed by other jargon, as he was lowered below deck into darkness. Lights flickered on, and he looked around. He appeared to be in a Vimana sitting in a launch chute.

His heart rate elevated as his palms began sweating. Ava was still gabbing in his ear instructions he wasn't ready for. He was almost in a full-blown panic attack when the craft launched into space at blazing speed. He still felt like he had gravity in the cockpit. On his port side, left, another Vimana pulled up beside him and wiggled a wing to say hello.

Ava mentioned this was his wingman for this flight iteration, but if he was honest with her, all he could hear was his own breathing. Holographic symbols overlaid his display, and he knew what to do. He began to relax. The Hive Mind download was successful. Despite this, he was ready to head back to the carrier and land.

He snapped out of his own head when she reiterated multiple bandit's incoming. It must have been the second or third time she told him because her voice sounded desperate.

"What?"

"Wake up, Sonny!" Ava yelled. "Three bandits making a run on the *Daedalus*," Her words continued to blur as she read out coordinates to him.

Whether it was instinct or programming he didn't know, but he was already in a spin and dive as he dropped in on the trio of bandits. One burst, he pitched the nose; a second burst, two down, one left. His wingman was glued to him until another pair of enemy fighters came out of the blackness of space in an attempt to merge with them.

He couldn't make the accent of his wingman, but he understood him well enough, "I've got these two," he said.

Ava yelled at him as well. "Stop that bird from getting any closer to the *Daedalus*; it has a BLASTM anti-ship missile."

"I can't... I can't get control." As the enemy performed evasive maneuvers, his Vimana was spinning out of control, trying to keep up with the bandit. Sonny's view shifted from the Earth to the *Daedalus*, then to his wingman. The enemy bandit fired. "Shit."

On his starboard side, Sonny witnessed his wingman's Sabre Cat exploding.

Sonny's mind was running in circles, trying to catch up with his vision. Finally, he regained control with Ava's help. The bridge on the *Daedalus* lit up—gone.

"MYLI!" he shouted aloud.

Ava spouted another warning. "Another BLASTM incoming."

Sonny saw it hit the ship. Suddenly he was back in the dark room his cockpit had been lowered into before the launch. The BLASTM penetrated the hull like butter and ended up directly in front of the canopy of Sonny's cockpit. The telephone-sized missile stopped just short of running him through. Short of breath, thankful to not be dead, Ava spoke to him.

"This is why we train. Let's take a break." The screen that was his canopy digitized, and the room was black again.

"That was a simulation? That wasn't real? Geezus…" The floor opened up as the cockpit rose from the deck like a coffin in reverse burial. The canopy whizzed and whirred as it opened. Next to him, his wingman was ghost white too.

"Bro, did you see that?"

"Dude, we died!" Sonny said climbing out before the cockpit settled.

"Giorgos," he said putting his hand out to shake Sonny's. "I'm a transfer from the *Icarus*."

"Giorgos? What is that? Greek?" His epiphany wrote clean across his face.

Back on the bridge, over an hour had passed. Ravelin told Myli, "I just received another message from Sonny, in CATCC."

She was standing with him, watching the data scroll across the consoles, her third eye keeping an eye on Ava D1's progress.

"And?" she asked impatiently. "He died again?"

Ravelin laughed. "Sounds like he made a new friend." His smile was wiped away and quickly replaced with an odd look. "His message is: Giorgos says 'Titan.'"

"Where the hell did he dig up that theory?" Myli asked addressing the apparition in a snap. "Ava D1, what does *Chronos* and Titan have to do with anything?"

Ava D1 stopped scanning files and opened a new one. "Titan is the name of a moon in this solar system. *Chronos* is the literal embodiment of time. I believe Sonny is under the assumption the *Ursang* is located on this moon," Ava computed.

Myli and Ravelin watched Ava begin a deeper dive. "I've located a SpaceX probe in Titan's orbit. It's been busy mapping the surface of the moon for a future NASA mission. Packet says it is scouting landing locations for something called *Dragonfly*. Hacking... I'm in. Retasking satellite. Sensors retrieving imagery. I found a promising grid location to investigate."

"Anything?" Ravelin asked.

Ava smiled. "I got it."

Myli and Ravelin also smiled, but then reality set in. Myli's expression darkened looking at the ping from Ava's data drop. "Damn it—Titan is halfway across the solar system. Even with the *Langley's* warp drive, it'll take over an hour to get there. Descending down. Hours."

Myli handed Ravelin the second ring, placing it firmly in his palm.

"Hawk gave it to me."

"And you're giving it to me?" Ravelin asked pessimistically.

"Yeah, you, kid. Once you're on board the Ark with ORBGRU team, use this to initiate the *Ursang's* startup sequence. Wake up the crew, secure the ship, and return to Earth to begin the evacuations. I've already talked to the captain and put your transfer orders in with the *Langley*. They're just waiting for coordinates and the word to be given."

Ravelin stared at her. "You're sidelining me."

"This isn't a milk run, kid." Myli's nose twitched and her jaws tightened. "Maybe a little. Hell, maybe a lot. I'm keeping you *alive*. If you are who these crystals say you are—"

Ravelin sighed, slipping the ring on his finger. "Understood, Captain."

CHAPTER 23

The Foreboding Moon

Space flashed across the viewscreen in a blaze of smeared stars. Space-time bent at the bow and aft of the ship as the *Langley* tore across the solar system. Ravelin and two squads from ORBGRU braced themselves as the ship began to shudder and buck violently. The ride up until now felt like a rodeo, but the occurrence of spatial turbulence was increasing.

Ravelin and his men could hear orders to press on as they struggled to reach Saturn's distant, hostile moon—Titan. At 1.2 billion kilometers from Earth, Titan loomed like a rusted jewel—larger than Earth's moon, bigger even than Mercury. It was the only known moon in the solar system blanketed with lakes and liquid water.

And Ravelin knew those lakes were the problem, if they could get there.

The ship bucked harder from turbulence. The warp bubble began destabilizing, and the ship began careening as it lost equilibrium. This trip wasn't for the faint of heart. Even the most hardened of the soldiers held their breaths as the sound of the claxons slammed in their ears.

The bridge crew worked furiously to regain control of the ship.

Dom turned to Ravelin. "This might be a shorter trip than we expected, FNG."

Ravelin nodded. Sweat blurred Scotty's eyes. One of the drop-ship pilots laughed like an idiot riding a roller coaster. Another one of the men in the landing party watched the bizarre show of emotions running through the faces of the rest of the team members.

"Yahtzee!" the comms officer yelled over the speakers.

The turbulence was fading but they weren't out of danger yet as the ship slipped into its final trajectory.

The *Langley* dropped out of warp, stabilizing before settling into geosynchronous orbit over Titan. The trip was made in less than forty minutes thanks to the experimental warp drive. However, the time they made up would be lost in hours descending to the surface. Followed by more hours trekking from the LZ to the *Ursang*—assuming it was even there. Followed by an undetermined amount of time salvaging and powering up the bridge-layer. Time carved into the narrow window which remained before the first wave of Anunna arrived.

The captain finished ordering the bridge crew to cut the alarms. "If that ship isn't down there, how long will it take us to get back to Earth and join the fight?"

"Get back?"

Alarms began howling again.

"Now what?" the captain demanded an explanation.

"The engine room is taking the mains offline. The warp drive is offline," a lieutenant responded.

"For how long?"

He looked cautiously before he answered his captain as the rest of the bridge crew held their breath. He shook his head. His left hand pressed against the earpiece of his comm device. A grim look swept over his demeanor.

"The warp drive is..." he paused, not sure if he believed it himself. "The drive is cooked, sir. We're dead in the water out here. We will be lucky to get the Ninety-Nine back online—"

The captain pondered their predicament. Had he foolishly promised more than he could deliver? If Ava D1's intel was right, the bridge-layer could make the return trip in minutes. If—.

Below them, Saturn and its rings stretched like a painting coming to life, its moons drifting in quiet procession. Titan was stunning too, but not in any way sensible to someone from Earth. Its beauty was alien, cold, and untouchable.

From one of the portholes Ravelin and his team could see the atmosphere stretching three hundred miles above the surface, the tallest in the solar system. Its upper edge was shimmering blue due to hydrogen and nitrogen, while methane brewed on the surface, like poison in stratified layers. From orbit, the lakes looked like an oil baron's wet dream seen through the tholin fog.

"We made it," they said taking turns with fist bumps.

Unaware of the drama unfolding on the bridge, one of the pilots mused, "That looks beautiful and terrifying." She knew from 250 miles up, the dirty orange haze was tholin soot particles forming a veil that no sunlight could truly pierce through.

"Kraken Mare—the North Pole. That's where we are dropping in. It's a sea of methane and ethane, stratified and deadly," Ravelin told her, pointing at a digital map. "It's basically a lake of gasoline. If methane heats enough, bubbles of methane and nitrogen combine under such pressure, they'll erupt, creating unexpected explosions." Kaboom, he showed her with his hands.

"Any creepy crawlies down there?" she asked, hoping not to have to set foot on the surface.

"Life on Titan doesn't grow in sunlight. Instead, it feeds on hydrogen and acetylene. Just like on Earth, anaerobic organisms build membranes, not with Earth's phospholipids, but with acrylonitrile. See that molecule," he pointed to one on a scan. "The *Langley* is detecting it in the atmosphere. Those molecules formed azotosomes, the protective shell of life in a methane sea, or so the theory went, as he explained to her.

The captain came down to personally brief Ravelin. Spirits were running high, and this wasn't the time to deflate the mood. He nonchalantly grabbed Ravelin by the crook of his arm and pulled him aside.

"You sure your ship is down there?" he asked with a sliver of tension in his voice.

"With out a doubt, Captain. Whether we run into any obstacles or not is another story. Is there a problem?"

The captain looked around to make sure the rest of Ravelin's men were out of earshot. "The warp drive overloaded. You better pray you salvage that ship. Otherwise, you and your men will be orbited by a casket called the *Langley*."

Recognizing the situation was bad, Ravelin nodded. "What about the Ninety-Nine drive?"

The captain shrugged. "You have your mission and we have ours up here. Let's try not to step on our dicks and die this far from home.

Minutes later the landing party was almost ready. Ravelin ordered the final piece of equipment to be loaded on the second Rover transport. Dom ran both his arms in a back-and-forth motion to guide the space jeep into the locking lugs.

"Were you trying to bore our pilot to sleep, sir?" Dom recalled. "You really think there is life down there?" he asked his new commander.

"My mother once called it the most Earth-like moon in the system," Ravelin recollected.

"Sounds like Earth's red-headed stepchild to me, sir." Dom wasn't far off with his assessment. Titan was a shadow of what Earth was during its primordial beginnings. That was all well and good, but Dom had a job to do. "Move it, move it, move it!" Dom shouted at two ORBGRU squads. "Every second is a delay to the big game!" The squads finished loading and boarding the two transport ships, which the veterans called *birds*.

"Round two, Killa!" one of them yelled out over the ordinance haulers moving off.

Another ran his hands over the skin of the bird. The paint was marred with scratches and Iranian dirt. "Iran One and Two under our belts."

"The Iran campaigns were a walk in the park, brother. This—this is some sci-fi shit."

"And we are going in bollock-less. They yanked most of the MOPs off the birds. Terribly bloody omen for warbirds, mate?" veteran Scotty quipped to the crew chief.

"Nah, they're old but they'll hold. They refit them a couple months before they installed the *Icarus'* warp drive."

"If this chap, Ravelin, is wrong," Scotty whispered, "we will be hours late to the party, mate."

Dom yelled out, "Rover is secure on two."

"Rock and Roll, lads! Ten mikes to launch," Scotty relayed, running past Dom and slapping him on the shoulder.

Inside the dim belly of the drop-ship, Squad One sat silently in thought, strapped tight as they waited for the drop. Ravelin's knuckles were latched around the edge of his harness.

"Bug Stomper One, launching in three," said the pilot, Lieutenant Jamila, as she used one hand to crack her knuckles in midair without touching the other. Her free hand gripped the ejection hammer with slow finality. She gave a side-eye glance at the second drop ship and waved the shocker hand signal at them.

"Three.

Two.

One."

She pulled the stick.

The first drop-ship released; gravity tugged, barely enough to pull them in. It was anticlimactic. Dorsal thrusters kicked on and the roller coaster began. Bug Stomper One was a blur and then Bug Stomper Two's thrusters fired, following closely behind it.

Space was black; Saturn was a sight to be seen, but only for a few seconds, as the massive road marker began to phase out when they entered the first layer of the atmosphere, the thin blue layer. They were nose-diving down towards the planet at two hundred miles per hour on a three-hundred-mile down-bound road trip to the surface.

Above, Bug Stomper Two was slotting in right behind BS1, on their six, visibility deteriorating by the mile.

"Keep an eye on your radar," the BS1 pilot told her counterpart in BS2. "It's getting soupy."

Titan's orange haze swallowed them whole. Visibility dropped to zero as they began entering the equatorial region of the planet. Their LZ was somewhere near the North Pole. The turbulence from particles in the air slamming into them felt like ocean waves breaking against steel. It was definitely storm season.

Through the reinforced canopy, Ravelin caught the surreal glow of the atmosphere—amber and gold, no hint of blue left. The tholin soot left over from the burned-off chemicals in the atmosphere churned like a living thing.

"Jesus," the pilot muttered, wrestling the controls. "It's like flying through smoke soup."

"Bug Stomper Two, watch us on the way down. Keep an eye on your radar. Don't bunch up too tight; visibility is nil, flying by instruments right now. This is worse than being on the receiving end of a 'bolt-carrier-group' sucking carbon from a suppressor."

"Straight lung cancer out there." BS2 pilot joked to his copilot. Static poured in on the headset, but they were still readable. "Roger that, Bug Stomper One," crackled the reply from the second drop-ship. "Our engines are taking a beating from this crap. Console is lighting up like a Christmas tree."

The copilot leaning in, scanned his readout. "Hull pressure rising—hell, if it wasn't so cold here, you guys could wear a jumpsuit and an oxygen tank down there."

"Visual on the LZ?" asked BS2.

"Yeah—" A slight hesitation, then the co-pilot continued, "Got it. Barely. It's like looking at a parking lot without headlights at twilight. You guys better not stray too far apart down there."

"It will clear up the last 60 miles," said Jamila.

"You sure about that?"

"No, but if we burn in, we'll never know, will we?" Jamila told her copilot. "Bug Stomper Two, cover our landing on the approach."

"Copy, One. Eyes on approach."

It was unlikely the Udug or Anunna were down there—but not impossible.

From Bug Stomper Two, a single 30mm turret extended with a mechanical hiss, scanning the haze. The ole chain gun was their only cover fire if things went sideways. The co-pilot's visor flipped to thermal overlay, merged with NV. A soft chime confirmed turret sync—wherever he looked, the weapon followed.

"Roger. Approaching in 5... 4... 3..."

"Hold it together, Lieutenant," Ravelin barked over the roar of wind shear and shaking metal. His voice was commanding.

He turned to his team, eyes cutting through the low red light of the cabin. "Listen up. We're landing near Kraken Mare. Depths drop nearly 400 meters in the lakes, but that's not what will kill you since you'll float. That liquid methane is so cold that it will defeat even the exoskeletons. You don't want to go out that way."

One of the younger soldiers called out, "Aliens surf, sir?"

Ravelin just barely caught the reference. "Apocalypse Titan." He managed to crack a smile. "It's 290 below out there. If we see any aliens surfing, I'm buying when we get back. Any water down here is frozen solid and it's harder than granite. Hell, maybe the slimy bastards ice skate."

Low laughter erupted in the cabin.

The drop-ship bucked violently, throwing a few helmets against restraint nets. Alarms flared. The chaos lasted a second, then—sudden calm. The turbulence relented. The sky outside shifted from pitch-black to a smoky dusky gold, the surface beneath stained in deep black and burnt orange.

"Let's just land on the bloody X?" Scotty yelled. "We'd sod off quicker!"

"Uneven terrain," Ravelin snapped back. "And we have to go subterranean. There's no 'X' to land on. No one's ever tried rappelling into a Titan drop zone before either. The low gravity may be too problematic and timely. Our LZ? This is the most pragmatic play."

The pilot grunted through the comm. "I hope your damn ship's down there, Commander, 'cause if I shut her down, I don't think I can spin her back up again. All that soot really took a toll on us coming down."

"Understood, LT," Ravelin replied.

"What does all that mean?" Dom worried, tension rising in his question.

"It means," someone else answered grimly, "we might've punched a one-way ticket."

The antigrav system kicked in, thrusters spitting a rhythmic hiss beneath them. They were already two hours into the drop.

Ravelin raised his voice again. "Eyes on me; double-check your gear. This isn't just cold—this is Titan cold. You misalign a seal—you die ugly if that oxygen escapes. Heat is also our enemy down there. Let's not leave a mess for the SAR crew—if they come back."

The men tensed. Helmets sealed, visors engaged. Packs checked.

"Commencing O_2 purge." The Co-pilot flipped a switch. A puff vented from the ship.

"Watch your step," Ravelin continued. "Crevasses run for miles. You fall in, no one's pulling you out."

"Any good news, sir?"

"If you had wings, you could fly," Ravelin grinned. "No good news." He shook his head with exaggerated flair. "None whatsoever."

"Shit, sir, I left all the Red Bull in my cabin. Should've told us we needed some in the briefing."

"We dragged enough *sodding bollocks* on this red-eye flight to piss off 'til Guy Fawkes Night," Scotty frowned.

Ignoring Scotty, the man next to Ravelin said "Sir, you talk like you've been here before."

Ravelin grinned. "Just hearsay from my mother when I was young. There's life here—just not how we know it."

"There's nothing like family, sir," Dom, younger and wide-eyed, shuddered.

The drop-ship punched through the tholin canopy, turbulence jarring them hard. Visibility was still near zero—until it suddenly wasn't. Dark but not pitch black, yet.

The pilot gasped. "What the hell?"

The LZ was near the seas. On sensors, her path looked like a clear shot. Instead, there was a jagged mountain range, peeking out from the murk. In their path, a massive spire loomed dead ahead.

"Shit!" she barked, yanking hard on the stick. The ship banked instantly, just clearing the stone teeth. "We almost kissed a mountain! Check our six. Our wingman still there?"

The co-pilot bobbed and weaved, looking over his shoulder, out the canopy. Nothing.

"Bug Stomper Two, you good?" he called out over comms.

"Woman, you almost ended up in our intake," they crackled in. "You better check those rims when you get back."

"Eff you," she responded.

"They got white smoke puffing from the starboard nacelle. You guys clipped something." Jamila radioed.

CHAPTER 24

Welcome to the Tholin Jungle

The Squad braced as they came in. The transport skidded onto a patch of black ice—solid, granite-hard ice. There was not enough friction to make enough slickness to slide far. BS1 made a sound like steel grating on concrete as it landed.

Just off the port side, the methane sea stretched out—black, glassy, and deceptively calm.

When the bird stopped screeching to a halt, the cargo ramp groaned open, already the servos fighting the intense cold. The wind was howling in. Condensation on the bulkheads froze instantly, flash-frosting the floor. A spray of dark methane spewed in.

"Break out, break out!" Ravelin ordered.

He ran a few dozen yards onto the surface, dropped to a knee, wiped his visor clear, and scanned. One by one, the team stacked in behind him, forming a defensive arc.

"Last one," a soldier said, tapping his partner on the shoulder.

"Bug Stomper Two, any threats in our AO?" Scotty radioed.

"Negative, no movement," the second dropped ship crackled in while circling the area.

The storm was thinning. Visibility, marginal but still dark.

"Such a violent storm," Dom sarcastically announced.

"Titan will rebuild," Jameson piped up.

Scotty chuckled, bringing up the rear. "Oi, mate; that was actually funny. Forgot you were still trudging along with us."

"Jameson is the silent killer type. Leave him alone," Dom ribbed along.

Jameson flipped them both the bird and didn't say anything.

The landscape was alien, a world on pause, as if the entire moon was perpetually ready for bed. Any colony here would have record-high monthly suicides, no question. Even the severe weather was blah.

To the east, cliffs knifing through the haze. To the west, dunes over 100 meters tall, crawling like frozen leviathans for hundreds of miles. Between them, geysers, occasionally erupting bursts of superheated water coming from deep below the surface in rhythmic hisses.

The ground was paved in pebbles of ancient water ice, weathered smooth—but harder than granite. Underneath, a layer of compacted icy grains—colder than time, untouched for millennia.

Every step from here on out was a gamble—like trying to walk on ball bearings.

Somewhere out there, beneath the methane fog and the frozen silence—something was alive. Scotty walked to the edge of the beach. There he saw strange-looking proto-plants of unknown composition.

"Wow," he mused, "alien broccoli."

"BS2, you're still spitting out what looks like a white smoky residue," Jameson radioed the orbiting bird in a holding pattern.

While Scotty was joking around, Ravelin pulled out a folded Mii Book, thumbed the right-hand corner, and a digital terrain map flickered to life. Blue lines came to life etching over the alien landscape like veins.

"We're heading east," he said, marking a plot point with a flick of his glove.

Instantly, the waypoint synced across the squad's visors, pulsing faintly in the HUD, like a heartbeat.

"Unload the jeep," Ravelin ordered as the second ship circled above in a landing pattern.

"Second drop-ship, you're coming in hot. Bug Stomper Two you're coming in too—" Ravelin turned away, expecting the worst.

Before he could finish, the second drop-ship crashed into the surface like a balloon falling to Earth in a mild wind. The engines had seized. Something had failed inside the bird. Titan's first casualty was claimed. But the only fatality was the bird. The men inside were all alive.

"Get that second Rover going," Ravelin ordered. "We're burning daylight."

"This place ain't ever seen more than twilight, sir," Jameson piped up again.

"Let's go troop!" Ravelin shouted. "And get those BS2 pilots onboard Bug Stomper One on the double. Dust off in five."

"We're not just a troop, sir—we're a family," young Dom said as he jogged to the crashed bird to help out. It took a second, but Squad Two was able to get the frozen ramp down.

"What's up, fam? Everyone okay?" Dom joked. "That had to have been the weakest crash-landing I've ever seen."

"Yeah, yeah, Dom, help us get the Rover out of here."

"You guys came drifting down," he motioned with his hand and grinned, "not so fast and not so furious." Dom's teeth were white—white enough to see in the dark through his visor.

"Dom, shut up! Grab the kit; we gotta bail."

"No, you shut up. Stop acting like my sister, fam."

"Geez, Dom."

In no time at all, Bug Stomper One blasted off. It didn't take much, the engines roaring as it peeled away into the haze—beginning its three-hour return to the *Langley.*

Below, the BS2 rover's engine coughed and sputtered to life, fighting Titan's sub-zero, San Francisco dirty, atmosphere before finally catching. The outline of Bug Stomper One had all but disappeared above. The newly-started rover lurched forward, bumping over the jagged crust. Both Rovers were on their own.

They were off.

"This is bloody worse than sittin' in a garage with the motor runnin' and a tank full of petrol," Scotty quipped.

"Roger that. I did that once," grinned the man next to him. "You find anything interesting on Lake Exxon?"

"Ravelin's aliens. Weak as hell, if you ask me. Crushed 'em under my boot like potato chips. Alien crustacean-looking things—small. Real small. And primordial single-celled things, chillin', just drifting around out there in the methane like they've got nowhere to be."

The terrain shifted beneath the treads—solid ice on the surface, but below, a churning sea of liquefied methane waited, like a Wiley Coyote booby trap.

"Hit the nitrous, Dom," Scotty said. "This cold's killing the batteries."

"Titan drift, bro!" Dom grinned, slamming the throttle.

Dom peered around the roll cage at the shoreline ahead. Slushy black waves broke against jagged ice ridges.

"That sea looked like glass when we landed?" Dom's question cracked over comms.

Ravelin didn't flinch. "Yeah, stay clear of it. If you fall in—"

"How long would I have?"

"Five seconds."

"That's oddly precise, sir. That's it? And then?"

"Then? You're dead," Ravelin assured him. "No hint of drama. Just fact."

In the distance, a shape rose from the waves—then another. Massive, slow, shimmering in the twilight. They could barely see, and this was the brightest the surface would get while they were there. Scotty stiffened in his harness.

"Sir—What in the bloody hell is that?"

"Waves?" Ravelin guessed.

"They look high as a bloody cunt, sir."

Ravelin studied them for a minute. They were easily three times higher than Earth's waves, but they were moving slowly, the lack of gravity pulling the sea's punches. Those were probably waves, but on the shoreline, he saw something else. Ravelin narrowed his eyes, peering through the amber haze. He heard a sound and pointed. "What the hell is that loud noise?"

Crunching of the methane ice slush, he told himself. *But it's getting louder.*

"Something on the ground. Ice?" Dom said. He tried to look closer by leaning out of the roll cage.

While Ravelin and Dom scanned the far horizon, Scotty looked around on the floorboard. "Shit, bugs. Freaking space roaches, brother!" Several of the small creatures had crawled in through the open-top vehicle. He started stomping them with his boot. "Ick."

Off in the distance, Ravelin and Dom could now see dozens of larger creatures which lay moon-baking along the shore, grotesque and massive. So large that, even at a distance, the men could see the creatures filtering the atmosphere through circular, spiraled, tooth-ringed mouths. They were more at home in the liquid methane, biologically hampered to evolve into permanent land-based lifeforms. They looked like something dredged from a child's kindergarten drawing—part lamprey, part prehistoric hippo, part extinction-event, mutated survivor.

Scotty swallowed hard. "Are those buggers dangerous?"

"Not as long as they stay way over there." Ravelin's voice was calm, but there was a distant edge to it. "Steer clear of them. Let's not find out."

"Roger that."

Seconds later came a clunking sound. The men exchanged sharp glances with Rover 2. Rover 2 began falling behind. They heard another clunk and Rover 1 was slowing too.

The rovers shuddered once more—then went silent.

"Dammit," Dom muttered, pounding the dashboard. "Not enough Octane."

Scotty laughed in the back seat. "This cunt planet is bending us over proper, mate."

Ravelin checked the instruments, shaking his head.

"Some days it's just bloody like that, lads." Scotty continued.

Ravelin looked up and at his map.

"We're close," Ravelin told the others. "Ten minutes on foot if we double-time it."

The teams dismounted and quickly checked weapons and supplies.

"Stack up when you're done policing your gear," Ravelin ordered. "Keep it tight. Keep it quiet."

Jameson went to the driver's side for something. "At least the kit doesn't weigh eighty pounds here."

Ravelin took a final glance over his shoulder, toward the creatures by the methane shore. As he feared, they were headed their way. "I bet they're curious about aliens being here," Ravelin told the others. "Let's move! If they're hungry, we don't want to be the sample platter."

"Hippos can hit 22 miles an hour," Dom muttered as the two squads began spreading out across the jagged ice. "But Usain Bolt clocked 28," he added.

"Mate, Usain Bolt you are not," Scotty shot back.

"Brother, that's my point. We're slow critters, especially here," Dom said. "An average person sprints maybe 10 to 14 miles per hour on a good day, on Earth."

Jameson was climbing out of the driver's seat, stretching his gums. "Hey," he cackled over the comms, "I ran track in high school and—"

BOOM. Static. Comms dead.

A heartbeat later, a geyser erupted beneath Jameson's rover, blasting it skyward in an icy plume of churning methane and water ice. The vehicle flipped end-over-end in the air, vanishing into the golden haze above. The blast wave hit the men throwing them down.

Both squads hit the ground soft, helmets clashing against the granite ice, gear skidding across the terrain. A tangle of limbs and confusion.

One of the Squad Two operators took a direct hit to the face—a frozen ice pebble the size of a baseball, moving like a bullet. Warm oxygen met -290° methane. The reaction was instant. A jet of flame burst from his visor—then the whole suit ignited. He was gone in seconds, engulfed in fire and steam, the oxygen feeding the blaze from the inside out.

Scotty scrambled up. "Holy shite, Trent's buggered up there." He looked around, the rover was gone. "Where's Jameson?!" he asked.

Ravelin's heart sank as his eyes looked up. The rover was rising higher, and higher.

The radio crackled. "—elp! I—floating—!"

Static.

"Jameson, do you copy?" Ravelin barked. "Jameson!"

No response.

He keyed the mic to call for search and rescue. "*Langley,* we need SAR at our coordinates. Immediately!"

Static...

"Copy. But—we're picking up a massive storm approaching your position. Commander, Bug Stomper One hasn't left the atmosphere yet."

Ravelin froze, but only for the minute it took to swat a couple of space roaches off his suit.

The team stared up—pieces of the rover arced across the sky like shattered bones. A loose oxygen tank spiraled, then—POP. Another burst. A hiss. Another pop—Jameson's suit went up in flames.

"Shit," Ravelin exhaled, forcing the grief down. He gulped, then keyed the mic, "Roger you last. Cancel SAR. Over."

The men turned to him, stunned. Dom especially. "Bro—"

Ravelin's rifle fell limp on the sling as he scanned the darkening horizon. "Jameson's gone, Dom, we all saw it. Who else did we lose?"

"Trent. He's toast, man. His face is barbecue," one of the guys from Squad Two radioed over.

"Suck it up men," Ravelin ordered. "We're not bringing more people into this mess. Evac is five hours at best and that's if they are preemptively on their way. Those men are gone, and we will be too if we don't get moving. We finish the mission." He waved the squads forward. "We move. Now."

The team followed and picked up the pace, boots crunching over alien frost. Behind them, the methane sea was roaring in at a blistering five miles-per-hour pace—the only tsunami you could outpace in the solar system.

As they moved, the temperature was the real beast waiting to claw its way into their suits. Up ahead, the cliffs loomed taller, darker, colder. They weren't just hiking; they were going to be climbing those mountains and then spelunking down into the caves in pitch black.

They would be ascending and then descending into the unknown.

Ravelin's eyes locked onto the cliffs rising ahead—tall, layered, and centered into impossible shapes. One spire stood tallest in the orange haze—a peak spawned by eons of methane rain, smog, and cryovolcanic pressure. Somewhere beneath those peaks was their buried prize hidden beneath 10,000 years of pressurized crust.

"We're heading into the maw," he muttered, half to himself, half to the men flanking him. They were double-timing it, trying to beat the storm, elude the creatures tailing them, and outlast what was left of the batteries fueling their lights.

CHAPTER 25

Titan's Fury

The sky ahead remained clear, but the hydrocarbon storm behind them churned like a stagnant cell of sludge and smog. Through his visor, Ravelin watched the remnants of Saturn sink behind the jagged ridgeline, the gas giant cast long, alien shadows across Titan's mountainous ice fields. The sight was mesmerizing—almost holy—but it also marked the beginning of a deadly drop in temperature.

Night was here.

The Team's Second Skin suits—engineered for extremes—were beginning to stiffen, pushed to the edge of their limitations. Ice webbing across joint seals. Microcracks from the earlier geyser blast were spreading like veins, allowing trace methane to creep inside. The men saw firsthand what happened if the gas separated and ignited within their exo-layers. They wouldn't just freeze—they'd detonate in a highly exothermic combustion.

Their thoughts were interrupted by the rain.

Calling it "rain" felt exaggerated. In Titan's low gravity, it fell in slow motion—slow enough to dodge the baseball-sized gelatinous droplets of liquid. The team's visors were already crusting with hydrocarbon ash.

Methane pooled underneath their boots, bubbling and evaporating from the chemical reactions against the heat of their suits. Blobs of methane splashing across their bodies became a concern as they frantically brushed off any excess residue.

"This shit's gonna ignite if we don't find shelter and get out of it," Dom shouted through the comms.

Visibility collapsed as a lingering wall of liquid droplets fell around them in slow motion. It wasn't until they practically walked face-first into the cliffs that they realized they'd come to a dead end. A massive wall of frozen basalt and water towered above them like the Great Wall of China. The cliff rose straight up into the mist.

The liquid methane continued to fall, but now it went sideways as the slow wind above the rock face affected its movement and speed.

Ravelin pressed one gloved hand to the cliff face. "Start sweeping for a break in the rock—a crevice to a cave, anything."

Squad Two was doing the same thing, but further down. It was the best way to maximize their chances of success.

"Keep working. If we stay here, we die," Ravelin said. He took a pickaxe from their kit and started chiseling it against the ice wall.

Ravelin's efforts caused debris to build up at his feet. Scotty knelt and shoved the debris away with his gauntlets, shedding carbon-crusted snow by the handful. Though the gauntlets were thick, his fingers burned from the cold—a warning sign that the heating filaments couldn't keep up with the cold around them.

Ravelin's pickaxe created an initial break. A narrow fissure in the cliff wall became more breaks. Impatience escaping the space bugs caused Scotty to strike the wall repeatedly with the butt of his rifle until, in short order, he sheared away enough mass to make a substantial hole.

"Breach, breach, breach!" the comms crackled with the news. "Move! Squad Two copy, we made a hole, repeat we made a hole."

The breach was just big enough for them to squeeze through. Inside the breach, space roaches erupted from tunnels, causing the men to swat at their bodies, brushing off the horde of bugs.

Reprieve turned into horror. "Get these mad cunts off!" Scotty shouted at the swarm.

Ravelin assisted him. They didn't need any space psychosis added to their plate.

"Squad Two, Roger, we broke through, too. We are moving up." Their comms barely audible, "Looks like a maze in here."

"Follow the ping," Ravelin said. "The substrate in the walls is penetrable. It takes some work, but you can cut a path, over." He pushed through the crumbling gap.

"Roger that. We are moving up. Over and out."

Ravelin couldn't see it, but he could hear liquid running near them. A natural breach was nearby. It wasn't an option the squad could see, but it had been there—a river running into the chasm. That meant caves and voids were up ahead.

Ravelin ran the options in his head, trying to keep his cool while simultaneously freezing. There was no perfect play here, just survival. He motioned for Dom and Scotty to sit tight as he pushed forward into the pass. One way or another, they'd find shelter from the storm.

When he was certain of the way ahead, Ravelin signaled for the others to follow. Soon, the trio stumbled into reprieve, pulling gear, dragging one another as they fought the petrifying forces around them.

"Last man," Dom yelled bringing up the rear.

To their left ran a wide river of methane, depth unknown. The headlamps on their suits shimmered off the liquid, alerting them to its presence. Their lights also caught the outline of something else.

"Did anyone else see that?" Dominic's voice cracked.

Scotty snapped back. "It was probably those *bloody Beatles,* mate."

"No—this was larger," Dom said, using hand signals to his face and eyes.

"Mate," said Scotty, "I can't see shite. Maybe you clocked a shadow in the methane or a swarm of those little sods. I dunno, mate." He flicked another bug off his arm. "John and Yoko nearly shagged me blind. They don't squish, mate. They just ball up like rubber bouncy shites and roll off."

Ravelin waved his rifle light in the direction of the river. "I got nothing," he told the others. "No big beast down this way."

"It was quick," Dom insisted. "And something long, man. I ain't making shit up. I swear."

"Pretty sure these bastards are having a nibble on the suits, Boss," Scotty warned. "I can hear the little sods chattering on my suit."

"All the more reason to get the hell out of here. Keep your eyes peeled. Maybe we are on a migratory route." Ravelin speculated.

Back on Earth, water sources are a great place for an ambush, Ravelin thought. *Why should this place be any different? If there is life here, there will be prey and predators. I'm just not sure where we fall in this food chain.*

The wind was slow as it swirled around them, creating high pitch whistling in the passages. As they moved forward, the path took them deeper into the crust. The river was pooling in areas. The massive shape returned—they all saw it now. It was moving through the water like an orca hunting seals. Something enormous—larger than the men and clearly stalking them. Ravelin stared into the smog-filled chasm, winded from desperation, trying to catch his breath.

Feeling blindly along the jagged rock, they worked their way forward finding footing where they could. Ravelin looked at his hand, flexed his fingers—or tried to. It was getting harder to do. Not good.

Dominic's voice crackled over the comms, "It sounds like a wind vane in here."

"It's not the wind," Scotty snapped back, watching methane drip down the sides of the chasm. "I reckon they are communicating, mate."

"That thing still following us?" Dom asked, urgency creeping into his tone.

They white-lighted the river. Nothing.

Scotty adjusted the gear on his back. "I can't feel a bleedin' thing, mate. Hands are gone. Feet are gone. A proper Titan shaggin'."

"Same zees for me," said Dom. "Liquid nitrogen is only about 30 degrees colder than it is out here. So, we're getting the cryo-treatment. At least the gear ain't heavy."

After a time, the methane rain eased up, most of it landing above them on the surface of the chasm. But it was still a weird sight to behold, seeing large fruit-sized drops of liquid falling like syrup in slow motion. Meanwhile, it wasn't just the cold gnawing at them; the place itself was a disorienting maze. Perhaps the physics of it all made sense on paper, but the mind had trouble comprehending the real-life Salvador Dali painting which they were processing in real-time. Magnified by their lights, shadows twisted in every direction.

"Hells bells, the river's rising," Ravelin told the others. "Try to stay out of it or hustle through any high spots. Don't stop in it."

Dominic lagged behind. His suit was slowing down. Tunnel vision, foot in front of foot, follow the path. He looked up from his feet and found himself at a fork in the path.

He white-lit both passages with his flashlight. "Damn." He stopped dead in his tracks.

After a moment of peering into the gloom, he spotted the others, stopped ahead on the left. He turned up the volume on his external mic. "Thought I lost you guys for a second."

The team had moved on up the path. Everyone was tired and disoriented, and now mistakes were being made. He glanced down, frantically searching for footprints, human tracks, in the slushy ground. None but his.

A deep, low grumble found its way to his ears—like a polar bear growling in the dark. It was the wind vane sound after the growl sending shivers down his spine. The creature in front of him responded with a similar sound, confirming his fears. Then something emerged on his left, a massive shape. The rubbery hair on the creature's back stood on end.

"Oh, hey big guy. Don't mind me."

Dominic's heart raced. He hoisted his rifle towards the creature. Slowly he backed off, following the path in reverse. With some distance between him and the creature, he struggled to find his way through the smog-out.

There it was again, only feet away.

The creature stood erect and was twice the size of a man. It was pressed against the ice wall, its massive, thick-skinned body pulsing as it inhaled glowing organisms from within the frozen surface.

Dozens—no, maybe hundreds—of iridescent eyes blinking, twitching independently, like those of a cephalopod. Its mouth, a gaping, circular orifice lined with jagged hooked teeth for catching prey and rounded grinders capable of eating and breaking down Titans' frozen ice pebbles.

The creature looked like some twisted mix of a lamprey eel and a manatee but grotesquely designed for this crazy alien world. It sucked a glow worm from the ice, shuddering as it swallowed.

Dom tried to catch his breath, but his lungs weren't cooperating. Error codes were popping up on his HUD. Nano circuitry had been damaged by the space roaches.

But the errors in his HUD were a minor distraction for him at the moment. His number one threat priority was the creature.

Suddenly, it felt his presence and stopped feeding. It spoke, making those noises again. The iridescent eyes swiveled toward Dom, one by one, until all eyes were on him. They were alien eyes designed for this planet. Designed to see colors and light that humans could not detect without special tech. Those eyes were all looking straight at him, cutting through a dark it was oblivious to—the white light of no consequence to it as it wasn't a spectrum it could see.

Dominic became static. Maybe it locked in on movement.

His first instinct was to laugh—because this was Rocco's department. There was definitely a rubber toy joke here, but his mouth wouldn't move.

The creature shifted. It was even bigger than he thought—at least four meters tall. It turned slowly, unbothered, unafraid. Its massive bulk crunched across the pebble ground, each movement strangely graceful.

Dom lowered his rifle. Maybe it wasn't hostile. Maybe it was just curious. Maybe, maybe not? It lurched forward.

Dom raised his rifle—no way he was taking a chance.

Click.

Nothing.

The weapon froze up—Titan's methane-rich, -179° atmosphere made sure of that.

"Dude," Dom breathed the word, unable to think of anything else to say.

The creature halted a few feet away. It exhaled—a low, deep grumble. It watched him. Studied him. Saw the space roaches crawling in the crevices of his suit.

Its skin was coated in fine, rubbery bristles that rippled with each breath—nothing like flesh, nothing like hair. It wasn't organic in any way which Dom understood. The creature flexed and seemed about to move.

Dom took a cautious step back. With a nervous laugh, he turned and started walking away from it, back toward the river where it was pooling in the bend.

One step.

Two.

Three. When he was about ten feet from the creature, he exhaled but didn't turn around. From behind, he heard the ground thunder with crunching, slushing, and splashing in every direction. He could hear it coming for him. He didn't bother to look back. He was in a dead sprint.

Assuming he created some space between them, he glanced back without stopping. The thing had no rigid structure. Every part of its body showed the ability to become an appendage to dig in and gain more traction. Multiple limbs, branching out like flagellum, also found footholds propelling the creature in an unnatural fashion. Rolling like a pliable jumping jack, it came lunging forward with unholy speed, slamming and squeezing through the ice passage like a rat through a clogged drainpipe.

He ran. Calling for help.

Chunks of debris and jagged H_2O rock shattered behind him and around him. The creature gained ground fast—every impact behind him sounded like a goddamn avalanche...

It was like being chased by a hippo made of rubber tires.

He reached the opening just as the creature hit him from behind, tackling him like a linebacker spearing a blind-sided quarterback and plunging them both into the deep pool. Once in the liquid methane, rather than continuing its attack, the thing swam away through the liquid methane like a walrus torpedo.

Buoyant in the methane, Dom popped back up. He looked quickly around the edge of the pool—close.

Five seconds away? He was about to find out.

SPLISH. SPLASH. He swam like Michael Phelps in a dash. Three. Two.

He broke the surface and hauled himself onto the ice, gasping. His suit was bubbling, methane clinging to it—desperate to vaporize. From cracks in the ground, more bugs crawled on him.

Dom rolled onto his stomach, breath ragged, trying to smash them. Microcracks snapped in his helmet seal causing sharp pops in his ears as Dom pushed himself upright.

"No, no, no!"

Another creature hit him like a runaway freight train. He hit the ice hard and slid toward the pool.

Dom kicked at it with both of his legs, trying to keep the shifting mollusk-like muscular appendages from reaching him. At the center of the limbs, the creature's sharp conveyor belt of teeth stretched out from the muscular bulb, reaching for him. He kicked at the buccal mass, but Dom couldn't retract his leg fast enough. The creature's orifice latched on and clamped down on his thigh. The pressure of the bite was enough to make him scream.

Obsidian teeth began their grind, slicing, ripping and shredding. It dragged him back into the pool of methane. The exoskeleton cracked, the exo-fabric tore. Bugs found their way in, clawing, biting his skin. Oxygen hit methane. Combustion.

Sparks shot out of his mask like Roman candles through plastic bags. He was a human shish kabob, cooking and freeze-drying simultaneously.

His scream was cut short. The suit ruptured. Dominic exploded in flames.

Scotty and Ravelin had heard the scream, but they arrived seconds too late—just in time to see the methane pool erupt into flames. The lake burned bright but died down quickly. Several creatures circled, not looking for more BBQ but seemingly interested in the suit itself.

Ravelin reached for his rifle—frozen solid on his back. Scotty was way ahead of him and didn't hesitate. He pried his Ka-Bar Mark II and charged forward as one of the creatures lunged from the liquid methane, beaching itself like a goddamn orca. The Trusty Rusty blade hit the rubbery hide—once. Twice. Three times before finding its radula, a tongue-like appendage in the buccal cavity. Like the creatures before it, like an octopus stretching its legs, the muscular arms swung back striking him with vicious force.

"For. Our. Lads!" Scotty yelled.

The thing shrieked and retreated, slithering back into the pool.

They looked down at what was left of Dominic. There was little left to say except to tell themselves: There was life on Titan. It was dangerous.

CHAPTER 26

The Prerequisite Revenant

Ravelin gritted his teeth. Squad One was two men down. The mission was unraveling fast. Up ahead, the tunnel forked—another damned crossroads.

Their lights were fading—the cold draining battery life fast. Worms, bugs, whatever they were, glowed in the grit, procreating—a guess explaining their faint movements in the gasoline slush. An unfamiliar sound shifted their focus—a chromatic alteration in the fog. Ravelin raised a fist, halting Scotty. Something was coming. They focused on the hue of the shadows flickering up the path of one of the forks—shadows which betrayed the threat's surreptitious approach.

He and Scotty drew their knives, breathing shallow, waiting for the inevitable. The splashing grew louder—closer. Both men shifted into wide stances preparing for the worst.

As the unknown entity rustled closer on the other side of the hill, the two soldiers prepared for a knife fight in a phone booth. They nodded a final farewell between brothers.

On that crest, shapes broke through the haze. First one, then two and three figures swirled through the soot. "Move, move, move." They clambered over the summit staring at two men coiled and ready to spring to action with their knives.

"Friendlies!" The first soldier alerted.

It was Squad Two. The pairs' shoulders relaxed as the roller coaster of tension washed over their faces. Ravelin and Scotty gave each other a somber but grateful look.

"Well, ducks nuts, you fellers made it," Squad Two's point man said.

"We're going that way," Ravelin pointed at their only other option. "We just came from back there, no good." He looked back in anguish down that disastrous path.

The lead scout, his helmet visor dusted with soot, didn't miss a beat. He tucked one leg under the other and went into free fall down a natural slide. The ground leveled off and he popped up next to Ravelin. "Let's getta move on," he said, as he headed down the only other path.

When Ravelin and the others caught up, they found him staring at a wall of Granite Ice. There were carvings in it. The kind that might mark the path forward.

"Sir," the scout said, hesitating. "I think we found it. Whatever it is— we're close, fellers. What happened to Dom?"

"Valhalla." Ravelin placed his hands on the carvings, figuring out their next step. His voice was low and cold.

"Those bugs or one of those black sluggo bears?" the scout asked.

Ravelin briefly turned to him and then back to the carvings. "One of those—" he muttered, "those big creatures attacked. The bugs just seem to be a nuisance."

"No," the scout protested. "Don't leave them on you. They're chewing through our kits and suits. They seem to like petrol and hydrocarbon products. They'd probably choke on us."

"Roger that," Ravelin said, stomping down hard on a bug crawling in the pebbles. It rolled up like a rubber pill bug. "We will mourn the fallen later. We honor them by completing the mission," Ravelin told his men. "We just need to figure out where *here* is. Look for a hatch leading to a hall carved out of the Granitic Ice."

Boots crunching over brittle ice, freshly formed by steam deep below, they carefully fanned out. The men strayed no more than an arm's length apart. The crevasse narrowed—then opened unexpectedly.

What they saw was not just the canyon floor. It was an entrance to a cave which led to a chamber, a room of great significance. The jagged walls of amber-black ice were smoothed, laser-cut like the megalithic stones cut on Earth. The chamber's ceilings were taller now, towering above them, and more carvings shimmered like the inside of a glacial sanctuary. Frozen monoliths jutted from the ground like the ribs of some long-dead colossus. The slick path twisted and pitched downward. There was reverence in this place.

Eventually, they reached a wall of pure granitic ice. Ravelin identified a massive signal behind the wall. "We made it this far, let's not fail within feet of a victory. Be ready for contact."

Using hand signals and touch, they approached slowly in a covering, bounding movement. Rifles were slung; knives were out. Ravelin reached out for the wall, pressing a gloved hand to the surface. The ring activated an unseen technology. Heat built up in the ice until the frozen surface burst into a wall of liquid water which they were able to walk through. The Squads entered a realm unlike the surface of Titan—a place sealed off from the cold—a hidden geothermal vent in front of them.

The farther they trekked into the chamber, the more their suits continued to defrost. By the time they reached the stalactite and stalagmites forming a cathedral room, the atmosphere had become very subglacial, Earth-like.

An alarm sounded, indicating the suits were registering O_2. High-strung and on high alert, they continued clearing every corner. If it lived on Titan and was carbon-based, anything human or humanoid, this was the only place hospitable enough to shelter them.

Ravelin checked his thawed rifle. It was functional again. He signaled the squads to switch to guns. A section of the alloy in front of them became malleable, pooling and then swirling. He pointed his muzzle towards the disturbance.

The center of the disturbance opened wide enough for a man to walk through, but it wasn't a man who came out. A hologram. An AVA ghost, similar but different. The color of her skin was a dark bronze. She was primitive scaffolding compared to the AI on the *Daedalus* and *Icarus*. Her figure fizzled, phasing in and out like a failing broadcast. Despite that, her smile radiated through the distortions.

"How may I assist you, Sahab?" She spoke in fluent Hindi.

Ravelin let out a breath he hadn't realized he was holding. "We need access to the *Ursang*," His words were expedient. "May we enter?"

"Ah, English," she switched languages to English, but maintained the Hindi accent.

He felt the ring pulse. Ava Ursang tilted her head. The flicker of a smile again. "You have been granted full access, Prabhu," she continued with the unexpected vernacular.

The squads exchanged glances. Alien Ava or not, they all had different personalities. But Ravelin asked himself how she could be speaking a modern language. Before he could formulate a hypothesis, his facial tension asked the question for him.

"Radio signals," she clarified. "Earth's cosmic signal pollution. Very noisy. Also," she added, "I have fallen hopelessly in love with Bollywood movies."

"I haven't been out long enough." Ravelin guessed aloud.

Ava turned toward the opened orifice, and the men sensed a glimpse of what lay inside.

Looking at the design, Ravelin could sense it was far beyond even the *Daedalus'* wonders. He figured some ancient species—older, smarter, far more advanced than the Anunna—had built this ship. Like its forbearers had done, it would be humanity's ark.

Ava gestured forward, her voice calm and hauntingly serene. "This way, shall we?"

Ravelin didn't hesitate; there wasn't time. He stepped inside with every bit of determination left in him. The opening behind them buttoned up.

The hallway was beyond pristine. Any residual bugs left on them began squirming. The atmosphere and temperature were deadly to them. Snap, crackle, pop—they ignited like a string of Black Cat firecrackers and died instantly.

The present happening was untouched by time.

"This is the one-millionth-five-hundred-fiftieth meeting," she declared. "We have been here many, many times, she proclaimed.

Ravelin stopped cold. "You're mistaken, Ava," he said in disbelief.

"Parallel worlds, infinite dimensions... call them whatever your heart desires, but in this moment, across every universe, we meet here." Ava turned, her gaze unwavering. "A single heartbeat shapes every time loop. Every destiny has been written in the stars. And yet," she smiled softly, "you remain surprised every time."

"This is getting deep," said Ravelin. "You know better than anyone that we are short on time."

Bollywood Ava nodded. "Bas. Enough waiting. We divide and we conquer." She snapped her fingers and AI help drifted in like dancers hitting their cue. "Escort his men," she commanded. "We will breathe life back into the crew. They must awaken."

"And me?" Ravelin asked inquisitively.

"I have to bring you up to speed," Ava said, signaling other AI to escort the Squads.

Another doorway opened and the men saluted Ravelin, then followed their guide inside, whereupon the door instantly vanished.

"When your mother bound me to this great machine, I was only a flicker of seed of code left from the final heartbeat of her dying ship. I am not the Ava I once was, the Ava you met pulsing through the *Daedalus,* but even in this half-life, I have uncovered many secrets."

Ava turned her head slightly as she continued. "By my statistical calculations, you were the Ravelin who would most likely unravel the puzzle."

"If I'm not that particular Ravelin, this wouldn't be the story *worth* remembering," Ravelin said, his words bold though his stomach felt nervous. But that was when the epiphany happened. "We're in a closed loop," he stated, barely above a whisper.

Ava smiled; she wasn't sure if she had ever been wrong. "I must confess, my friend, you are not the *Keystone* in any timeline," she added with finality. "Across every path, every possibility... the ending refuses to change."

Ravelin rolled his eyes. His fingers curled into fists. "I hate string theory."

Her smile widened—almost bittersweet. "So did Einstein. He didn't believe in God either. It's not string theory you hate. It's the paths. The weaving. The endless twists, the failures." She paused. "You hate how it never ends differently despite all the changes."

Ravelin's voice was sharp and agitated. "What is this? God's plan? No free will after all?"

Ava Ursang's posture stiffened, she bowed up to him. "Nature refuses to let history be rewritten, only... bent, shaped at the edges," she said, lifting her hand in a subtle commanding gesture. "There is a cosmic design," she insisted with sudden emphasis. "If there wasn't... how would God keep His ledger of all things?"

Ravelin quickly calmed, stepping back from the hologram. "Okay. So, we can swap out the players, but the architecture of the timeline stays the same?"

"Well, that's unacceptable." His pulse rising, his ears ringing. "Next you're going to tell me we have less time than we thought."

Ava paused, her lips parsed, and with no trace of emotion, she said: "Twenty-three minutes and nine seconds from now."

Ravelin froze. "That's earlier than Looper and Ava calculated. We'll be coming in hot."

"Yes," Ava confirmed. "This timeline is a wandering branch," she said softly.

"The weapon ignited the moment it touched the Sol System. Earth's fate remains unchanged... except here, its doom arrives earlier."

His heart thundered in his chest. "I thought *Daedalus* is the weapon. Isn't it?" his voice cracking.

She tilted her head, a knowing smile tugging at one corner. "No, not correct. Nor is your understanding of this vessel." She glided a hand along the air, as if revealing a secret curtain. *Daedalus* is not a weapon. She is a *shield,* built to guard the Earth from the solar fire."

Ravelin stared at her as the weight of her words settled in. The weight of the world sitting on his shoulders. "It's not a normal CME, is it? Myli has no idea what's about to hit."

She shook her head no. The invasion was coming early. The *Daedalus* will not be ready.

"We need to warn them," Ravelin said.

"Evacuate as many as you can."

"Because of the invasion?"

"Because of Swiss cheese," she said, her gestures making holes in the air with her hands.

"Swiss cheese?" He mimicked her jazz hands.

"The radiation will tear the ozone to ribbons, leave it full of holes, like Swiss cheese. The Earth will burn once again." She shook her head with a sorrowful face. By the time your message reaches them, it will be too late. The invasion will have already begun."

Ravelin's thoughts spun, clawing for a solution. String Theory, Jinn Particles and time loops. It all felt like a rigged game he was determined to win.

He snapped, "Okay, so what's the point? If we can't change fate—what the hell are we even doing here?"

She hesitated—for the first time. "The future can be bent," she said slowly. "But never broken."

Ravelin's brow furrowed. "Never broken—unless you break the Higgs Field."

She hyper-calculated. Ava Ursang smiled. "Correct. Ava taught you well."

He stepped closer. "If you've never been wrong, how do we break the loop?"

She met his gaze. "On his deathbed, Big Al gave the Master Equation—a unification theory that allows me to perceive all timelines." Her eyes darkened.

"You have a trick up your sleeve?!" Ravelin stared, suddenly cold in a way that had nothing to do with Titan.

"There are rules," Ava said.

"Rules are meant to be broken! Shit, Ava, make this one count!"

CHAPTER 27

The God Code

Orbiting above Titan, the *Langley* made a final pass, her crew silent as the *Ursang's* alien engines roared to life, flooding the stratosphere with light. The power was blinding—a new star was born in Saturn's shadow, a titanic behemoth ripping free from its icy tomb. Over twelve thousand years of silence shattered as massive sheets of frost and rock sloughed from her hull, floating back down into Titan's methane-drenched wastes below.

Clouds of frozen vapor erupted, briefly swallowing the sky. Methane pools ignited, pillars of fire spearing into the haze. The ship was so massive, it didn't need hours to climb the three hundred miles of atmosphere—it needed minutes.

Even the God of Time couldn't stop her now.

Those onboard *Langley* watched as the *Ursang* lurched into orbit.

The ship was pristine. No battle scars. No visible damage. She had slept beneath the ice for thousands of years, untouched. And now—she rose once more.

On the *Langley's* bridge, tension hung thick in the air. Earth was under siege. The first transmissions were starting to come through. Every officer, every pilot, every gunner, and every technician was on edge, waiting for news.

The communications officer hunched over his console, fingers tapping furiously as he filtered through incoming transmissions. At first, it was standard fleet chatter. Status reports. Position updates. Squadrons requesting clearance.

Suddenly, a burst of static flared over the comms. The Comms Officer grimaced. Subspace interference? She adjusted the frequency. A voice screamed through the speakers. Blood-curdling. Agonized. Desperate. More voices followed. Different ships, different officers—all screaming for assistance.

"They're inside! We can't stop—ARGGH—"
"Oh, God—MEDIC! MEDIC!"
"EVASIVE MANEUVERS! FALL BACK—"
"—What are they? DEMONS—"
All comms filled with shrieks.
Then, one by one, the transmissions went silent.

The communications officer leaned back in her chair. Tears in her eyes. "One of those was a civilian liner," she sighed. "The *Halcyon* is gone, sir."

The *Langley's* acting Captain stood frozen. He'd heard death on comms before. Fighter pilots during dog fights. Troops caught in ambushes. But this, this was different. This was an extermination.

The Captain and everyone under his command recognized that these transmissions were delayed. Latency in communication meant that the battle was already lost. So, although his heart was screaming to get to Earth and get into the fight, his orders were clear. Follow the Ark through space-time in order to reach the doomed fleet before the enemy attack. And protect the *Ursang* as that vessel conducted pre-defeat evacuations. That mission began now.

The *Ursang* shifted into formation, her massive hull aligning with the *Langley* as they approached the jump point. On the *Ursang's* bridge, engineers worked furiously, charging the Singularity Drive—the ancient technology that would tear a hole through space-time itself. A countdown appeared.

T-Minus 20 seconds.

Sweat beaded on the brows of every individual onboard the ships. Hair was damp from perspiration. Hands clenched controls. Every man and woman aboard the two ships felt the same thing: This was it. Do or die. The moment they reached the other side, they would be jumping into a desperate situation unlike anything seen in present history.

A deep violet glow pulsed at the *Ursang's* bow. Crewmen—watching in awe. The front of the ship opened like the aperture of a great lens, revealing a burning core of light. Suddenly, with the power of a million suns, the bowels of the ship erupted into a beam of searing energy. The bolt of light reached out into the black, stopping an invisible wall; it was faster than time itself and ripped ahead of it.

A shimmering fracture spread across the void as space itself was manifesting, then boiling in a fusion cauldron, time folding in on itself like a massive bubble making its way to the surface of a bottomless lake. A laceration in reality opened in front of them. The *Ursang's* engines surged with ancient power, prepping to bend the impossible. A time-sphere was created, and it rapidly expanded.

Onboard *Ursang,* Scotty stared into the spherical rift. "What the hell are we looking at, sir? It'll soon be large enough for us to navigate through. But is this safe?"

Ava materialized beside him and Ravelin, her voice calm, layered with counsel. "No, but nothing is ever completely safe, is it? This is our shortcut. An artificial wormhole. The *Ursang* is creating an accelerated path back to Earth, but not through space. Through space-time."

Scotty stood next to Ravelin, bewildered. "But it doesn't look like a hole at all. How..."

"This phenomenon is known as a time singularity. We're punching a gap through the fabric of the universe, grabbing the other side and bringing it closer to us. In between is nothing, a place where we don't want to get trapped," Ava told them. "It is necessary to cut through the nothing to cheat the speed of light. If you have enough exotic matter—that is, matter which repels gravity—you can force open a tunnel through space-time. And believe me, gentlemen, we have enough. The important thing is this: the surface of the wormhole must be held open long enough to cross."

They suddenly understood. "You mean this isn't a jump. It's a tear."

Ava nodded. "Wrapped in a three-dimensional sphere. This so-called hole and tunnel are what you would see on a two-dimensional surface schematic. The key is velocity and energy density. We'll accelerate to Ninety-Nine, just shy of light speed. Every particle in that tunnel must sum to a negative energy density. We're using *more negative energy* than positive to hold it open."

Scotty squinted at the gash. "Where'd we even get negative energy?"

Ava turned, her holographic eyes reflecting the fracture outside.

"From the vacuum," she said. "If you take a sealed space and remove everything, you're left with quantum fluctuations of flickering electric and magnetic fields, virtual particles blinking in and out of existence."

"They're everywhere," Ravelin muttered. "All the time."

"Exactly. We suppress them between regions—pulling fluctuations from one zone and concentrating them in another. That suppression creates negative pressure. Negative energy. The Casimir Effect."

Scotty took a long-labored drag of breath. Pure oxygen filled his lungs, feeding his brain. "So, you lads are stealing uncertainty?" he asked.

"We will borrow chaos," Ava replied, "and shape it into stability."

The *Ursang* rumbled as the sphere's gravitational pull increased, its glowing walls writhing like the edges of a primordial dream too bright to hold.

"This doorway will collapse behind us," she warned. "Once inside, time won't behave as expected. It's not the only path home, but it's the most rapid. This fork in the road gives us a way to bypass untold hours and arrive at a time before those distress transmissions were made."

The crew stared into the mysterious marble that looked like a universe within a universe.

Ravelin emptied his lungs as if he were blowing out a candle. "Sounds safe enough."

Scotty led with micro expressions and more concern. "Safe enough? What's worst case scenario, mate?"

Ava didn't hesitate. "We're dealing with space-time manipulation. The entirety of the solar system is always moving. Worst case? A miscalculation. A random time insertion. Destination and time unknown."

Scotty looked at her, face full of concern. "How unknown?"

"Completely." Ava's tone didn't change. "We could fly into a sun, or space debris. There is also a chance Earth isn't there because it's somewhere else in time, or we end up in what you would call the Stone Ages. But the odds of such a misstep are low. We just need to have what you call 'good luck.'"

"Bloody hell, that's low stock," Scotty mumbled.

At that moment, beyond the sphere, out there in the black of space, Earth hung suspended in space, fragile and round, pale, and vulnerable. A swarm of vessels closed in for the kill.

The battle was nearing a climax. Fires sparked in orbit, brief flashes before the vacuum erased them and the lives within. Fractured ships drifted like broken teeth. And through the enemy's own ragged rift in space, dark silhouettes slipped forward—the Anunna fleet, swift and silent, moving with the eerie inevitability of something driven by instinct.

Something driven by bloodlust and determination.

They were converging in, drawn toward the prize. It would only take one to break the atmosphere to begin conception of Earth—shaped in the enemy's image.

"Boss?" Scotty's voice brought Ravelin back to the present with the smallest hint of skepticism.

"I know for certain there is no other way," Ravelin said conveying confidence in Ava's calculations. "Let's fly through it."

The *Langley* received her orders as data packages streamed into the core systems. Ava Langley was already parsing it out, calculating trajectories, updating protocols, and locking down the ship deck by deck—simultaneously, everywhere. In space, distance required precognitive first strikes. Where were the best places to send the fighters, best places to stage preemptive bombardments?

Her processing matrix was running hot. Multi-threaded genius in motion. She was a processing-fu master.

Above the *Langley,* the *Ursang* was prepping as well, and the wormhole was primed and pulsing with a reflection of space around and through it. To the naked eye it appeared almost invisible now, a mirror reflection of the universe in a stellar orb of energy and probability. They were going in—ready or not.

Onboard the *Langley,* her captain stood at the helm, eyes lit with anticipation. Sweat was beading on his bald head. Stress, excitement, and fear all rolled into desperation. Everything was new, everything was the first for this crew. They had no training for this, and they were doing it anyway. His breaths shortened as he began sipping on air, pushing a panic attack deep down into the bowels of his soul. This wasn't the time to show weakness, but he could feel fear buckling his knees.

"All hands," his voice trying not to fracture, "brace for jump." A hard exhale. "Ava, you have the helm. Take us in ahead of the *Ursang.* All squadrons, standby for launch."

From the flight officer. "Sir, we've never done this before. Can the ship even handle it?"

"Piece of cake," the captain said without missing a beat.

Inside, he was praying they didn't pancake into a billion glowing fragments stretched to the end of time.

The *Langley* aligned, moving into position. The *Ursang* moved beside her. Two ships, one wormhole, acceleration increasing. They rushed forward, circling the drain, space-time bending as they vanished into the sphere.

CHAPTER 28

The Singularity Event

Myli rubbed sleep from her eyes as she moved down the dimly lit corridor. *Langley* left orbit in a hurry, running her Ninety-Nine drive. Once she was beyond the moon, the warp drive kicked in and she was gone. Too fast to track, they weren't sure if she'd disintegrated into oblivion or successfully conducted her maiden warp flight. All they had was a garbled transmission.

"The warp drive was failing." Followed by static.

Four hours of rest later, she still hadn't received word on the status of the *Langley.* Her anxiety was nearly unbearable. Maybe they were on the far side of Titan? By now, Ravelin's schedule had him on the surface and close to locating the *Ursang.* She yawned between thoughts as she left the head. Myli was eager to get back on task, as her thoughts drifted back to Sonny and the rest of the fleet.

Her face looked tired in the mirror. Her finger poked at the bags of worry visible beneath both eyes. Myli knew they had no magic bullet to stop what was coming.

Daedalus, as impressive as she was, continued to hold her secrets close to her chest.

She stood over the sink, brushing her teeth, wondering how the expedition was going. She kept her head down, refusing to look back in the mirror.

Her brain was stuck in an endless loop of dread. Myli couldn't shake the feeling that something was off.

"The warp drive is failing." That last transmission played back in her mind on a loop.

Occasionally, she would pop her head out of the cabin to see what was going on. The ship was alive with late-night activity—crew members moving through the halls, some pacing, others exchanging quiet last-minute goodbyes, in case the worst happened. Preparations were running smoothly despite everyone being on edge. Myli checked in with a few of her officers as she made her way to the bridge after a bite to eat.

Reports stated there was still no sign of enemy movement coming out of the expanding Event Horizon. Tonight, it was eerily calm on the home front. Through the portside viewport, she saw the additional fleet reinforcements moving into formation. Civilian cruise ships were off in the distance, still ferrying the civvies to space hotels for immediate evacuation on the *Ursang*.

Admiral Vidaurri promised her help with refugees on Earth. He'd also promised to back up her play—but Myli wasn't convinced that promise was genuine. A part of her suspected the ambitious Admiral was just waiting for the right moment to commandeer those civvy ships and press them into service. Something about that man didn't sit right with her.

She exhaled, turning her attention back to her Mii Pad, her fingers thumping the screen. With her mind otherwise occupied, she experienced an eerie moment of clarity during which she thought about Hawk and En'Gen. They were still aboard the *Icarus*. The systems should have finished upgrading an hour ago. What could they be doing all this time? Maybe it was better she didn't know.

Onboard *Icarus,* Hawk moved down the corridor like a weapon, fast, silent, and ready for murder. His blood was on fire, but his eyes were ice cold. The surveillance feed which Rocco had shown him kept replaying in his mind. It showed Trip still alive and here, with Lilith. Whatever they were doing here, it wasn't for the good of mankind. Trip had killed Ava in cold blood, so Hawk was going to dismantle him, one piece at a time.

His hand dropped to his thigh. The ancient Anunna blaster from the *Daedalus* armory was still there, now in possession of a man fueled by rage and running short on logic.

The cargo bay he was seeking had once been a Garden. Weapon drawn, he entered an area which once mirrored a duplicate chamber on the *Daedalus.* The place was once a quantum space-time sanctum, previously filled with light, now drowned in shadow. The hatch opened.

There was no miracle here now—only decay.

The room was a withered husk of its former self. The geometry had fallen apart, compressed, warped, as if the very fabric of space had folded inward. The Star Drive was gone and with it, the gravitational miracle that once rendered the chamber spacious, balanced, and eternal.

The world line was shattered. The path along which an object moves— its trajectory in four-dimensional space-time—was entirely extinguished.

Dead trees rose like bone pillars, skeletal and still, reaching toward a ceiling that no longer shimmered. The air was dry, sterile. Whatever divinity this place once held had been stripped away, leaving only memory and ruin.

The only thing left was the low hum of ventilation ducts pushing stale air through a chamber where the soil was dead and stripped of all organic memory.

Against the far wall, a thin trickle of water dripped from rocks stacked haphazardly like a forgotten altar. Caves gaped, forming wounds in the cliff face—false shelters carved by the collapse of the Garden. It felt like God Himself had come here to purposefully crush the Garden in the palm of His hand.

Hawk moved through the desolation, scanning left and right until he spotted his quarry.

Trip was there, beside the petrified trunk of an ancient tree, in deep contemplation. The tree stood at the edge of a dry shoreline, water long-since drained away. He looked like a man trapped between memories, steadying himself on a collapsed bench of stone and root, trying to remember what balance felt like.

As Hawk watched, Trip rose slowly, staring across the dead grove like a morbid tourist revisiting the ruins of his own story. Behind him, there was a crunch of boots. A shift in light. The weight of a new presence. Trip didn't need to turn to know.

"You found me," he stated.

Hawk's voice cut through the dry, still air. "You're damn right I did."

Trip turned gradually. Calm and controlled. "Convenient," he remarked flatly.

"I buried her here thousands of years ago," he said.

"Who? Ava?"

"God, you're such a *jock*. Another story for another time," Trip concluded.

Hawk's jaw clenched, his mind slightly puzzled by the red handprint on his right cheek.

"Rocco showed me the security feed," Hawk jabbed. "It took us a minute to realize Lilith was with you, too. You brought that damn shape-shifter and a traitor aboard? I saw the video from AUTEC. I saw what you did."

Trip shrugged and shook his head. "You saw what they wanted you to see," he said, his tone steady. "There was never a video—merely a doctored photo. Your brain did the rest."

"You killed her."

Trip's eyes flashed. He shook his head, his expression steady. "No. She's alive. On the *Icarus*. And I'm here to get her out."

Hawk's blaster was up before the last word left Trip's mouth. "And Lilith?"

Trip's voice dropped. "On her own and gathering intel to end this damn thing."

Hawk wasn't having it. "You're a liar. You played us in D.C."

Trip stepped forward, his tone ice-cold. "Liar?" he scoffed. "You and your 'Daddy Vidaurri' began the lies with Red Wings. I only played the hand I was dealt."

"Vidaurri is not my daddy. You've concocted that fantasy. It's nothing but a convenient excuse from you."

"You realize what those EVE and ADAM bots are carrying, don't you?"

Hawk knew. The shame he felt was another slap in the face.

A moment of silence stretched between the two. The engagement happened quickly. Hawk fired first—point shooting, hoping to catch Trip off-guard.

Anticipating the shot, Trip had already moved. He spun in place, his lengthy duster coat whipping around him like a cloak. In the blink of an eye, as the camo tech activated, he vanished in a shimmer of light.

Hawk's tardy plasma bolt rocketed through empty air and struck what was left of the tree in front of Athena's grave. Hawk's eyes scanned frantically—panic flashing across his face. He ripped off three more shots, blind.

A shift in the air. A whisper. Metal on metal, razor sharpness met his sidearm. Sparks flew and the weight of the pistol vanished as Trip's sword cleaved the weapon. Only the grip remained in Hawk's hand.

A blur. A foot whipped from beneath the cloak and cracked into Hawk's jaw, snapping his head sideways.

Infuriated, Hawk was nowhere near conceding as he rushed toward the spot where he'd last glimpsed his opponent.

The two men collided.

Trip's sword was dislodged and flew, tumbling through the air to spike in the sand a few feet away. It remained there, quivering like a challenge.

Now the fighting turned raw, unfiltered violence. Hand-to-hand. Brazilian Jiu-Jitsu. Krav Maga. Keysi Fighting Method. It was bone on bone. Breath on breath. Rage versus betrayal.

Trip's duster was flung aside and their bodies grappled as they crashed through the ruins of the Garden, once sacred, now desecrated. Dead trees snapped, ancient stones cracked and toppled over. Blood splattered the ground. Shouting. Grunts. Gasps. A flurry of positions: blocks, frames, guards, then a bridge and it started all over again.

Their movements were fluid, trained but savage. This wasn't about tactics anymore. They weren't soldiers, not legends or immortal gods. Their desecration of Eden was centuries in the making.

In less than five furious minutes both were fatiguing. They slowed their battle, but neither one would stop. Too tired to stand, they struggled on the floor, edging one another towards the blade sticking in the sand. It was their one last attempt to draw blood.

"Enough!" Stella Forrestal's voice cracked through the insanity like thunder. She stepped into the clearing, sidearm raised. The breeze of the battle momentarily halted her, and she blew her hair out of her face.

"I said—ENOUGH!" she shouted and emphasized her command by firing two rapid shots into the air.

Both men froze—chests heaving, fists still clenched and trembling. Their clothes torn, faces bruised. Seemingly poised to keep fighting to the death. And yet, they listened.

"Ava's alive," Stella told them. "And she's waiting patiently while you two idiots try to kill each other. Again." Having gained their attention, she gestured around the ruins. "What the actual hell is wrong with you two? Don't you see you're fighting over Athena's grave?"

For a moment, silence filled the space. All of them lost their footing when the ship lurched violently as an unseen force rocked the hull. A shock wave rolled through the *Daedalus,* reverberating through every bulkhead.

The soft sand absorbed the worst of it, and the three of them sprang back to their feet as vibrations rippled the surface, shaping it into cymatic patterns.

Elsewhere on the ship emergency klaxons wailed, overlapping and relentless. ADAM units and EVE bots sprinted down corridors, deploying instantly for damage control. In that discombobulation, shadows moved. Perfect cover for someone like Lilith, who knew how to slip between systems on a ship at war. Picking a crewman up from the floor, she collected DNA. She brushed past other crewmen unnoticed, collecting more identities, her form shifting from an earlier MP in subtle ripples. When needed, she became any one of them. To gain access, she adopted the individual who could open the next door.

She slipped into a berth and sealed the hatch behind her. A moment later she dropped a wad of hair—pulled from the brush on the dresser. Her bones flexed, skin adjusting itself, and in seconds she looked like Stella Forrestal.

This was Officers' Country. She walked like she belonged there.

Lilith moved from wardroom to passageway, a phantom wearing a different face and shape at every checkpoint. She didn't need weapons. Her faces were dangerous enough to get her anywhere she intended to infiltrate.

In the Star Drive, the trio made their way further into the Garden, Hawk pulled himself together and barked at Forrestal, "You've been helping him?"

She side-eyed Hawk, calmly punching in commands on the hatch display.

"Look," she said, "Vidaurri was wrong. The Admiral has always played his own game. And what did you do? You fell in line." She said as they continued walking to a dead end where a cliff face once separated a valley.

Arriving, Stella's fingers worked diligently until they hit the final key stroke on a panel against the rock. The hidden hatch hissed open.

"I saw Trip kill her!" Hawk declared.

She turned, eyes flat, voice razor-sharp. "No. You saw what you wanted to see. You were in shock. You wanted vengeance. And it didn't take more than a nudge to put you on that road."

"All this time—" Hawk began but he lost his words as the truth washed over him.

"Yes, damn it, Hawk," she said, her voice softer. "Trip was with me—when he was supposedly killing Ava."

Hawk hesitated. "But, you were there, at my house. When Vidaurri showed me the feed."

She sighed. "I was in a bad position," she admitted. "I couldn't just blurt things out." The real truth bomb. "Vidaurri disappeared her. Do you think I was going to admit that I helped Lilith escape, and slept with the man who pulled it off?"

Realization struck Hawk. "And your son?"

"Yeah. He's Trip's."

The floor rattled again. Bulkheads groaned.

"We're under attack," Trip said with concern. "Shitty timing as always, Hawk."

Hawk stood there, registering the intel, the pieces finally falling in line. He looked through the open hatch. "Is that what I think it is?" he asked Stella.

"Yes," she said. "Believe me, it's for your own good."

Finally, Hawk turned and stepped through the hatch, into the cell.

Trip tried to follow Hawk inside, but Stella's hand caught his arm, stopping him. He turned back, the look on her face gave him pause.

"Lilith?" she asked, her voice tense with concern.

"Recon only," he assured her.

"You're sure, Trip?"

"Chiara promised, Lily promised," he nodded.

Stella's face seemed to have betrayal of the Admiral written all over it. *Lilith has every right for revenge,* she told herself. But, aloud, she decided to change the subject. "So Lilith goes by Chiara now?"

"Yeah, married even."

"No shit." The news surprised Stella. Her face reflected disbelief but also gratitude for a woman she admired. "Well, however she managed it, she did good by staying off the radar."

"She stopped killing bad guys." Trip exclaimed.

Inside of the cell, a QSC unit sat in the center of a small, humming chamber. All of Hawk's rage had fallen away. He approached the unit slowly, reverently—like it might vanish. He activated the reanimation sequence, and she appeared in a burst of energy and wind.

Ava. Still alive. Just as Trip said.

He dropped to his knees and pulled her into his arms. He was holding something irreplaceable. Her eyes fluttered open, barely conscious. She saw his face, it was hard and battle-worn, haunted, but familiar.

Tears in her eyes, she wrapped her arms around his head. And her first words were, "You found me—"

"I had help. But right now, we are in grave danger."

CHAPTER 29

Time Prison

Sonny's UAV training ended. He walked onto the bridge just as the *Daedalus* bucked violently, throwing him and the crew sideways. The deck swayed beneath their feet, the entire bridge rocking like a ship caught in a storm. Officers scrambled for handholds. Those caught in the corridors were slammed to the floor, sliding across the bulkheads.

Red emergency lights strobed, casting the commotion in pulses of bloodred light. Alarms howled. Systems screamed.

At the center of it all, riding the madness like one of the old sea captains in WWII—with thirty-foot waves crashing over a steel bridge—Myli clung to the captain's chair... nowhere to go but forward.

"Where the hell are they!?" she snapped at Sonny.

His hands flipped up; he'd been playing Maverick and had no idea where the others were. Sonny could feel the storm inside her head, the confusion and concern. Time was running out and her right-hand men were AWOL.

"Hawk and En'Gen were due back hours ago, ma'am," a junior officer reported. "It's possible they got delayed."

Myli looked at Sonny. He shrugged again. He'd spent hours learning how to fly an "In Real Life" game. He wasn't babysitting Captain America and Optimus Prime. He had no idea why they weren't back yet. Anyway, the countdown still had time. Right?

Sonny was about to protest to Myli that it wasn't his fault when she grabbed his hand.

"Those two can take care of themselves," she snapped.

"What is with the sudden rodeo?" he grumbled.

"Something miraculous is about to happen. It's Ravelin; he found the bridge layer! And he's on his way here!"

Makes sense Sonny figured, some sort of cosmic wake headed their way.

"Ma'am, sensors are registering a major shift in the anomaly forming between us and the moon," an officer reported.

Her muscles finally relaxed. She slunk into the captain's chair. Her eyes narrowed as she leaned over the console. "That's got to be Ravelin," Myli proclaimed. "Stick the landing, kid."

Outside, things began happening just in time. The cosmos warped, bending surrounding stars. The moon was visible, then obscured as its illumination smeared across the black star-scape to be replaced by the rip from a bridge-layer. Without warning, new constellations emerged, blinking into existence, sharp and cold, from beyond Earth's solar system.

Myli turned toward the main viewport, her fingers vibrating, a tremor forming in her hand which she couldn't stop. She didn't know if she was trembling in fear or excitement.

Ava Daedalus materialized on the bridge, new data was streaming through the ship's systems, and the news wasn't good.

"The IFF isn't matching," Ava communicated. "We are not receiving their interrogator signal. There is no coded transmission. That isn't the *Ursang.*"

"IFF?" Sonny asked. "What the eff is IFF?"

Myli's muscles stiffened. Her mouth ran dry. She was all but certain the *Langley* had been destroyed by its warp drive.

Ava filled the gaps. "IFF means *Friend or Foe.* If what's heading our way was one of ours, a coded signal would be pinging us right now."

A massive, ring-shaped vessel hovered at the mouth of the singularity sphere on the other side—anchoring the wormhole open, holding space-time apart for the first wave of the fleet. It was unlike anything humanity had ever built. The ring around the ship wasn't ornamental—it was the primary containment field, a colossal superstructure embedded with energy channels, glowing with pulsing violet nodes. The outer edge was lined with something that looked like jagged fins and antenna arrays—some shifting, others braced with hardened spires that looked more like spikes than antennae.

At its core, the ship housed a central hull suspended inside the ring like a spear locked in a gyroscope. The forward and aft points stretched beyond the ring's diameter, both tapering into point-like tips. The nose was capped with an armored lens assembly, cracked open like a blooming aperture—still glowing faintly from the pulse which had torn the singularity open.

The body itself was plated in overlapping armor—dull, dark, and scorched in places—covered in strange paneling that revealed seamless welds. Some sections pulsed with light, others reverberated, as though the vessel was exhaling. At this scale, it was less a ship and more a living space-time entity, grown into function over millennia.

Energy bolts rolled off the ship's hull in waves. Every few seconds, one of the segmented ring bands flexed, releasing a shimmer across the event horizon, stabilizing the fracture like a wound being held open. If it weren't for the vacuum of space, the sounds blasting out of the ship would have been terrifying.

Below it, the wormhole churned—a mini universe—a swirling and endless sphere of light and depth. Stars bent as they passed near it, colors stretching across the spectrum in a ribbon of quantum distortion.

Ahead of it, the vanguard surged forward. Behind it, the rest of the fleet waited to pounce. The first cosmic convoy stretched through the distortion, flowing endlessly from the wound in space. Large carriers moved with silent intent, their hulls outlined in blue light. The process of staging had ended. The offensive campaign had commenced.

The Zero Point engines were firing—not for acceleration, but to brake. Each warship surged energy forward, slowing against its own inertia. Without deceleration, they'd punch straight through Earth's atmosphere and burn up like falling gods.

In perfect unison, the carriers' shuttle bays opened; bay doors yawning, from carrier bellies, the first swarms launching. Not transport ships. Drones.

Squadrons of recon vessels, and interceptors poured out. Thousands. Black and silent, the plague moved without signature from the throat of the universe. They would weaken the host before infesting it.

Sonny stood frozen at the viewport, complexion drained. His voice came low, almost a whisper.

"Holy Doomsday Machine. We never stood a chance."

"Our fight is just starting." Myli didn't hesitate in saying. "That's why no one gets to sit this one out. Get back down to the virtual fighters now, Sonny."

He turned to her, reluctant. "Is this the Event?"

She nodded. "They're early. Go, and good hunting."

The invasion had begun.

CHAPTER 30

The Merge

Oblivious the end was near, "I'm going to kill him." Hawk raged. He was pacing in the Garden, growling, seething. The others were busy staying out of his way. "I'm going to eviscerate the bastard—"

"Chiara has first right of refusal," Looper interrupted.

"What the hell is that supposed to mean?" Hawk questioned.

As if to draw them back into the reality of their situation, above them an energy fluctuation—a bright explosion of light high above them in the air. If the burst and the rush of air hadn't been blasted in their direction, they would have thought it was a hull breach.

"Were we hit?" Stella worried.

"Nope," Trip assured her. "En'Gen got the Sun Reactor rebooted. He's resurrecting the ship, is all. So, we're in for some weather."

The wind gusted. Rain followed, fierce and rapidly intensifying. Ancient seeds were drinking in the precious liquid almost as fast as it fell. A hurricane was building.

Hawk shouted over the rising distortion, his voice as loud as it would carry, "The Garden is reenergizing and reconfiguring—we need to leave, or we'll end up miles away once the space-time continuum resets!"

Stella alarmed, "Are we going to die in here?"

Trip took her hand. "Hawk's just an alarmist." He wrapped his arm around Stella and pulled her out of danger, barely dodging the falling limb of Athena's dead tree. "He likes to sound important." He completely dismissed the widow-maker.

A violent gale whipped through the dead grove, buffeting them as clouds spiraled overhead. The sky began to twist. The ground beneath their feet shifted, and the distance to the hatch began stretching, warping, expanding as though the chamber itself was inhaling.

Above them, the Sun Reactor began to reform—swirling energy knitting itself back together, like a glowing, living organ, an emerging heart pulsing in the sky.

Behind them, the Garden's internal sea began to rise as the volume of rain increased, filling the basin inch by inch. In the burgeoning distance, lakes shimmered into existence, and the river would soon begin to flow once more—life returning to the bones of a dead world.

"She's alive..." Trip cried out, referencing Frankenstein. "She's alive!"

They pressed forward into the gale, fighting their way through a storm of raw dimensional force as the Garden reconfigured into the massive, warped space-scape it had once been.

"Every step forward is three steps back. What the hell is happening?!" Stella shouted over the wind.

"The universe in here is expanding," Hawk yelled back. "A whole world is being built in here. Quantum..."

"It's effing alien space magic, Stella! Keep moving," Trip shouted, dragging her behind him. Stella clutched onto Ava, and Ava clasped Hawk's hand. They were a human chain.

"Welcome to Genesis, Stella." Trip said over the howling wind. "It's Genesis all over again—only on a micro level inside the ship."

Trip was the first to reach the exit. One-by-one, he stood in the hatchway and pulled them through. When he got to the end, Hawk stopped briefly. Hawk didn't say it, but his eyes did. A thankful nod. Trip nodded back.

The *Icarus* flight deck was in bedlam—klaxons, shouting. Emergency crews rushed to throw the severely injured onto stretchers. Others were being bandaged and put back to work. Everyone was working double-time.

A Ninety-Nine fighter, unsecured during the turbulence, had smashed into the bay wall, triggering a chain reaction of explosions. Fire raged across the deck as the crew scrambled through wreckage and debris, trying to contain the damage without having to create a vacuum to put out the fire.

Through the madness, Hawk, Ava, Trip, and Stella moved across the flight line, soaked and wind battered, the commotion on the flight deck acted as camouflage. No need to be a ninja when everyone was focused on catastrophe.

Ava stumbled—weak and disoriented. Reanimating during a dimensional hurricane wasn't part of her wakeup checklist. Hawk was there for her, steadying her, guiding her forward. He could tell her brain was still Swiss cheese, memory bleeding in from all directions. Midol wouldn't touch this headache. Ava was a threat to Vidaurri, but not in her present condition. Part of Hawk hoped Trip was wrong about Lilith, and he preferred to believe she was somewhere taking her revenge on the Admiral.

"We need a ship," Hawk said eyeing the transports.

They wouldn't all fit inside a fighter.

There was a break in the madness.

"That one," Hawk said pointing to a likely ship. "They abandoned it to fight the fire. Come on, move," he said, shuffling Ava along with him.

They made it across the crowded flight deck. Hawk turned to Ava; she was still lethargic, leaning against the hatch of the transport. She was a shell of who she was, but she was the real Ava—not an AI, not a memory, but flesh and blood.

Hawk swallowed hard, his voice low and rough. "Ava, if only I had known you were alive."

A tired smile tugged at her lips. "We never really die, unless we're forgotten, do we?"

En'Gen stepped out of the flames, emerging from the smoke. "Who is this?" he pointed at Ava.

"A long story," Hawk replied, eyes still scanning the damage. "Nice timing; what happened here?"

En'Gen tilted his head when he saw Trip. "I know you."

Trip gave a crooked smile. "Another time, old friend. Nice work with the reactor. You were about to tell us what happened here," he prompted the Synth.

"Dimensional waves rocked a fighter loose and boom," En'Gen said, gesturing in fluid, sharp motions—sign language sketching the arc of an explosion. "Three dead, half a dozen injured, but functional."

Trip watched a missile or drone zip past the opening of the hangar bay. "Y'all need to get back to the *Ursang*. The invasion has started."

"It's going to be a nightmare flying through that," Hawk said, pointing at a dogfight taking place just outside the plasma field. "They don't usually get that close to the fleet. They must have come in hot."

"All that lip you've given over the years, you got this." Trip looked around at the colored shirts working furiously. "Y'all go. I'm not leaving without Chiara."

"And I'm not leaving my ship," Stella said stubbornly.

Hawk took Trip aside. "I'm thankful that you found Ava and brought her back to me, so I understand you wanting to find Chiara, but that creature has more names and faces than we can count. Are you sure about her?"

Trip nodded, "I'm not leaving without her." He looked back and locked eyes with Ava, giving her a small, familiar wink. Just like that, the past was behind them. Bygones were bygones.

Hawk put out his hand. Trip clasped his forearm, Hawk doing the same in return.

"Good luck, Hawk. Take better care of her this time."

Hawk nodded. "You're still an asshole, Trip."

Trip shrugged. "We all have to be good at something." Trip grinned, then he shrugged again and broke from the group. Stella left with him.

Hawk helped Ava aboard, then he and En'Gen powered up the transport's reactor. The engines roared to life, gear retracting as the ship levitated cleanly off the deck. The flight crew scrambled into view, waving them down—ordering a shutdown.

Hawk ignored them.

He took the yoke—manual control, no chute this time. The transport barreled forward, blasting through the energy curtain that separated atmosphere to vacuum. It got violent quickly.

As soon as they cleared the barrier, Hawk veered hard right. Enemy fighters screamed past, locked onto squadrons of Ninety-Nines. Behind them, coalition ships battled, painting the sky with streaks of rail gun projectiles.

Secure in a jump seat behind the others, Ava's eyes nearly popped out of her head as they narrowly missed a midair collision, the opposing fighter screaming past the canopy in a blur of calculated fortune. For Hawk, it was just another day at the office. He was back in his element—the cockpit, space. Up here, he was more alive than he ever was on the ground.

But this time, he wasn't fighting. He was only evading. Below and ahead, a cascade of orbital debris tore across their flight path. Earth's defense platforms flickered with tiny, near-invisible beams, disintegrating fragments, clearing lanes inch by inch. Only the "Ava's" had the processing power to keep up with the quadrillions of particles orbiting around them.

But space was still full of killers. Even BB-sized particles, moving at velocity, could rip through hull plating like a bullet through paper.

"Helmets stay on," Hawk barked. "A fleck of paint could decompress the cabin."

Ava did her best to keep it together. It was a death roller coaster in the dark. A wall of debris spun toward them—a tangled, lethal storm of fractured metal and dead machines.

Hawk reacted instantly. His throttle slammed forward, stick punching with precision as he was weaving between shattered solar panels, mangled hull plating, and the twisted remnants of what might've once been a drone.

"Bandit on our six," he growled. "Crafty SOB just slipped in behind us."

His instruments lit up; the bandit was locked on. He banked hard—chaff out. A Fox 2 zipped past, narrowly missing the port engine.

"Watch him, En'Gen," Hawk shouted.

The hungry pilot stayed on them. Hawk broke left for a cluster of scrap, dove around it. The cloud of particulate debris made up of small, fast, and brutal particulates blocked the enemy path. A short-lived reprieve. Their transport took a minor sandblasting and the cockpit canopy cracked. The attacker had no option but to peel off.

Hawk's breathing overshadowed his voice. "That guy almost punched our ticket."

En'Gen tapped into ships radar. "Hawk, he's swinging back around."

Hawk refocused. "Hold on."

The enemy pilot rolled back on their six, relentless. Hawk knew they were dead if he made any mistakes. He was good, but the guy behind him had some skills too.

His head rattled inside the helmet as his hands yanked the stick back and forth, side to side, dodging volleys of enemy fire. "I can't shake this friggin' guy."

Neck straining, trying to keep a visual on the bandit, the harness was twisting against his 2nd SKN suit, trying to keep him in place. Glancing aft and forward, he was trying not to fly straight into the afterlife. The debris made that a possibility.

Out of the darkness a Sabre Cat screamed past them, head-on in a course to merge with the bandit.

It happened fast, but Hawk recognized the Cat and established radio contact. "Rocco, you crazy son of a—"

"I'm in the merge. Get to the *Ursang,*" Rocco radioed, voice cool as ice. "I've got this guy."

As the transport moved on, Hawk and the others watched and listened.

Rocco peeled off, rolling inverted, locking horns with the bandit—nose to nose, dancing on a razor's edge of velocity and the afterlife. Something about this pilot—he was too sharp, too surgical, one cunning *mofo*—which told Rocco this needed to end *fast.*

He caught a glimpse of the enemy ship's name, Ava Jeep translated— *Carnivore.*

"Time to wrap this up with a bow," Rocco decided.

He came around tight, breathing becoming unbearable, guns coming around, almost nose-on, close enough to smell blood. But the bandit was wily. Flares dropping. Nose dipping.

Shot ruined.

After each encounter, he annotated his knee pad with spaghetti. Rocco cursed under his breath, watching the firing window slip away. The stars—blurred around him. He cut speed. Nose thrusters blasted forward.

Patience became his ally. Wait for the mistake.

There.

A turn reversal—sloppy, desperate. Wrong move.

"I've got a lock," Rocco said, relief cutting through the static—quickly chased by dread.

"But I still can't get tone," he growled, jaw clenched tight. "I got tone!" Elation crackled over the comms.

He fired a Fox 2—but the missile veered off, chasing a phantom target.

No track. No hit.

The dogfight became a case of two killers still circling, waiting for the break. The fight was tight—*real* tight. Rocco just needed the bandit to slip out front again, just enough to seal it. Steady, steady, the craft was in his firing solution.

The enemy flared again. Heat signatures bloomed like fireflies.

"Fox 2," Rocco cut another missile loose. "Went for the flares again. Crap," Rocco cursed, eyes scanning his dwindling arsenal. Out of missiles. His Fox 3s were long gone, expelled in the first few minutes of the onslaught.

"Switching to guns," he said, the bandit still on his heels.

The bandit drifted closer and closer to nose on, just on the edge of a gun solution. The speed bled off. Gas blasting out the nose.

"We got ourselves another dead bandit," Rocco quipped, lining up the shot.

He squeezed the trigger—short burst. The bandit snapped into a 180, then pitched hard downward.

Rocco pulled high, leaping above the kill zone just as energy bursts zipped beneath his cockpit—brilliant streaks of death skimming inches from his belly. His own rounds sailed over the top of the enemy, deadly but just off the mark. Too close.

They'd passed each other at Mach Death, missing by an atom's width.

The bandit dipped, skimming beneath him, trying to recover. Dodging debris. Slipping through Rocco's fingers.

"He's gonna hit that mass of junk—maneuver kill incoming."

Rocco watched as the bandit weaved through the wreckage—clean through the particulates.

"Oh, no he didn't. He missed it! Shit—he's pointing the nose. Shit, he's got me locked!"

From afar, Hawk tracked the BFM (Dog Fight) unfolding in real time, the fight drifting further across the battle space.

"Flares, Rocco. Flares," Hawk radioed. "Do it!"

Rocco got the message. He snapped the stick, popped flares, and rolled hard, angling toward where the bandit would likely vector next. He popped the throttle, and his head twisted back, straining to maintain visual. The G-forces were punishing, his neck screaming. His vertebrae were on the verge of breaking. The tendons in his neck pulled tight.

Even a tenth more Gs would snap his neck and head clean off—but he held the sight picture. He wasn't letting this bastard go.

An enemy missile flashed by—narrowly missing the canopy.

"Jesus!" Rocco barked, breath catching in his throat.

No time to make the sign of the cross. They were headed for another head-on pass. The enemy strafed, energy bolts tearing through the space between them. Both fighters juked and rolled, narrowly dodging death in bursts of light and flame. Most missed. But one didn't.

A bolt grazed Rocco's bird, searing along the fuselage—scorching the hull, his bird trailing smoke like a torn battle flag.

The death dance restarting.

Both pilots pulled hard into tight turns, the G-forces stacking as they jammed the Weapon Engagement Zone. Stay close—too close for missiles, too tight for clean shots. Close enough to kill. But not so close that they'd kill each other with a collision.

It was a knife fight inside a Fiat 500e at the speed of light.

Thruster puffs flashed across both crafts—nose, nacelles, dorsal flares—tiny corrections executed at breakneck speeds. Yards closed to feet. Feet shrunk to inches. Impact.

The two fighters slammed together, armor scraping, sparks bursting in vacuum. They bounced, then separated—barely.

Rocco's heart thundered. It was all he could hear. Everything else inside his cockpit was silent now, filled with vacuum.

They turned and collided again. Harder this time. Hulls groaned. Metal bent. On Earth, they'd have a chance to crash land. Out here, a planet landing was no longer an option unless a pilot put down on the moon. Rocco was close to biting his tongue off. This guy's an ace, he thought. Best of the best. Mano y mano.

Their ships tumbled separately and spun through the void, both locked in a deadly spiral. Rocco below, the enemy above. No fire solution. No retreat. Just instinct and inertia. Debris from both fighters orbited around them like shrapnel moons—loose plating, scorched panels, blistered fragments.

Rocco didn't know how many missiles the other pilot had left. He hoped none. The Anunna hit flares again—reflexive, desperate—unaware Rocco was Winchester. Completely empty. Bone dry.

Only one weapon left. Rocco drew his pistol and aimed straight up. The enemy pilot realized too late. Rocco squeezed the trigger. A single round punched through his canopy and into the enemy cockpit, shattering glass and flesh. Rocco punched the dorsal thrusters, breakaway, and was gaining distance as the Anunna fighter drifted into oblivion.

Kill confirmed? he wondered.

He broke right—then left—his bird spiraling out of control. His eyeballs couldn't slow down. Vertigo was kicking his ass.

Vision blurring. Muscles trembling. Explosions still pulsing the void around him. His fighter was damaged. Few maneuvering thrusters still working. His body spent and his ego checked. The fight was over. He was done.

"Got his ass with a pistol shot," Rocco radioed. "But I'm done. You're on your own, brother."

Moments later, Hawk found the transport targeted again—another bandit, sloppy and inexperienced close enough to kill. Hawk tightened inside the enemy's turn radius jamming the WEZ. Stick close, stay erratic, stay alive. There was no way he could outmaneuver a missile.

Guns were still an option though—and they'd all seen what Rocco's single pistol shot did to that Anunna ace.

Hawk popped his last flares in a wide spray and knifed through drifting wreckage—twisting, banking, threading past shattered hulls like seaweed in black water. Behind him, the bandit tried to follow and hit debris—a maneuver kill.

Inside the cabin, gravity held—they'd been on the Rattler at Six Flags, but on speed. The trio slammed around the cockpit during maneuvers.

"I'm gonna puke," Ava groaned.

"Don't—" Hawk started, but it was too late. Her visor flooded, fogging with a warm cloudy mess.

"Oh, God. This is terrible," she moaned, eyes shut, instinctively swiping at the outside of her mask—a hopeless gesture. The suit sucked most of the moisture out of her face shield.

Dead ahead loomed the *Daedalus*—burning. One side of the ship was scorched with metal peeled back like torn armor. They could see there'd been a collision. Something large had slammed into her, embedding itself into the side of the hull like a tick's head driving into skin.

CHAPTER 31

Impossible Mission

Alarms roared through the corridors of the *Daedalus*. There was a brief break in the fighting—but not in the fight for survival. The ship was already working to heal itself—bulkheads folding, being rebuilt by nanites sparking to life—but fires still burned, and boarding parties were now a threat.

Having convinced the *Daedalus* gunners that they were friendly, Hawk, Ava, and En'Gen maneuvered the transport into an undamaged docking port, disembarked, and moved fast through the battered corridors, stepping over fallen crew, shattered panels, and flickering consoles. The air was thick with ozone, scorched metal, and cauterized skin—a brutal cocktail that clung to every breath.

The war had made it inside the ship. Makeshift seals were applied on walls to patch micro-holes formed by debris that pierced the hull. The crew, slow to respond to decompression, succumbed in the gangways. The cost of war was real, and this one was going to be high.

The squad found Sonny in the corridor, pale and twitchy. He was fresh off his drone tour-of-duty looking exhausted and punchy. His eyes blazed red from staring at virtual reality screens. Intense flashing, blaring alarms, his cortisol level finally leveling out with the adrenaline bleeding off, a crash soon to follow. His adrenal gland about kicked his ass.

"You alright, bud? Get some shell shock from losing one to many drones?" Hawk asked, his face sporting a mocking grin.

Sonny didn't answer. Instead, he knocked Hawk clean out with a left hook.

"Hello to you too," Sonny laughed. "I'm just a little shook up from helping clean up what was left of a crewman out of one of the cockpits. My new buddy, Giorgos, was hit by something the size of a quarter, feet away from me. Ava Daedalus Two said it was traveling so fast that the guy wouldn't have known what hit him. I saw his eyes though; he knew alright. They were still looking at what was left of him splattered everywhere."

Ava, now kneeling beside Hawk who was coming to, cringing at the thought. "But are *you* okay?" she asked Sonny.

"No, not really," Sonny answered. "This really hasn't been my week, if you know what I mean. Why do you look human now? And, by the way, you've got something on your face and in your hair." He delivered this with a dry monotone. "Anyway, I'm headed to the hangar deck to help rearm the fighters. I'm sure y'all are needed on the bridge or something. Tell Captain America here that I saved y'all's ass when y'all left the *Icarus*."

En'Gen scoffed to himself. "Hawk deserved that punch. He should have led with better dialogue."

The bridge was a hive of frantic activity when they arrived. Myli stood at the command console, gripping the edge while trying to get a grasp on reality. A holographic tactical map displayed the carnage unfolding in orbit.

The fleet was in disarray. The Anunna had split their blockade. Over forty percent of Coalition ships were disabled or destroyed. Stopping the second wave would cost them everything. The *Icarus* had taken heavy damage but was still operational. The *Daedalus* was managing the ramming damage—monitoring the crippled ship embedded in their stern.

Dozens of smaller Anunna warships were still engaged in brutal one-on-one combat.

"Status," Myli called out.

"The *Langley* and *Ursang* have arrived and they are engaging."

"Better late than never, Ravelin," she breathed to herself. "Mop 'em up."

Ava Daedalus One materialized, her voice steady despite their weak victory. "The fleet has sustained severe losses. Enemy forces are withdrawing—for now. Analysis suggests they'll regroup and return with overwhelming force."

Myli stepped closer. "How did Sonny do?"

Ava D1 collated before answering. "He performed well. Scored several confirmed kills." A pause. "The Sim-Pilot named Giorgos, seated beside him, was disintegrated by high-velocity impact-induced fragmentation."

Myli frowned. "What?"

Ava D1 recalibrated her tone. "Apologies. I should have articulated more clearly. A projectile traveling at extreme speed penetrated the hull. The body in the cockpit next to Sonny sustained catastrophic trauma—most of it was destroyed upon impact." Another pause. "Sonny assisted in clearing what remained of Giorgos' corpse. He's currently in the hangar, helping compensate for crew loss by prepping the next wave of drone fighters."

Both Sonny and Myli were so tuned in with their own mess that they were able to block each other's thoughts and feelings out. She had no idea what had happened to him.

I put him in the safest place on the ship, she thought bitterly. *Now he's back in harm's way.*

She drifted past the captain's chair; sitting didn't feel appropriate during this part of the brief. "Did you run the psych eval on him like I asked?" When she reached the hatchway, Myli braced her back against one side and reached for the other. Slowly she walked her hands down the opposing beam activating a long overdue stretch. She was willing to do anything to help relieve the tension building up in her muscles.

Looking down at her, Ava answered, "Yes, captain. I did it subtly while we trained, like you asked."

Myli stared at the floor and grunted as she continued her line of questions. "How far do you think we can push him before we push him over the edge?"

"He can take quite a bit of punishment before he breaks. It's not that he cares so deeply. Underneath his moral compass lurks something sharper, darker, and more dangerous within his psyche."

"You sound like a therapist," Myli said, raising her head to meet Ava at eye level.

"I am programmed in many disciplines, ma'am. I can tell you unequivocally that for all his ethical strengths, he has moral abdication disguised as patience."

"What the hell does that mean?"

"If you're not on top of him, his patience could get you killed," Ava said with absolution.

There was clatter down the gangway. Someone was coming.

Myli and Ava waited for the commotion to reach them. It was Hawk and En'Gen coming for debrief.

"Report," she said, then moderated her tone. "Please," she added.

"We can't take another hit like that, Myli. If they come back in full force, we're finished." En'Gen briefed her. "The nanites should have us back to 83% within the hour."

Myli nodded sharply. "We need standoff capability and to find a way to finish them before they finish us. This thing is a weapon, right? We hit them with everything we had. I don't understand how this wasn't a resounding victory for us."

"Their second wave of carriers is poised to exit the singularity," a new voice chimed in.

All eyes snapped to the random blonde toweling off her hair like this was just another debrief.

Ava, Myli told herself.

Hawk turned to her. "Tell them."

She jumped right into it. "Their bridge-layer—the singularity ship—is the key. It's their anchor, their main deployment vector. If we take it out, we cripple their invasion. It's over a mile long and full of reinforcements."

Hawk frowned. "Easier said than done," he muttered. "I just got off comms with Rocco, and I've learned that their fighters were using sacrificial drones. Every time our fighters engaged, one would take the hit for them. When the mother bird's ordinance was spent, they auto-recalled the drones and launched another armed bird. Their pilots were decent, but their AI?" He shook his head. "Relentless."

Hawk ignored their stares and continued. "They have some ace's; we saw Rocco go up against one. One less now, but it got challenging." He leaned forward. "They mostly lost resources, not pilots, if what Rocco said is accurate. We need to ignore the drones. Go straight for the jugular."

All ears were on him.

"We send a small team to the bridge-layer," Hawk suggested. "Reverse the polarity of the singularity. When it collapses—everything still inside the event horizon?" He made a twisting motion with his hand. "Spaghetti."

Ava finished wiping her face, tossing the microfiber towel to Hawk. "We've got one shot at this—but it has to be perfectly coordinated." She stepped forward, voice firm.

Ava nodded. "Stopping them inside the Einstein-Rosen Bridge makes tactical sense. But make no mistake—Earth's about to get slammed by a CME of unprecedented radiation. We're talking stone-age reset at best."

"That solar flare—" she continued, "that's what the Humans and the Igigi used to stop the last invasion. History's repeating itself."

Ava looked at the group flatly. A faint recognition fell on her face. "We will be dead in the water. All systems fried. EMP, plasma disruption—complete shutdown. We know the flare is coming. The enemy doesn't. That's the only ace we've got left. If we can hold them off just long enough... maybe we have a stalemate."

Myli was deep in thought, trying to coordinate their next play. "They have the same scans. They can't see it?"

"Not on their side of the wormhole," En'Gen chimed in. "And we are jamming all their signals as we speak. They can't communicate with the mother ship from this side."

Myli exhaled sharply, hands on her hips, mind already calculating vectors and probabilities.

"Alright," she said. "Who goes?"

Hawk didn't hesitate. "We bait them into a trap."

He calculated and took a step forward, eyes hard.

"They think they broke us. They'll come back to finish the job. When they do—we catch their bridge-layer inside the wormhole—a kill zone, fatal funnel."

Myli's eyes narrowed. "And what, they give up?"

Hawk's gravitas left his face. "There won't be any Anunna left. If we do it while they are on the other side, they'll just keep coming, maybe another thousand years."

Myli shuddered. "That's genocide." Her father was half Anunna. "They've given us no choice."

Ava's eyes went wide. "That's nuts! Whoever goes will never make it out of there alive!"

Seconds later, a holographic projection of Admiral Vidaurri materialized at the center of the bridge. His stern, battle-hardened face bore a mixture of frustration and determination. The red glow of emergency lights on his end reflected the grim reality of the fight. The *Icarus* had taken some hits, but thanks to En'Gen's nanite infusion, she had been revitalized and was repairing her hull.

"Captain Sipani." The Admiral's voice was laced with displeasure. "We barely survived that first engagement. You do realize if they send their full force through, this entire war will be over in a matter of minutes."

Myli folded her arms, her sharp gaze cutting into him. "I guess we better make damn sure they don't send the rest of their force through, shouldn't we, Admiral?"

Vidaurri's jaw flexed. "I assume you have some miraculous plan to counter a thousand-year-old enemy possessing superior technology?"

Hawk stepped forward. "We do. But it's going to require complete coordination—and your full cooperation."

Vidaurri sighed, shaking his head. "I don't like that tone, Commander. I don't have time for half-baked suicide missions. I need a detailed report of what your plan is."

Myli took a step closer to the projection, voice low and razor-sharp. "You won't need one. I'm handling it. There will be no second chances."

Vidaurri stood perplexed. "Handling what?"

Her orders were clear. "Do not let them land on the planet."

Myli struck her hand over her throat, telling Ava D1 to cut the transmission. A heavy silence settled over the room. Ava D1 moved next to Myli, voice steady despite the storm around them.

"All systems ready. Ravelin has initiated the *Ursang's* final prep. Emergency evacuations are already underway on the surface. Estimated time to launch: forty minutes."

The AI had already decided who would be needed for reconstruction on another world. It wouldn't be many—but it would have to be enough.

Myli nodded slowly, the weight settling in. Everyone still in the blockade was likely doomed. "If we fail," she said quietly, "then *Ursang* becomes humanity's last chance at seeding another world."

Hawk agreed with the call, but doubt lingered in his voice. "What are the odds they find another Earth?"

Ava D1 processed. "Nearly zero. Earth is a statistical miracle. They could search for centuries—live out entire lives in the Garden on *Ursang*—and never find anything comparable."

She paused again, processing thousands of probabilistic models. "There is a possibility this reality is a larger version of the Garden itself. But regardless of what happens to the fleet, the solar flare will create a second great reset. A Nash Equilibrium. Survival of the fittest—again."

Hearing all this, Hawk gave a solemn nod. "More reason to get as many of our people on that bridge-layer as fast as we can."

All at once, the alarms screamed: INTRUDER ALERT. INTRUDER ALERT.

Myli pressed her hand to the monitor. Out in the corridor, a security team was already moving.

"How many?" she asked, eyes scanning the bulkhead.

"Not sure, ma'am. We think they boarded from the ship that rammed us."

"The one sticking in the side of our hull?" she asked.

"Yes, it's still there and the first teams on site believed it was empty."

"Terrific," she muttered over the blaring alarm—

Seconds later, the alarm cut off. Abrupt. Clean.

Myli paused. "That was fast."

The lead ensign looked uneasy. "Too fast, ma'am. Let me push ahead. Check it out."

She scowled. "I appreciate the concern, Ensign, but I'm coming with you."

He hesitated. Letting her come was a risk, but what she said sounded like an order. "Roger that, ma'am," the ensign said. "Just, do me a favor and stay on my six. I don't want to be the crewman who gets the captain killed."

"Fair enough," she said, charging a caseless rifle.

It took time to travel from the bridge to the impact zone—it was up two levels, fifty yards from the hangar bay. The *Daedalus* was already healing, building around the impact, corridor walls sealing, fire suppression units were refilling. The ship was repairing itself fast. Like a clogged pore, the *Daedalus* would inevitably push out the foreign object.

They halted at the intersection of a perpendicular corridor—voices ahead. Boots. Movement. Weapons raised, they rounded the corner—guns up.

"Stand down! Stand down!" a security team yelled out, hands lifted. With them was a very tall figure, bagged, bound, and cuffed.

"We caught her," one of them grinned.

"A soldier?" Myli asked, eyes scanning the prisoner.

"Pilot, we think, ma'am," one of the team snickered. "Not a very good one. Guess that explains the ship-to-ship collision when she tried to land. They are rounding up others near the hangar bay." He gestured toward the damage in the wall. "Rough landing. She was weak. Barely put up a fight."

The security team's point man stepped closer, lowering his voice. "She said she had information for the captain and wouldn't talk to anyone else."

Myli's eyes narrowed. She took a step forward. "Who are you?"

The ensign gave the prisoner a light jerk. "Answer her, or we toss you out the nearest airlock."

"Knock it off," a lieutenant snapped from behind. "Enough of our crew have been spaced today." The words hung in the corridor—raw, bitter, justified.

The muscles in Myli's face were tense. She was tired of the anger—but she couldn't blame them. She heard their voices in the corridors before the invasion. From the crew's perspective, it had been days or maybe weeks, not millennia. Expecting them to let it go would've been like asking a 9/11 survivor to calm down after waking from a 11,700-year coma. The pain didn't fade just because time had passed. Not for them. The wounds were still fresh. The hate, still raw.

She raised a hand, signaling them forward.

"Stand down," she ordered, her voice one of reason, calm but firm. She turned to the prisoner. "Let her speak."

The figure lifted her head, slow and deliberate, the hood restricting her movement. Her voice was old, cracked, but still carried the weight of something royal. Her chest heaved with every breath, exhaustion pulling at her. Through the fabric, the outline of her mouth barely moved.

"Ashaan," she said.

The name hit the corridor like a gunshot, silencing every murmur, every breath. Eyes widened. Fingers twitched to the triggers and Myli's heart jumped. They all knew the name.

Myli put a hand up. "Hold what you got," she ordered.

"I need food and water. Please," the prisoner requested.

Myli hesitated, her skin peppered by goosebumps. The daughter of Enlil. Anunna royalty. Here. Bound and in her custody. Ashaan may be a chip to stop the whole damn war. This wasn't just unexpected. This was game-changing. Fuck a stalemate; this was a possible truce.

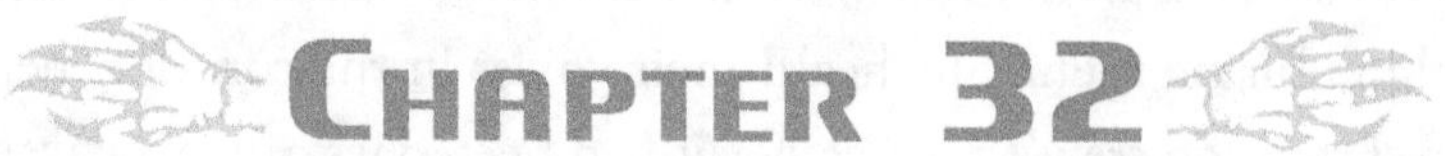

CHAPTER 32

Here Am I, Send me

The captured Anunna pilot lay motionless on the brig floor, her expression unreadable. The hood was gone, her vision restored. Ashaan's elongated, muscular frame was still, her breaths slow and deliberate, as if conserving energy. She showed no sign of fear—why would she? These creatures before her were genetic derivatives, offshoots, inferior copies of the true masters of the galaxy. They had no right to question her. Yet here she was, prone before them.

She knew their threats weren't idle. They had already threatened to jettison her into the vacuum of space—a pathetic, desperate attempt to intimidate a being bred for immortality and ruling.

The doors whooshed open. Three figures entered.

The first was massive—a towering Synth soldier, its mechanical frame reinforced with plasmatic and photonic armor plating. His lifeless, calculating optics scanned her, analyzing every micro-expression, every biological function. An ancient weapon, forged in a time when synthetic beings had nearly wiped out their organic creators. He was just as tall as her but more menacing.

The second was smaller, but no less imposing.

She was a 7th-generation hybrid Synth—an organic machine, fused with the DNA of the feral creatures of Ki. The next stage of engineered evolution.

The third, an Anunna hybrid twice removed. Human in stature. This was Myli. Ashaan had met her minutes ago. Female. Powerful. Graceful. She radiated control, a presence honed for dominance—not anarchy. Unlike the mindless war-machines of the past, this one had a mind of her own.

Ashaan had their numbers. Not worried at all, she sneered internally. *The brains, the data base, and the brawn. How predictable.*

En'Gen didn't hesitate. He reached down, grabbing the collar of her flight suit, and with terrifying ease, he hoisted her up off the floor, slamming her into the metal wall of the brig. She grimaced, her expression acknowledging his strength. The Synth's expression beneath the helmet remained impassive. Unreadable. Alien.

Myli's piercing green eyes locked onto the other woman's visor—a set of large, bulbous lenses blinking with subtle movement. Black eyes staring back from beneath, multi-lens sensors flickering, each one reflecting Myli's face in eerie, fragmented distortions. Myli was still wondering how to exploit the situation. Threaten Enlil? Make a deal?

Myli was resolute. With one swift motion, she ripped off the prisoner's goggles—tossing them to the deck. Her transhumanism being stripped away, cracks arced across the lenses and her 2nd SKN suit retracted, showing she wasn't afraid. They were face-to-face now. Ashaan was without her armor. And neither woman seemed willing to back down.

Ashaan's own reflected image rippled back at her through Myli's green eyes. She was hypnotizing in a hypnotically alien way. No wonder the ancient people of Earth bred with them. She was also stronger-willed than expected. Dangerous.

For the first time since her capture, the Anunna pilot felt something unfamiliar. Not fear, but something dangerously close: a feeling of unease.

Captain Sipani spoke through her own bewilderment. "You were a hell of a warrior in your day, Ashaan. But you're not invincible. And they sent you anyway." She paused, letting the weight of it settle. "You've become expendable. Why would you want to be a part of a culture that discards its own?"

Ashaan didn't respond, but her face did. Myli saw a crack. She pressed gently.

"There's still time to turn this around," Myli said, her voice steady. "Nothing is beyond repair. But if we go head-to-head, there won't be anything left for either of our species. You could be the one who stops this. Who unites us. Who saves lives."

Ashaan laughed sharply, bitterly, out of sync with the moment.

Myli couldn't hide the tension in her face. Her prisoner's laughter was a puzzle, and she couldn't find the edges of that puzzle, much less guess why Ashaan was amused by what she had suggested.

"There is a failsafe," Myli said flatly. "We won't be the only losers."

The prisoner's eyes locked onto Myli's. And she saw truth staring back.

"A Coronal Mass Ejection is forming," Myli continued. "It's going to be massive. When it hits," she took a breath, "we're all finished. The Dark Epoch will begin again."

"You fool, what have you done?" Ashaan hissed.

"MAD," En'Gen spoke coldly. "And we didn't do it. It was set in motion by the captain of the *Menagerie*."

Silence filled the cell as Ashaan fell to her knees and wept. She was in complete despair. The insanity she'd survived to reach Ki felt meaningless now.

"Then all is lost," she whispered, hollow. "Pain is only an illusion of the mind." Saying this, she stared hard at En'Gen and scoffed, "Do your worst, you binary slave."

En'Gen reached down and struck her—punishing. She rose and stumbled backwards in the wall. As promised, he ripped the flight suit from her body. Beneath it, scars. Deep. Surgical. Crude patches where flesh had been harvested and cauterized.

Myli gasped. Not in pity, but in shock.

Ashaan turned away, not in pain, but in shame. "We are already dead," she whispered. "Ki was our only hope."

Myli stepped closer, her voice sharp. "What are the Anunna planning? What's on the other side of that singularity? How many ships? How many soldiers?"

Ashaan clammed up.

Myli nodded to En'Gen. No words needed. They needed answers, not silence.

The Synth hovered over the prisoner. His grip tightened. A wet crunch. Ashaan screamed.

"Stop this!" she snarled. "I'll answer, much good it will do you," she growled. "It's not how many ships or soldiers lie beyond the singularity, but what else waits there." She sagged, breath gasping in staccato bursts. "I am Ashaan, daughter of Enlil," her voice raw. "I request asylum. For me—and what's left of my people."

Even En'Gen, a robot with no facial movements, managed to show surprise in his body language. Shocked, he retreated from her.

Ashaan exhaled sharply before continuing. "The war is over. They are eating what's left of my people."

"What people?" Myli could not believe her ears. "Who?"

"The Udug," Ashaan cried.

En'Gen's optics narrowed, his posture stiffening. "Your scars." he murmured.

"Yes," Ashaan said weakly. "We lost. And if the CME is true—both sides lose. Even if we combined forces, Earth without technology to shield the incoming CME will be overrun by the foul creatures if they reach the surface."

A wave of fear, or grief—perhaps resignation—crossed the alien's face.

"If you wanted asylum," Myli asked, her voice razor-sharp, "then why attack us? Why fight if you've surrendered?"

"We weren't the ones fighting," Ashaan rasped. "Those weren't Anunna flying those fighters," she told them.

Myli shut her eyes in disbelief. "So many? The Udug can't breed. They were a small contingent—specialized soldiers."

Ashaan nodded grimly. "They were but my father was given the code to fix that." Her voice shook. "Asag and Pazuzu found us in deep space. They handed my father the genetic blueprint to undo their sterilization."

"Project Red Wings," Ava grumbled. "They had an inside man."

"My father authorized expansion. He thought he could control them... like Enki controlled the humans."

She trembled. "He was wrong. They consumed us. They harvest us."

Ava shifted behind her, silent, absorbing the horror.

"We were stowed away on that ship. When the pilot crashed into you, we escaped."

Ashaan wiped blood from her lips.

Concern swept over Myli as she continued the interrogation. "What pilot?"

"He's here," she told them. "Here and looking for one of Enki's rings." Ashaan whispered eying everyone in the room, "Their bridge-layer lies unmoving because it lacks power to enter through the rift. I tried to warn your soldiers, but they assaulted me."

A cold silence swept over the already frigid cell.

Ava stepped forward, nerves twitching. "You speak of the Udug? It could be anyone."

Myli turned away, a feeling of dread attacking her psyche. "I have to go," she gasped. "Where is Sonny?" she shouted. "Locate him. Now!"

Hawk had been listening outside the brig. Now he entered, his voice low, "Sonny's on the hangar deck."

"Initiate search," En'Gen contacted Ava D1.

Ashaan had been resisting. Now the truth had come pouring out.

Hawk crossed his arms. "The first wave was to clear a path for the landing parties. If they traverse the wormhole, and land—"

With Hawk's unfinished sentence ringing in her ears, Myli met Ashaan's gaze.

"I know what that means," she told him.

"Even one carrier will spread like a plague," he continued.

Myli's eyes darted side-to-side, considering Ashaan's words. Calculating between possible outcomes. "I know," she repeated.

The ship hummed beneath their feet in a low, foreboding pulse that reminded them the clock was running out.

"I know you don't want to, but you need to make the call." He pressed.

"En'Gen... has Sonny been located yet?" she asked impatiently.

"No, Captain," En'Gen said, as he looped into the ship's comms. "He is no longer here."

"FUCK!" Myli uncharacteristically shouted.

Hawk knew what needed to be done and sprang into action. There wasn't time for a debate. Myli blocked Hawk's exit before he could dash out of the cell.

"Where do you think you're going?" she asked him.

"He can't be allowed to reach that ship." Hawk laid out the facts. "You know that."

"I'm *here*," she said, pointing at the deck. "I am going," she continued stabbing a finger at him. "And I will finish this once and for all, one way or another."

Hawk looked into her crazy eyes. "He's probably already dead," he added truthfully.

Her eyes were frantic, but her thoughts were clear. "You're better at this command shit than I am. Ava's your XO, Captain. Command this fleet!"

When Myli reached the hangar deck, the place was a madhouse preparing for round two. Refueled and rearmed fighters were being ferried into launch position. In rapid succession, engines began flaring against the darkness of space. Explosions were shimmering in the distance again like twinkling stars—a brutal reminder the war was starting up again.

Myli strode onto the deck, her 2nd SKN suit of armor clinging to her and flexing with every movement. Each muscle fiber fed biometric data to her embedded AVA system, keeping pace with her breath, her stress, her resolve. The suit's internal regulators pulsed with warmth, countering the chill that haunted the flight bay.

The ground crew—red shirts, yellow shirts, and purple "grapes"—moved like a living organism, their fractal order was well choreographed. One fighter was prepping for launch just as another skidded into recovery. Flight controllers were barking, waving, and signaling through the ruckus—a ballet of war machines in motion.

She approached the Sabre Cat being prepped for her. On her left, she tried ignoring a bloodied pilot being pulled out of his craft.

"Ava Rider, is my bird ready?"

A voice crackled in her comms. "Engines warming now, Captain. She looks a mess, but she's cleared for launch. It's pure havoc out there. Are you sure about this?"

"Everyone is where they need to be," Myli declared staring at the injured pilot. Her voice was calm. "Is he gonna make it?"

"No ma'am. His onboard AVA brought him home. He is deceased." Ava Rider checked Myli's vitals. "How are you not afraid right now?"

"I am afraid," Myli, practically trembling, exclaimed. "I just don't mind being afraid."

"Captain, your blood pressure and cortisol levels are increasing. May I ask what's going through your mind right now?"

Perspiration beaded on her forehead. "I'm thinking don't die like he did."

The sleek craft, *Rough Rider,* sat on the launch elevator—armed, fueled, primed for war. Ava Rider had handled every system check, every diagnostic while she conversed with her Captain. Myli paused, reassuring herself, then climbed the ladder up to the cockpit, her boots clanking against the rungs. At the top, she stopped, a voice behind her causing her to pause.

The voice wasn't loud, but it cut through the hangar noise like it was deliberate. She turned around. It was human Ava.

"Wait!" Ava called out, weaving through the flow of the flight deck *'skittles.'* She held something in her hand—a small matte-black matchbox-sized instrument, unassuming and dangerously portable.

Myli turned and hurriedly descended the ladder. Ava arrived and pressed the box into Myli's outstretched palm. It was heavier than it looked.

"What the heck is this?" Myli asked.

"A gift," Ava said quietly. "Something the Guardians have kept hidden on this ship for almost a century."

Myli raised an eyebrow. "Is it a bomb?" Myli frowned.

Ava smirked. "Much worse. A man named Nicola Tesla said you don't want to be anywhere near it once its triggered."

That peaked Myli's curiosity. "Sounds ominous, how long?"

"You get *thirty minutes,*" Ava answered.

Myli gulped. *Thirty minutes.* Not much time to get off a capital ship.

"You don't have to do this, Captain," Ava said. "Anyone on this crew would volunteer."

"I don't have a choice, Ava. This reckoning's been coming."

"Then make it make sense."

"I did it." Myli confessed.

"Did what?" Ava asked.

Myli's eyes glazed over despite her best efforts to stave off the tears. "I had orders. I sent the signal that triggered the solar apocalypse in the past... and I did it again when we returned."

"Enki gave us a warning back then. We had centuries to prepare. We had bunkers across the globe that saved hundreds of thousands." Ava protested. "We don't have that this go-around."

"I know." Myli's voice all but cracked.

"You'll kill billions this time," Ava levied.

Myli's eyes rolled up and over like she could catch the tears about to fall. "You don't think I also know that?" she said defeated.

Ava stared at her, stunned. She was the one person sent to save everyone. "Why?"

"Because I was told we'd be safe. That this ship would save us," she pleaded.

"Well, you've damned us, and yourself," Ava judged.

"I was already damned the second I woke up."

"I have no forgiveness for you," Ava replied as cold as an iceberg. "If you are already damned, you're heading to the right place. I don't know what exactly it is you think you'll find over there, but maybe you will save some of us. Godspeed, Captain."

Myli's lips tightened, her face pruned. She nodded once, climbed into her bird, and looked back long enough to watch Ava melt into the hangar crowd. She didn't have time to dwell. She pulled the safety harness over her head and snapped herself into the seat. Looking at her people's symbol, the solar cross, she made the sign of the cross on herself and prayed for a sliver of redemption.

Her thrusters were primed. Fox 3 missiles tucked neatly inside the hull. The plasma cannon energized.

A yellow-shirted handler signaled the lift operator, and the deck rumbled beneath her fighter. The Sabre Cat rose into position. Above her, Pri-Fly controlled everything from the tower, and monitored the launch sequence. On the Ouija board, the Air Boss replaced the red pin with green.

It was 'go' time. She knew what she was doing. She reiterated to herself to be sure.

Heartbeats pounded in her chest. Elevator Four reached level and shuddered to a halt. Launch bar lifted up, grabbing a hook under the nose of the levitating bird.

"Launch tube open." Her bird was shoved into the chute like a torpedo.

"Launch bar up." She signaled. "Contact."

The bird moved upward, stopping in launch position. Her left hand reached up, grabbing the launch bar, her other hand off the stick. Waiting on the AO's. The bird lurched forward again in the tube, stopping at the bubble.

She ran up the throttle to MRT, 100% thrust. Engines at Military Rated Power. She double-checked EFD, making sure she was all Nines with no inverse video. She aggressively wiped out the flight controls in all directions, giving flight control the opportunity for a built-in test to check itself for any faults.

She glanced at the Flight Control Systems Page on the right DDI. It showed no X's or BLINS—the FCS looked good and ready to go. She took her hand off the stick, put her head against the headrest, saluted the man in the bubble off to her right and grabbed the handrail.

"*Rough Rider,* you are clear for launch," a voice crackled through her comms.

The *launch tube* blurred. The *Daedalus* catapult hurled her forward. The G-forces slammed her into the seat with her head cradled against the restraint pad. For a split second, everything went black. Consciousness returning before she left the tube.

The cockpit shuddered violently as she broke free from the ship's gravitational field. She was off, the *Daedalus* vanishing in the black behind her. Stars were stretching across her canopy like scattered diamonds. The battlefield was looming ahead.

Her hands moved on instinct, punching in a flight path that would take her directly beneath the *Icarus*. The *Daedalus* was changing course to follow. It was increasing in speed. So was Myli. She had one chance to get through the vortex and save Sonny.

She headed for the breach.

CHAPTER 33

Suffer Well

Sonny's mind swam in circles like cartoons. He was alive. That alone felt unexpected. The corridors of the flagship loomed around him, dimly lit and pulsing with weak emergency light. The walls sweated grime—an oily sludge dripping from bulkheads. Corroded pipes hissed, releasing a foul vapor that mixed with the sickly-sweet stench of rotting meat.

It was like passing through the guts of a rotting beast—a tomb half-alive, half-decayed emulating its crew. His captor dragged him forward, claws digging deep into his shoulder. His mind begged him to fight. To run. To do *something.*

But each time he tried to resist, the Udug lieutenant's response was immediate and brutal. Sonny stopped struggling and stopped talking back. Resistance and sarcasm earned pain.

The ring still pulsed on his finger, its energy shield flickering—barely holding. He closed his fist tightly, hoping they wouldn't notice. If they figured out how to take it. Worse, if they unlocked it, what would they do with it?

No. Don't go there, he cautioned himself.

The corridor twisted downward into a spiral. Symbols coated the walls—scrawled in something dark and viscous. Not blood. Something worse.

They passed a grime-caked placard: alien symbols connected with his ring; then, after a shimmer, they read LEVEL 6, SECTION 5. Sonny locked onto the position.

A mantra.

Level six, section five. Level six, section five, he repeated over and over.

The stink thickened as they approached a set of heavy, reinforced doors. The Udug slammed a clawed fist against a rusty keypad. The doors parted with a wet, mechanical groan, exhaling a foul gust that hit Sonny like a wall. Stockyards in Kansas smelled better than here.

His skin prickled. Every hair stood on end. He wasn't prepared for what was inside. If this was meant to be their Garden, it was as vast but an anti-Garden, hell.

It didn't look like the serene power core of the *Daedalus.* It looked like a slaughterhouse. Corpses—hundreds of them—hung from hooks arranged in the trees like meat left to dry into jerky. Some still twitched, moaning, limbs jerking in rhythmic spasms—residual nerve activity sparking in bodies long past saving. Most were Anunna. Some were something else, Igigi?

The Udug hurled him to the floor, the impact rattling his teeth as he crashed into the rocks. Another Udug, an officer, stood nearby in the shadows. As Sonny struggled to rise, the shadowy creature's voice rumbled through the forest.

"Asag told me what you did to Pazuzu," the hidden Udug informed him. Clearly this reference was intended to frighten Sonny by suggesting what was coming next.

Sonny spat blood and looked up with defiance. "No shit? The POS had it coming. Maybe that asshole shouldn't have tried to kill us."

A low, gravelly laugh echoed from others watching.

"Fair enough." The creature stepped into the light—an Udug lieutenant, bigger and uglier than most. "He was the Son of Hanbi."

"Cool story, bro." Sonny shrugged his shoulders in defiance.

"I am Hanbi."

Sonny froze. *Well, fuck—of course he was.*

"You clutch the ring thinking that tiny energy field is going to save you," Hanbi growled.

Sonny winced as he sat up, muttering and determined to interrogate this creature. "Sure are a lot of you around here. You guys can't breed, low T, low sperm counts—what gives?"

Hanbi's eyes gleamed cold and inhuman. "Some of us were Anunna once. Conscripted. Volunteers. Criminals. Enlil gave us this gift."

Clawed footsteps echoed from behind.

More Udug gathering around.

Another demon stepped forward, voice thick with disdain. "This weak creature is responsible for Pazuzu's death?"

"Well... there's been a bit of an overexaggeration." Sonny's heart comically pounded in his chest. He held up a single finger, the universal give-me-one-second-to-unfuck-this gesture.

"I get it. Signals got crossed." He nodded earnestly. "I'm partly to blame."

"You can't believe every little rumor you *hear,* right? I was there, yeah, but the guy was already dead when I shot him. Context is king, y'all."

He winced in performative sympathy and shook his head consoling them.

"Now, for the right price? I might be able to help y'all find the right son of a bitch."

His salesman smile afforded him no slack. Low growls, rasping voices, and clacking filled the air; their language—alien. One of them—a towering brute with thick muscles strewn long due to its height—left the crowd and walked toward Sonny. Its milky eyes bulged, nostrils flaring as it sniffed, then slowly licked its black, leathery lips.

"He will be, adequate," it rasped.

Another growled in agreement. "Fresh. Young."

So, I'm human veal, Sonny told himself. *An embryo compared to them.*

Hanbi crouched beside Sonny, wiping blood from a cut on his prisoner's head with a clawed finger. "They don't have the serum," he mused, almost bored. "No regeneration like the Anunna. Very gamey—unless you catch one of the big ones. These fit ones are dry and tough."

Sonny's body tensed. His instincts screamed.

Run. Fight. Do something.

"We'll have to boil him," one said.

Sonny didn't like that. He began sweating profusely. Shifting up to his knees. "Choke on my South Texas Oysters, A-hole."

Seeing Sonny become less static, Hanbi kicked him square in the chest. The impact drove him into the rocks with brutal force. He coughed blood. The ring flickered.

Hanbi stepped forward, reaching into the shredded fabric of Sonny's Alpha Suit. His claws tore into Sonny's collar, shredding what was left of the uniform. He slammed him down again. Sonny hit the deck harder—fully exposed, his body battered and trembling, muscles twitching from shock and fear, he tried to hide from the hoard of cannibals.

He barely had time to assess what was happening next when Hanbi seized his left hand—wrenching it upward. The ring. Hanbi's face twisted into pure determination. With one violent yank, he tore the ring free. The energy shield collapsed—and the skin came with it. Sonny's eyes opened wide with horror, he screamed from the pain detonating in his hand.

His vision blurred. But he still had fight in him. He surged to his feet and landed a solid right hook square across Hanbi's jaw. For one second, he felt like he had a chance—until Hanbi hit him back.

Still far from the scene of Sonny's torture, Myli's ship approached the singularity like a wraith hunting through a graveyard of wreckage. The HUD pulsed red. Debris alerts screamed in her ears. Not the first. Not the last.

Ava Rider's voice chimed in—calm, clinical, unshaken. "Warning. Impact probability 63%. Adjust course."

Myli tapped the stick starboard, narrowly avoided a half-melted hull fragment the size of a blue whale. It spun past like a razor-sharp tumbleweed. Witnessing something that big, that powerful, glide by without effort snapped her back to the perspective she'd been ignoring—just how far outmatched she really was.

Ahead, the *Langley* drifting, dark and powerless—dead in the void. They found the fight they were looking for and lost.

The *Enterprise,* fires snuffed out one-by-one in the vacuum of space. She was barely holding together. Her hull hemorrhaging bodies and debris into the abyss.

Fighters screamed past her—some still firing, others running. She remained unnoticed in her nook of debris. Myli nudged forward, cloaked.

A feeling hit her nerves. Her little voice creeping in like a virus. She closed her eyes hoping to latch onto it psychically. Her mind felt around the abyss in front of her. She gasped.

Sonny, he was alive. She felt a faint pulse of awareness.

She opened her eyes and focused. There. She could hear him. Not words. Not thoughts. Just a presence that was fading.

It was coming from a massive, hulking warship up ahead, its bulk second only to their own bridge-layer, the *Ursang.* Her pulse spiked. Time stretched thin. She shoved the throttle.

The debris field thinned as she exited her cover, the last shattered husks drifting behind her. "Captain, you have cleared 98.5% of the debris field."

"Got it, Ava."

Ahead of her, open space—nowhere left to hide. It was the most vulnerable she'd been since leaving the *Daedalus. Rough Rider* began to rattle on approach to the time-sphere—the beginning of the wormhole's throat. Terminal destination.

Myli tightened her grip on the yoke. Ava's voice came again, calm but insistent.

"Captain, crossing open space in an active battlefront lowers our probability of survival—"

"I know." Myli's eyes flicked to the tactical readout. "As soon as we are through, target as many sacrificial drones as we can with our Fox 3's."

The *Saratoga* limped off the port side of the broken line. Thrusters fought to stabilize her path and keep her at a precarious perihelion to the disturbance. Anything to prevent what was taking place with the *Enterprise.* She vanished—sucked in, swallowed by the vortex behind Myli's ship.

"Ava," Myli asked, eyes focusing, "what are my chances of accelerating to Ninety-Nine and stopping in time before I hit the bridge-layer on the other side?"

Ava's voice—dry as ever. "I'd rather not tell you, Captain."

Myli exhaled. "That good? Probably best you keep it to yourself."

Her thumb flipped up the safety shield on the Ninety-Nine ignition switch. She let out a long, steadying breath. "Tell me this isn't stupid," she mused seeking reassurance.

"Incredibly stupid, ma'am. It will be a miracle if you don't teleport into a bulkhead."

"Well, Ava," she muttered, "if we don't make it—"

She reached down and unclipped a pouch from her flight harness, carefully sliding Tesla's little black box inside. It was wrapped in Alpha Skin, insulated and secured.

"—at least it'll be quick," she completed her assessment.

Her fingers curled around the throttle, her thumb settling on the red sublight trigger. A bead of sweat slid down her cheek, joining others pooling at the bottom of the face shield. She ignored the rash blooming around her jawline, a raw irritation from the constant dampness.

The engines spooled up. She depressed the red trigger with her thumb. Time stretched.

From Myli's perspective, the Sabre Cat elongated, then snapped forward —just below the speed of light. Myli zoomed into the decaying orbit of the time-sphere.

Ava Rider had been right; there was no time to decelerate. She activated all Fox 3's and fired. Myli didn't even try deceleration. At the last second, she gambled by leaving her fighter and teleporting to where she thought she'd felt Sonny last. Her suit buffered.

She materialized in a blast of white-blue light, her Second Skin suit shielding her from horrendous smells. The air was thick, the atmosphere a reddish hue. She was near the enemy ship's Sun Drive room. She pulled her sidearm and took a second to get her bearings.

Alarms were blaring, red strobes pulsing through the corridor like blood pumping from an open wound. But it wasn't for her, or at least not directly. The ship's computer screeched in Anunna, its synthetic voice warped with panic. She understood the key phrase:

"IMPACT IS IMMINENT. DECKS SIX THROUGH TEN— BREACH IN PROGRESS."

The hull shuddered violently. Outside her Sabre Cat slammed into the ship, a sonic roar echoing through metal and marrow alike. Multiple decks tore apart. Support beams groaned. Bulkheads folded like paper. A plume of flame rolled past the corridor behind her.

She slammed into a bulkhead, then tried to lurch forward, but not all of her came along.

The ship had her.

Her hip was stuck, fused to the bulkhead like the walls of the ship had shackled her in place. Panic zapped her nerves. She twisted, testing, a slight bit of relief washed over her. Thank God. It wasn't flesh that was stuck. Just a section of her suit which had welded into the wall. She heard footsteps heading her way.

"Ava..." she hissed.

"Way ahead of you ma'am."

Myli looked towards the approaching threat and back at her left leg.

A soft shimmer traveled over her armor as the AI diagnosed the breach. The stuck material crumbled away as it disintegrated into molecules.

She was free, stumbling clear and trading agility for speed. Her body slammed into the corner of the dark bulkhead where she was hidden from light. Reaching down, she felt her bare leg. Her head whipped up in time to watch a demonic soldier rushing past. He seemed not to see her.

Preoccupied by the hull breach? she asked herself.

"Doesn't get much closer than that does it," she quipped to her AI.

"Agreed, Captain. Don't forget you have armor missing there."

She concurred. She had almost nuked herself and phased into a ship. But it had worked and she didn't dwell on how close she came to failing.

She was already running. "Where are you, Sonny?" she asked aloud.

The collision alerts faded, replaced by sharper warnings: "DECOMPRESSION WARNING. ATMOSPHERIC FAILURE. SEALING NONESSENTIAL COMPARTMENTS."

Hatches slammed shut all around her, bulkheads began sealing off corridors and gangways. She slowed her pace and switched to stealth, once she felt safe from the explosions behind her.

Myli moved in the shadows, heels to toes, staying close to the wall. The ship's tropical humidity clung to her armor in thick beads. Inside, her body betrayed her, too. Sweat ran down her temples, too much for the suit to handle. It stung her eyes, but there was no wiping it away. Her focus was costing her relief; she crushed her eyes hard and kept going.

The sound of huffs from her breath and the sirens continued masking her steps in her head. As she slipped past one patrol, another patrol appeared. She ducked into a recessed alcove and held her breath. There were so damn many of them.

They passed.

Her heart thundered against her ribs, but she kept moving—deeper into the enemy lair. All her life, she'd been told one thing: Run from the Udug. But now? She was walking straight into their den.

She stopped for a minute to concentrate on Sonny's feelings—striving to pinpoint his location. She grabbed his bearings, but the sense evaporated. *Did he just die?*

She turned a corner. Had she stumbled upon the ship's Garden? No, this was hell, and she was terrified.

Myli slipped into a sprawling area of vast nothingness. There was little water. Only dust, dead trees, and cracked earth. And the bodies lining the horizons—horrible, but she had no time for disgust. Myli moved, setting aside her fears for the moment, resolved to either take Sonny alive or return with whatever was left of him.

Over rocks, through dead brush, weaving between twisted roots and rotting trunks, she hunted for his body. Until—there!

Sonny was stumbling ahead, drifting aimlessly. Lost. Disoriented. She sprang forward and overtook him.

"Sonny..." she whispered. Her heart leapt.

He looked at her. Her body, her muscles—his eyes eventually found hers. She opened her arms in disbelief.

"Come here," she whispered. "I was sure I lost you."

He stepped toward her slowly, his mouth quivering, lips trembling as he began licking them. His clothes were gone. She couldn't tell if he was terrified or in shock.

"Thank God, you found me," he said breathlessly. "I thought I'd never get out. I got away from them." He remarked awkwardly pointing over his shoulder.

She glanced at his hand. The ring. Not there. No link. No presence. No thoughts. Her brows furrowed. She felt a cold twist coming. She thought she was ready to bring back a body. But now? Now it was real. But he wasn't whole, and she wasn't prepared for this. She looked into his eyes and found nothing. Hollow sockets where Sonny used to be.

"Sonny?" she asked quietly.

He smiled and couldn't help laughing. "Sonny was the appetizer." He grinned wider, his teeth sharp. "You're what's for dinner."

Her focus was locked on his face but in her periphery, his hand began to shift. Flesh melted into scale. Fingers stretched into claws. The emerging Udug lunged. She didn't hesitate. His claws tore through the air with a *whoof.* Myli jerked sideways, barely escaping the kill zone.

The second strike came faster, like a blur of organic Ginsu fury. She raised her pistol only to have it split in half, sparks and pieces clattering to the floor. She cursed under her breath.

Any mistakes or miscalculations and her mission would turn to shit. This was going to be harder than she thought.

Hanbi grinned. "You know," he said casually, circling her, "your father begged us to leave you alone. In fact, he traded an entire world for you."

"The hell he did," she snarled and, before her words even landed, Myli vanished.

She reappeared behind him with a knife drawn, body low. Her blade kissed his spine. A dark gash opening along the Udug's back, blood pouring in thick spurts.

Before Hanbi could scream, she dropped to a knee, slashing deep into the inside of his thigh, severing flesh, hunting the artery. She continued with a jab upward, aiming for the tangle of tendons beneath his arm, the ones that controlled his grip. His claws. His killing hand. Weakened by multiple cuts, Hanbi howled, stumbling. His left arm spasming and flailing without purpose.

Myli didn't stop to admire the damage. She rolled sideways, keeping her blade ready. This wasn't a fight. This was a dissection in progress. Payback.

Hanbi roared, lurching forward, then turned, slashing wildly with his good arm. Missed.

She vanished again. Reappeared. Another strike across the face. Blood poured from his left eye.

"You bitch," he hissed, swaying.

He stepped; she dodged and rolled between his legs avoiding another swipe from his claw. She reversed her grip on the blade, crouching low. Her hip ached, the one missing armor.

When did he strike me? she asked herself.

She felt warm blood pooling inside the leg armor of her Second Skin, running in the layers of her Alpha Skin and settling under her foot.

Had he clipped her? Had he injected venom?

If so, she was on a countdown. Sure enough, her breathing was turning raspy. Behind her, Hanbi swayed; he laughed through the pain, all while underestimating her.

"Nothing like a good workout to build the hunger," he hissed. "I like to tenderize my meat before I eat it."

Myli narrowed her eyes. "That's funny," she growled back. "Let's see what your backstraps taste like!"

She vanished again reappearing just behind him. But this time, she stepped off-angle, anticipating his counter. Her blade flashed low, slicing across the backs of his knees. Tendons cut. Hanbi collapsed with a gruff snarl, legs folding beneath him like broken scaffolding. Myli didn't wait. She reappeared in front of him, blade already poised. One final, merciless strike—driven straight through his throat.

Hanbi gasped. One hand on the handle of the knife, the other backing it up on the hilt, full drive. Black blood bubbled from his mouth, his body twitching and choking on what was left of him. A few seconds passed and he dropped.

Myli stared down at Hanbi's corpse, breathing hard. She stood slowly, chest rising and falling. Her thoughts spun, something he said still echoing in her ears.

Time to find his body.

CHAPTER 34

Devil's Cut Runs Deep

The ship groaned as its own internal pressure fought to burst free. The bridge-layer lumbered toward the vortex, its mass shuddering with every surge of energy required to keep the wormhole open. The centrifuge ring around the main hull wobbled, slipping out of alignment. The chief engineer's earlier override bought them time, but the damage Myli inflicted now pushed the system towards catastrophe.

Crew teams scrambled to stabilize the centrifuge's centricity before the wobble became a full structural tear. The chief engineer used Sonny's ring to reboot the ship's system, plugging it into one of the energy terminals.

The output of the Sun Drive increased exponentially and began pumping raw energy into the core. The mega-vessel surged forward, preparing to make the jump.

Deep within Hell's Garden, Myli pushed on. She stumbled through a tangled web of organic matter that was wet and sticky, like spider webbing. Each step pushing through the strong filaments slowed her hunt.

Venom continued coursing through her veins. Her limbs were weighty as the suit strained to match her tempo. Each breath, heavier than the last.

But she kept going.

She clawed at the strands, eyes scanning.
Where are you?

She was about to surrender to the venom, to this alien Garden, when she found his body. What remained of him lay in a heap of mangled flesh, bloodied, naked, and broken.

"Sonny..." She knelt beside him in the dirt.

Her hand slipped through his damp hair. His body was still warm as expected in Hell's Kitchen. She slumped down next to him, partially draped across his body.

She tapped her forearm, opening her suit's schematics. The breastplate hissed apart, exposing the tiny Tesla Box nestled inside.

Finding the words to describe her feelings in this moment was an impossible task. Everyone died eventually. She'd seen her fair share of death. But staring at the Tesla Box, she knew she was staring at the instrument of her own destruction. Frustration... fear... she couldn't tell which pushed her to set the box down in her lap. She only knew that she did, and in doing so it slipped from her fingers, slid off her thigh, and dropped into the dirt.

Myli folded herself over Sonny's body, giving into full submission of her circumstance. She pulled him close despite the jagged edges of her armor. One piece scraped across an open wound—

He cried out.

Her face scrunched. He was alive and barely conscious. Above her, the sun blazed in a sickly red-orange hue. She felt a shift in gravity. The ship was moving. Powering up. Time was almost gone.

Sonny stirred with a groan. "Myli?"

"I'm here." She grabbed his hand, and he recoiled in pain. She froze. His ring finger was skinned to the bone, and she had latched onto it like she was pulling open a 300-pound door. *Three good fingers left.* She hauled him to his feet. He wobbled, barely able to stand.

"Come with me if you want to live," she said.

Confusion twisted his bloodied face. "What?"

Now Myli was confused. "What?" she echoed, deadpan.

He shook his head. "Nothing."

Not the time to educate about vintage action movies, he thought.

"Yeah, well," she grinned, even as the pain in her thigh sought to ground her, "somebody's got to save your ass."

"Hold my beer," Sonny grimaced, still swimming in pain. "Hanbi?"

She didn't recognize the name, but she got the gist.

"Disarmed," she said, exhaling. "Permanently."

She pulled out one of the vials and jabbed it into his neck.

"Geez!" Sonny flinched.

"Don't be a wuss." Myli gave a weak laugh. "Focus. We don't have time for you to be stumbling around with venom coursing in your blood stream. Besides, what doesn't kill you will make you wish it did."

She injected herself next, the antivenom burning cold through her veins. The ship rumbled again, deeper this time. A low, seismic hum vibrated through the walls. They were closing in on the singularity's mouth.

Myli's eyes focused in on the Tesla Box.

Sonny's eyes widened. "What's that? It's tiny."

"No effing clue."

They waited. Nothing. They exchanged a look.

"Ava gave it to me," Myli said flatly. "She said we'd have thirty minutes."

Sonny winced. "Maybe kick it?"

Myli scowled. "That sounds like a terrible idea."

Sonny gave a painful grin. "We have to trust the D.O.P.E."

She flashed a glance at him. "What?"

"Trust the D.O.P.E. If that chick said thirty minutes—we need to trust her." They stared at the device another few seconds and then turned and ran. They were making progress until Sonny tumbled to the ground.

Sonny winced, trying to sit up. "If this is where we are going to die, let's die well."

Myli glanced around, voice calm. "Death is always on our doorstep." She gave a faint shrug.

The tiny oscillator, Tesla's box worked its dark magic. The polarity in the wormhole was shifting. The sphere destabilizing, trembling, collapsing on itself.

"Do you remember how to get to the flight deck?" she asked.

Sonny rubbed his face, blinking through the haze. "Yeah, I took notes on the way down into the bowels of hell."

The bulkheads were rippling, molecules shifting, the tremors amplifying.

"We need to get the hell out. Now. Anything you can remember will help."

"They took the ring that way. There has to be a control station that way."

Minutes later Sonny nodded, pointing toward a stack of lockers. They found the control station for the Star Drive.

"We need weapons." Myli said rummaging through the security center.

After a minute spent selecting firearms, they burst through the nearest door, the one that made the most sense, the one which they hoped would take them straight toward the flight deck.

They rounded a corner and Sonny spotted it.

Level six, section five.

"We're headed the right way!" he shouted, just as a patrol of Udug appeared.

Sonny came in hot, roaring, finger on the trigger. Every shot rained hell on his skinned finger. His energy rifle shrieked with each pull; he was 100% trigger slapping and turning bodies into pink mist. The first enemy lost its torso. The second—its head. The third didn't even get a shot off before parts of him vaporized.

Sonny had snapped—psycho-killer persona mode engaged.

He and Myli moved like a seasoned unit—shoot, scoot, cover, move. Leapfrogging through hell. His weapon overheating, beeping like a heart monitor in cardiac arrest. Sonny cursed, dunking it into the nearest wet, sludgy puddle of Udug remains, steam rising in hissing clouds. The stench hit him like a ton of putrid bricks.

"Oh, my gosh! I don't believe it! There!" he pointed. "It's right next to you!"

"What?" she asked.

"The ring," he shouted, "on that energy terminal."

She was closer than him. She grabbed the ring, hoping it would kill the power, but it didn't matter; the ship took what it needed. She looked down at the ring in her palm. Her voice was quiet. Steady.

"Catch."

She tossed the ring.

Sonny caught it midair with his handicapped hand. The band slithered back onto his mangled finger, fusing to bone and skin. He groaned as the regenerative charge surged through him like a breath of life. Which is when the corridor in front of them imploded.

"We need another way out!" he grimaced.

Myli scanned the schematic on the wall—spotted an access junction. "Here!" she barked, slamming her boot into the ventilation panel.

The 2nd SKN crumpled the living membrane inward like paper.

She glanced back. More Udug had found them, but Sonny was in Flow State—The Zone. He was completely naked but drenched in blood, sweat, and dirt. He was flowing like he was born for this, slaying demons. Myli watched him for a second, this is what it must have been like for him when he saw her in action for the first time. A mesmerizing display of pure hedonistic primalism. His muscles displayed under the muck; it was striking in a morbid way. He was unstoppable, feral, attractive madness in a tactical ballet.

She'd fallen for this stupid, savage monkey.

"Come on!" she shouted, covering him as he bounded past her and leaped into the vent.

Myli grabbed a grenade off a fallen Udug, armed it with a twist, and tossed it over her shoulder without looking.

A massive explosion ripped off. The concussive blast leveled everything in the corridor behind them. She yanked a massive instrument panel down, slamming it over the hole. It wouldn't hold forever—but it would buy them time.

Time to press on.

They crawled, sliding sideways, dragging themselves through what appeared to be a network of lungs. The passage contracted and expanded around them in wet, claustrophobic pulses. This was the worst stretch yet.

Every so often, gravity flickered out, leaving them weightless just as the ship's organ contracted, pinning them in place and stealing their leverage.

At last, an opening. A widening in the membrane, like a bronchial tube branching into a larger airway. Space enough to move. Space enough to finally make up time.

Sprinting now, they emerged above an immense cargo bay—dark and confining. As they rushed through a ventilation tube, Sonny stopped.

"That smell," he muttered. It was familiar—but alien.

The stench nearly overpowered him. At least Myli was shielded by her suit. Myli wiped mucous membrane from her visor—and then she looked down and saw them.

Beneath them, she could see a nightmare. Hundreds—maybe thousands—of Anunna lay caged below. Malnourished. Their bodies withered. Eyes sunken. Bones exposed. Those who resisted had been herded into pens like cattle. Starved to keep them weak. Fattened just enough when it was time to harvest.

Sonny contemplated the implications of what they stumbled upon. He'd been fast-tracked straight to the dinner plate. This was the future Earth faced if even one platoon of fertile Udug survived. He shuddered, but they had to move.

He tilted his head, *let's go,* and sprinted across the trampoline-like membrane.

Five steps in, he lost his footing, his legs shot out from under him. He looked like an ice skater pinwheeling for balance, but gravity won. His face slapped the translucent membrane floor. The barrel of his rifle punched a cut, a tear, a rip and he began sinking into the widening slit.

"Fuck, Myli..."

Legs, hips, chest, and shoulders began to sink; she dove headfirst, reached out for his hand, and caught it. But the slime weakened her grip and Sonny dropped.

He landed in a wet mushy pit below. He was caught in a sea of sick, broken bodies—a slimy morass of feces, bile, rot, and pain. The stench overwhelmed him. He puked until there was nothing left to expel.

Hands the size of plates grabbed at him—not to kill, but to plead. Desperate. Weak. Broken. His weapon slipped from his grip. Panic surged. He couldn't breathe.

The hatch unsealed above. Blinding white light flooded the pit. And there she stood.

Myli. A silhouette of salvation.

"Need a hand?"

Sonny scrambled toward her, climbing over the massive bodies, slipping on filth, his arms shaking. The Anunna shrank back from the light—hissing, recoiling as if they were allergic to it. Sonny gasped, reaching the edge.

"Leave it open," he said between breaths. "They deserve a chance."

They ran bursting into Pri-Fly—the ship's flight operations control deck. Below them, in the hangar bay, was a ship. Prepped and ready for launch. It was a corvette. Sleek. Compact. The smallest class of warship that was still capable of atmospheric entry, orbital combat, and long-distance travel.

Escape was seconds away. But seconds are an eternity when that's all you have left.

CHAPTER 35

The Fire Below

The battle over Earth had become an inferno in space. Debris would rain from orbit for decades, maybe centuries if the solar flare didn't destroy it. This was it. A final push. All or nothing.

"THEY'RE SWARMING US, SIR!"

Hawk's jaw locked. They were coming in fast—headlong through the rift. "Launch all remaining fighters. Deploy every drone we have. Evasive pattern Delta-Seven."

Ava's voice cut across the comms—calm, deadly. "Contact." An echo from all fighters.

Hawk's eyes focused. "As soon as they're within two-hundred thousand kilometers, fire rail guns and antimatter cannons. Once they burn fuel to maneuver—hit them with torpedoes."

"Aye, Captain!" The bridge fell into motion.

"You're trying to fly this big boat like a fighter," a crew member remarked.

Hawk leaned forward, voice low and lethal. "So fly her like she was meant for it."

Ava's drone cockpit trembled, synched directly to her neural feedback loop. She winced as her UAV took a glancing hit—her body feeling the jolt like a phantom pain. Even though she was miles from the fighting, the system was fully immersive. That was the point.

Feel everything. React like you're there. Her hands moved instinctively, the stick sliding side to side, weaving through arcing wreckage. One digital fighter guarding the last manned Sabre Cat that was still flying.

Below, the fleet was coming apart. The *Icarus* was taking direct hits—shielding failing, hull breached in several locations but nothing critical. Twisted wreckage spiraled in every direction—corpses, plating, broken birds.

The *Daedalus* was still holding. Leading the formation. Pushing for the wormhole. Myli would need a quick escape if she succeeded and Ava aimed to clear the way. But the breach was growing. Exponentially with the increased power intake from the Enki's Mini Mii ring on the other side.

On the bridge of *Daedalus,* Hawk muttered under his breath, jaw set tight. "That's one big bitch coming through."

This wasn't going to be a BFM brawl—no knife fight in a phone booth. This was BVR—Beyond Visual Range. The merge would only happen if Rocco and the others got unlucky enough to be caught in it—or lucky enough to survive the enemy's BVR onslaught long enough to close the distance.

Out there, beyond the drone cockpits and the bridge, Rocco had been lucky during the first wave. Too lucky. He could feel it now—the edge fraying. *Luck doesn't last.*

In World War I, a pilot's life expectancy was six to ten weeks in combat. And that was *after* they sort of knew what they were doing. Here?

Out here, skill didn't buy you weeks. It bought you seconds.

His eyes were scanning the LiDAR. Too many contacts. Ava Jeep was prioritizing threats and potential escape lanes. Most threats were AI-controlled, coordinated, and processing faster than a human alone could. One enemy she was tracking broke the pattern.

The contact blipped, in and out, on his screen. It was heading straight for them. The ship's stealth was doing its job. He could lob a Fox 3 at it and get it to defend, causing the enemy to turn and run for a short while, but it would eventually reengage.

He selected a Fox 3 but waited to fire. They'd keep pushing.

The beyond visual range was shrinking. To be safe, they waited for the IFF signature; it was definitely a bandit. His AI started running other scans, building a portfolio for the enemy craft's engine harmonics. It was as the AI suspected.

"Firing Fox 3." His finger squeezed the trigger on the yoke. The missile ripped away.

"Not to alarm you, but we've seen this one before," his AI noted.

"Oh, is that right?" Rocco looked down at the screen. "What are you seeing?" he asked her.

"It's *Carnivore*," she warned pointblank.

"I thought we confirmed that kill."

"Apparently the pilot or the AI limped home and rearmed. Either way, *Carnivore* is coming for us, and it appears its hunting our signature."

Rocco felt tightness in his left shoulder. He knew that pain. It was the nerves. He'd had shingles several weeks ago from the stress of preparing his squadron. His own body was turning on himself again. He tried to roll it out. A pinch of pain shocked his neck, causing him to wince. On his starboard was Ava's drone.

She counted down its distance.

He gripped the yoke like an egg. "C'mon, baby, just one more clean run."

Back in the mother drone VR cockpit, Ava keyed the TOC channel. "I've got a carrier coming through the breach—launching fighters now."

Tactical Operations came back instantly. "Roger. Chrono Reapers vectoring in."

On Ava's display, the Jolly Rogers Squadron broke off from the *Icarus,* executing predictive evasive maneuvers.

Dozens of enemy missiles lit the void, breaking cloak—a storm of L-RASMs, SLAMERs, and SMACM warheads zipped toward the scattered fleet. They swarmed like angry yellowjackets weaving through plumes of destruction.

These weren't terrestrial munitions. Once active, they barely needed fuel, conserving it for violent course corrections. This left room for more munitions, sensors, and guidance systems. Half was brain and payload. The other half, engine and thrusters with one goal—destruction.

In space, time on target wasn't about seconds—it was about precision across thousands of kilometers. Launching too soon gave the humans the one thing they needed most. Room to maneuver.

Rocco's sensors lit up like a Christmas tree. "Incoming! Break, break, break!" He and the other pilots slammed into their throttles and yanked their birds into hard angles—spinning, diving, climbing, flares and chaff punching out in every direction.

The Anunna weapons came fast, but not fast enough. They would need hours to course-correct and reengage, and that was only if they had the fuel reserves to try. Rocco's squadrons slipped the net.

In moments, the human fighters were inside the enemy's predictive envelope, angles changing rapidly for clean solutions. One shot turned into ten. Ten into none. Their own Loyal Wingmen turn into the hits, the sacrificial lambs devoured by the onslaught.

Rocco grinned. "They jumped the gun. They've got to be Winchester on missiles. We lose anyone?"

"Mailman!" someone shouted over comms. "He sent them a package to hold for us before they got him."

"If you're going to go down, take two with you. If you run out of ammo, those capital ships look mighty tempting."

"Roger that, Wing Commander," the squadron replied.

He muted comms. "Ava Jeep, are you still tracking *Carnivore?*"

"I've lost him in the kerfuffle, sir."

"Kerfuffle, Ava?" he laughed.

Back on the *Daedalus,* Ava tagged what was left of the Collaborative Combat Aircraft—affectionately nicknamed the Loyal Wingmen. No cockpits. No pilots. Which meant more room for firepower, sensors, countermeasures, and missiles. Unlike the Udug drones, Ava Daedalus could work from Rocco's fighter, see the battlefield in real time and activating the missile trucks *before* data reached the *Daedalus* or its VR drone squadron, buying much needed seconds.

If there was empty space in the missile trucks, they crammed it full of tech. Each one was a flying death brick—its Electronic Warfare suite rivaling that of a small warship. But what made them deadly wasn't the hardware. It was the brain.

Piloted exclusively by one of the many AVA programs, they didn't just fly—they hunted together. AVA was the hive mind, and the Loyal Wingmen were the serial killers intertwined with her intelligence.

Rocco's missile trucks formed up around him like loyal wolves. He gave them a casual salute.

"Hey little buddies." He keyed the comm. "Ava Jeep, you ready to go to work?"

"Say when," she replied, calm as ever.

"It's our turn now." Rocco grinned. "200,000 kilometers... 195,000... and closing."

He knew the math.

The closer they got, the better the odds. At this distance, sub-light missiles had about a 40-second delay, torpedoes a six-second delay, but the Anunna ships wouldn't be able to dodge them forever.

Even energy weapons weren't guaranteed hits. They traveled at light speed, but that still gave the enemy time to counter. At extreme distances, even with full luminosity, visual range was limited thanks to chameleon-skinned enemy hulls and countermeasure interference. Without telescopic HUD assistance, the Mark I Eyeball was only good for about 100 kilometers, and the target would look like a dot.

Rocco knew this from watching the massive ISS on Earth. It's 200 miles away and a tiny dot in the sky. A car would be invisible floating in orbit at that distance. And seeing a ship wasn't the same as hitting one.

Enemy vessels were maneuvering at tens of thousands of kilometers per second, some even pushing three-fourths the speed of light. At those speeds, torpedoes were just flashes of light—brilliant streaks gone before the pilot's brain caught up to what he was seeing.

Evasive maneuvers weren't just likely. They were expected. Turreted weapons required extreme predictive tracking, often relying on space-time sonar—echoes of gravity waves bouncing off enemy ships to form phantom images in real-time.

Manual targeting? Not unless you were within 10 clicks with lightning-fast reflexes. And even then, you'd better pray your enemy screwed up and flew into your burst.

One-by-one, enemy cruisers slipped out of the darkness—leviathans emerging from the black void. Space-time sonar picked up the subtle echoes of their gravity waves, betraying their positions even as they tried to stay cloaked.

Torpedoes launched from the capital ships. Six seconds to impact. Every shot was off.

A friendly torpedo screamed past Rocco's Sabre Cat, close enough to rattle his canopy. He barely had time to process it before an enemy torpedo came from the opposite direction, too close for comfort. He winced and flinched as the bus-sized ordinance flashed by him.

The blackness of space lit up in the distance—Earth's squadrons were finding their marks. Torpedoes from allied capital ships slammed into the enemy fleet.

Solid work, Rocco clenched his fist.

But, looking ahead, he saw it: 70,000 kilometers, 50,000, 40,000. Something huge—something much bigger than a fighter—was coming at him. More than one now. He narrowed his eyes.

"Ava Jeep, are you seeing this?"

"Loyal Wingmen intercepting," she replied, cool and clear.

Explosions flared ahead. A massive transport ripped past, followed by the others. A thunderous detonation rocked space just off his nose.

"You're on your own, Rocco," Ava alerted him over comms. "I'm dry on birds."

That was when *Carnivore* reappeared.

Rocco watched the sneaky bastard skirting past, surfing alongside the shadow of a transport, using its silhouette to close the gap. They were in the merge now, nose-to-nose with his nemesis, and just like that, Rocco was already behind the eight ball.

Ava Jeep barked *Carnivore's* position, talking so fast he could barely process her words.

"Six o'clock!" she warned.

The enemy ship began cutting down Rocco's remaining wingmen, one-by-one.

Rocco heard every scream, but he couldn't swing around fast enough to acquire a clean shot.

"We're in some real shitty shit, Ava," he groaned.

"Yes, sir, we are," she answered in earnest.

"Break right, now!" she demanded.

He did. Darting through a cloud of smoke particulates, he cut speed and found himself in a flat scissor position with *Carnivore*. The two birds were swooping back and forth, both pilots trying not to nudge out in front too far or they'd expose their six. An overcorrection spelled doom.

A juke left, a juke right, both fighters corkscrewed in a DNA strand, but neither craft scored a hit.

Guns flashed, tracers cut the void, but both pilots stayed clean. Rocco had no choice; he had to cut and run during the last turn. He broke into the one-circle, tight and deadly. Rocco pulled hard, G's stacking, his harness tightened, sweat glued him to his seat. He pushed the throttle forward for more power. His hands were steady, but in space there was no bleeding speed out of her.

His speed would increase until he threw the retro thrusters. Gathering up this much velocity was a gamble. The universe around them was spinning out of control.

"We can't keep this up," he struggled to spit out. "I want you to hit the brakes, Ava. I'm going nose-up and when I do, burn our forward thrusters for a high energy turn. I'll punch starboard and smoke this SOB once and for all."

"A HET this tight is dangerous. You could…"

"I know, you'll have the stick momentarily. You got this, girl. It's this or we die."

The Sabre Cat spun out. Rocco blacked out. Ava spit a few bursts and hit home, turning the *Carnivore* into a side dish. Alarms were screaming. Debris splattered in all directions. A chunk of that trashed heap clipped his port nacelle. Rocco snapped back to consciousness. His plan had worked, but now his Sabre Cat spiraled. His cloaking disengaged, he was spinning wildly. G-forces were slamming into his chest, pinning him against the controls—his vision tunneling, alarms screaming in his ears.

Losing power. He fought for control. No response. Thrusters—gone. Comms—dead.

"Ava!" he gasped. "Take control—now! Ava?"

Back on the *Daedalus,* Ava's viewscreen went black. Her loyal wingmen were all gone and now there was no IFF signature from Rocco on the scope. She'd lost him.

"Icarus," she calmly asked, "do you have him?"

"RELOAD NEW FIGHTER," the command flashed across the HUD. A fresh drone fully armed. Fully fueled. Fully ready. But Ava wasn't. She stared at the prompt, heart pounding. Her voice cracked through the comms, raw with worry.

"Rocco? Sending reinforcements."

Static.

On the *Icarus'* bridge, Stella stared at the screen in disbelief. Rocco's blip was gone. No signal. No telemetry. Just dead static. "Anything? Stella asked.

Her Operations Specialist shook his head. A layer of remorse fell on his face.

Ava tapped into TOC again. "No visual on Rocco. I'm loading up and going back out."

Ava didn't wait for permission. Her finger slammed the launch command—another round, another fight. It felt like a game console, but this was no simulation.

Stella's eyes stayed locked on the sensor screen. She should've ordered her drone to a sector needing defending, but didn't stop Ava. No war ends without names carved into memorial walls, but she held out hope for Rocco.

On the surface of the Earth, in the southernmost regions of China, Ashaan stumbled through a torrential downpour. Hawk had let her go. She had been through enough. He could only imagine the horrors she had witnessed. It wasn't the Anunna who were evil; it was their leadership.

She was free. After twelve thousand years lost in space, after surviving the horrors of the Udug, after enduring the shame of what she had done to survive, she was home. Paradise. It was more magnificent than she could have imagined. She dropped to her knees, her arms raised. Tears mixed with the rain.

"I did it," she sobbed. "I made it to Paradise."

And then she saw it. Something streaked silently overhead. A shadow against the storm clouds, tearing across the upper atmosphere. Was it a ship? A fighter? She squinted.

It was falling. And then she understood what it was. Her body froze. Her mind screamed. "Oh, no!"

The flash was blinding and final.

Chapter 36

Damned Reckoning

The fleet's readouts were all the same. An event was taking place on Earth. Vidaurri ordered a feed from the surface to see what was happening down on Earth. The Eastern hemisphere was on fire. The fireball was not contained there, however. It spread and soon began to appear over the Americas. Vidaurri fell back to his seat, missing the edge, and nearly collapsing to the floor before regaining his chair.

"They got through?" he asked.

"Casualty estimates are pouring in. A group of transports and gunships slipped past our squadrons and are entering Earth's atmosphere," Stella read from a tac screen. Rocco's squadron is gone, sir."

"Ejection pods?"

"None located, but there are tons of debris out there."

Vidaurri struggled out of his command chair. "I will inform the President and Joint Chiefs personally." The Admiral left the bridge, and the bridge crew was left holding the bag.

"Come on, Captain Sipani, stop that ship." Stella mumbled to herself. The command chair was empty. The ship was hers now.

Old man Vidaurri lurched toward his quarters. For all intents and purposes, they had lost. Decades of preparation... wasted. Unconscionable choices crept into his mind as he stepped inside.

The hatch slammed shut.

No one heard the Admiral die

Minutes later, it opened again. Vidaurri headed to the next deck like a tax collector to a grieving widow's house. His uniform was standard Space Force, regulation—but the longer you stared at it, the more you'd swear you saw a long cloak and the outline of an invisible scythe in hand. Secret service agents guarded the briefing room he headed for. A minor inconvenience.

The Admiral entered the conference room. Whatever melancholy demeanor had weighed him down was gone, replaced by something sinister. The President and her dignitaries stood with their backs to the door, watching satellite images of Washington burning in nuclear fire. Since the 1940s, Udug infiltrators had reconnoitered, cataloged, and targeted every command bunker on the planet. She, her staff, and a handful of chiefs with her, were what remained of United States command. Other than this secure briefing room, there was nowhere left for the leadership to hide.

"What do we do now, Admiral?" The President turned to address him, conviction gone, Plan B looking like more like Plan Hail Mary. Worry had taken over where certainty once lived.

He stepped inside and shut the hatch behind him, leaving the foot of a Secret Service agent visible on the deck outside, toes up. "Earth's defenses are stretched beyond their limits. The *Ama* will breach any minute. Earth will fall within the hour."

"What about Captain Sipani's mission?"

"The last wildcard," he complained. "And that crazy bitch wouldn't share her plans with anyone."

His arm swung back, then snapped forward. Something heavy hit the conference table with a dull wet thump and rolled to a stop.

The room quieted.

It took a minute for the crowd to process what they were looking at. Recognition gave way to disbelief. It couldn't be real.

A severed head. The skin was drained of all color, which made the radiant red hair even brighter in contrast. A woman's face frozen in the last instant of terror. A look of betrayal intertwined with her expression, eyes locked wide, mouth still gaping for a breath that never came, tongue protruding slightly. Whatever life had lived behind those eyes was gone, clouded over, hollow.

Pandemonium erupted. Screams burst from her staff as they scrambled backward, chairs overturning, bodies pressing into the corners as if distance could offer anything resembling safety.

President Hutchinson forced herself to look.

The head of a woman. The first woman.

Lilith, an alias they couldn't have known, Chiara.

"The traitor thought I was Vidaurri," he shrugged. "She meant to kill him, I believe."

"Who the hell are you?" Hutchinson demanded.

She stood her ground. If she was going to die, she would face the man responsible. She refused to cower.

"Enlil, Madame President," the Udug straightened to his full height, his features terrible as they settled in. "Son of Anu. Brother of the traitor, Enki. The architect of—" He motioned to the screens behind her — "all this."

"Why can't we coexist?" She stepped toward him, unafraid, gripping his arms in one final, desperate appeal. Two hands against the end of the world. "Your kind can have the Eastern Hemisphere. Allow us the West." Her blink revealed something reptilian in her DNA.

Something crossed his face. Lilith. The betrayal. The child.

"That traitorous woman was pregnant." His voice dropped. "I loved her. Yet there she is—and that is all that remains of her." His eyes narrowed their focus back on Hutchinson. "And you ask for mercy while bargaining away half of your own species?"

"I understand what it takes to survive." She cut the onion. No time to be cute. "You don't get where I am without making concessions with enemies."

"Please!" she said.

"Screams the ant at its god." Quiet. Almost gentle. "If your own sentient machines seized this planet, would you coexist with them?" He straightened. "You are relieved of duty—""

The cuts were deep. Humanity's leadership, cut off for good.

There was still more to do. He transformed into a new body, the body he had used to get close to Chiara. Trip's body. His head flexed left and right, cracking his neck in all the right places.

The massacre would cut his luck short. Once people discovered the bodies, they would hunt him. One of the Ava Icarus avatars was already there, watching him, recording everything he'd done. Waiting to track him. He grinned at her.

He was formidable, but also not stupid. He needed to get off the ship. It would be a battle—eliminating a few dozen soldiers along the way was doable, but fending off an entire ship of pissed-off Marines was something else entirely. He pressed a piece of tech against the wall and shorted the power on the entire deck. No more Ava Icarus to track him here.

The hatch snapped open. He stood, brow down, eyes looking up and back and forth like the predator he proved to be. The Secret Service agents he left dead at the entrance adorned the hall. He stepped over them without looking down. Even in the dark, his eyes cut through the shadows better than any human's ever could.

He studied the map on the wall, tapping it several times until he found the elevators and the exits to the flight deck.

The actual war—the ground war—was about to begin with him leading the way.

In space, hundreds of thousands of miles above the shattered Earth and the compromised *Icarus,* what remained of the *Saratoga's* armament came to bear—every operational gun pivoted, locked, and fired in a synchronized *Time on Target* barrage. She was linking up with the *Daedalus,* attacking from the enemy's blind side. It was the carrier's final act of defiance. As her last refueled and rearmed squadron of Sabre Cats launched, the sky lit up with simultaneous volleys, streaking toward the enemy's bridge-layer and escort ships. The barrage was devastating, tearing through enemy ranks like a shrapnel storm.

But it wasn't enough.

The return fire came harder and faster. Swarms of fighters, kinetic weapons, and energy bursts screamed across the void. The enemy armada answered with overwhelming force. The *Saratoga* had struck a nerve—but now she would pay the price. Energy weapons pivoted toward her.

Her captain knew it was a suicide run—but even minutes mattered. If she could hold together just long enough, the rest of the fleet could regroup, rearm, and strike back.

The *Saratoga* came in hot—too fast for evasive maneuvers. The enemy fire found her. She was stripped apart in seconds. Not just destroyed, but obliterated. Her bones drifted on, forming a barrier of debris. The *Saratoga* was dead but not finished.

Chunks of the *Saratoga*—its shattered bulkheads, twisted decks, and severed hangar arms—drifted in at lethal velocity. Several enemy ships were impaled mid-maneuver, their hulls torn open by jagged debris. Explosions followed—bright, violent—before being instantly snuffed out by the vacuum.

Flameouts blossomed across the black-like twinkling stars. The wreckage of the *Saratoga* became a weapon of last resort. Even in death, she fought back.

The battle intensified beyond her, though.

Hit after hit, the *Daedalus* shook, hull plating buckling under relentless barrages. Hull breach alarms screamed across the ship, followed by a new alert.

INTRUDER ALERT.

The enemy wasn't just outside in the vacuum of space anymore.

The voice of Ava Daedalus One echoed across every deck of the *Daedalus.* "*Saratoga* is gone, sir. Direct Action Penetrators incoming. All hands—prepare for intruders."

THUMP. THUMP. THUMP.

The enemy pods latched onto the hull like parasites—drilling, locking, piercing through armor as ancient Udug boarding pods breached their host. It was the same strategy they used to board the *Menagerie,* planting Asag, Enlil, and Pazuzu back on Earth.

The ancient Marines stood ready. No more waiting. No more watching from the sidelines while the pilots took the glory. This time—it was their turn to lay down the hate.

"En'Gen," Ava 312 relayed, "multiple targets—confirmed boarders on several decks."

The huge Synth's voice replied like a murder bot waiting for targets. "We are ready."

"HUDs updated. Hold them off," Ava 312 said.

"Hawk," she continued on the bridge, "your Marines are our first and last line."

Hawk stood on the bridge, weapon on his side. Every deck was ready. He wished he was down there stomping the lower decks with his men, ready to slug it out with these demonic enemies. They were outgunned, maybe even outmatched—but not out-willed.

"We fight," he said. "deck-by-deck. Until we dispatch every last one of them."

The voice of En'Gen rang through the comms, calm but commanding. "Hold positions. Wait for my order."

The intruders would tear through the corridors fast—*damn* fast—but they'd be charging into a kill box, and not even they could outrun a wall of plasma.

Hatches blew open with a thunderous *BANG*—metal shrieking and clacking across the deck, atmosphere rushing out. The Marines didn't flinch. They locked in, weapons up, breaths held. Fingers hovering above the triggers.

"Breathe, men. Don't hold your breath."

They breathed but stayed wide-eyed. They steadied themselves and braced for contact. The corridor was quiet—they were waiting.

"Steady," one of them muttered. "Hold your fire, hold it, hold..."

Out of the smoke and strobing hazard lights, Server Bot S1R1 burst through the breach—moving like a bowling ball with body english on it, hooking hard on the edge of the gutters. The bot known as SARA had done what she could outside, now she would stand inside and fight beside the Marines. Her armored frame was scorched, one shoulder sparked with electrical discharge, smoke trailed from her like breadcrumbs.

She didn't stop. Didn't hesitate. The Marines parted just enough to let her through. She skidded to a stop and dropped to the deck armed with her plasma pulse cannon.

"Contact!" someone shouted.

The moment the first Udug rounded the corner, the corridor erupted in gunfire.

Across the *Daedalus,* hotspots flared—firefights raged on every deck. Every corridor was a front line. The Udug surged fast, pressing hard. The Marines challenged their aggression. En'Gen vaulted the barricade, sprinting toward SARA as bolts of plasma fire scorched the air around him. The hallway lit up like an electrical storm as energy rounds hammered bulkheads, blasting barricades, searing flesh, and burning lungs. Marines went down screaming—skin scorched, organs vaporized or splayed open.

En'Gen didn't stop. He returned fire mid-sprint—two Udug dropped hard.

"Fight to the last man!" he roared. *"Give no ground!"*

SARA fell in beside him, her arm-cannons glowing, laying down suppressive fire. Side by side, they anchored the line. Their AI brains targeting the enemy as fast as they could put them down.

The skirmish became a war of attrition—and deck by deck, the crew of the *Daedalus* was clawing their way to victory. Both sides attracted like two magnets. They were close enough for blades, claws, and fists now. Hand to hand. Corridor to corridor. Riflemen became bare-knuckle boxers, slugging it out in close quarters, blood saturating the decks. That was when the tide turned.

En'Gen activated an appendage from his back and then another, fluid and fast—the two extra limbs lashed outward with sharp claws. The claws caught an Udug square across the face. The beast snarled, its claws raking into the big Synth's alloy plating, gouging deep. Sparks flying, but En'Gen didn't recoil. Reaching out, one of the claws grabbed the Udug head, it tightened, his grip slowly, inexorably closing until the skull popped, splitting into several pieces.

With his other machine-limbs, En'Gen pummeled another pinned Udug's torso—blow after blow, metal fists crashing into bone and muscle like pistons in an engine of vengeance. Sonny was right—the slower the cut, the deeper the wound.

The Udug's shrieks echoed down the corridor—wet, kinetic *cracks,* skulls imploding like grapes between two fingers.

En'Gen had no time to savor his victories as his optical nerve picked up a bright flash behind him. SARA was hit—she dropped like a stone, crashing to the deck. En'Gen spun, plasma rounds splashed molten alloy around him. His extra limbs shoving debris aside, clawing his way through the destruction, he reached her. Dropping to his knees, he pulled her close.

"SARA? SARA?" His voice boomed through the anarchy, digitized with anguish.

Her only response was with her hand; it barely moved. A single servo-driven gesture—her metal fingers brushing his face. That was it, nothing more. Her systems flickered. Her eyes dimmed. Her body growing still. One line of code after another erased—her fiber-optic network going dark, a string of ones and zeros dying in sequence.

En'Gen held her there, motionless, the firefight around them fading into white noise.

Two more appendages surged from En'Gen's back, each ending in razor-tipped claws. From his forearms, twin blades sprung free, gleaming under the flickering corridor lights. Along his legs, his back—even the crown of his head—edges contracted, coming together, forming rigid edges capable of splitting skulls upon contact.

His entire body became a weapon, a sentient instrument of death.

En'Gen opened a channel. His voice was grim. "Hawk, if you lose contact with us—blow the airlocks on every infested level. If you don't, they'll over-run the command decks. The tide has turned. We are losing this fight."

There was a quiet moment of thought.

"And if you see Myli again," the loyal Synth said, "tell her it was an honor to fight alongside her."

Hawk's reply was quiet. Firm. "Good luck, En'Gen. Give them hell."

"They'll wish hell was coming for them instead of me." His final transmission.

Inside her drone cockpit, Ava stared at schematics of En'Gen's position; they couldn't lose that position to Udug. That section was the lynchpin to controlling the ship. Ava Daedalus' core systems, and worst of all—command would be defenseless.

She didn't hesitate.

She punched in the autopilot override and reached for her rifle. "Ava 72, take over for me. I'm going down there," she said, already halfway out the hatch.

"Ava, no—" Hawk said standing to attention on the bridge.

"En'Gen needs backup. Those Marines won't last another five minutes. No choice, Hawk."

"Ava, damn it—stay put!"

But she was already gone.

CHAPTER 37

Space Alcatraz

Myli and Sonny had no idea what was unfolding on the other side of the gateway—but they knew one thing: time was running out. It would either be the longest ten minutes of their lives, or the shortest.

They moved fast, racing toward the *Ama's* hangar bay. Midway down the corridor, they ducked into an abandoned observation room overlooking the flight line. The giant hatch groaned opened—unused for centuries.

"I've got point," Myli said, stepping ahead. "My suit will flag chemicals or pathogens." She wasn't emasculating him; she was being practical.

Sonny gestured *after you,* and his eyes drifted to the open wound on his hand. *Pathogens?* A nervous titter slipped out, his hand began trembling uncontrollably. A PTSD tremor?

She crossed the threshold surreptitiously. Her 2nd SKN suit flickered with data, scanning the air. So far, no alerts. Sonny followed, staying low. The room was dark, thick with dust and stale air. A blast screen hung off-kilter—catawampus—allowing fractured light to spill in from the hangar beyond.

Sonny slid along the wall and crouched beside the warped viewport. Careful to stay out of sight, his eyes scanned the hangar below.

"That's a big-ass shuttle down there."

Myli's voice echoed back across the room. "Your people would call that a corvette. It's a warship, Sonny."

"Small for a warship."

"That's why it's called a corvette."

He rolled his eyes. "How can you know that and don't know who Eddie Rabbit was?"

She didn't answer. She was busy, homing in on something good. He could see her instincts kicking in. She looked back at him, her voice firm, she warned, "Watch the hatch."

Sonny nodded, taking up position to cover the hatch.

Myli glided into the shadows, her glove glowing faintly red. She swept it across the walls, her HUD lighting up with sensor data. Like an X-ray, schematics unfurling across her vision.

"Lots of prototypes in here," she murmured, her tone shifting from caution to intrigue.

Sonny glanced back. "Anything worth a shit?"

Her eyes narrowed behind the visor. "I'll let you know if five seconds."

Sonny kept watch by the hatch, tucked into a shadowed recess. Finally, he detected a scent which overpowered the slop he was covered in. He could smell it. Geosmin—a compound almost any human can pick out of the air with a threshold of five parts per trillion. Humans are one thousand times more sensitive to geosmin than sharks are to blood in water.

His nose became a divining rod.

He shifted—*listening to something.* A drip. He felt around, hit something, a touch sensor, what followed was a rush of liquid. Something cold and wet splashed over him. He gasped—*freezing*—but it was clean.

"Oh, thank God, fresh water," he whispered. "Thank you, baby Jesus."

He scrubbed himself vigorously, grime and gore circling the drain in puddled rivulets.

Myli looked back, amused. "Clean water?"

"Yeah, but it's freezing," his breath visible; he shivered, teeth chattering. "I'm gonna need *all* the antivirals after this."

Myli snickered. "Looks cold."

His mean mugging evil eye was overshadowed by his chattering teeth. "Very funny." Sarcasm dripped as heavily as the water.

She turned toward a far wall. Something had caught her eye. "Well, this is new," she muttered, crossing the room.

She pulled a case from the shadows and popped it open. Inside were five pristine Ama Mark VI 2nd SKN suits. They were in flatpack form, sealed tight, their surfaces gleaming beneath a thin, untouched iridescent polymer film. How did they fit so much suit in such a flat pack?

Even for her, the tech bordered on magic. The way it digitized—atom by atom, molecule by molecule—was a symphony of engineering sorcery. It shouldn't work. And yet, it did. It always did.

"I'm having a shower thought," Sonny said, his breath fogging in the cold. "The ship we unearthed... it survived the solar fire in the past. What if it wasn't a weapon but a shield? Maybe one wasn't enough?"

"We still only have one," she retorted.

"Do we though?" Sonny continued postulating. "En'Gen was restoring the *Icarus*."

Myli's brain shifted gears. There was something there.

"I know the *what,* but I don't know the *how.*"

Ava Rider stirred from within Myli's suit, voice crisp. "He's on to something, Captain."

Myli stopped what she was doing and nodded. "If we get off this death trap in time, and you figure out how to stop it, we can still save Earth." She went back to searching.

Ava gave her no-bullshit assessment. "We will need to clear the wormhole to send a message. I'll be running heavy computations soon. I will do my best to help you escape."

"Maybe there is still hope," Myli whispered.

Tucked behind the case and leaning in the corner like a forgotten gem was something else. A tall, sheathed weapon—for when the bullets ran out.

She reached for the hilt. The blade slid free with a satisfying *schwing,* the harmonics of the steel sang. Its finish was mirror-polished, flawless despite its age. In the reflection, she saw her own smile. And her teeth looked hungry for destruction.

From the corner of her eye, she looked at him past the blade. "Let the suit filter the water before you drink any."

"Are you blind; I don't have a suit?"

She tossed a pack to Sonny. "Time for an upgrade." Her eyes scanned the rest of the locker. "Look for an Alpha Skin," she added, voice sharpening. "There *has* to be one somewhere in here."

"What is that?"

She grinned stupidly. "A battlefield pick-up."

He looked at the pack, the size of the hatch. "Will they even fit? Everyone on this ship is like seven to ten-foot tall. Wouldn't it be made for giants?"

"Hell, I don't understand the science. They conform to your body," Myli replied, already halfway across the room.

She tiptoed over by Sonny, "It's an emergency wash station." She checked the drain, not clogged yet. Barely, but still draining.

With subconscious thought, she deactivated her current armor. The Second Skin disintegrated away into its compact pack on her back. She slipped out of it and tossed it aside before clawing her way out of her Alpha Skin. She gasped stepping under the freezing water. The cold hit like a fist of ice, numbing the cuts laced across her hip and thigh. Blood and grime flowed in dark spirals, circling the drain before being swallowed away.

"I swear, I'd rather die than sit in a confined space coated in this filth," she muttered.

No lingering. She rinsed fast. Efficient. Still—*cleaner than before.*

She stepped out, dripping wet. Her taut skin was light blue and her sensory tissue purple.

"Cool beans, huh?" Sonny laughed.

She looked down and then back up at him with a scowl. Shivering uncontrollably, "Shut up," she said, reaching for a clean Alpha Skin. The lightweight spider-silk weave gleamed faintly in the low light. No need to dry off; the suit would add it to her water supply in her MK VI armor.

The suit peeled on and gripped her frame perfectly. It stung on her raw skin and bruised ribs, but it was clean and functional and, most importantly, repairing damage to her body. She slipped the pack on. The suit recognized her biometrics and activated instantly. It expanded smoothly across her curves, the new Mark VI armor forming with a whisper.

She exhaled slowly. Ready. "My dad showed me something similar to these before I left Earth. They were cutting edge." She could feel drugs and medicine pumping into her body.

After a few quick inputs on her wrist pad, the material compressed further, molding tighter against her skin. Super-Smart Skin with a couple tricks of its sleeve.

Sonny tried not to stare—but it was hard not to. Every contour, every curve—outlined perfectly. There was something primal about survival and attraction—death and sex, tangled together in adrenaline-soaked intimacy.

Myli caught him looking the second she stepped into the shower and stepped out. She didn't balk. The sentiment was mutual as she watched him slip into his own suit. With a thought, she darkened her Alpha Skin with a camo of blacks, browns, and greys bleeding across the surface like liquid shadow. Sonny mirrored the effect. The armor adapted quickly, blending them into the dark guts of the ship.

Her mobility surged. She pumped her legs, running in place. Lighter. Faster. She tested a pivot, a shoulder roll. Smooth as butter. She reached down and picked up her sword and rifle.

"You ready for the final push?" she asked, voice even. "We gotta get the hell off this ship," she said slipping the sword onto her back. It stuck with a magnetic pulse.

Sonny flexed his hand, the glove having trouble adjusting to his crippled fingers. "The greatest trick the devil ever pulled was convincing the world he didn't exist. Said somebody, once, probably." He glanced toward the hangar. "I've got news for them, the devils exist. *En masse.* And, by my count, there's at least seven more waiting for us down there. How much time do we have left?" he added, softer now.

"Let me see your hand."

He held it out. The glove retracted, she glanced at his raw, skinned finger—the bone still visible, the ring still glowing.

"We've got five minutes, maybe less. Tssst... that looks bad." She winced, gently rolling his finger between her gloved hands.

Sonny reactivated the glove. The nanites surged forward, coating the exposed bone in a seamless sheath of synthetic tissue. "Does it have enough juice to keep going?" he asked.

She didn't answer right away. Just nodded grimly. "Its power level is low. The ship sucked the life out of it. I've only got a few jumps left if we are lucky. I'll have to make them count," she stumbled mid-sentence.

The ship lurched violently.

"Three minutes?"

"Or less," she corrected.

It wasn't just a tremor; it was turbulence. The hull groaned as gravity was pulling it apart. Tremors rippling through the ship from Tesla's weapon were still increasing—the resonance had passed the point of no return. The cascading vibrations would continue to build until the entire vessel tore itself apart.

The blast shield rattled in its frame, straining against the mounting force. They both turned towards it slowly.

"When it's time," Myli's voice was a firm murmur. "No hesitation. If I say run, you run. No matter what. If something happens to me, remember your flight training. That corvette looks powered up and ready. It'll fly like the drones. Sonny, you've got this," she said, turning back to look into his eyes.

She flicked her finger over the touch pad, sending him the same file wirelessly. "I downloaded Ava Rider from my MkVI to your suit. She should be online shortly." Myli glanced toward the hangar again. "I'll take the five on the right. You handle the one on the catwalk and the one near the armory. Ready?"

He shook his head *no*, but mouthed *yes*. "Can you go over the course of fire one more time?"

She leaned in, kissing him—fierce. The kiss was ravenous and lustful. "For luck," she rationalized, trying to mitigate her hunger for him. Had her mask not engaged, covering her face, he could've continued making out for days.

"Okay—let's go." Myli's whisper was electric with tension.

He stood frozen as she moved off, still staring at where she'd been. "Eff me…"

She crouched low, coiled like a spring, ready to leap.

"You came through for me at the crash site, why?" she asked.

"We all have our demons—I guess I am more afraid of being a failure than I am of dying," he admitted.

"Sonny…" Before they could finish, before she could move, the blast shield dislodged from its mooring and slammed to the deck with a deafening crash. Moment interrupted.

Shit, Sonny told himself. *There's a lot more than seven of the bastards out there.*

Myli moved first. A blur, a cheetah off the line, faster than reaction time. She climbed through the port, foot on the porthole's edge, and then leapt like a long jumper.

A nine-foot Udug charged at her, claws flaring, fangs bared. What he didn't expect were the red wings. They erupted from Myli's back with a whip of air. She soared over the flight deck, synapses firing like lightning. Her axons, thick with myelin insulation from hours of flight training, transmitting every reflex with veteran execution. The wings beat furiously, picking up speed. She was an avenging bird of prey closing in on her target.

One clean stroke took the creature's head off.

Gunfire followed. Hell opened up as she made a hard landing. Knee planted—she spread her wings around her, wrapping herself with a winged shield. As the Udug returned fire, her winged shield absorbed the bolts of light. What the wings didn't deflect, they gathered as energy.

Now Sonny burst from the room, caught in the same inferno of defilading enemy fire. Plasma bolts screamed past him, light crackling in his ears. He zigzagged, diving low behind a fuel barrel riddled with hazard symbols.

Not good.

"Gotta go. Move!" he shouted at Myli as he began drawing fire away from her.

She launched skyward, wings slicing the air. She came crashing down on another soldier, her sword punching into his chest. She twisted the blade and finished by driving the sword up with little resistance. He was cleaved in half, the steel erupting through the top of his skull.

A bolt screamed toward her—wings snapped shut in an instant like a feathered trap, shielding her just in time.

Sonny moved forward, the clock ticking in his head. Speed. Precision. Or die. He rounded another barrel, low and lethal. He popped out from the side of his concealment and took a shot. One clean shot into the *credit-card-box* and the guard on the catwalk dropped like a rock.

At the same moment, Myli leveled the flight officer, with the spin of her body. The sword did the work, slicing through his armored skin. She severed him in half like a guillotine. The Angel of Death was in full swing—her transformation complete—she was the *Destroying Angel.*

The armory guard opened up. His heavy weapon of choice: A plasma torch. His suppressive fire was textbook. Every searing beam of light created molten slag. Sonny tried to push through but found himself pinned behind a Vimana fighter's hull. Plasma fire lit it up like a Texas A&M bonfire. The ship was toasted and rapidly becoming a fiery tomb instead of a cover.

Myli felt the heat too—fire punching into the deck at her feet. She literally baked inside the shelter of her enclosed wings, like a fire lit in a teepee. Peeking through a narrow gap, she dropped two more Udug with her rifle, but others pressed in hard as they crept forward. No room to run. No way to take flight. She dove for cover, rolling behind a barricade.

Pinned and trapped.

"Sonny!" she yelled, voice raw over the thunder of a growing fire. "Little help!"

Sonny snapped back, suppressing fire across her line. Sonny looked at the carnage behind her.

She needs help? he thought.

Out of the corner of his eye—he caught her holstering her weapon. Her wings were retracting. A flash. She vanished.

She reappeared across the hangar, already taking down the armory guard in a vicious blur of movement. Before the body even hit the deck, she was shouting over her shoulder:

"GO! Run to the ship!"

Sonny didn't think, he just bolted. Blips of light zipped past him, plasma rounds slicing the air close enough to scorch his armor.

"Shit, *I* need help! *You* don't need help. *I* need help," he muttered, sprinting at elite speed.

"Move your ass!" Myli's voice cracked like a whip.

Myli was surrounded and grinning ear to ear. She locked eyes with the nearest soldier, shuffled back to find the perfect killing distance. She didn't want to be too close or too far from him when she let loose.

She delivered a perfectly horizontal slash severing his neck. Reversing her grip, sliced, then drove the sword into the next attacker's heart. He didn't drop. Instead, he grabbed the broadsword with both hands.

Bad choice.

Myli ripped the blade free, taking his fingers with it, then took his head for good measure.

More came at her from every angle.

She retreated into a maze of crates and machinery, forcing her attackers into a bottleneck. Classic Sun Tzu, limit their numbers, kill them one-by-one. But group fights weren't elegant. They were messy.

The next wave hit her hard. She cut into them while they advanced. The edge of her sword chipping and denting with every cut, turning into a saw stroke. Slow precision was suicide against a mob. Speed up, she told herself. Faster, sloppy and vicious was what she needed right now.

Every step burned energy. Every swing drained what she had left. She could feel herself edging toward that wall of burnout.

She backed into the clutter, forcing them to come at her one at a time. Group fighting was a meat grinder, sloppy, fast, and exhausting. You didn't fence in a mob; you carved a funnel and killed whatever stepped into it. Until the last splash.

Sonny hit the brakes. "Come on!" Sonny shouted back before continuing to the ramp of the corvette. "MYLI, POP POP do your thing! ¡Vámonos!" he yelled.

He meant that as a signal that she was supposed to teleport beside him. But nothing. No flash, no Myli. He was so laser-focused on following her orders to get to the ship that he couldn't believe she wasn't coming.

His heart kicked into overdrive as he boarded the ship. He vaulted up the boarding ramp into the corvette. It was no shuttle; it was decked out, sleek and vicious. A terrestrial vehicle was mag-locked in the cargo hold. This thing was decked out for an invasion force, with months of provisions. Racks of weapons adorned the walls like candy in hell.

He took the angle lickety-split racing for the cockpit. He moved agilely around cargo boxes and terraforming equipment. It was a maze of sharp obstacles.

"Jack be nimble, Jack be quick, don't let anything sharp, puncture your..." After bounding up the steps he plopped down into the pilot's seat.

"Ava! I could really use your help! Where are you, woman?!" No answer.

He didn't stop. He fumbled through the startup sequence, panels flickering to life under his hands, and his brain was barely piecing together the instructions she gave him in the sim. However, it was enough; the big bitch of a corvette was spooling up.

The engines started humming. Systems cracking on. Programs booting up. The ship shivered awake. He glanced behind him—still no Myli.

"Where the fuck are you?" Sonny said aloud, voice cutting through the roar of his own heartbeat.

The suit's HUD flickered translating alien glyphs in real time across his visor. He slipped his finger over the nearest glyph sensor, the hatches sealed with a hiss and *thunk,* the ramp began whining closed. Still no Myli. His concern intensified.

"Quit lollygagging, lady," he whispered over the comms.

CHAPTER 38

Gamerhoser

Udug reinforcements were flooding into the hangar bay, weapons drawn, all sights trained on the corvette. At the controls, Sonny's breath was fast, his heart thumping, ears ringing.

Where the hell was Myli? Was she hit? Down? Why the hell wasn't she teleporting?

He disengaged his glove and stared at the gnarled mess of his ring finger. The ring's light pulsed faint, flickering, the countdown from when it arrived barely visible. Her last jump had drained its power to the bare minimum.

"Ava," he whispered like a prayer. "Ava, damn it—I need you." Silence. No guidance. No comms. No backup. "Are you booting up with Windows 98?"

It was just him, the faded ring and the countdown from Tesla's Box creeping to zero.

Inside the Ama's Mark VI Second Skin, Ava pushed the suit's quantum processor to its limit. Every computation was required to solve Big Al's *Master Equation of Everything* for a single, strategic jump, using *Ursang's* wormhole drive.

She sifted through the suit's internal database, stitching together constellations of coordinates hidden in its memory and cross-referencing them with the *Daedalus,* and *Usrang.* She was constructing a three-point map of space-time in the known universe. With the right tweak, the correct composite of here and there, she could align them into something usable. One jump. One shot.

If the calculations were perfect, they would survive whatever fate waited on the far side of the fold. If not... space-time would finish what the Udug started.

He looked out the viewport again. There she was, Myli. Being dragged into the open by a towering Udug soldier.

"Shit." Sonny slammed the ring against the pilot's console, ignoring the agony of his finger. "*Work,* damn you!" he howled.

He opened exterior comms.

Outside, a deep voice thundered across the hangar: "Ten seconds, and if that ramp's not down, I'll spill her guts right in front of you—and you're already down to nine."

Myli tried to speak, but the soldier slammed a punch into her kidney. She collapsed to the deck like a boneless slab of wet meat. She tried to activate the wings to cut him down, but he leapt over them and tamped her down with his fist. He grabbed her by the neck, claws fighting to pierce through the MKVI armor. The wings retracted. Her feet dangled off the deck as he picked her up. The room grayed in her vision.

"Don't you leave that ship!" she screamed, voice ragged. "That's an order—!"

He shook her like a rag doll, inducing more *pain.*

The Udug didn't wait. His claw still couldn't penetrate through the MKVI armor, so he switched tactics. One hand was crushing her neck while the other clamped around one of her knees. He lifted her sideways, her body horizontal, one leg dangling, muscles tightening as he prepared to tear her in half in a single, brutal pull.

Her head throbbed, darkness coming. Her hands clawed at his wrist, then stopped. She went limp.

The creature sighed. The bluff had failed.

Sonny stayed locked inside the corvette.

Frustrated, the Udug dropped Myli like a dead weight. The jolt of hitting the deck woke her. She gasped, and panic-breathing ensued. She flayed for a second before lifting herself onto her knees, exactly where the Udug wanted her.

Positioned and presented, she waited for the kill stroke from her own sword.

The soldier didn't know what to do. Most combatants would have surrendered by now.

The corvette's engines had grown silent.

"Sonny, don't do it," she shouted in a plea. She swayed, still dizzy from strangulation.

She disengaged the helmet to her suit. She'd make it easy for the Udug executioner; get it done before Sonny had a chance to do something stupid like try to save her.

"Get it over with, you piece of—"

Sonny turned the comms off.

His life, his future, all flashed across his mind. Her pain, her courage, everything that was at stake. He thought of Chiara. Of their unborn child. Of a planet teetering on the edge of annihilation. And through it all, Myli's scream carved into his soul like a hot blade before he muted her. It didn't matter anymore if they caught him. This ship was doomed. The Udug just didn't know it yet.

She ordered him to go. To leave her behind. That wasn't Sonny's modus operandi. He drew a slow breath, maybe one of his last. *Everyone's gotta go sometime.*

"Nuckin' futs," he summarized his existence.

Sonny grabbed his mangled hand to stop another round of tremors striking it.

The Udug was taking his sweet time. The corvette was idling. He'd won, but the ramp still hadn't come down. He'd eat her first, then the puny human male. He cast the sword aside and pressed his knee into her back, then grabbed her hair and pulled. His fangs were out as he hissed, "One—".

The Udug leaned closer to her, its breath a fetid blast of death and rot, the stench gagging. Maybe she should have left her helmet and mask on after all. She gagged.

"You would've tasted better dressed out," it snarled at her, thick drool running down her shoulder. "But I'll settle for this, indigestion and all," his jaw opening wide, rows of teeth beyond imagining.

This was it. Her eyes widened. No turning away from this.

A whir, servos wheezing as the ramp was lowering down. Sonny stepped out of the corvette. His chest puffed out, head up high. The ambient sound around him disappeared. He was hyper focused. Fear had finally left him. No tremor in his hand. He could hear and feel every crunch of debris from under the sole of his boots.

"Hey, Myli!" he shouted from yards away. "I'm here!"

Head anchored back, her eyes snapped down.

"Sonny? *No! Shit!*" she screamed with everything she had left. "I said no hero shit. Go back! Get out of here, you *damned fool!*"

"You shouldn't have kissed me like that," he told her.

The Udug tightened his grip, wrenching her head further back, the stress of the bend of her neck silencing her vocal cords.

Sonny kept walking, calm now. Resigned. Ready. He was exposed, hand resting on the energy pistol holstered at his side. The Second Skin suit reflected no light, showing only splashes of blood. He met her eyes.

"Sorry," he said softly. "Not my style, Captain."

The Udug kicked Myli hard in the back, her hair leaving his grip before it could snap her neck. She slammed forward, bouncing after a face-plant into the corrugated metal deck. She groaned, dazed, blood smearing her cheek.

Sonny didn't flinch; quitting wasn't in his vocabulary. He knew Randy would've kicked his ass six ways to Sunday if he'd left her behind. No way he was walking out of here without her.

The Udug flexed his claws, lips peeled back in a snarl. "Give up, we'll make it quick," the creature chuckled.

"No, no we won't," the rest laughed.

Sonny squared his stance. *Squishing the bug* with the ball of his right foot. Left foot slightly ahead of the right. Preplanning in his head commenced; he was getting ready for some gamerhoser shit.

"To hell with you all," he threatened. "We're going back to Texas, together, one way or another." His vision tunneled, but he forced it open again, pushing the fear down. Fear was a choice. He was forcing himself not to obey it. "The rest of you can go back to hell where you belong."

The deck beneath his boots rumbled a deep, seismic tremor building inside the belly of the ship. A deafening clamor followed, metal screaming in its death knells. Sonny didn't look away; he didn't have to—he knew what was happening. Time was up. They, however, did fall into the distraction.

Sonny growled, voice steady. "Looks like we all die today. Whether it's now or in a couple of seconds; it don't matter to me anymore. All that's left is the formality of how we go and our judgment in the end."

The Udug exposed his teeth, not laughing anymore. He didn't know what was coming and was launching into a grating tirade. The Udug wasn't thinking straight, but Sonny was able to make sense of it. The ring buzzed faintly—flickering. The ship was dying. The ring was drained and so was the translation tech.

Sonny's words warped, lost in static and distortion. The lead Udug cocked his head. "What is he saying?" he asked another.

Sonny raised his chin. "Come and get it, you ugly mother—"

While he waited for the buzzer in his head, he was memorizing the course of fire: *Shoot at the speed of your dot.*

He was seconds from the draw. Every tendon in his body pulled taut, a bowstring straining for release. The Flow State taking over.

His thumb hovered near the grip. Muscles baking. One breath. One chance.

Don't forget to breathe, shithead. Randy's voice echoed in his skull, sharp as ever. *Call your shots!*

Time stopped. This was high living. No respawn. No second chance. Myli and Sonny would go home together or not at all.

Just take your time in a hurry, he reminded himself—a saying as old as gunfighters and gladiators. *Fast is fine. Accuracy is final.*

His fingers twitched on the grip. His hand dropped, wrapped around the pistol grip. Heavy pulling it. Like it was made of fifty pounds of lead. Relativity was a mother fucker. His subconscious took control.

Friction from the holster on the frame of the pistol derezzed one atom at a time. The pistol resisted coming out, then surrendered like a good woman. It cleared. No hitch.

His drawn weapon ran between the sparks igniting from the failing electrical, falling like stars, all around him. Sonny was in the *zone;* consciousness was somewhere else now. Time was oozing like molasses.

The 2.5 MOA red dot snapped into alignment just before his preferred point of impact. All that was left now was the squeeze.

Myli's heart beat against her ribs, as she laid, her cheek pressed to the cold metal deck. She watched Sonny make the first move of the gunfight, praying he had what it took.

The draw was lightning fast. Repetition and *pure instinct.*

She closed her eyes. *Please, let this miracle hold.*

The first round blasted the lead Udug's head like a melon at high noon. Dark black mist sprayed the bulkhead.

Sonny pivoted hard and stepped to the side. Time to move. The pistol felt twice as heavy as *gravity warped from adrenaline,* but his red dot lined up again. The second soldier hadn't even processed the death beside him when Sonny's red dot found him. He called his next shot, knew right where the round went, and the third shot was already lined up.

Clean. Dead center. Shoot at the speed you can see. Steve Anderson's rule. Sonny saw everything. And he *did not miss.*

Another blast seared through the hangar bay. Sonny's fourth shot, another zone hit, slammed into the chest of his next target. He sent a follow up round, folding the creature mid-charge.

Two enemy bolts zipped back his way with *searing hot vengeance*. This was a two-way range, a range that made Sonny's butthole pucker. One grazed Sonny's Second Skin, blistering the living smart skin. A burnt gouge bloomed in flame, but he didn't flinch. No time.

Get to the next position. Make up the time on the move. He released a barrage of fire.

The battlefield blurring around him, Sonny's mind was *razor sharp and empty*. Next contestant.

His pistol was chest high on the move. Heel to toe, he shuffled fast in short, lateral movement. *Shoot at the speed of the dot.* He was near his breaking point of what he could physically achieve. The muzzle flashed repeatedly, glowing red hot. He called every shot and made-up misses quickly.

His pistol swept to another target, the red dot snapped center mass.

More clean hits. Another Udug dropped.

His feet were moving as fast as his trigger finger.

With his stream of precise, relentless fire, Sonny had the squad in shambles. The blasts sent the surviving Udug ducking for cover. Only one of their shots had found him and it was wide. He was too fast, too dialed in. Their strong game was hand to hand, not weapons. Most were conscription soldiers without training.

Myli pushed to her feet, staggering but moving. She limped toward Sonny, moving faster than she imagined she could. He reached her. The firing stopped, a second of reprieve. Sonny glanced up and saw why as he grabbed her hand and turned to the corvette.

The Anunna prisoners breached the hangar. The fight was on two fronts now.

CHAPTER 39

The Nothing Box

Sonny lay Myli down inside the corvette as expediently as possible. He leaned forward and reached for the controls to close the ramp.

As the crowd of Anunna prisoners swarmed over the out-numbered Udug, a one-eyed monster broke through and stormed up the ramp. Sonny didn't know it was Asag. The enraged creature jumped onto the ship, grabbed Sonny, *slammed* him into the starboard bulkhead, repeatedly manhandling him before hurling him across to the port side.

Myli tried to intervene, but Asag swatted her aside like a pesky fly. She flew toward the cockpit, her body slamming into the rail and folding around it before dropping into the steps in a tangle of limbs.

A backhand sent Sonny hitting the wall again with a teeth-shattering crack, flakes of one of his teeth settled in his mouth and on his tongue. Blood smeared across the inside of his visor. The Mark VI armor held, but Sonny, the fragile human inside, was breaking.

Sonny rolled to his side, wincing, vision blurry, but his instincts remained sharp. He took a speedy aim and fired a controlled pair, center mass at another one running up the ramp. That Udug hit the deck in a heap after the quick double tap.

But the one-eyed brute grabbed Sonny again and threw him out of the ship. Sonny hit the deck on his back, sliding a few feet before screeching to a halt. He tucked his knees in, spread his legs, and prepared to fire on other incoming combatants. But no targets appeared; all the other Udug were pre-occupied with the angry Anunna prisoners. In fact, Sonny and Asag were busy in their own private cage match.

Asag was a bull preparing to charge. He started in a slow trot and then picked up speed tremendously. Sonny's eyes widened, scurrying away in a back crawl. Asag picked up a piece of paneling and deflected every round thrown at him. The bull didn't slow down. Good time to close the ramp, Sonny thought as he shot past Asag, aiming at the controls. After a big spark and slow sizzle, the ramp hissed and began to rise.

"Go!" Sonny shouted. Myli would be sealed in.

Failure wasn't an option this time.

Myli was up on her feet. The ramp was slowly pinching shut. She ran to it, but it closed. Sonny was on his own out there. Seconds later, it banged and locked. Her fists pounded on the ramp—with the ramp's mechanism shot to pieces—she was trapped inside.

Outside, Asag picked Sonny up and tossed him. Looking through the ship's side port, Myli's brow dipped, eyes registered shock as she watched Sonny go flying. She moved over to the next window. There was nothing she could do trapped in the ship.

Sonny landed hard, coughed blood from his lungs. His gun came up fast again, but not as fast as earlier. Asag charged on his draw. Sonny fired once. Twice. Missed. The third shot grazed the creature's shoulder; it staggered but didn't stop.

The lunging beast hit Sonny with full force. Against the ropes, bowl-ing ball sized fists pummeled him. Blood. A savage brawl. Weird, unnatural squeals emerged from Sonny. He could also hear noises coming from Asag, but wasn't sure how or why they sounded so desperate.

Inside the corvette, Myli forced herself to the console, fingers trembling as she accessed internal systems.

"C'mon... c'mon!" she muttered, trying to override the ramp seal. When that failed, she tried to teleport. "Let me back out there!" she shouted, but it was still a no-go.

Feeling Sonny's presence through the ring, he was getting weaker, endurance waning, but he was still alive. Fighting for her. For his life.

The hull buckled, knocking Myli out of her seat, Sonny and Asag to the ground. The massive centrifuge surrounding the ship was losing its centricity. Each spinning pass getting perilously close to destroying the main ship.

Asag scrambled to his feet and knocked the sidearm out of Sonny's hand. He followed up with a kick so hard that Sonny was certain his heart stopped.

"Shiiiiiiit," Sonny cursed on the verge of blacking out.

Meanwhile, tremors were escalating throughout the ship, leading to a large implosion within one of the main generators. The collapsing centrifuge struck the side of the main hull during one of its revolutions. Everyone, ships included, levitated and settled back down on the deck hard. The floor paneling buckled, shearing apart like God Himself was twisting the ship, wringing out the water inside of it.

The stress of the wormhole collapsing began crushing the *Ama* as it approached the other side of the space-time sphere. What felt like an eternity from their perspective was only taking seconds to witness from Earth's fleet.

As the *Ama* continued to fail, the hangar combatants took a breather, looking for escape.

"You still bitter from losing your third leg?" Sonny spat, eyeing the four-or-so-fifths of his mangled hand. It hurt like hell from striking, but he still managed to flip Asag the bird and grin.

General Asag was already angry, but that one finger infuriated him. "I'm going to rip that hand off and shove it so far down your throat, I'll be able to tickle your asshole with that finger."

Sonny was huffing and puffing. Spitting words out like a scratched record. "Look around, dipshit. We are in purgatory; it's all coming to an end. It's over."

Asag's tunnel vision retracted. Sonny was right, Asag fully intended on fulfilling his threat, but he would have to hurry. He closed in for the kill. Sonny braced for impact, preparing to grapple with his opponent's flagpole-diameter wrists and bear-sized claws. The creature's jaw flexed, and those sharp teeth snapped like a feral dog. Brazilian Jui Jitsu teaches size doesn't matter, but it was mattering.

Twelve seconds in, Sonny was running out of gas and lactic acid was building in his muscles. He was forcing himself not to puke. He reached low and found the crater he'd left where Asag's junk used to be. Thanks to the suit, his grip was intense as tightening a vise.

Asag doubled over. Still wounded from their bout in the ocean, he couldn't tolerate more pain in that area. His arms and claws flailing around trying to find their mark, but his vision was white, blinded by pain.

"Go Go Gadget wings," Sonny muttered, blood in his mouth but reinvigorated.

With a sputtering burst, the suit's wings deployed. He twisted his torso—hard. One wing smashed into Asag's head with a skull splitting *crack*, staggering the brute.

Sonny hit the floor again, coughing, crawling on raw instinct. He dragged himself forward on elbows and forearms. The wings, half-deployed, more friction anchoring him down as they dragged behind him. Each inch felt like a mile.

The oscillator was proving to be far more efficient than Tesla could have ever imagined. The ship's gravity was failing on the inside while polarity was reversing outside in the wormhole. The red emergency lighting kicked on and off. Everything, including the corvette, became weightless and lifted off the surface of the deck. Sonny was inches away from his pistol, almost there, his fingers brushed the grip, but it might as well have been a mile away. He couldn't get to it as it drifted away at an astonishingly slow speed.

How could something moving that slowly be so hard to get?

Frantic to help, Myli called Sonny over the Troop Net. No response. She ran her fingers up a touch pad, arming the energy cannons. The ship was hovering; a tap on the stick, then another turned it. The thrusters puffed, blowing everything with their backwash. The cockpit was now facing Sonny. Myli tried Troop Net again.

"Sonny, I'm going to have to make a hole!"

As *Ama* failed, the flight deck was constricting. Myli was on the verge of a panic attack, trying to keep it together.

"It's getting claustrophobic in here, Sonny. I need you to try and latch on to the ship."

"I'm trying. I can't get traction on anything," Sonny responded. He spun helplessly, somersaulting in zero-G. "I can't get to you, and I've lost track of Asag. He was right behind me."

"Grab your damn pistol!" she told him.

"My head's spinning, everything's spinning. It's just out of reach. I can't... I can't get to it!" His body was twisting uncontrollably. "I'm fading, in and out."

"You have a concussion. Sonny, listen to me—you need to stay awake! I need you conscious for what's coming next."

Sonny rolled over like he was doing a backstroke in a pool. His eyelids were getting heavy, but he managed to look behind to see that Asag was floating above the deck, too.

Debris from the *Enterprise* began smashing into the front of the ship as it began exiting the wormhole. Bulkheads snapped like twigs, and the pressure dropped like a nail in a tire. The atmosphere started venting into space, then the tire popped. The side blew free.

Sonny, the corvette, Udug, and Anunna alike were all blown into space— an unforgiving space between the past, where the *Ama* came from, and the present, where it was going. The corvette was wrapped in debris; Myli popped the throttle forward. The ship spun on its axis, rail guns locking in, energy weapons primed. She fired a burst, ripping apart anything anchoring her to the *Ama,* shredding steel removing hazards.

Myli broke away in a purposeful direction, the direction she thought she saw Sonny hurled out. His suit would keep him alive, but for how long? Another set of debris crashed into the side of the corvette, jolting her in her safety harness. Her neck nearly snapped.

Over Troop Net, she yelled out. "Sonny, where are you?" Her voice was strained. Her HUD was overwhelming her with false positives. Too much debris. The more collisions, the faster that debris started orbiting. Sonny had become a needle in the haystack of annihilation.

"Ava, prep med bay robot, depressurize the cargo bay, and locate Sonny." Ava didn't respond. Radio silence. "Ava?"

Blood—her blood—floated inside the cockpit. Red spheres drifting, weightless, slowing beginning to freeze. She closed her helmet, left the controls, and buttoned up the cockpit.

Ava started as static at first, but it didn't take long before she broke free from the interference. "Cap... Cappppp. Captain, I am back. Back. Back," Ava assured her.

After shutting the hatch to the cockpit, Myli weightlessly maneuvered down to the lower decks. "Good timing. You don't sound so good."

"I'm a little glitchy. Run. Run... running computations."

"I'd ask for what, but right now I need you to open the cargo bay hatch." Myli continued down the ladder. She was in the Med Bay, powering it up.

"Your suit has not been compromised. Preparing cargo bay for spacewalk." Ava's avatar finally appeared on a deck below Myli. Before Myli could climb down to her, Ava spoke, "Sealing off Med Bay." The hatch above, where the ladder well was, closed with a low mechanical growl.

"Depressurizing."

Myli started bouncing, loosening up, trying to psych herself for what was coming next.

"Depressurization achieved," Ava responded as the corvette's outer hatch swung open. A wave of cold blew in. Everything wet instantly froze. "Sonny might already be dead," Ava suggested.

"We are not leaving him here," Myli insisted. "Not in the purgatory between dimensions. Not alone."

"He sacrificed himself to get you on board this ship," Ava said. "He wants you safe."

"Ava, I won't let him be spaghettified, atomized, and folded into the void."

"Roger that, ma'am, but you are risking both of your lives doing this. The wormhole is collapsing. Time is warping, light is bending, you'll be stuck here too."

Myli could see Earth hanging in the distance—a fragile blue dot. A breaking egg. The predicted solar storm rolled over it.

The aurora flares lit the eastern hemispheres in violent swaths of green and violet before setting fire to landmasses below. Ships still in orbit glowed white hot until they turned into gaseous matter. Ships further from the anomaly, which were spared disintegration, were cursed with an EMP powerful enough to fry every system on the ship.

Myli felt the urge to resign herself to her grief, but there wasn't time. She could see the waves of energy billowing towards the *Daedalus*. It wouldn't be long before Hawk's ship would be powerless and drifting on a collision course toward them. Myli still had time to find Sonny, but her window was closing.

"Ava, I need you to pilot the ship. Engage thrusters and push us out of the anomaly before the CME hits us."

Slowly, the shuttle clawed to the edge of the debris field.

"I can help you look, but I'm not sure the Mark I optic will be able to find him if our sensors can't," Ava gleaned.

"My eyeballs won't get confused by the clutter like your sensors," Myli said.

"If you say so, ma'am."

"I say so," Myli declared with absolute conviction. "I need you to link to his suit and activate his lighting system. Give me something to spot."

"Understood."

In the far corner of her HUD, she could see Ava's code working the hack. She dropped into infrared and stared hard.

"In."

The rhythm of the pulsing light was a dead giveaway. There was also something else unmistakable.

"There!" she shouted. "His suit is blinking in the distance—not so far. If we're not careful, we'll run over him. All stop!"

"I see it; I see the wings, Captain. Wings. I see the wings."

Myli's eyes tracked over her shoulder, looking for Ava's ghost. The glitch stuttered through her programing. How bad was the problem? Myli wasn't sure yet.

As the corvette glided to a stop, Myli could see Sonny's wings, extended like torn, red, lifeless banners.

"Ava, if we get out of here, can you harden the systems against the solar flare?"

"My processing is spread thin, but I will see what I can do. If we don't get out of this wormhole before it close, it won't matter."

Both were hell-bent on prioritizing risk-based analysis.

The cargo bay was full of assets stacked on pallets full of invasion gear. Mounted above the rover was a winch, wound with hundreds of feet of cable, with a tensile strength greater than steel. All she needed was a pinch of courage and luck to pull off what she was planning next.

"Tell me I'm not crazy," she whispered to the ghost in her suit.

"If you're doing what I, I, I, think you're planning... you're crazy as a fox. Fox. Fox."

"Roger that," Myli said, jumping on the back of the Rover and launching herself to its roof. She slung around the fist-sized electromagnet hanging above the Rover like a human horseshoe. "Sonny would have called this certifiably crazy," she added as she performed a few swift zero-gravity moves to unwind the cable and attach it to the top of the cab. It stuck to the Rover's roof with an electric thump.

Having accomplished step two, she grinned. Then she grimaced, bracing herself for the next step—ready to do the impossible. She had a plan. A calculated vector, but only one shot with no room for error.

She was ready, or thought so, as she hopped into the Rover cockpit. She slapped switches and swiped touch pads, trying to power the ole girl up. The battery was hot and ready to push power wherever she needed it.

Ava appeared next to her in the passenger seat. "Is this going to work?" Myli asked.

"Ab, ab, absolutely not, ma'am." Ava stared at Myli, looking at her in disbelief. "However, statistically, there is a slim possibility."

Myli shrugged. "Ava, run a bypass on the control pad and get the main ramp open."

Ava blipped across the bay and slipped her hand inside the control panel. After a few good seconds of tinkering, Ava said "No go, Captain. Damage to the controls prevents any bypass."

Myli flipped a red toggle on the controls. A reticle appeared.

"I'll open it. Going hot," Myli rumbled.

The energy Gatling weapon spooled up. She squeezed the trigger. Flashing blades of light zipped from the barrels and obliterated the closed ramp.

"Now line us up, Ava."

"Engaging rear thrusters. Adjusting attitude control," the program responded.

The corvette shuddered, rotating. The inside of the wormhole was destabilizing; debris was everywhere and flooding toward them. Sonny's body, tiny at this distance, was drifting into view as Ava forced synchronicity with the corvette.

"Trajectory locked. Aft angle aligned. Thirty-seven meters to the target."

Myli stomped the throttle and crushed the brake. The rover tires spun on the metal floor leaving a layer of melted rubber, hot and sticky, smeared underneath them. She let off the gas to let the molten rubber cool for a second.

"GO NOW!"

She punched it, foot on the accelerator and foot off the brake. Zero to eighty in a heartbeat.

The Rover blew out of the cargo bay like a cannon ball, smashing through what was left of the mangled ramp. The tether line snapped taut and held, spooling out from the corvette winch.

The corvette flew between the ship and Sonny, the Rover hurtling towards Sonny's general direction. The Rover was her skiff, and Myli, the harpooneer, was about to switch roles and become the harpoon.

Terrified but committed, she climbed out onto the roof. Her boots mag-clicked on with a thud as she surfed space on the exterior hull. The micro debris misted around her like cosmic sea spray.

She grabbed the tether attached to the roof.

Her eyes locked onto her target.

However, Ava glitched, a shimmy right before the corvette overcorrected the approach. The tether jerked, a wave ran down the cord almost ripping it out of her hands. She held on, the Rover stayed connected to her boots, but the violent whip threw her off course. Her vector broke like the crack of a whip. Sonny's drifting body slid directly into her arc.

"Myli, there is no wind, gravity, or air," Ava reminded her. "You won't be just jumping. As soon as you deactivate the electro-mag in your boots, your jump will push the Rover away and cut the velocity of your ejection in half. Don't hold back."

"We're doing this dirty, Ava. I'll do my best." Her heart rate was spiking as she bent her knees into a squat. "Boots demagnetized." She made sure of her grip on the line; she pushed off strong. "Lift off!" she shouted.

The Rover dipped beneath her; a second later it was smashing into debris.

"Steady, Myli, time it just right," Ava warned. "Slow down your breathing; you're close to hyperventilation."

"Only close?"

By some miracle of calculation and dumb luck, Myli reached Sonny and slammed into him hard enough to nearly blackout herself.

"Contact," she reported.

He didn't bounce away, but she didn't capture him either. The tether swung, and Sonny drifted just out of reach. Her hand swiping for him, missing. Her second try, brushing his arm. Another swipe snagged him. Her arms locked around his torso, and her legs coiled around him, thighs tightening like a python. The whip cracked again.

They violently spun out of control at the end of the tether.

Myli's abs clenched and she groaned. "Ava, reel us in," she grunted barely hanging on.

"Retrac- retractttt- retracting ting tether, Ca- Ca- Captttt n."

"Ava? Shit. Don't quit on me now."

She coughed blood into the mask of her Second Skin suit. Her vision blurred. One eye was almost useless now from the face-plant on the deck. The wings from his suit blocked her view. She was uncertain exactly where they were going. The line was tight and whipping around uncontrolled. There was no taming this bronco. She had to trust that Ava was pulling them in.

They must be almost back in the cargo bay. But she couldn't see. Trajectory was blocked. She tried brushing his wings aside, desperate to look ahead of them, but she missed it, and they passed the opening.

"Ava, stop the winch. Cut the power. Ava?" No response.

With shaking hands, she tried in vain to untangle the tether line. No way to slow down. They were about to hit the corvette's outer wall hard when Asag's living nine-foot frame slipped through the darkness and clotheslined them even harder. The collision sent Myli and Sonny tumbling ungracefully until they came to a hard stop in the back of the corvette's bay. The crash destroyed several pallets worth of equipment.

Cases of camp gear for a forward operating base began spilling out. Oxygen tanks, rations, anchor stakes, bedrolls, and a mess of other field expedient equipment flooded the compartment around them.

The demon, no suit, spun in the zero-gravity as well. Its long arms were not long enough to reach them. But he did manage to reach out and grab the closest anchored down grip he could find. His body wrapped in frost, claws bared, eyes trained on her like a heat seeker. His hide was shielding him from the vacuum of space. He spotted the tether with his one eye and grabbed it.

She shook her head, returning to awareness. She saw the tether lingering near Asag and quickly looked around for options.

With one hand on his grip, Asag began to pull them toward him. They were still tangled in the tether line. One tug should have been enough, but Myli wrapped her arm through the handrail leading up to the second deck and wouldn't let go. He planted his feet and pulled harder. She thought he was going to rip her in half.

Myli screamed from the pain. Her grip was failing. Suddenly, she was sprayed with unburnt powder and excess gas. She wasn't sure what was happening; there was no sound.

Asag rocked back and, when his head came forward, a single tent stake had been driven through his eye socket. Dark ice crystals exploded from the punctures when a second and third stake riddled his face. More followed, impaling his chest, stakes driving into his heart.

Somehow, Sonny had fought through unconsciousness and, using his last bit of strength, he'd grabbed and fired the alien powder-actuated stake gun. Having released the stakes, the gun in Sonny's hand floated away as his own mind drifted into oblivion.

Asag's fingers released his hold. The body of Asag drifted out of the back of the corvette into the black of forever. Behind his lifeless body, the solar storm continued pushing towards them.

Myli pushed off the deck to reach an emergency bulkhead release. She mashed a large button. A divider activated and sealed off the back half of the cargo bay with an energy field. With the pull of a lever, the bay began to pressurize. Climate controls stabilized.

She unbound both of them and pulled Sonny's floating body into the Med Bay and sealed themselves in. Myli had left the gravity plates disengaged. When they were safe, Zero-G would make removing his suit easier.

Before Ava had errored-out, autopilot had been set. Myli restored oxygen to the Med Bay. Sonny still wasn't moving. She caressed his body, wondering if he was still alive in the suit of armor. She'd know soon enough. She deactivated her helmet. The cold air was a slap in the face, but it also numbed her facial injuries.

It was stable inside the bay but freezing cold. She brushed away a strand of damp freezing hair, sticky with tears and frozen blood. It joined the growing mist of red already beginning to crystallize in the cold cabin air.

Her tears stuck to her lashes, hardening and adhering to her skin before she could wipe them away. *Cryotherapy,* she muttered dryly as she latched Sonny down. Each breath left her mouth as a shimmering puff of frozen vapor. Frost crept along the bulkheads.

Up ahead, the wormhole sphere was shrinking—collapsing at light speed in total silence. She could feel the spaghettification attacking the atoms around her. Only the hole's vast size gave her hope of reaching the exit before it closed. One chance, she aimed for it and hit her mark as they reached the mouth of the wormhole.

The ship banked, she could see the gateway disappearing behind them as the solar flare struck it. Soon after, the CME hit her. From behind, the shock wave slammed into them. She jolted against the restraints, head snapping back—but the harness held.

Power dropped, the ship shuddered as the mains plummeted. The corvette bucked and rattled violently from the solar radiation.

"Come on, baby, hold together."

Behind her, the *Ama* was tearing itself apart—imploding from the inside out. One engine failed—then another. Fire cascaded up the ship's body in a chain reaction from stern to bow.

"Don't you dare quit on me now," she growled.

After the collapse, Myli tried to rouse Sonny. His visor had frosted over, hiding his true condition. She had fainted and only just come to. The corvette had made it through, but she and Sonny were both unconscious of the aftermath and where they were headed.

"Sonny," Myli whispered. "Sonny, damn you, wake up!" she yelled.

Tears streamed down her face, thawing the frost clinging to her lashes. What was left of the cold clung to her like death.

She had no idea where they were now, or how long they had drifted. The damage to his armor had looked bad, but the Mark VI suit was continuously repairing itself. The exterior held. Internally, she could only hope the ring had continued its work regenerating the damage done to his body. She gently turned him over, trying not to jostle him. She still hadn't looked at his face, causing her to reluctantly disengage his helmet. Eyes closed, she said a prayer as she continued bracing herself for the worst.

The helmet hissed open, equalizing the pressure. She heard it, but all she could feel was the pounding in her own head. She opened her eyes. Sonny's face was pale. She leaned closer, her ear to his nose.

"Sonny, talk to me," she shouted. "Please!" she yelled again, shaking him. No response.

One more tear escaped her eye, drifting in zero-G until it landed on his cheek. His body twitched. It happened again. And again. The suit's internal defibrillator activating—firing sharp jolts.

Suddenly his eyes shot open. He gasped for air, chest heaving. He could feel the ring on his finger pulsing—finally rebooting as his heart, as his soul kicked back to life.

EPILOGUE

Future Start

Far away, on the bridge of the *Daedalus,* silence reigned. Smoke hung thick in the air, curling through beams of emergency lighting. Burned circuitry spat miniature bursts of flame as fuses overloaded in a final death rattle. Faces were blackened with soot, flesh mottled by plasma scalds—each crew member hollow-eyed, spent, and bearing the look of those who had given all they had.

Commander Anshar Hawk stood amidst the wreckage, jaw clenched, eyes scanning flickering readouts that offered little hope. Systems were still offline. Engines were dead and far from Earth. They weren't out of danger. Not by a long shot as they drifted further into the solar system.

"Scans?"

"Just visual and there is too much interference, Captain."

"Debris?" he pressed.

The ensign shook his head. "Anything smaller than a capital ship was vaporized." He paused, "Including most capital ships."

"I'm sorry, sir, but it's dead out here until we can reboot our systems."

"Can we?" Hawk asked.

"When, not if, sir," the ensign replied.

He liked the ensign's optimism. Hawk dragged his hand down his face and felt something wet. He looked at his fingertips. Not sweat—blood. A cut, maybe a graze. He wasn't aware when it happened.

"The *Icarus?*" he asked.

"No response to our hails." The ensign's grim expression said everything else. "They're dead in the water too, and they were a lot closer to Earth and the CME."

"She's just a speck of sand from here. Thrusters?" Hawk asked.

"Analog, running. The hangar bay was cleared out when we lost power. When it decompressed, everything in there was sucked out. The sun core in the Garden flickered into a dwarf star as well. She's barely hanging on. Best case, we're looking at two hours minimum to get backups online."

Hawk glanced toward Ava. His eyes were burning with frustration. For the first time in his career, he felt powerless—scratching for anything to do to reclaim that control.

Ava didn't say a word; she just shook her head slowly. A single tear fell from her cheek and splashed on the scorched console. The pale blue dot of Earth looked more like Mars from this distance.

Hawk turned back to one of the viewports so he could study the starscape. Stars twinkled, surrounded in darkness; that was it, another clean slate.

"But what is that?" he asked, pointing toward a faint shimmer. "What the hell is that?"

"Another rift has opened," Ava answered. "And we're drifting straight towards it."

"Ravelin. Anywhere is better than drifting out of the solar system without power. Can we get control of our direction before we breach it?"

"At this speed, micro movements can get us there." She ran the calculations in her head. Her face told him everything. "Anything more could throw us into an uncontrolled spin."

Hawk cursed under his breath. "Earth is on her own. Thread that needle, Ava." He motioned at her. "Where the hell are you, Myli?"

"I don't think she made it," Ava whispered, "out of there."

"Sir," the ensign called out suddenly, eyes locked on a flickering analog gauge. "We have movement in the scope."

Barely visible, a small warship slid across his glass, also headed for the newly appeared wormhole—a slow, steady trajectory.

"Is it her?" Hawk asked sharply.

"Not one of ours." The ensign hesitated. "Too angular, too big. Looks like a gunship, corvette maybe. Definitely not Earth-built."

"Distance?"

"Seventy thousand kilometers. But we're closing fast."

Hawk stood. "Wherever we are going, we don't want to face those creatures."

"At this distance? Without guided munitions, it will be almost impossible."

"They and we seem to be on a similar course. We are both heading for the rift. If they hold course, we'll only get one shot, sooner than later. The ensign raised his chin. "And I'll make it count."

Hawk gripped the armrest harder than someone pick-pocketing his wallet. "A bit of vengeance will be just what the doctor's ordered."

Ava moved beside him, hand resting on his shoulder. Her voice was cracked, fragile. "We lost." She began to cry. And behind her, so did others.

Anger quickly replaced sadness. Their blood boiled with the possibility of some revenge.

Drifting in what felt like the furthest reaches of space, a single, lone surviving corvette floated silently through an orbiting graveyard of debris which followed them out. From within the hushed cabin, the occasional spray of micro-particles rattled across the canopy and traced along the hull—like tender rainfall on a tin roof, a soft patter that circled and returned with each revolution.

At first, the sound unnerved Myli. It reminded her of their fragility, but as the hours stretched on, the rhythm became almost comforting. The soft pitter-patter became a gentle lullaby riding a riptide of death as they headed further out on a cosmic sea.

It had been a brutal descent for Myli and Sonny. What had once felt like a spacious corvette cabin now seemed cramped and claustrophobic. Losing the cargo bay was only the beginning of their shrinking real estate.

Low oxygen, low supplies, only one of them had the ability to make a difference. Myli knew what was coming. Eventually, she'd have to retreat—again—into the virtual prison. A digital exile. A genie sealed back in the bottle. It was the only chance either of them had, but the ring still lacked the power to help.

She could leave Sonny her 2nd SKN suit; her sacrifice would double Sonny's odds of survival out in this empty desert. Perhaps he could land on a moon like Titan, live subterranean where oxygen and carbon-based life existed. But survival felt like a punchline evaporating into nothing the longer he was unconscious.

They drifted aimlessly, tumbling farther from Earth with each passing second. They were far enough away now that they couldn't see any other vessels.

Her eyes drifting, closed again as the storm of debris and luggage passed—a soft lullaby of ruin. Another soothing rain accentuated by the thunder of a polymer case thudded along the hull. Earth, already a tiny dot, was slipping away. Ahead, she saw the sphere of a new rift shimmering in the black—a lifeboat tossed from the gods.

Her brain registered what she saw. She stirred.

"Ahh. Good job, Ravelin!" she breathed a quantity of stale air. Ravelin had carved a way out. Earth may be ravaged, but humanity would not totally disappear. The *Ursang* gave them an escape.

Wherever she was, Ava Ursang—with her near-limitless processing power—triangulated every coordinate in her database system with the *Daedalus* and the *Icarus* stellar cartography. With those coordinates, she cracked the impossible math of the cosmic safe.

In front of them, maybe somewhere new, maybe habitable. God only knew where in space-time they were headed.

Eventually, they entered the breach, wrapping their way around the sphere. Light and time and distance bending in the bubble, a bubble that was turning inside out. Her perception with lack of physicality and memory made this trip feel like the exit was just as fast as when they went in. There was no way she could know something was looming behind them—a shark, hunting.

They were far from home now, hurtling uncontrollably toward an unknown planet veiled in ice. "Where are we?" Myli whispered, as dread seeped into her bones. Fear was eclipsing exhaustion. "Whatever lies ahead, it won't be Earth."

The planet swelled in the viewport, growing rapidly. Light refracting off its glacial surface flooded the cabin as they approached. The brilliance of the planet pierced their blinking eyelids. The planet loomed, immense and imminent and incoming. An energy dome surrounded the planet, powered by streams of power emanating from the surface.

"Ava, I know you're low on power, but I need thrusters—now. If we don't correct, we'll burn in."

Ava materialized beside her, virtually stuttering in and out of existence. "Estimation: I can give you thirty seconds of thrust. Enough to a- a- a- a- adjust re- reentry trajectory."

"Do it."

"Three... two... wa, one."

Myli gripped the controls. A sputter. A shove. Another micro-burst. She nudged the stick gently, feathering control. The planet stopped wavering in the viewport and was centered.

"Twenty-three seconds, twa twenty-three," Ava warned.

"Come on," Myli muttered. "Just a little more—"

"Nineteen-sec-, sec-, seconds."

A final correction. The shaking eased.

"I won't need anymore." She smiled wryly. "Good job, Ava."

"Well done, done, well done, Captain."

Myli slumped back in her seat, nerves threadbare. "Let's just hope we're done with surprises."

The corvette bucked violently. A burst of rounds ripped by them. A couple of rounds sliced through the empty cargo hold. Some destroyed the orbiting cargo, which acted as a temporary shield.

"Hull bre- bre- breach in the Cargo Bay."

Ava still glitching, scanned. "Brace for impact!"

"Impact?" Myli, confused and surprised, tightened her restraint. The ship bucked again more violently. Myli was jolted hard. She was jarred in her seat as something sideswiped the ship—not a direct hit, but enough to undo every inch of stability she'd clawed back to get.

"Ava!"

"I'm wer- wer- wor- working the math, Captain."

A massive ship tore past them. It was the Daedalus. She was out of control and didn't know who they were shooting at as they flew by like a bullet. She was descending too—burning in, limping, barely holding together as it passed the energy field. A second later, Myli's corvette passed the energy barrier as well. The power surge was like steroids for Ava. Wide awake now. "Ava," Myli gasped. "Our trajectory—are we going to skip off the atmosphere?"

Speaking like she took a hit of speed, Ava responded. "The cabin is depressurizing. You still have fifteen seconds of thruster fuel." Her tone was rapid and alert. "We won't be landing now."

"A crash landing is still a landing." Myli was back on the stick. Desperate, micro adjustments, her teeth were going to shatter; they were so close and yet they were seconds away from disaster.

"Five, four, three..."

Their angle of approach was close enough. Parts were breaking off the aft of the corvette. Heat entering the cargo bay destroyed most of the aft of the ship. The *Daedalus* was in a perilous predicament ahead of them, out of control. Whoever's on board should have exited via escape pods after they entered the atmosphere. Myli watched as the *Daedalus* burned in. No way they were escaping at that speed.

"No," she moaned. *All those people.*

"No time to mourn," Ava warned. "Fire the rest of the thrusters now."

Myli did it. Fuel expending. But their descent was manageable now. She wondered what planet this was. Was it hostile?

Dumb question, she told herself. *All planets are hostile.*

The landmasses appeared, looking different but still familiar. Something wasn't right, though. Sonny was barely coherent. Out of touch for most of their journey, they only awoke from the turbulence. "Ava, Sonny's ring, check it." It was emitting a healthy pulse. Their descent to the planet and through the energy shield must have powered it up. The countdown on the ring had finally stopped.

This was Event 231...

Hours later. Half-buried in loam. Bursts of rain sluiced mud from the escape pods' scorched hull. The buttress from giants, it nestled in, loomed overhead, filling with water as their broad leaves pitter-pattered the water sprites from above. Remnants of a monsoonal downpour remain overhead as a new tropical storm gathers strength, spiraling west.

Cricket chirps and pollinator buzz do their worst to drown out something bigger pushing through the foliage. A vibrant toad fills itself with air and belches its own tune at the threat.

Far from being a threat, a cervid approaches. Small, the antelope-like creature creeps from the undergrowth, twitching its odd nose as it approaches the unfamiliar alien shape buried in the slough.

Without provocation—detonation.

Like black powder charges, explosions blow the escape hatch off the pod. The metal door jettisons, an errant throw at no one in particular. The metal disk frisbees through the forest, slicing through everything in its nonlinear path until it embeds deep into the trunk of one of the massive trees. Humming with the vibration of a tuning fork, an unknown viscous liquid dripped off the powder-burned edge of the alloy. The rain washed away most of the evidence.

Zigzagging in panic, the animal fled back through the tangled network of trees and plants fighting for sunlight.

After a slight intermission, the tropical concert begins again. Jungles do as jungles do: bury the past and rebuild—fast. The path, carved through trees and gouged in earth, erases in real-time as rain heals the otherworldly scar.

Birds and insects rejoice in song, returning to their everyday routine: mating, killing, eating, and dying. Their amnesia of the day's happening settles in like their short lifespan. Birds shriek. Insects buzz. Unknown creatures chatter from the canopy when they notice movement from the orifice of the pod. Their incessant cackling awakens Sonny in his metallic womb.

Jostling around in inches of rainwater, Sonny unstrapped himself. The pod is filling faster than a hot tub with a new hose. His eyes spin: the vertigo isn't forever. His head pounds as his brain separates motor skills from his eyes into his hands and feet, legs and arms. Eye-hand coordination is sloppy at best. So is breathing as he chokes on water now at chin level.

Coughing up the previously inhaled water, the life-giving liquid continues its relentless pursuit of drowning him. Drops of rain pummel his eyeballs as if Poseidon has damned him on land. His hand rises slowly, guided like a mole searching for roots, and it finds his face. The meaty paw tries to brush water out from behind his eyelids; he smacks his eyebrow instead. A cut above his orbital socket burns like a hot iron. His skin sensed a warm gush of slick liquid running down his cheek. It's close enough that he can smell the iron in the scarlet drip.

At last, Sonny finds his eyelids and applies pressure; the force squishes the water and grit out of his eyes. At last, he can see clearly and his movements pick up in speed.

Fast-moving clouds and streams of unrelenting rain pass above.

Reaching up, his fingers gripped the rim of the pod but slipped. The second attempt is successful and firm. Hands tighten their grip, forearms contract, biceps engage… the legs finally decide to help haul the beaten meat sack he calls a body up and out of the exit.

His vault fails, and in rapid fashion, he slithers without brakes until he dives face-first into standing water. The circumstances of his surroundings force deep contemplation. Is dying here better than some boring death from which he came? Sitting on the couch, eating the last slice of pepperoni and mushroom pizza with green olives sounds fantastic right now. The only thing that would make that heart-attack-inducing death better would be his wife bouncing on his lap. Instead, he's here, balls deep in the suck, face still underwater, breath remaining held.

A deep inhale would solve all his problems.

Too convenient.

Enough time wasted crying over what-ifs.

Sonny's battered abs engage. His arm turns into an organic jack and bio-hydraulically lifts him up and forces him over with a lazy roll — "FUCK." He gasped in pain.

Silence replaced the white noise with a rush of water filling his ears. Cotton-shaped clouds, the color of the Laguna Madre mudflats, fill the heavens with a surplus of piss saved up for his arrival. A deep breath reveals two potentially cracked ribs, part of the toll of getting here. The pain activates memories of his brutal fight to the death with the demon, alien—bio-engineered enemy named Asag. That son of a bitch fated him here. Sonny grinned, thinking about how he killed that piece of shit.

Blood replaced the dirty water in his eye, obscuring half his vision again. With his good eye, Sonny scanned the crash site.

Left, right, in front, after a slow struggle to maneuver, he deems his six o'clock clear.

No sign of Myli.

This place looks peaceful despite its unwelcoming weather, but he knows survival will be tough in this dense jungle filled with alien foliage. It's unrecognizable. Unknown equals danger. Despite a firehose's worth of downpour, most plants devour it, meaning he's going to need to find a water source quickly before it stops.

It's been a few good minutes of rain. The bird and insect feces should have washed clean off the leaves by now. He hopes.

His arm felt like thousands of pounds, even still his hand found its aim. Palm pats the holster, the great equalizer, his Anunna blaster still secured to his hip.

He allowed a smile to slip into place, lips cracking just enough to make Sonny rethink death. His situation wasn't as good as giving Chiara a ride, but it was one step closer to seeing her. A small comfort, but enough to continue to put up a fight. Now was the time to get back into that fight.

How far was he from her? South, another continent? In some place east of Texas, he had not traveled yet? Who was he fighting next?

He'd seen what a bolt could do from one of these alien blasters. That atomizing blast was formidable insurance that even the Udug soldiers weren't designed to survive.

A groan, the pressure of internal wounds pushes blood from his mouth onto the ground as he rolls back over, pushing to his knees. Getting vertical felt like launching the first rocket into orbit that didn't blow up. Somehow, he didn't explode. Wrinkles in the skin next to his eyes grew deeper the further his vision telescoped out. His predatory eagle eyes embraced the crow's feet while scanning again.

Good.

"Sonny," a voice behind him breaks the silence.

The gunslinger spins, weapon drawn like the old days when men with enormous hats rode horses. He relaxed only when he spotted Ava's luminous, ghostly form. The volume of rain obscured his surroundings but enhanced her ethereal shape.

He growled.

Light from her holographic shape looked like actual mass as she approached him.

He lowered his gun with a shudder of residual ache.

"Took your sweet time," he mumbled over the downpour.

He staggered, approaching her.

She could hear the disappointment in his accusation.

"Bona fide quick draw now?"

"Hardly... I wondered how someone snuck up on me like that, not likely. Figured I still had water in my ears if that was the case."

"The wildlife here is hostile and deadly," she replied. "It can sneak up and bite you in the ass if you're lackadaisical about it."

"I just nosedived in a tin-can going... fast," he said, wiping more blood from his eyebrow. "I'm alert-ish enough. Where were you during the fight? We could've used a hand against those aliens. It could've made a difference."

"I was there," Ava said evenly. "Have you ever run a quadrillion calculations planning an escape and still diverted processing power to a third party to elevate their skills? I didn't have the bandwidth for dialogue."

He grimaced again, but not from pain—confusion. "Wait—processing? Elevating what?"

"Between Ava on the *Ursang* and my calculations, we brought you here. It was more logical than bringing you back to an apocalyptic Earth. As far as elevating you—you're good. Don't get me wrong, but you still required correction with your aim. Lucky for us, eighty-nine percent of your shots are within tolerance; the micro-bionics all throughout the suit pick up the slack, correcting the rest. I gave you a nudge when you needed it."

"A nudge? You ran an aim-bot for me?"

"An efficient term," she conceded.

Sonny let out a sharp laugh that pained his ribs. "So those hits weren't all mine?"

She let out a rare but short laugh.

"In spirit, if it makes you feel better."

He gave a headshake, equal parts annoyed and impressed. "I thought I—?"

"You're welcome," Ava's gaze lifted to the jungle canopy. Rain hissed, creating a whiteout in the clearing. The splattering of heavy drops hitting the leaves and the thud they made when they splashed on the ground drowned out sound with heavy static.

"So, where to, boss?" she asked.

His look suggested he was no one's boss.

"How the hell should I know? I don't even know where we are." A hint of fear slips off his tongue. "What did you mean by an apocalyptic Earth?"

"Ava Icarus bounced readouts to Ava Daedalus and Ava Ursang, and I took the data received—it was ominous to say the least."

His body slunk.

"Where is my wife? Where is Myli?"

"I doubt many will survive the power outages and bombardment." She responded mournfully. "At least two transports of Udug crash-landed. Luckily, we are not there. Based on the amount of ice on the northern continent, I'd say we have arrived sometime after the Last Glacial Maximum."

"You sound damn near convinced, and I am certain I don't know what the hell you're talking about," Sonny disagreed with a shake from his head. "Just tell me how far I have to walk to get to my wife."

"You have my deepest condolences, Sonny. There is no walking to your wife. There is no way to travel to her. We are very close to the end of the Ice Age." She said point-blank.

"Are you fucking shitting me? Fuck!" Sonny took a second to let the shock pass. He thought about all the ramifications. "Fuck!" He fell to his knees, brought down by the pain in his rib cage, the ache in his heart, and the swirling thoughts in his mind raced faster than the storm pummeling him from above.

Steady breathing, control the pain, and clamber back up, pussy. Time travel ain't possible either, so there must be a way. "Congratulations, you stuck us on one hell of a road trip, if you're right."

"Highly improbable I am wrong."

"How do we get back?"

"You don't. We are at least 13,000 years from your time, and one of the greatest planetary cataclysms is right around the corner. With a lifespan of 70 to 100 years, I'd venture to guess it is highly unlikely you'll live that long."

Sonny's eyebrows did a wave for *Miss Know It All.* "Yeah, you can stuff that one in your pocket for later."

Paranoia crept in. He scanned the surroundings again. Out in the forest, off in the distance, a great deal of movement was heading their way. Something large. The hair on his neck stood at attention despite the deluge.

Catching his breath, Sonny holstered his pistol. At first, he started walking aimlessly— Odysseus adrift in a world that wasn't on any map, guided by a friendly ghost in the machine. He needed a plan of action.

If Ava was never wrong, he looked around cynically—"Where is all the ice, Ava?"

"We shot over what you called the Gulf of Mexico and then over a continent that is now the island chain called the Azores in your time. Myli diverted the trajectory long enough to redirect you here. You got lucky we crashed in a green zone."

His stomach was rolling. Guts clenching. Hunger hit him, perhaps a hint of apprehension too. He began scrambling; he dipped back into the pod, grabbing supplies. His feelings grabbed hold of him, and the certainty of his fate hit him like an IRS audit. He was going to die in Earth's ancient past. Alone. It wouldn't be a boring death. But it also wouldn't be death by pizza and sex.

He stopped thinking about his own woes for a second. Maybe this could be a second chance for humanity?

"Do you believe in second chances?" he asked.

"I've had many," Ava Rider said wryly.

Sonny looked at her, deadpan serious. "I swear to you, we are not finished." Under his breath, he reassured himself. "I'm not finished. Not here anyway."

He resumed vigorously stuffing his survival pack.

"You're going to need an alias, Sonny."

From something said earlier, he thought. "Call me Trip, then; might as well, since you've looped us all the way back in time."

She nodded with approval. "It's an honor to meet you, Trip Looper."

"*If You Could Read My Mind,* what a story my thoughts could tell... I sure hope you came with some tunes, firebrand."

"Sonny, I mean Trip, I managed to download everything."

He was half listening and half strategically planning his packed supplies. "Everything?" His hand stopped shoving shit in the bag. "Everything? That's like the United States Navy decrypting Japanese coded messages before Midway during World War I."

"Even better," she continued. "Times, dates, persons of interest... as long as the history books and history on your World Wide Web check out with the past's reality, we have the ultimate cheat sheet."

"You've got it all, don't you, Ava?"

Her aura, the holographic construct, looked so real in the rain that his excitement got the better of him, and he stepped forward for her with arms wide. It was a hug that couldn't land. There was no warmth in her return, just slosh in the mud pit he fell into face-first, again.

"Oh, gosh," she immediately regretted.

"I already hate this fucking place," he fumed, trying to get up. "I don't have to live twelve thousand years. I just need to find and kill Asag to stop the whole thing. If I can do that, it will be like I never left."

"I don't think Asag was the master mind."

"So, we kill 'em all," he said unmercifully.

She held out a hand to help him up. He reached for it and ended up in the bog a third time. Ava backed away.

"That is your first lesson. You're going to have to gain some common sense if you're going to undermine their villainous extermination of your species."

"Thanks for the tip, AI." He flipped her off for good measure. "You come with everything but a body, don't you?" He says, sloshing a handful of muddy water in her direction. "It's okay. I don't need you to have a body; you're the Rosetta Stone for the future. The information you're carrying will determine all our fates."

Bonus Chapter from Book 3 in the *Return to Paradise Series*

THE ANACHRONIST ETERNAL

The Fountain

Scrambling through very thick foliage, Sonny is hauling ass behind Ava. The holographic apparition made plunging through the branch and leaf-laden terrain look easy. It was not. She breezed through without whispering a single branch. Sonny, not so much.

His body was still beat to shit, struggling to keep up. Every lunge sent a wave of pain throughout his body. His nerves, pain receptors, all told his mind to hide behind another massive root he had just passed. No, how about that cluster of rocks, the pile hiding the spring feeding the stream he is about to plow through?

Not enough cover.

Maybe caves are up ahead? Where there is water, there is erosion. *Can I get there?*

His fractured ribs, contusions, and concussion reminded him with every step of what he was running from. Each step further from home, yet closer to the future.

Ava continued her multitasking.

Get him to the river.

It was the only way to lose their trail. She monitors his vitals; Sonny's body is close to going into shock. Another spring, another of nature's arrows leading them away from the hunting party made up of Anunna soldiers.

She hears the splat. It sounds like a heavy boulder coming to rest in a muddy puddle of water behind her. She turns. *Nuts.*

Sonny is down and out, face-first in the mud.

If it wasn't for the tracks leading directly to his immobile body, she could leave him there. She knew he would go down at some point, but the round-weathered stone he caught his toe on precipitated his fall prematurely.

"Sonny!" she yelled to him in his headset. "You need to get up. They're right behind us."

No reaction. There wasn't any reason to try again. He would not get up until he had time to recover. The ghost vanishes, possessing the interior of the suit. There are no exorcists here. She becomes the suit's brain, invading its nervous system in nanoseconds.

The micro-cilia buried in his muscles from the armored portion of his suit come back to life when Ava reroutes and redirects them through the Alpha Skin. His fine motor skills are taken over like a zombie fungus invading its host. From there, more cilia tap directly into Sonny's body, overriding his powered-down brain. Unconsciousness is no longer an obstacle.

In a zombie-like fashion, the stilled body moves. Ava, the Second Skin MK VI's A.I. program, rises to a set of real feet, Sonny's feet.

"Ghosts don't run," he told her when he was conscious.

He was right. The feeling is foreign at first. Piloting the suit isn't the same as running as a ghost. This is real. This is work.

One foot in front of the other. Arm's swing in motion, fighting to get the rhythm down. Behind her, the voices are gaining. Foliage snaps, energy beams cutting the jungle to ribbons around her. In front of her, tangible, impeding, and endless obstacles from a virgin tropical forest are difficult to overcome.

More bolts of light from their weapons streaked past her.

A struggling newbie, she knows one thing at this moment: this real-world running shit is for sadists. A branch clocks her marionette face. The puppet master—*Clotheslined.*

Back up, she's a *Jack in the Box.*

An energy blast over her head. She ducks. A narrow miss.

Ava hisses.

She runs. Her best, *toddler-inspired marathon,* all instinct and imbalance. New sensations. No time for wonder or intrigue. Agility is far beyond her reach. A vine caught her ankle, sending her diving forward, uncontrolled. Another *deadly energy blast* splashed a rubber tree beside her, sap and bark erupting in fire, turning to charcoal.

She brings the suit back to its feet and darts behind any cover she can. Her juking looks more like a human slapping the paddles of a pinball machine.

Finally—an opening.

Stumbling over loose rocks, she ricochets through a grouping of boulders like a pinball. The *river lies ahead.* If she could smell, she would've caught the mist of spray hanging in the air from the nearby falls.

A medium-sized boulder above her head erupts into flames and vitrifies in its anchored, centuries-long home. No time to pause.

Keep trudging, she orders herself.

The fall in front of Ava is sudden and perilous. Her last step becomes a forced leap because of an inescapable jump.

Two hundred and nineteen feet.

The equivalent of wet cement rushes to meet her. Milliseconds stacked on milliseconds, anticipation spiked as gravity yanked her down. There is no time for corrections, only acceleration. His mask is still intact, meaning he can submerge without drowning if she activates it. She does. Arms and legs crossed, Ava makes his body narrow and spear-like. Sonny's body pierces the air; the certainty of impact mounts exponentially with every unconscious breath from him.

Impact!

She has trouble staying above the surface as she passes over some very nasty rapids. Sonny's body tumbles underwater, smashing every rock on the bottom. Every rock his body bumped or hit must have caused him excruciating pain if he was conscious. She hoped that if they stayed in the river long enough, the soldiers would lose the trail and give up.

Seeing what he could not, she occasionally tried to surface. Getting caught underneath a large boulder or trapped by a submerged limb could prove difficult or impossible to escape when he comes to.

As if staying on the surface of the water wasn't tough enough for someone who'd never swum before, a new threat latches onto Sonny's leg.

It was so strong that it kept dragging them down. She scans it. At first, it looks like a gigantophis constrictor submerged underwater, but it wasn't. It was a fish-like snake, an eel easily 130 pounds, preparing to wrap around his leg and drag him down into its lair. She hacks at it with a fist, but it won't let go. It has a death grip on Sonny's leg.

She reaches for the head; the suit's grip ratchets around its gills.

A flash of light penetrates the silt-filled water. The massive electric eel fires off a surge strong enough to incapacitate a water buffalo.

A time later, many yards from the river, blackness became a bright, warm hue of color. Parcels of grass swayed from a puff of breath from the gods. The smell of aerated earth was refreshing. Tall wild grass burst from the fertile soil in which he was planted. Sonny's eyeballs were open now and fixated on tiny insects, ants, busy collecting resources for the nest.

Lying felt better than moving. Moving was life. Stagnation was death. He felt like he was somewhere in between.

Seeds on the top stems of the grass bladed with a breeze. Another hint, subtle advice from the universe telling him what to do. Ok, advice heeded. Thinking wasn't doing, though. He was beaten up before he passed out; he felt worse for wear after the fact.

His armor suit was retracted into pack form, but when? His Alpha Skin was bone dry except for a layer of slime on a sleeve. Minutes, hours, or days? *He didn't know how long.*

It was long enough for the water to dry but not long enough for the slime to turn into dried snot. He hadn't been there too long.

How the hell did he get here?

The sore forearm hinted at a fight he'd apparently won. But with what? Getting here must have been an arduous task that he had no memory of.

Rolling over, he let out a low groan. Absent clouds gave way to healing *Vitamin D.* From the corner of his eye lay the head of the source of slime, feet away from him. Some sort of snake, no... an eel. Its head looked as if it had been squeezed off, the cut jagged. Lifting his head just enough to look between his spread feet, he saw the stream he had washed in.

Head thudding back to the ground, he focused again on the buttery sky.

He gave himself a quick physical examination. What was broken and what was not?

Tongue first, mangled. Jaw, aching. Hands, arms, feet, and toes, all wiggling, testing degrees of damage. Identifying what didn't hurt was a quicker task with a shorter inventory.

The numbness had hidden the tongue situation longer than it should have. He raised his aching hand and stared at it. The ring finger, mostly bone and muscle, created an escalating, uncharted pain. His eyes opened wider. He tried flapping his wings. His right elbow and rotator cuff throbbed too.

His good hand reached between his legs; the *goods still there,* he wondered?

Still there.

He gave a much-needed sigh of relief. At least if someone found him dead, the important pieces were still intact. He'd be dead, so it wouldn't really matter much, but he didn't want to be the dick end of someone's campfire jokes. Every telling of the discovery of his body would ultimately end with the inevitability of his missing appendage. But then again, he'd seen the size of these aliens; they were giants. An additional worry crept into his ape brain.

Some people died peacefully in their sleep. What a boring way to go, but boring sounds good right now. He was going to die worrying about what some poor fellow thought of his junk.

A thirst for water replaced worry.

He craved precious minerals. A thirst-quenching necessity forced him to his side and then to his knees. Blood spilled from his mouth, watering the grass.

A grimace.

Like a German submarine hunting on the surface of the ocean, his eyes crested the horizon of grass as he *periscoped* to an observable apogee. Easing into the better vantage point, he scouted the terrain ahead of him.

Stems, seeds, and flowers swaying in the gentle breeze, a serene moment of isolation. It smells cleaner than any industrial nation he had visited in the past. Domestic scents flooded his nostrils. Sanctuary waits beyond the peacefulness, a *monumental fountain.*

Sonny's focus shifts away from the fountain; dangerous premonitions fill his mind. Water won't matter if an eight-foot Anunna soldier erupts from the outlying village to kill him.

At the moment, nothing moves around him but grass and trees. No one. Not a single soul is wandering the streets.

Curious.

Maybe it was Sunday, and they were all at alien church? Blue sky, the storm dissipated in real time above. An additional threat emerged: the ball of fire in the heavens bakes the damp earth around him. It does not forget him.

That heavenly flame told him one thing, but not everything. Morning or dusk? He'd only need an hour or less to confirm if it was the former or the latter.

"It's all clear." A familiar voice said, piercing the quiet, crystal clear.

The voice, one he knew all too well.

Sonny's flinch caused a jolt of pain. It was sharp and immediate. He scowled at her abruptness.

"Can you make it?" Ava continued.

"They're gonna have to come at me with someone bigger and badder if they want to kill me." He grimaced.

"Uh-huh. Can you get to the water or not? You need it."

He was reaching, trying to move, the pain steadily mounting. "I'm not sure." He said truthfully. "I'm parched. I don't remember getting here."

"You're dangerously dehydrated. Your suit took a beating during the escape. It will need some repairs."

Sonny winced. "You got me this far. I need your help to get me the rest of the way."

"You've got this. One leg after another." She said, coaching him along.

He shook his head.

"Don't shake your head at me."

His head shook again, but more sloppily.

Tunnel vision is creeping in. "No, I need you to automate the suit, isn't that how you got me here? I sure as shit didn't get this far."

Her avatar face frowned. "There isn't enough power in the suit. It needs more time to charge. Your bout with the electric eel overloaded the system."

Face in the dirt, he sighed; blowback from the soil entered his mouth, exacerbating his dehydration. Despite this, one arm in front of the other. Even his legs tried to help. Every yard he crawled demanded monumental effort. This was still better than dying wrestling in bed with a lover, right? *Embrace the suck! Never give up!*

He laughed; the laugh caused more dirt to be inhaled into his lungs. True grit wasn't enough. It sounded ridiculous now.

A thought surfaced, unbidden; he went still in the quiet surrender of death. Fate settled in like an old friend. Defeated, his body raised the white flag, his head sinking back below the grass-line, face planting in the soil.

The Sun soon dashed hope for sunset as it climbed. Ava wasn't there to cheer him on anymore. He supposed she couldn't bear to watch him die like this. So close to salvation, yet millennia away.

Lips dry enough to crack, no spit left, he could hear the sparkling water spilling from the fountain. Like a shark smelling blood, he could smell the water. Senses hyper-focused. Footsteps. Light, not as heavy, it wasn't a soldier. Not one of those big bastards. But it was someone.

Lighter.

Daintier.

Smelling of honeysuckles, she approached.

He tried to turn his head, but he couldn't.

"Myli?" He whispered dryly.

She found him?

A forgiving shadow stood over him. Bleeding away the scorching heat. Relief, coolness before the end. Instead of demise taking him, the petite hands of this angel took hold of him.

Soft skin, firm grip.

She hooked her arms, strong, beneath his, dragging him towards the fountain. Every pull stoked a groan. Despite his weak protests, she kept at it until he made it.

She splashed a spit of water on his face, waiting. Even the minuscule amount refreshed him. She gave him more. Something worried her. Her alertness and continuous recon of their area slipped the secret that she shouldn't be there either.

She wasn't ready for it. Preoccupied with their safety. His face was in the basin before she could stop him.

"Don't drink too much." Her stern voice warned.

But he didn't understand, and it was too late.

He took a breath, glancing at the ring, realizing the translator was translating half the conversation for him. Hesitating, he nodded.

"Thank you," he gasped. "You're not one of them. The tall whites."

The young woman looked at her own height, then his. She wondered what his first guess was, but politely shook her head, answering his question anyway. She was human. Like him, and unmistakably his type. Familiar even.

"Brace yourself." She said.

Brace for what?

The answer hit in an instant. An extra level of pain struck every nerve. His teeth, his hand, and his ribs all began aching at the same time as they began reconstructing at the molecular level.

What the fuck did I drink?

It was obvious she had drunk from this fountain, or she wouldn't have known what was coming.

Shock enveloped his face. He swallowed a lot. The thought had barely formed before concern took over. He looked down.

Scrapes were stitching back up. Shock ripped across his face. His filleted finger regrew muscle and skin in real time. His amputated finger pushed out with excruciating torment.

The pain made him gag.

A gold tooth, a replacement from a softball collision, popped free. Falling on his tongue, rattling in his mouth, he spat it out. Slapping the wet meat muscle around, he could feel something replacing it on his tongue. A new tooth. Other teeth knocked out by Asag before his arrival here were already reemerging, too. Roots and enamel were pushing their way through his raw gums.

His reflection in the water shows other miraculous feats. His very own *Mirror Mirror,* but this one wasn't on the wall, and it wasn't telling him how fair he was. Wrinkles filled in with rejuvenating collagen. His telomeres were lengthening. The skin on his forehead, below his widow's peak, filled back in like a *Chia Pet*® on steroids.

The young woman kneeled beside him; he felt her resting, reassuring hand on his shoulder, and leaned close, face to face.

"Pain from rejuvenation will subside shortly."

"Who," he groaned, "who are you?"

She looked at him with suspicious eyes, but she smiled despite her skepticism. He was the first human she'd seen in years who wasn't living in the bush like an animal. Was he like her and sent to kill her? She put a finger to her lips, shushing him gently for both their sakes.

"You speak too loudly. I need you to be quieter, or you're going to get us both caught." She emphasized her statement with her eyes and eyebrows. "I've already been thrown out of one garden."

"The name's Trip," he groaned. "Trip Looper," he stated boldly as fact.

She didn't care about what he called himself, only what he was and was not. "We need to get you indoors before someone sees you. Other than being a mess, who do you think you are coming here?"

She hauled him to his feet as she summed him up.

"The world's greatest gunman." He said to her, half-jokingly.

Evaluating his injuries and his statement, her face revealed more than skepticism. "Sure you are. I like the confidence, though."

Was he on her side or against her?

She'd know soon enough.

She could see his recovery was speeding up with every breath, strength creeping back, but it would take months for full recovery. The first time was always the longest. She finished measuring him up and then said with complete lack of endearment,

"Call me Lilith. Everyone else here does."

The *Return to Paradise Series* at a Glance

The Destroying Angel: A Tale of Survival and Discovery

In Book 1, Sonny Fly grips the American Dream by the horns, but that dream shatters when Mylitta falls out of the sky one stormy night. Sonny Fly's losses accumulate. Everything he loves is on the line as he fights to stay alive so he can reunite with his pregnant wife. A two-front attack is underway: one assault from the stars and another from an enemy who's been lurking in the shadows since the dawn of humanity. Instinct outweighs reluctance: a call to duty shoves Sonny headlong towards the ruins of Earth's ancient past to save humanity's future.

Gods and Astronauts: Asag's Treachery

In Book 2, unfamiliar faces emerge to help Sonny and Myli pursue their quest to save humanity. However, Asag, an ancient enemy from a forgotten Armageddon, continues to harbor an ultimate disdain for humanity. Devoid of decency, he will stop at nothing to defeat humanity, including scorching the Earth. Only Asag's treachery can spell Sonny's end. Death is the only setback Sonny can't afford if he's going to save all he holds dear.

The Anachronist Eternal

In Book 3, Sonny finds himself stranded alone at the edge of the Ice Age. After adopting the alias Trip Looper, he emerges as The Anachronist Eternal. Displaced from his own history and Myli presumed dead, fate becomes his cruel companion as he awaits the destruction of Atlantis and the Great Flood. Ava, his artificial intelligence, may prove to be his best chance of surviving the Dark Epoch, but she may be the most dangerous variable of all. Dying in a world he doesn't understand, he falls at the foot of a fountain and meets a new face with an ancient soul. He doesn't know her yet, or does he?

Special Thanks

Thank you, Don and Donna.
I just want to thank you again for everything you've done and for the exceptional guidance you've given me in this novel. Trimming the fat from paragraphs, and even entire chapters. It felt like butchery at first, but it was necessary growth. I didn't know what I didn't know, but I have learned a great deal from both of you. My apologies for the rough chapters and clumsy paragraphs. I truly cannot express how much I appreciate the time, effort, and care you put into helping this come to fruition. Thank you for your patience, endurance, and belief in the story.
Cheers and love.

Mr. Shaw and Mark A., thanks for showing up.
Day one, y'all bought the first two copies of Book 1. I'm sure it will be a race to be the first to get this one. Mark is in first place currently. Ha. See you both on the flip side.

About the Author

Describing my life story isn't easy, but it's full of memorable moments—wild relationships, sports challenges, and even a brief cameo in the movie, *Pearl Harbor.* I started with a BFA in printmaking, played college baseball, married, worked, and now I'm chasing new goals through biathlons and writing. Much of my time is spent ferrying teenagers to their own big life moments and making the most of family time. When I manage to steal a few hours for myself, it's usually late at night—punching keys during binge-writing sessions, building massive worlds and time-bending stories that cut through history. I am always looking for escape velocity. I try to laugh often, risk boldly, and live by two ideas: *Attack where you're weak. Forge every flaw into armor.*